Winds of October

by

Alan Gibbons

The Library
Kirkham Grammar School
Ribby Road
KIRKHAM, Lancs.
PR4 2BH

Circaidy Gregory Press

Copyright Information

Winds of October text © 2017 Alan Gibbons, cover photo Rhiannon Barton © 2017, cover design and content under this cover © 2017 Kay Green. All rights reserved. No part of this publication may be reproduced, stored in a retrieval system, rebound or transmitted in any form or for any purpose without the prior written permission of author and publisher. This book is sold subject to the condition that it shall not be lent, resold, hired out or otherwise circulated without the publisher's prior consent in any form or binding other than that in which it is published.

ISBN 978-1-910841-45-7

Printed in the UK
by Catford Print

Published by
Circaidy Gregory Press
45 Robertson Street,
Hastings
Sussex TN34 1HL

www.circaidygregory.co.uk

About the Author

Alan Gibbons has been a published writer for 26 years, mainly in the children's and Young Adult field. He is the winner of The Blue Peter Book Award 2000 'The book I couldn't put down' for his best-selling book Shadow of the Minotaur and he has won seventeen other awards.

Before becoming an author Alan was a teacher for 16 years. Alan is a full time writer and independent educational consultant. He is the organiser of the Campaign for the Book, which promotes libraries and the culture of reading for pleasure. He is a member of the Speak up for Libraries coalition and initiated National Libraries Day. He is the recipient of the Fred Jarvis Award for services to education. Alan visits 150-180 schools and libraries a year in the UK and abroad, working with young people to encourage their interest in reading and writing.

If you would like Alan to visit your school, library or youth group email: mygibbo@gmail.com

Winds of October is Alan's first adult novel and is the first volume of the Revolution trilogy.

Two other novels, **Reason in Revolt** and **Spurn the Dust** will follow.

Contents

About the Author
page i

Glossary of historical characters
Page iii

Part One
February's Child
page 1

Part Two
April's Messenger
page 79

Part Three
October Mists
Page 161

Glossary of real life figures in Winds of October

Some real-life participants in the Russian Revolution appear in this novel. The author has made every effort to portray them accurately. Where their words are included in the novel, they are re-imagined using their real-life speeches as a basis.

Maria Leontivna Bochkareva, commander of the Women's Battalion of Death, a regiment raised to support the Russian war effort.

Lev Davidovich Bronstein, member of the Bolshevik party and organiser of the October insurrection.

Viktor Mikhailovich Chernov, a founder of the Socialist Revolutionary Party and member of the Provisional Government.

Joseph Vassirionovich Djugashvili, Bolshevik Central Committee member, known as Stalin.

Lev Borisovich Kamenev, Bolshevik Central Committee member.

Benyamin Nikolayevich Kayurov, Bolshevik militant at the Erikson factory in Vyborg, Petrograd.

Jessie Kenney, working class activist in the Women's Social and Political Union.

Alexander Fyodorovich Kerensky, Prime Minister of Russia from July to October, 1917.

General Sergey Khabalov, Commander of the Petrograd Military District at the time of the February revolution.

Alexandra Mikhailovna Kollontai, leading Bolshevik party member and writer.

Julius Martov, leader of the Mensheviks.

Vyacheslav Mikhailovich Molotov, member of the Military Revolutionary Committee and Bolshevik militant.

Emmeline Pankhurst, founder of the Women's Social and Political Union, known as the Suffragettes.

Larissa Mikhailovna Reissner, Bolshevik activist and writer.

Fyodor Fyodorovich Raskolnikov, leader of the sailors at the Kronstadt base and Bolshevik. Married to Larissa Reissner.

Anton Vladimirovich Stankevich, military figure. Later joined the Bolsheviks.

Alexander Gavrilovich Shlyapnikov, Bolshevik militant and trade union leader.

Vladimir Ilyich Ulyanov, known as Lenin, main theorist and leader of the Bolshevik faction of the Russian Social Democratic Party, separating itself completely during the revolution as a distinct and separate party from the Mensheviks.

Grigory Yevseevich Zinoviev, Bolshevik Central Committee member.

Part One

February's Child

Raisa

'What's this little whore got in common with Mother Russia?' Bagrov chuckled, ushering Raisa forward so that the stranger could examine her. 'They're both about to get fucked.'

Raisa knew better than to scowl – after all, she was not going to get paid if she subverted her employer – but her azure eyes blazed briefly with revolt because he was right, she was a whore to be bartered with. Bagrov was a pig, but he was a pig that put bread in her mouth and kept a roof over her head. Dry and fed in a whorehouse was better than cold and wet and hungry on the streets, and the street had been her home far too long.

When Bagrov's attempt at a joke fell flat, his moist, fleshy smile vanished. He kept calling the gent in the expensive winter coat 'Your Honour'. Raisa considered the perfect creases along the man's trousers, the frock coat, the shiny, leather shoes, the gold signet ring, the perfectly manicured fingernails; rich didn't cut it. She was about to turn a trick with a right toff. What if he was a prince or some such? For a moment, she entertained thoughts about him falling in love with her and taking her away from the cheap brothel that had been her home for the last six months, but the crazy dream faded before it could even take form.

She inspected His Honour's cold, pale blue eyes – almost as blue as her own – and his milky white skin. She became aware of his soft, dainty hands and oddly thin wrists. He had never done a day's work in his life, at least not what somebody of her background would call work. Some might say she hadn't either, other than lie on her back and spread her legs for the next pathetic loser who could scrape together enough cash to buy a few minutes of her company.

His Honour took Bagrov aside to make payment. Raisa watched the men talk and gave a little grimace. She saw money changing hands, but she couldn't work out how much. What did it matter? Bagrov would cheat her anyway. She did the work and Bagrov skimmed most of the profit off the top. Lev, the stooped, rheumy-eyed caretaker said the way he treated the girls was nothing short of slavery, but he never dared say it loud enough to get the heave-ho. He wasn't that stupid. There was a cold, heartless world beyond those walls where people died on the street and in the trenches like so many unwanted dogs.

His Honour was younger than he seemed at first glance. He dressed like a bourgeois, a merchant or a banker, maybe a factory owner with investments on the Vyborg side, but look beyond the expensive clothes and commanding gait, and the man before her was only a few years older than she was. The haggling was taking longer than usual. His Honour must have special requests. Some of the punters made her stomach turn, with their "extras". Dirty perverts! She had learned to cope with the ones that wanted to beat her. She had been beaten half her lonely, squalid life. It was the sad, withered bastards like old Yuri with his dog eyes and flaccid prick that made her puke. Some of them even wanted her to pray with them.

Don't look for absolution from me, she told him in words unspoken.

You're the sinner.

Live with it.

What would His Honour's appetites be? There was something about his face that made her skin tingle with unease: the waxiness of his skin, the thin, uneven moustache that reminded her of an adolescent's first attempt at growing facial hair, the full, almost feminine lips. She was only sixteen but he was more of a child than she was. He might even be a virgin. Yes, that was it, he was one of those overgrown babies who would expect her to show him how it was done, even where to put his lousy, unused prick. Here came another reluctant cock to jerk to life. Christ, men were such wretched creatures, and so cruel. Between Bagrov and the punters, she felt like a crane fly having its legs plucked away one by one by naughty boys.

While the negotiations continued, her gaze drifted to the grimy windowpane and the falling snow outside. In February, Petrograd was as cold as the wastes of Lapland. Its citizens shivered in temperatures fifteen degrees below freezing. The blizzard veiling the street was thin and light and fast, not like real snow at all, more like mist. It reminded her of the steam from a kettle. The storm painted the world white, a parody of innocence. Beyond the snow, men were perishing in their thousands, maybe millions, mown down by the German machine guns, ripped apart by their superior artillery. She had seen them returning from the Front, heads and eyes bandaged, limbs missing, hideous disfigurements transforming handsome young men into grotesque, sideshow freaks. She had watched an argument just the previous week. A father, a sad-eyed muzhik from some village in the sticks, had been scolding his son, a bag of skin and bone with a leg missing, demanding to know why he hadn't died on the battlefield. What use was he now he had lost his leg? He would be a burden on his family. That's when Bagrov broke in on her thoughts.

'Look lively, wench,' he snapped. 'His Honour hasn't got all day.'

Raisa stared at Bagrov with startled, incredulous eyes. His Honour was opening the door onto the street, letting the snow swirl inside. He couldn't be serious. Was she meant to go with this boy-man in his expensive coat and polished shoes? This had never happened before. Usually, she took her punters to a corner of Bagrov's filthy hovel and let them screw her there, behind a clumsily-hung curtain. She knew every crack on the ceiling, every pattern on the pock-marked wall. That's what she did while they humped away at her, getting their joyless satisfaction. She focussed on some minor detail, imagining she was a little girl again, watching shadows play and imagining they were night ghosts. She had to do this or she would have thrown up all over the twisted, ugly scum who came to empty themselves into her. It was a strange thing, these men were supposed to get pleasure from their visits, but invariably they walked away sour-faced or ashamed. They came to her expecting relief from their burdensome lives, but they always walked away as unfulfilled and lonely as ever. The world was full of losers.

'Get a move on, Raisa,' Bagrov urged. 'You're going with His Honour. You'll be getting paid double for this.'

That got Raisa wondering just how much the brothel-owner would be pocketing. It had to be a pretty penny. His pig-like eyes were fairly sparkling. One day, Raisa promised herself, I will have money and I will leave this shithole a hundred miles behind. I will never look back.

'He lives nearby,' Bagrov said cheerfully. 'It's only for an hour, two at most. He'll whisk you back here before you know it.'

Whisk her back? So she was Cinderella now and this randy dog her Prince Charming. As for "lives nearby", fat chance of that. His Honour was bound to live across the river on the Petrograd side, in a fine house in its own grounds. There weren't many of them round here on the wretched streets of the Vyborg, heaving as it was with careworn people. When Raisa was a little girl, she was innocent enough to believe she would one day live in another place, somewhere the wind kissed her cheeks and the night sky was so black and cold she would be able to see all the stars like glittering gemstones. When you are a child, there is a kind and caring God who takes you in his arms and keeps you safe. You lose your innocence when a bitch called cancer takes your mother and throws you to the wolves. That's when you realise life is a scourge with a hundred stinging tails.

Bagrov was talking to His Honour again. 'You've picked a good one here, Your Honour. Our Raisa is a blank page. She's a girl with no past. You can put your own stamp on a willing girl like this. Isn't that right, my lovely?'

Raisa thought for a gut-wrenching moment he was going to pinch her cheek. She painted the usual mask of indifference on her face and screamed inside.

'Cat got your tongue, Princess? Come on, tell His Honour something about yourself.'

Not a word left Raisa's lips.

Bagrov winked. 'She doesn't talk much, but she'll show you a good time.'

For a toe-curling moment, Raisa thought Bagrov was going to list her services, but His Honour cut him off in full flow.

'Be quiet! Just... hold your tongue.'

Raisa cast a curious glance his way. Was he trembling?

'Forgive me,' Bagrov babbled, sensing he might just have blown a lucrative deal. 'I meant no offence. I...'

His Honour raised a delicate hand, silencing Bagrov with a flick of the wrist. As Raisa followed His Honour outside, Bagrov met her eye and pulled a face. She blanked him. What, he thought they had something in common? She was going to give him a conspiratorial smile as if they were bosom buddies? Did he really expect her to treat him like a brother? Go fuck yourself, you leering piece of shit. Raisa followed her wealthy punter outside and did a double take. He was leading her to an automobile, a shiny, black Russo-Balt. For a moment, wonder replaced disgust.

'Is this yours?' she asked.

'It is. Do you like it?'

She stared. 'I have never been in a car.'

Her eyes stung with emotion. The car spoke of a life so beautiful and so remote she wanted to sink to the pavement and weep.

'There is a first time for everything,' he said.

His breath misted in the cold. The blizzard had almost blown itself out. A few last snowflakes danced in the air. Raisa sensed something in his words, a double-entendre, a sinister promise. She went to climb in the back, but His Honour shook his head.

'Sit in the front with me, my dear.'

Suddenly, she was aware of her thin, worn clothes, her unkempt hair, the shoes that let in water and allowed the cold to strike through the thin soles. She wondered what passers-by would make of the gentlemen in his finery and the wretched waif beside him. The leather seat was chilly against her back and she gave an involuntary shudder.

'You are cold.'

'Yes, Your Honour.'

She was offered a blanket.

'Wrap yourself in this.'

She snuggled into its woollen warmth. It was a small enough gesture, but it cheered her momentarily.

'Thank you, Your Honour.'

That earned her a disapproving stare. 'Don't call me that.'

'Bagrov did.'

'Bagrov is a scoundrel and a fool. How would he know how to address a gentleman?'

'You use his services. What does that make you?' She could hardly believe the fiery words had come from her own lips. Maybe he was going to boot her out and leave her to walk back through the driving snow. Bagrov wouldn't be happy if she turned up on his doorstep, leaving a disappointed customer to demand his money back.

His Honour lowered his eyes. 'Yes, I frequent brothels. All men are sinners.'

'What about the women who meet your needs? Are we sinners. Or are you one of these men who think we are fallen angels? Do you want to save me?'

For a moment, he looked startled then he composed himself. 'You will call me Andrey. For the time being.'

She wondered what pet name he would want her to call him when they reached his house. She had heard them all, even "Mummy", for fuck's sake. When he looked away to start the engine, she wrinkled her nose. You *will* call me Andrey. This was a man who was used to giving orders. Andrey turned the steering wheel with his dainty hands, now swathed in kid gloves, and accelerated down the road in the direction of the Nevsky Prospect. The wind snapped around them like a whip. Raisa waited a beat then put a question to him.

'Do you really want me to use your first name?'

He was squinting into the wind. 'I said so, didn't I?'

'And Andrey is your real name?'

He seemed surprised by her boldness.

'It is.'

In spite of her instinct to treat the men who used her services as alien beings to be anonymised and reduced to nothing more than groping hands and pumping hips, Raisa was warming to the man beside her but she struggled to call him Andrey, even in her thoughts. It implied intimacy. How could that even be possible? Andrey came from another world. Just because you fuck some rich prick, it doesn't mean you're suddenly best friends. It took half an hour to reach their destination, a substantial building overlooking the river. Raisa peered upward.

'Is this one yours?'

'That one,' Andrey said, pointing down the street.

When Raisa frowned, wondering why he had parked a hundred yards away, Andrey leaned across and opened her door. 'Wait here until I call you.'

She stood shivering in a doorway while night curled up over the drab, dark Neva like a self-satisfied cat. A gate opened and Andrey drove his Russo-Balt inside. Presently, a stooped, elderly man shuffled past without giving her a second glance. He must have seen her. Raisa dropped her eyes. It didn't take a detective to know that Andrey must have brought other girls here. Another couple of minutes passed then a light shone out on the pavement and Andrey gestured for her to approach. The snow was starting again, this time fat white flakes flickering against the backdrop of the river and the bleary gaslights beyond.

'That man,' she asked, 'does he work for you?'

'You ask too many questions,' he answered disapprovingly. 'You need to remember why you are here.'

Raisa brushed her hair from her face. She swore months ago never to let a punter get to her. Penetrating her body was one thing, entering her mind was quite another. Her fine resolution had just crumbled to dust. She fought to put the mask of indifference back over her wind-scoured features.

'Get inside before you attract attention,' he ordered.

Raisa nodded and followed him meekly inside, but not before she had peered into the murk of Petrograd, wishing Andrey's servant had not left for the night. Instinctively, she knew that there would be no servants to attend to the master and his guest. It was all down to her now. Silence awaited her beyond the polished oak door, but there was something else in there, hiding its face. Reluctantly, she left the rumble of the city and the sigh of the wind behind her. She noted the walls hung with photographs and wondered who they were, the expressionless faces that stared out from them. The little boy standing in front of two ghost-people, was that Andrey as a child?

There was a dining table with a crocheted cover on which there was a vase and a rosewood box. Andrey reached past her, the way he did to open the car door. She smelled his Cologne and heard the lock click shut. She realised she would rather be lying underneath some balding slob like Yuri, reeking of cheap vodka, sweat and self-pity. She had never met anyone like Andrey. After this night, she would avoid such men like the plague. Bagrov had better have negotiated a bloody good price. Double, he said. All the while she was following Andrey up the stairs, relishing the carpet's thick pile underfoot, she could feel the quiet of the house heavy on her shoulders.

'Are we alone?' she asked.

'We are,' Andrey answered. 'Does that worry you?'

She had to sound brave, much braver than she felt. 'Of course not. Bagrov knows where I am.'

Instantly, she felt a rush of heat down her spine. What made her say that?

'He doesn't, you know,' Andrey told her. 'My dear, do you really think I would grace that oaf with personal information, such as my address...or my name?' He snapped his fingers. 'You may prepare yourself in there.'

Raisa's heart was pounding. What nonsense was this? 'Prepare myself?'

Andrey peered down his nose at her. 'You don't think I would receive you in those clothes, do you?'

She burned with shame as she saw herself through the eyes of the bourgeois.

'A bath is drawn for you. There are three dresses on the hangers. Choose whichever one takes your fancy.'

'How did you know my size?' she asked. 'You have never met me until this evening.'

'Like most men,' Andrey answered, 'I have certain tastes, height, build, hair colour.' He hesitated. 'Eyes. I give the merchant the specifications I require. He furnishes the goods. Your eyes, my dear, are...precious.'

'Is that how you think of me, Sir, *goods*?'

'Isn't it how you think of yourself?'

Raisa must have communicated her unease because Andrey opened the door to the expansive bathroom. He indicated the key in the lock.

'Do you see?' he said. 'You are in control of your own privacy. Besides, I would not intrude on a lady at her toilet.'

Raisa wondered whether he was mocking her. The men called her many things. Lady wasn't one of them. 'I will be waiting in the drawing room.'

Her face asked a question and he answered it with a wave.

'The second door down.'

Raisa gave the ghost of a nod and crossed the threshold into the bathroom. It was almost as big as Bagrov's entire whorehouse. She ran her hand down the dresses Andrey had left for her. The material was both flimsy and beautiful, like the wings of a butterfly. The décolletage was deep and plunging. She imagined herself in this dress, her plump, growing breasts adding contours to the garment, stirring lust in Andrey. He was a normal man after all. Raisa found that reassuring.

She returned to the door and turned the key as quietly as she could. It was stupid, but she thought it might offend him if he heard the rasp of the metal. It might communicate distrust. She reviewed the various bath salts. There was one incongruous item among the items laid out for her. There was a shaving brush and cut-throat razor. Maybe this served as Andrey's bathroom from time to time. Undressing herself, she slid into the warm, soapy water. As the bubbles coated her skin, she removed the stoppers from the various bottles lined up on a shelf by the bath. She slid down and allowed the water to cover her chin, mouth, cheeks. Pinching her nose, she immersed herself entirely, imagining what she looked like from above, naked and pale like a sleigh track. She was picturing herself through Andrey's eyes, trying to enter his mind. The image disturbed her and she sat up abruptly, looking around. There was nobody there. Thank God there was nobody there.

She pulled the plug and watched the frothy water, slightly discoloured with the grime from her skin, gurgling down the drain. Imagine if that greyish water constituted her departing sins. Imagine if this was the last time she ever succumbed to some stranger's lust. Something about this entire farce made her smile. It was all so silly. The war had made a whore out of her. Now the brothel had made her into a princess for one night, bathed, scented and desired. It wouldn't last, of course. Andrey was after one thing. Once he had satisfied his appetite, he would return her to Bagrov and a life of bare subsistence, earned from nights on creaking bedsprings. Raisa padded across the cold, tiled floor in her bare feet. She liked the sensation of cold air on bath-cossetted skin.

'I am pure,' she murmured then giggled. 'The purest little whore in Petrograd.'

She dressed and admired herself in the mirror. Quite the cutie. Yes, she scrubbed up well. Bagrov and his clients hadn't ruined her, not yet. She saw the hairpins on the table and arranged her hair in what she imagined to be the style of a lady, a princess, a Romanov. The pilgrim Rasputin came to mind and she played the part of the Tsarina. The word on the street was it that she did more than discuss her religious faith with her mad monk. Raisa gazed at her reflection and she was the Tsarina giving the ragged madman the come-on.

'Do you want me, Grigori Yefimovich? Would you like to run your hands over my body? I'm sure you would. What's stopping you?'

Then she laughed out loud, just a little too raucously. What would Andrey think? There were three pairs of shoes against the far wall, one to go with each dress. She slipped her feet into the matching ones and admired the effect. It disturbed her that she had been selected to fit these outfits. Andrey had very precise tastes. Did he search the bordellos of Petrograd to find his latest princess? Was he that choosy? She was about to go when she noticed the jewel box. There were earrings and a necklace. Were these meant for her too? It was just too good to be true. If she pleased him maybe, just maybe, he would let her keep them. Then she shook her head.

'Fat chance!'

Before leaving the bathroom she hung up her pitiful, drab clothes, marvelling at the contrast with the dresses she rejected. Like Cinderella, come midnight, or morning perhaps, she would be stripped of her finery and returned to the uniform of a drudge. With a snort, she reflected that the world was short of Prince Charmings. She wiped the bath and put the stoppers back in the bottles.

Raisa unlocked the door and stepped outside, feeling very alone. Did Andrey leave while she was bathing? Along the passage, there was a door standing ajar, the second door, the one to the drawing room.

Through it, she could see a porcelain chandelier casting its eerie, yellowish light on a carpeted floor. She frowned. Maybe Andrey was still in the building, but playing hide and seek. If only he'd just get his stupid, bourgeois pecker out, seal the deal and have done with it. Should she call out? But what was she supposed to she call him, Andrey? Your Honour? She twitched her little finger. Maybe she should call him Pecker. The thought amused her for a moment. As she reached the drawing room, gramophone music filled the house, a Russian folk song.

'Your Honour?'

Raisa walked slowly, her gaze travelling round the drawing room, inspecting the rich furnishings. Surely the sofa, armchairs, wallpaper and curtains were chosen by a woman, or should that be *for* a woman.

'Andrey?'

She lifted the needle to still the music, but Andrey's voice interrupted her.

'Leave it on.'

Raisa turned. This was going to be a long night.

'Where are you?'

She was pretty sure he was talking from behind the silk screen. What was he playing at? Was he about to he leap out, dressed in nothing but a necktie, a pink ribbon round his cock? She adopted a playful tone of voice.

'Do you want to play, Your Honour? Do you want me to seek you out?' She reached out, wriggling her fingers, the way a parent does with a giggling child. 'I'm coming to get you.'

Andrey's voice crackled across the room. 'You will call me most excellent and sovereign prince.'

By now, Raisa felt like laughing out loud.

'Am I the Tsarina?' she asked. 'Am I Alexandra to your Nicholas? Do you want me to speak in a German accent, *mein liebchen*?'

There was fury in Andrey's voice when he spoke again.

'Stop it! Stop it, I say. You will call me most excellent and great sovereign prince Pyotr Alekseyevich, the ruler all the Russias: of Moscow, of Kiev…'

'I can't remember all that,' Raisa protested, before realising what he had just said. Now it made sense. Any minute he would be wanting her to call him Peter the Great and praise his magnificent, tumescent schlong. 'Do you want to play Peter the Great? Is that it?'

That's when Andrey stepped out from behind the screen. Raisa almost burst out laughing. He looked ridiculous. He was wearing a shirt, a coat and knee-length breeches. The outfit was set off with a lace jabot and cuffs, leather shoes with buckles and silk stockings. Andrey did not join in the laughter. His eyes didn't look blue anymore. They were black marbles. His lips were pressed tightly together. He was not amused.

'Oh, give me a clue, Sir? What is it you want from me?'

'You will submit,' he said.

'What, now?'

Raisa was becoming impatient. Men and their their pathetic insecurities. Andrey reached for something and Raisa's heart slammed. He was holding a knout – a rawhide whip.

'Oh no,' she said. 'I don't play those kind of games.'

'You are being well paid for this. You will do exactly as you are told.'

'There are limits, Your Honour. I draw the line at violence. Please don't be offended.' She was managing to sound obedient. Truth was, she wanted to rip his balls off. 'Take me home, Sir. Bagrov will give you a full refund.'

'Be quiet!'

The shout wasn't masculine at all. It resembled a woman's scream or the shriek of some wild, terrible bird.

'Please let me go. I'm a good girl. I swear, Your Honour. Don't hurt me.'

'Hurt you?' He roared with laughter, taking the whip in both hands. 'This isn't a game. Is that what you think? You misunderstand me, Raisa. It is a holy duty. I was tasked by God to drive out sin. You are to be purified as Mother Russia will be purified. Do you understand me, sinner?'

Raisa remembered her earlier doubts. She was not here to satisfy Andrey's desires, at least not those desires. Andrey drew back the whip and lashed out with it. The rawhide tail snapped across the room, missing Raisa by inches and shattering the porcelain lampshade so that shards of glass fell on her like rain. She squealed in spite of herself. That seemed to please him.

'With this knout, I will end your career of sin and you will join the others. Bitches like you don't deserve to live.'

Others. Terror clawed its way down Raisa's spine.

How many girls had left Bagrov's employ without explanation? What was their fate? Did some of them end up here? Did they fit Andrey's specifications? Were they *purified*? Andrey was preparing to wield the knout again. Raisa turned and fled, escaping out into the passage just as the whip brought a large portrait crashing to the ground. She was at the door. She was frantically scrabbling at the handle. It was rigid. There was no key in the lock. She spun round, panting with fright and a stirring sense of fury and injustice. War, misfortune and loss, hunger most of all, had led her to Bagrov's door. She hadn't deserved to be "broken in" by the brothel-keeper. She didn't deserve the nights working on a soiled mattress. She didn't deserve a twisted monster like Andrey.

'Where's the fucking key?' she screamed.

'You will not use foul language in my house,' Andrey shrieked, that feminine voice echoing around the walls. 'I forbid it.'

'You think you can order me around, do you?' Raisa shot back. 'You know what, Your Honour, Your Can't Get it Up, You Bourgeois Prick! I'll use any language I want and you'll pay me for it.'

'Shut up! Shut up!'

'Make me. What, you don't like the language of the streets? Well tough – cock! Prick! Shit! Fuck!'

'Be quiet, you whore!'

'You don't tell me what to do, you impotent filth.'

For a moment, she felt in charge. She half-expected him to crumple to his knees, sobbing for forgiveness like the spoiled brat he was, but she had misread him. He flicked the whip again. It snaked out and struck her on the shoulder. The blow slammed her back against the door and she slumped to her knees, winded. Her skin was broken and blood was staining the dress.

'You bastard,' she panted. 'You cut me.'

But he was about to attack her again. Her thoughts focussed on the bathroom and the razor. You want to cut me, do you? Well, I will fucking cut you back. I'll saw your balls off, you monster. She started to run. The knout pursued her through the door, sweeping the bottles of bath salts to the ground where they smashed. She had the razor in her hand, gleaming under the electric light.

'You want me, do you?' she asked, chest heaving with terror and just enough defiance to keep her fingers wrapped round the razor's handle. 'Come on then. You're bigger than me, stronger, better armed. You want to break me. Do it. You're a big man, you're the Tsar of All the Russias. Well, what are you waiting for, your stinking, puke-faced Excellency?'

Andrey roared and raised the knout to strike. Suddenly, there was a demon inside Raisa, a thing that had been growing inside her all those miserable nights at Bagrov's place. She scampered forward, ducking under his swing and swept her arm left to right. She heard his flesh grind then watched, fascinated and appalled as a scarlet line, like a mouth with badly applied lipstick, opened wide and blood pumped, cascaded, stained the aristocratic garments. She looked with curiosity into Andrey's shocked eyes. Then she surprised herself by laughing.

'That took you by surprise, didn't it, you pig?'

She listened to his gasping and wheezing.

'Listen to you grunt.' She turned on dancing feet. 'All Hail Pyotr Alekseevich, founder of Petrograd, Tsar of all the Tiny Peckers, Emperor of Stuck Pigs.' She whirled before his dying eyes. 'I got one over you, didn't I, your Imperial Gobshite.'

She saw his eyes roll back in his head and she knew he was in his death throes. She put down the razor and poked him in the chest.

'To Hell with Tsars, to hell with bourgeois, to hell with war and to hell with you, you dirty bastard!'

Andrey's legs finally gave way and he crashed to the floor, supine like Mother Russia under the German jackboot. His arms were stretched wide in crucifixion as the blood pooled.

Kolya

The students turned the corner onto the Nevsky Prospect, singing the *Marseillaise*. They had red ribbons on their coats, and scarlet banners bobbed among their ranks. Surely they were asking for trouble, marching along the Nevsky Prospect like this? Kolya eyed the familiar plate glass windows of the luxury shops. The one before him was English-owned, with Fortnum and Mason hampers and Huntley and Palmer biscuits, the one over there French. There were tailors, dressmakers, milliners, glovemakers. The marchers passed Brocard, the perfumier and another shop, the exclusive Brisac. This was the Petrograd of the wealthy and powerful, cultured, well-dressed, multilingual. The workers' barracks were a long way from there, on the other side of the river.

'I wonder if we'll see the Tsarina in there,' Grigory shouted. He spotted a sign. 'Ici on parle francais.' He gave a scornful laugh. 'Ici on parle merde.'

'See what an education can do,' Kolya said pointedly. 'You can spout filth in more than one language.'

His words earned a bray of appreciative laughter. Kolya took advantage of the other students' approval to twist the screw of class-consciousness.

'No food queues here,' he said.

'I wonder if the bitch took her mad monk with her,' Grigory said, loudly enough for the well-dressed customers to hear.

'She can't take the bastard anywhere now,' another student commented, 'not since they threw his sorry arse in the river.'

13

That earned him a glare from the lines of police.

'Don't antagonise them,' Grigory advised. 'The last thing we need is a battle with the Pharaohs.'

Kolya eyed the mounted Gendarmerie. Maybe a battle was exactly what was needed. One of the Pharaohs, a beast of a man with eyes like the scales of a fish, blew him a kiss, but Kolya looked away, disregarding the provocation. There was great excitement among the hundreds of students. The wind sighed with the voices of the battlefield dead in their many millions, the hunger of the people, the clang of downed tools. War and class struggle were winding together like the plaited components of a thick rope and something was stirring in Russia. There were whispers, rumours.

'The Putilov workers are on strike,' said one.

'It's not a strike,' another said, contradicting him. 'It's a lock-out.'

Kolya was in the know. It was the job of a Bolshevik to have the ear of the worker-intellectuals. There are just a few thousand of us in Piter now, he thought, but soon we will be a mighty, proletarian army. Soon, we shall be all.

'The Putilov went on strike for higher pay,' he explained. 'This is the bosses' answer. More fucking repression.'

'Down with the bosses and the aristocracy,' Grigory said, with a smirk on his face. 'That's right, isn't it, Kolya?' He raised his fist. 'Towards the socialist revolution.'

One of the Pharaohs pointed Grigory out.

'I'd take care if I were you,' Kolya warned. 'The bastard on the grey has his eye on you.'

Grigory didn't seem bothered in the slightest. There was a spring in his step. The students were outgrowing fear. Kolya didn't know what to make of it. There were millions of dead, millions more maimed for life, crushed like offal and bone in the jaws of war. Everywhere, there were queues for bread. Assault and murder awaited the unwary traveller. Yet here was Grigory, not the most class-conscious of men, laughing in the faces of the Pharaohs. Had he taken leave of his senses, like his namesake, Rasputin?

'Lighten up, Comrade Kolya,' Grigory said, teasing him. 'What's happened to the vanguard of the revolution?'

Kolya rolled his eyes. 'You talk too much. I swear, it'll be the death of you.'

'You'll be the death of me, Comrade Kolya. You're too serious by half. Why, the look on your face would sour milk.'

'Sour milk is what the scoundrels are selling these days,' somebody grumbled behind them.

'Pay attention to the Pharaohs,' Kolya advised. 'They could charge any minute.'

'Yes,' Grigory said, 'and if they do, we'll pull up every flag and cobble in the city and let them have it right between the eyes.'

'Will you keep your voice down?' Kolya hissed. 'Are you looking to get your head cracked wide open?'

'What's with you?' Grigory demanded. 'I thought you were the great r-r-r-revolutionary. You don't sound like it.'

That was too close to home. Ever since he had been a small boy, Kolya had been an outsider, the child who was the butt of the rough boys' jokes, the adolescent who had his nuts crushed down a back alley, humiliated for his shyness and awkwardness with girls. How many times had he dreamed of being one of the swaggering beasts who taunted him, those snarling braggarts without an ounce of self-consciousness or decency?

'Revolution isn't about mouthing off in front of the police,' Kolya snapped. 'It's about discipline. It's about...'

Grigory looked around those closest to him. 'I'll tell you how it sounds to me. It sounds to me as if you're getting cold feet.'

Kolya shook his head and pulled his muffler over his mouth. He had a cold everything else. Christ, it was bitter. It had been a hard winter and it wasn't just about the snow and the damp, heavy wind. Kolya looked down a side street to where the snow was piled like defensive ramparts. The Neva gleamed under the dimming light. The demonstration had reached the police lines and the students drawn up in the front ranks were shifting their feet nervously, wondering if it was their heads that were about to get cracked.

'Link arms, Comrades,' Kolya said. 'Don't rise to their provocations.'

That made Grigory's eyes twinkle. 'No, we're not Anarchists, are we, Kolya? We can't go provoking the poor little Pharaohs. They are such delicate flowers.'

There were more hostile glares from the riders.

'This isn't a game, Comrade,' Kolya told him.

Grigory hooted loudly. 'Oh, so it's *Comrade* now, is it?'

Kolya wasn't taking the bait. 'Do be quiet, Grigory. You're making a complete idiot of yourself. Until recently, you were saying protest was pointless.'

15

Suddenly, Grigory wasn't smiling. Kolya had touched a raw nerve. Grigory had always been the joker, more interested in booze and women than politics, but in the last few weeks there had been a profound change in him. 'Sometimes, life teaches you a cruel lesson, my friend,' Grigory whispered. 'My cousin had his legs blown clean off last month in a German barrage on the lines. The explosion took his balls too. What kind of life does he have ahead of him, eh, the eunuch of Kazan?' He glared at the line of police. 'If you can't get angry about that, what the hell is going to make you protest? They flog those poor bastards at the Front like dogs, talk to them like children then shove them into the bloody meat grinder.'

Kolya rested a hand on his friend's shoulder. 'You never said anything.'

Grigory shrugged. 'Good way to spoil a decent drinking session, don't you think? Heard the one about the kid with no balls and no legs? He arses about all day.'

They were pressing forward. There was apprehension now. The police had a fierce reputation for brutality. Fitful glances stuttered this way and that, trying to interpret the Pharaoh's intentions.

'Are you going to let us pass?' Kolya asked, coming to a halt in front of the Pharaohs' commanding officer.

The commander looked left, drew a breath, looked right, spat a gob of phlegm on the street.

'You want to pass?' he drawled. 'You can pass.'

Kolya smelled a rat, but he led the way, striking up another revolutionary song. He half-expected to feel a blow on the back of the neck for his pains, but none came. With each step he took, Kolya felt a deepening sense of unease, but still, the blows did not fall.

'What are they doing?' he whispered to Grigory.

'Nothing.'

'They must be doing something,' Kolya retorted.

'See for yourself,' Grigory told him. 'They're being as good as gold.'

A stolen glance confirmed Grigory's verdict. The mounted police seemed bored. What was going on here? The marchers were weaving northwards when Kolya heard a shout behind him. It was the police commander.

'Take care when you disperse. I wouldn't want any of you coming to any harm.'

'Don't let the Pharaohs spook you,' Kolya advised, his voice shaky.

Grigory whispered in his ear. 'I'm not the one who's spooked, Kolya. It's all right to be scared.'

Kolya made a confession. 'I am afraid, Grigory. I am no hero.'

Grigory squeezed Kolya's shoulder. 'It's not the fearless man who is a hero, you know. It is the one who overcomes his fear. I'll walk you back to your apartment.'

'I don't need a nursemaid.'

'You're not getting one,' Grigory replied. 'Let me do this, Nikolai Nikolaevich. You said they were watching me. I don't think so. These bastards have got their spies. They know exactly who organised this protest and that puts you in the frame.'

Kolya thumped a fist into his friend's shoulder. 'I wasn't the only one, dear Gregory, but please don't point out the others. We don't want to make it easy for the Pharaohs, do we?'

They placed themselves at the heart of the dispersing students then slipped down a side street. Grigory accompanied Kolya to the tram stop.

'Watch your back, Comrade,' he said. 'We need you.'

'You can stop taking the piss,' Kolya told him.

Grigory's stare was intense and emotional. 'I'm not.'

'You mean…?'

Grigory winked and raised his fist. 'Arise ye fucking starvelings. Down with the autocracy.'

Kolya waved away the gesture and boarded the tram. 'Well, isn't this a novelty? I never thought I would hear slogans dripping from your lips, Grigory the cynic.'

Grigory winked. 'I didn't dream that the Russian army would throw down its guns and walk away from the battlefield. Sometimes everything you thought was permanent melts away like the spring snow. The only thing I know is this, we can't go on living by the old rules. It just isn't possible anymore.'

The tram wheels squealed and Grigory's form retreated into the distance. Half an hour later, Kolya was taking his seat in a small room in the Vyborg district. His eyes stung from the fug of cheap cigarette smoke. He had tried smoking once, encouraged by Grigory. Kolya had very nearly vomited on the spot. He had always had a weak constitution, laid low for days by the slightest cold, reduced to a piteous wretch by a drinking bout. For all that, he had the admiration of his friends. His determination and single-mindedness had always earned him the respect of his fellows. Too bookish by half, but not the kind of man to back away from an argument.

Kolya was in a fever as he looked around the meeting, mostly workers. He wanted to report the atmosphere on the student demonstration, the way they shoved their way past the Pharaohs and owned the Nevsky for almost an hour. He would have to bide his time though. Advanced workers his comrades might be, but he still felt as if he must defer to them, these metal workers and machinists. Comrade Anishin was in the chair, giving his report.

'The Vyborg borough committee is opposing any extension of strike action,' he said, to the consternation of some. 'The mood of the masses is tense. The advance workers are combative…'

That provoked an interruption. 'Then we should place ourselves at the head of the movement. The people are weary of the war and privation. Is this not what we have been waiting for?'

Kolya joined the murmur of approval for the speaker. Anishin was having none of it. He stuck to his script.

'Any further strikes could lead to rioting and the certainty of repression. We are not ready.'

'So when will we be ready?' somebody demanded from the back.

Anishin raised his hand to quell the incipient revolt.

'The Party has not yet sunk deep enough roots. We have too few links with the soldiers. If we get ahead of ourselves we could be crushed before the revolutionary moment ripens.' He played his trump card. 'Who here will assume the leadership?' He started to point people out and mentioned them by name. One by one, they lowered their eyes or fell silent. 'Very well, I will put it to the vote.'

There was a majority for the Party keeping its powder dry and delaying revolutionary action until some moment down the line, when circumstances were right. Kolya held back from mentioning the students' action, but he approached Anishin as the meeting broke up.

'I saw something today,' he said, 'a new defiance.'

Anishin smiled indulgently. 'Is that right? Where was this, Nikolai Nikolaevich, in one of your seminars? What was the subject? Waiting for pocket money from Papa?'

Kolya took the taunt on the chin and soldiered on.

'No, I have just come from the students' demonstration. I mentioned it to you the last time we met.'

'Forgive me,' Anishin said. 'I have had a lot on my mind. So tell me, what did you see that was so new?'

Kolya didn't like the way Anishin was humouring him, but he pressed on.

'It was the way we defied the Pharaohs,' he said. 'The others were running ahead of me. I have a friend, Grigory…'

'I see,' Anishin grunted, 'a friend.'

Kolya ignored Anishin's dismissive tone.

'He has always been cynical about politics. You know the type. He would rather be drinking himself into a stupor or chasing a bit of skirt.'

'And you wouldn't?'

Kolya was tiring of the constant interruptions, but he ploughed on. 'He was fearless today, same as the others. He even expressed an interest in joining the Party.'

Anishin nodded. 'That is good. Of course it is. It doesn't mean we can leap from a single conversation or one student demonstration to revolution overnight, now does it?'

'Thousands have struck in Moscow. Surely that means something. We in Petrograd have always been at the eye of the storm, but now we are not alone. They are following us into battle. Something is happening. We should be striking at the roots of the social order now, before the moment passes. We can bring this criminal war to an end. We can send the two-headed eagle crashing to the ground.'

Anishin tugged at his beard. 'I see. Is that your considered opinion, Kolya, your Marxist *analysis*?'

Kolya suppressed the urge to yell in Anishin's face, to wipe the arrogant smile from his lips.

'It's what I think.'

'That we are on the verge of revolution?'

'How will we know if we do not test the water? *On s'engage, et puis on voit.* Why are we holding the masses back? I don't understand.'

Anishin passed over Napoleon's words and rested a fatherly hand on Kolya's shoulder, even though he was no more than ten years older.

'Well, that's good. I like a comrade who has some independence of mind, but the vote has already been taken. I don't remember you raising any objection. The advice to hold back came from Kayurov himself. Kayurov joined the Party in 1900, He has been a supporter of the Bolshevik faction since 1903.'

Kolya detested the appeal to a greater authority, but the conversation was at an end. There was no more to be said.

'I just wanted to express my opinion.'

'Of course,' Anishin said, 'and I thank you for it.'

With that, he walked away to rejoin his close comrades. Kolya watched the row of backs in their workmen's clothes. It was up to Anishin if he wanted to ignore the students, but Kolya had seen the fire in Grigory's eyes and heard the way his voice shook with emotion as he talked about his cousin's sacrifice. There was something in the air today on the Nevsky. It was as if some great behemoth was stirring beneath the pavement, its pulse beat throbbing from below whilst the others were laughing and joking. These were the advanced workers. Why was there no sense of urgency? They were the very nerves and sinews of the revolution. Yet they held back.

Kolya hovered at the edge of the gathering for a while, then mumbled his apologies and stepped into the night. He walked past the Putilov Iron Foundry with its chimneys belching smoke into the sky. Why was he not born the son of workers, here in red Petrograd, rather than the child of provincial schoolteachers? He imagined himself standing before the assembled masses, urging them to storm the very heavens. Instead, it was a mediocrity like Anishin calling the shots.

Kolya loved these Petrograd nights, warm in his fine winter coat. His parents must have saved for some time to buy it. He thought of them worrying about him in the great city on the Neva. He wrote to them regularly. He didn't say much about his political involvement, but they were able to read between the lines and their concern showed in their replies. Kolya looked back at the Putilov plant and slipped off his gloves for a moment to examine his uncalloused hands. He shook his head and continued on his way to his lodgings. He was crossing the road when a figure detached itself from the shadows.

'Are you looking for a good time, Sir?'

The speaker was of indeterminate age, but she was no spring chicken.

'No, thank you. I am going home.'

'It won't take long. You'll feel better for it. I'll make sure of that.'

She named her price.

'Really,' Kolya said. 'I have to go.'

The woman laughed.

'Are you scared of me, dearie?'

'Of course not,' Kolya told her. 'Look, I have to go.'

She was insistent. She walked right up to him and made a grab for his wrist. He tried to squirm free, but she clamped his hand to her scrawny breast. Instantly, in that miserable tatter of flesh, Kolya felt the hunger stalking Russia. He wondered when she had last eaten a hot meal.

'Please let me go,' he said.

She lowered her price.

'No, I don't want to bargain,' he protested. 'I just want you to leave me in peace.'

Finally, he succeeded in freeing his hand and shoved her away. She stumbled back against the kerb and sprawled on the pavement. She squawked something behind him, but he wasn't stopping, not for anything. He stumbled through the murk, boots skidding from time to time as he blundered on uncleared ice. He remembered the throb of fear he had felt on the Nevsky, Anishin's pitying expression, the whore's bony fingers pressing his hand to her shapeless, puckered breast.

What he hated most was that, old and wasted as she was, he really had been tempted. He pinched himself, as if pain could cleanse him of his impure thoughts. Socialism was rational, a cure for the ills of war and hunger in this lousy world. Why must he wade through this filth, why was he forever dragged down, dirtied and humiliated? He reached the river and gazed out across the ice. He clenched his fists. He had tears in his eyes.

'Life will be better,' he promised through chapped lips. 'I will drag you, Russia, screaming oaths and obscenities if need be, into a brighter dawn. This I swear.'

That's when he heard giggling behind him. There was a courting couple in a doorway. They had heard everything. Kolya blushed and hurried off home.

Raisa

Fifteen minutes after the slitting of Andrey's throat, Raisa was numb. She was sitting on the far side of the bathroom, her back against the wall, staring at his body. She was no stranger to death. She'd nursed her mother as the cancer devoured her. It was an experience that had stripped all hope from her soul, all belief in the future. Andrey's body lay accusingly before her. The razor had done its work well. The sharpened steel had showed her assailant some small mercy, in a way her mother's cancer never had. This bourgeois monster left the world with his dignity intact, going down like a soldier shot in action. He had probably been too shocked to feel much pain or to reflect on his own mortality. Not so Raisa's beloved mother. She had had to fight the growing tumour, day in day out for months. She had had to suppress her groans of pain to spare Raisa even more intense grief. Finally, Raisa glared at Andrey's body and forced out a single word.

'Bastard.'

On impulse, she scrambled to her feet and kicked Andrey in the ribs. It didn't have much effect. Her feet were small and shod in dainty slippers, more suited to the ballroom than the inflicting of pain. Pain? What are you talking about, you little fool? Tsar Peter was beyond pain, beyond sensation. All that was left was a lump of meat. Raisa did not believe in a life beyond this vale of tears. God had died along with her mother one terrible summer's evening not that long ago. She wanted to believe in the afterlife, if only so that Andrey could be condemned to twist and writhe in Hell, tortured by Satan's prongs and dancing fires. Yes, the Devil made a lot more sense than a loving God.

Raisa approached the mirror. There was a wound where the tip of the knout split her flesh. It wasn't deep and there was precious little blood. That couldn't be said of the stains that were marking her dress. Andrey's blood was all over it. It was on her cheek too, and her arms and breasts. She would have to bathe again if she was to avoid arrest. She couldn't walk into the street looking like this. Her gaze strayed back to where Andrey was lying on the tiles, eyes staring lifelessly at the ceiling. She couldn't bathe in here, next to her attacker's grotesque cadaver.

What then? She investigated the possibilities. She could drag the body out into the hallway and clean the place up. How long would that take? She searched for a clock and registered the time. Ten o'clock. When would the servants return? She thought it through. The master would want to eat his breakfast in a warm room so the fire would need to be laid by six o'clock. They would probably start work about five o'clock. There was time.

More minutes passed. She swung between her horror at the scene and rage at the fate Andrey had had planned for her. She was paralysed, wanting to turn back the hands of time. The wind sighed against the bathroom window, reminding her of the world beyond these walls. As her thoughts wandered through the events of the last few hours, a steeliness entered her soul. She would not let Andrey take her life.

Let's make the best of this, she thought. The bastard was rich, so she'd turn it to her advantage.

She discovered a master bedroom. There were two sets of clothes. They belonged to Andrey's parents. She wondered where they were, panicked for a moment at the thought of them returning from the theatre or the opera. Even now, they could be turning the key in the lock. Raisa scoured the building. Maybe there was a calendar, a diary, anything that could tell her what to expect. After some feverish searching, she located a dated letter on Andrey's escritoire, where she read: *...away for another week...thinking of you, my darling...hoping you are not at a loss for some way to entertain yourself while we are travelling.*

Entertain himself. He did that, all right, the dirty bastard. Oh, Mama, Papa, if only you knew what your little boy got up to while you're away.

Raisa fairly danced around the room. That is when she noticed the door to a small, ensuite bathroom. How many bathrooms did these people have? She drew a second bath and brought salts from the hellish scene at the other end of the passage. Her mind was suddenly as cold as ice. Her attacker was gone. What mattered now was her own life. She would survive. She luxuriated in the sweet-smelling bubbles and washed away the proof of her crime. Crime? Fuck that. It was self-defence. Sweet, fragrant Andrey would have flayed the skin from her bones. He would have butchered her like a farmyard beast. In the eyes of vermin like Andrey the Great, the poor were utterly worthless, about as much use as chaff tossed to the wind.

Emerging from the bath, she scrubbed her blond hair dry and enjoyed what she saw in the mirror's reflection. The city's hunger had not withered her. She had a good figure. She was Bagrov's prize asset, his little beauty. The punters gagged for her. She got enough to eat that her curves were not allowed to fade. When she had some bastard riding her, he liked a pair of tits to hang on to. What now? She couldn't go back, not after this. How the hell was she going to earn a living? At least with Bagrov, she had a roof over her head and the company of the other girls. Now, she imagined herself huddled in a doorway, soaked to the skin.

So began a painstaking search of the place. First, she needed something to wear. She dismissed the wardrobe in Andrey's mother's room, though she took a shine to a particularly fine winter coat, so beautifully padded she would surely be as warm as toast inside it. She assembled several pairs of boots and started to try them on. Rejecting the majority, she was left with two suitable sets of footwear. She was still naked and beginning to feel the sting of the cold. She discovered some underwear, a nightdress and dressing gown and resumed her exploration. Up a flight of stairs she found what she was looking for. A housemaid had left one of her outfits hanging in a wardrobe. It was plain but practical. Raisa wouldn't stand out from the crowd, wearing it. She would resemble any shop girl or waitress. There was a second change of clothes in another room. Now for a suitcase.

She discovered just what she was looking for in the room belonging to Andrey's parents. It was plain and unremarkable. Ordinariness, anonymity, would be the key to her freedom. She packed the clothes and added some accessories, a hairbrush, two bottles of perfume, some jewellery. She remembered the earrings and necklaces in the bathroom and added them to her treasures. She found money in some of the drawers and counted it. That should be enough to pay for some modest lodgings until she found a job. Raisa permitted herself a quiet smile. This was all turning out rather well. She should have murdered a client long ago.

She giggled like a schoolgirl, shocked at her own boldness. There was no guilt. Instead, she felt vindicated. Andrey had been going to subject her to the most unspeakable tortures before she finally succumbed. He got what he deserved. There was something else. She had crossed a line. In the aftermath of her mother's death, her days sleeping on the streets and scavenging for scraps to eat, she had lost any sense of dignity or self-worth. Washing up in Bagrov's stinking den was the logical result. He had taken her virginity and thrown her to the wolves.

'Well, fuck you, world, this is one whore who's going to survive.'

It was half past eleven. She would need a nap before she left, but the house of horrors was also a magical grotto of surprises. She needed money, lots of it, and a rummage through the drawers in each room produced a fair haul of cash. How casual the rich were with their wealth! Why, the girls in Bagrov's brothel would have stared with popping eyes at all this cash. She found a sewing kit and an idea formed. Gleefully, she deposited it in her suitcase. Before curling up in Andrey's bed – who else's – she gave his bureau the once-over and stopped short. One drawer was locked.

What was Andrey hiding? She searched for a key, but to no avail. She set to work with a paperknife. It slipped and almost sliced her finger open. She cursed and sucked away the little bead of fresh blood. After a few moments, she finally prised the drawer open…and whistled.

'Well well, aren't you a naughty boy, Andrey?'

There was more money, still in its paper wrapper from the bank, a fat, black pistol and an accompanying cardboard box of bullets. She weighed the gun in her hand.

'What did you want this for, my little Tsar?'

She slipped her hand inside the drawer and felt around. What was this? Her fingers had just come into contact with a leather-bound diary or notebook. She flicked through the pages and her eyes widened. It was a journal, no, more than a journal, a confession. In it, page after page, Andrey catalogued his self-loathing, his hatred of the streetwalkers he saw every day as he went about his business. Raisa devoted forty minutes to her reading. The narrative had the fast pace and over-wrought vocabulary of some cheap novel. She had counted four victims whose stories were told in the journal by the time she wearied of the morbid material and threw it down. Gazing at the pages splayed on the floor, she came to a decision. The world had to know what this monster had done. She chose a particularly graphic section and returned to the killing floor, sliding the open journal under the dead man's fingers.

'It looks like you will live forever, Andrey. Enjoy your notoriety.'

She spent the rest of her stay in his bedroom. She put six bullets into the gun's chamber and slipped it into the coat she had laid out to protect herself from the cold. The remaining bullets she put into a small pocket inside the lid of the suitcase. She finished her packing and placed the case by the door. There was one more job to do. She unpicked the lining of the coat and sewed some of the money inside. She sewed more of the notes into her skirt. Satisfied with her night's work, she ran once more through her plans. She would leave by the front door just before five am when the street was quiet. The servants would probably enter by the back door anyway. Raisa wound the alarm clock on Sergey's bedside table and set it for four forty-five. She curled up on the bed and snuggled among the bedclothes. She could smell Andrey's hair oil on the pillow. Before long, she was in a deep sleep.

The sleep of the just.

She woke before the alarm had time to ring, refreshed herself with a brief wash, dabbed a little perfume behind her ears and on the inside of her wrists. She submitted herself to one final appraisal in the mirror, running her palms over her slim waist.

'Quite the lady,' was her verdict. 'Raisa Alexeyevna Kulakova.'

She let herself out, looking left then right down the street before marching briskly though the white mist, swinging her bulging suitcase. There was bound to be a smart hotel open for breakfast before long. She killed a little time wandering the quayside. Her sense of freedom was intoxicating. Finally, she presented herself at the threshold of one inviting establishment. The doorman ushered her inside and guided her to a table.

'Will this be all right, Miss, or would you like one by the window?'

'Oh, the window please. I can watch the world go by.'

Raisa wanted to clap her hands with glee. Just look at the regard a few roubles, a clean dress and an expensive coat can buy you. Just imagine if she had draped herself in some of the jewellery she had concealed in the suitcase. She was actually able to pass herself off as a person of note. She cleared her plate, devouring her breakfast possibly just a little too greedily. The city came to life before her eyes as she sipped her tea; well, except for the throat-slashed, little Tsar. He wouldn't be greeting the dawn this side of Judgement Day. The thought of Andrey sobered her. They should have discovered him by now. She half-expected to hear whistles blowing, but there was nothing.

So dies a gentleman.

He would soon be worm food, just like everyone else.

Maybe the police had read his confession by now. Imagine the look on their faces! To the outside world, Mummy and Daddy would refuse to believe what was in that slim volume, but deep inside they would know. In private, they would tell each other that they always suspected something. Raisa tired of her speculations and called the waiter over.

'Do you know of any cheap lodgings? I need somewhere for a week or two.'

'How cheap?' he asked.

'Well, I want somewhere clean, nothing much, just a room to myself.'

'So you have no family in the city?'

'Not a soul,' Raisa told him.

She detected a question in his gaze, but he didn't put it into words. Discretion was part of his job.

'I will ask the concierge,' he said.

He returned a few minutes later and handed her a slip of paper.

'I think this will be suitable. Mrs Kuznetsova lets rooms to young, single ladies only.'

Raisa read the name of the landlady and the address. The price was included.

'Is that what you were looking for?'

Raisa smiled sweetly. 'This is exactly what I'm looking for. You are very kind.'

Then she did something she has always dreamed about. She tipped him.

'Why, thank you, Miss,' the waiter said. 'Are you sure you want to give me this much?'

'I believe that kindness should be rewarded,' Raisa said grandly, enjoying her newly discovered wealth.

'You're a true lady,' he replied. 'Stay as long as you like, Miss. It's bitterly cold out there.'

She took him up on the offer and ordered more tea. The waiter brought her a newspaper and she scrutinised every item. The war was the big issue, of course. It continued to consume human souls like some monstrous kraken.

She left the hotel just after nine o'clock. By the time she had walked to the lodgings, there was bound to be someone up and about to answer the door. She passed a long line of ragged women, shivering in the cold. Some were pinching their shawls under their chins. Others covered their heads. Jealous eyes followed Raisa along the street. What a turn up! Just hours earlier, she had been wearing drab, worn rags like theirs, but her old clothes were now floating down the river, where she had tossed them.

She wondered how long the women had to queue in the cold for a hunk of bread or a pail of milk. She heard a tram-car approaching, its wheels screaming, but it was packed to overflowing so she walked instead. She was in luck. There was a light in the window as she climbed the steps to knock on the door. She saw somebody peering out of the front window and gave a little wave. Presently, the door opened. She explained about the hotel.

'The concierge recommended you.'

The landlady beamed.

'Come in, my dear. Is it just the one room you require?'

Raisa nodded.

'Did they quote you a price at the hotel?'

Raisa presented her scrap of paper with its line of figures.

'Then we have a bargain. I am Mrs Kuznetsova. That is my door. You may knock at any time. I lived in Moscow many years ago. I know what it is like for a young woman to be on her own in a strange city. It can be a lonely, frightening experience.'

Raisa had just finished unpacking when she heard a noise from the street. She looked out of the window and saw people milling about, both men and women. A woman in faded, ill-fitting clothes caught her eye and waved.

'Come down,' she shouted. 'Join us.'

Raisa opened the window. 'What's going on?'

'It is International Women's Day. You're a woman, Comrade. Come down and march with us.'

Raisa hesitated.

'You've been hungry, haven't you?' the woman shouted. 'You don't fool me. I can see it in your eyes.'

This struck a chord. Yes, she had been hungry. She had been cold and wet, her body had cried out for bread. She had sold herself to the pig Bagrov just to live. You don't get much more needy than that.

'Wait for me,' Raisa said gaily. 'I'm coming down.'

When Raisa rushed out into the street, the woman greeted her with a broad smile. 'I am Svetlana.'

When her eyes sparkled like that, Svetlana was quite beautiful, a goddess in rags.

'I am Raisa.'

Red banners were sprouting around her. There were shouts.

'Bread!'

'Down with the autocracy!'

'Down with the war!'

Some wag shouted from the other side of the road. 'Down with the Tsarina's knickers.'

Somebody yelled back. 'You're too late, brother. Old Rasputin got there first, God rest the horny bastard's soul.'

The ribald humour earned a reprimand from one of the Vyborg workers sporting a scarlet armband.

'That's enough of that,' he scolded. 'Show some respect. We are celebrating the woman worker today.'

'Shouldn't you be at work?' came the retort.

'We're on strike,' the workers' steward explained, 'or locked out.' He shook his head. 'I'm not quite sure which anymore.'

The pace was quickening. Suddenly, a new stream of marchers, a second human confluence, joined the first. Crowds of women in shawls were descending on the street, shouting out demands for bread. Their cries were mixing with the slogans against the war. They were approaching the richer end of town. Raisa appreciated the irony. She had only just arrived from there. A few stones were flying. One woman picked up a chunk of ice and hurled it at the hated Gendarmes. The steward hurried up to the women.

'Comrades,' he said, addressing them in a loud, clear voice. 'Restrain yourselves. This is a peaceful demonstration. There are going to be speeches.'

'What good are speeches?' one of the women shouted. 'You tell me how my kids can live on speeches.'

'That's right,' Svetlana added. 'You can make all the fine speeches you like. It won't put any food in your belly.'

There were roars of approval. The steward looked concerned. The women's rage could quickly spill over into a full-scale confrontation.

'Please, please, Comrades. Listen to the speakers. They will have answers to your problems.'

'Can they bring my baby back to life?' came a cry, dark with pain. 'She died for lack of a mother's milk.'

'That's right. When a woman's breasts run dry, her child is doomed. Make a fucking speech out of that.'

'Listen to the speakers,' the steward said. 'We have a plan of action.'

Svetlana grimaces. 'You have nothing, Comrade, but we will listen.'

'Do you think anything will change?' Raisa asked.

Svetlana winked. 'Look around you, sister. Something has already changed.'

Kolya

Suddenly, there was little hesitation. Nobody was holding back. Kolya was at the factory gates, face flushed with excitement. It was happening. It was really happening. The women workers called this forth! Just as they give birth to children, so they had brought a great movement into the world. All over Vyborg, there were factory meetings. What he would have given to be in there, calling the masses out onto the streets, but that was left to the likes of Anishin; Anishin who had been counselling moderation. Kolya paced outside the factory gates, talking to other militants.

'They are coming out, aren't they?' he said, more by way of thinking out loud, than talking to anyone by name.

That's when the gates burst open and the marchers appeared. There were the blue caps of students among those waiting outside, but much more, oh, how much more, there were the workers.

'In defence of our brothers and sisters. They were killing innocent people. Long live the revolution!'

This was the moment Kolya had dreamed of for so long. Then there was Anishin, at the head of the great throng. He had put aside his caution. The Vyborg party was rallying to the women's cause. He caught Kolya's eye and wrapped an arm round him.

'Do you see?' he said without an ounce of self-consciousness. 'We are going into the streets. The word is, many more workplaces are walking out. What do you think of this, eh, Kolya?'

A murmur travelled through the crowd.

'What about the Cossacks?'

'They say they are not going to shoot.'

There were all kinds of banners rippling among the crowds as columns converged. Some talked about the Women's Day.

'Hail, women fighters for freedom.'

Others demanded an end to war, to the monarchy.

'It's not just about bread now, Comrade,' Arhsinin observed. 'This is about power.'

Kolya decided it would be grudging to remind Anishin of his previous advice to wait and see. Like everyone else, he was being borne along on the tide of anger and hope. Over to his left, somebody struck up a revolutionary song and it was taken up by hundreds, eventually thousands.

'Here come the women,' Anishin said.

There were hoarse cries, stories of the women textile workers marching from factory to factory, pounding on doors, rallying support. As if to confirm the swelling rumours, some of the younger women started pelting a factory's windows with snowballs. A pane smashed and the thrower clamped a hand to her mouth, unable to suppress a fit of giggles.

'You get a prize for knocking down a foreman, you know.'

'What do I get for a boss?'

Anishin had the answer. 'We'll strike a medal for you, sister.'

The mood continued to swell as the growing crowds move steadily forwards, pausing from time to time to listen to speeches: Bolsheviks, Mensheviks, SRs, Anarchists.

'For a general strike,' one of them roared. 'No more bread lines, proper rations for the soldiers at the Front, down with the autocracy!'

There was some heckling, a few disagreements, but mostly there was unity, the sense that a great change was underway, a bubbling wellspring that was going to sweep all before it. Before long, the human maelstrom was approaching the river. Then there was confusion, a slowing of the pace. Anishin pushed forward, jostling through the hesitating ranks.

'What is it?' he demanded. 'Why are you stopping?'

Kolya knew. He thumped Anishin's shoulder.

'There.'

The Pharaohs had thrown up a cordon across the approaches to the Liteiny Bridge.

'Bastards,' Anishin growled. 'So they think they can shove the cork back in the neck of the bottle, do they?'

'We can't let them stop us,' Kolya replied. 'We have to go forward.'

Even before the words were out of his mouth, the women workers were spilling over walls and parapets, swarming onto the frozen river. The ice was thick and winter-hard. Their boots on the compacted ice were like the beat of many drums.

'Well,' Anishin said with a grin, 'we're not going through them, we're going round them.'

Kolya watched the knots of protestors skidding their way across the ice. After some hesitation he followed, while another stream of humanity surged on towards the Troitsky Bridge and confronted the police lines. The *Marseillaise* was echoing through the city, summoning folk memories of the great French revolution. Kolya sang it in French then noticed some of the crowd staring.

'Student?' one asked.

Kolya blushed.

'Comrade,' he answered.

Before long, he saw a familiar face. It was Grigory. His fellow student was beaming with excitement.

'Do you know what I just saw?'

'I'm sure you're going to tell me,' Kolya replied.

'These lasses are wild,' Grigory said. 'A tram came round the corner.' He waved in the direction of Nevsky. 'One of them jumped on board and nicked the control handle. She took it just like that and lobbed it into a snowbank. What do you think of that, eh? I call that initiative.'

'Everybody should be doing it,' Kolya said. 'We'll bring the city to a standstill.'

'Our comrades are well ahead of you, Citizen Kolya,' Grigory chuckled, mischievous as ever. 'There are stranded tramcars all the way from the Sadovaya to the Nevsky Prospect. They're like beached whales.'

'That's nothing,' Anishin said. 'I just heard that tramloads of wounded soldiers are joining in.' He seemed a little self-conscious. 'Remember how I was talking about the need for worker-soldier solidarity, Comrade Kolya? Well, it's happening.'

It's happening. It's happening.

Kolya looked at the faces of the women. They were smiling. Faces that had been grey blanks in the bread lines just two days ago were glowing with joy. Eyes that had been dull sparkled with optimism. This wasn't how he'd imagined the revolution. In his mind's eye there had been stern, determined faces, the steely conviction of the proletarian masses, but this was jubilation. Again and again, people came running to report on what was happening. Anishin was handed a poster.

'What is it?' Kolya asked.

'Well, General Khabalov has a sense of humour,' Anishin answered. 'He has just informed the people of Petrograd that there are sufficient supplies of rye flour.' He roared with laughter. 'See, there's no need for a revolution. There is plenty of food to go around.'

'So we weren't hungry, after all,' Grigory said. 'That's good to know.'

'So much for all their excuses,' Anishin continued, his words directed at the women who had spent so many hours queuing for bread. 'Do you see? They were withholding supplies all the time.'

His words provoked a shriek of fury from a nearby phalanx of factory women.

'Give us bread! We want bread!'

'They're withholding supplies.'

Then the political slogans.

'Down with the Tsar.'

'Long live the revolution!'

Even as this elemental roar rippled through the floodtide of humanity, the Cossacks made their appearance, lances glittering in the sunlight. They could be seen galloping forward in an attempt to scatter the marchers, but the women reformed, defying the spear points. The mounted Cossacks came again, lashing out with their *nagaikas*. The short whips swung at heads and shoulders, but there was no retreat, just a steady ebbing and flowing of defiance. One woman offered the riders a bunch of red roses.

'Do you see?' Kolya said breathlessly. 'They are not cowed.'

Then there was something even more remarkable. One of the Cossacks removed his hat and waved it at the crowd. Kolya stared in disbelief at the jaunty salute. Competing shouts reverberated this way and that.

'Down with the police!'

Then there was a cry he never thought to hear. 'Hurrah for the Cossacks!'

A shower of stones and chips of ice forced the Pharaohs back, but there was no such hostility being directed at the soldiers. There were men and women chatting to them.

'Fraternisation,' Anishin said, with a knowing look. 'Well, Comrades, we've got our revolution all right.'

There were people crawling between the horses' legs, slipping past them, filtering through the Cossack lines. There were swapped looks, even smiles. Kolya had imagined that the revolution would come like a great tidal wave, sweeping all before it. Instead, it trickled through the defensive barriers of the reaction in meandering tributaries that soon came together and crashed over any obstacle in the way.

'I never thought I would live to see this day,' Grigory murmured. 'We are watching the crumbling of an ancient power.'

'You're right,' Anishin said, surprised at himself. 'There's no shooting. They could be cutting people down, but they aren't. Do you know, I think Khabalov is a general without an army.'

As if to prove the truth of his statement, a young woman hurled a snowball, knocking a Pharaoh's black, horsehair busby from his head, an act that drew gales of laughter. And what did the Cossacks do, they cantered forward without any serious intent. It was a game of cat and mouse.

'It doesn't feel real,' Kolya said. 'It is more like a horse show than repression.'

They stood watching the spectacle.

'Here we are,' Anishin said, 'proud revolutionists all – and it is a crowd of women who are showing us the way. Would you believe it?'

'I believe it,' Kolya said.

Grigory spoke even more simply. 'I believe.'

Faces around them shone with pride. Snowballs knocked off more police hats. Suddenly, one of the Pharaohs reacted with fury, lashing out at the nearest woman. She yelped with pain as he delivered a fierce blow to her temple. Instantly, a forest of hands clawed at his uniform, dragging him from his saddle. Fists flew and boots rained down. Anishin watched for a while, curious to see how things were going to turn out, then he waded in, pulling the policeman from the melee and booting him up the backside. His reputation as a Bolshevik and a worker-militant gave him the authority to save the Gendarme any further punishment.

'Clear off or I will let them finish you off,' he barked. 'The next time you are tempted to beat a woman, remember this moment.'

The grateful Pharaoh limped away, nursing his sore ribs and buttocks. Anishin gathered some of the Bolshevik cadres around him. Kolya and Grigory crowded in eagerly.

'We haven't had a single report of gunfire. Do you get that? None. There will be no Bloody Sunday, no Lena. The tide is turning. Fuck me if this isn't the revolution.'

'You can't be telling us the autocracy is going to lie down and let us take everything from them,' Kolya protested. 'The autocracy has much blood on its hands.'

'Will you listen to our student comrade,' Anishin scoffed, 'trying to teach his granny to suck eggs. What I am saying, Nikolai Nikolaevich, is that the autocracy has no vitality. Do you want to hear something funny? I have just been handed another poster.' He read from it. 'All gatherings on the streets are absolutely forbidden.'

Laughter followed.

'*Absolutely* forbidden,' Anishin repeated. 'Listen. The lower ranks of the Cossacks are reluctant to crack skulls. Some of them are even chasing the Pharoahs off the street as if they were naughty schoolboys. Imagine if the Tsarist police were to shoot one of these women. It would be like tossing a firecracker into a barrel of gunpowder.'

'So they are powerless?' Grigory asked.

Anishin shrugged.

'Judge by the evidence of your own eyes. The old order is having a fit of nerves.'

'And the new order?' Kolya demanded. 'What of that?'

'Let's not run ahead of ourselves,' Anishin said. 'You know what the muzhiks say, make hay while the sun shines.'

A beam of sunlight broke the grey cloud.

'Well, the sun is shining on us today, Comrades.'

Raisa

'You take care of yourself, young lady. The neighbours are saying that more trouble is brewing. There is another rash of strikes. Imagine that. When our poor boys are facing the Germans, some of them without even a decent pair of boots to keep their feet dry. Two days it's been going on now.'

'Do you have a son at the Front?' Raisa asked.

'No,' Mrs Kuznetsova said sadly. 'My only son died in the war with the Japanese. My poor husband passed away two years ago. I am quite alone now.'

She went on to set out in detail what it was like surviving as a widow when everyone was trying to swindle you. Did Raisa know that some of her guests vanished like thieves in the night without paying their bills? Raisa allowed Mrs Kuznetsova's words to wash over her like a shower of raindrops.

'Don't you worry yourself,' she said in a voice that was almost carefree. 'I am only going for a walk. I am not the kind of girl who goes getting herself in any trouble.'

She couldn't help but tease her host with hints at her past. It was a game she liked to play. Mrs Kuznetsova, like a gossiping child, was oblivious.

'Oh, I know that,' Mrs Kuznetsova said. 'I could tell you were a fine, upstanding young lady the moment I saw you.'

Raisa almost burst out laughing at that. She thanked Mrs Kuznetsova for her advice and walked out into the biting wind. Though it rasped her cheeks like a metal file, she was warm in her layers of clothing. Her new coat was everything she hoped it would be, comfortable and quite impervious to the wintry gusts. She walked briskly, enjoying the freedom Andrey's unwilling largesse had given her. She revelled in the sting of the wind. How rarely had she felt, actually experienced, true sensation since she fell into Bagrov's groping hands? Her every day in his establishment had been spent in a kind of torpor, sleeping, trudging around in a tattered housecoat, getting screwed.

She appreciated the irony of her new-found respectability. She could have been an anonymous, blue-marbled corpse, washed up further down the Neva and now here she was, two days on, striding down the street in a fine, new set of clothes. She glimpsed her reflection in a shop window and smiled. Mrs Kuznetsova was right about the weather. It was cold, but less so than on previous days, less so than when Andrey directed her to the room where she was meant to die. There was gaiety in her stride as she approached the river. She looked across to the Vyborg Side and the Finland station.

'What a turn my life has taken,' she sighed straightening her fine, fur hat – another gift, courtesy of Andrey's household.

The money she had taken from Andrey's death house wasn't going to last forever, though. She had the jewellery, but she had no idea what it was worth, or how to turn it into cash. She was about to walk on when she overheard two women discussing a particularly grisly crime.

'...Yes, that poor young man had his throat cut in his own home. They are saying it was a burglary gone wrong.'

Raisa stiffened. So the news had hit the streets at last. 'I heard there was no evidence of a break-in. You know what that means, don't you? He must have known his attacker. It hardly bears thinking about. I swear, our Petrograd is becoming a wanton, lawless place.'

'How dreadful! I think the city is going quite crazy, my dear. What with the war and the shortages and all these strikes, people are being driven to the edge of insanity. We are all going to be murdered in our beds.'

Raisa wanted to follow them and eavesdrop on the rest of the conversation, but that would have been unwise in the extreme. They said nothing about Sergey's confession. Raisa was about to turn around and retrace her steps to her lodgings when she heard the sound of galloping horses. She tensed.

The thunder of hooves grew louder and she saw a troop of Cossacks galloping towards her, sabres slapping against the flanks of their mounts. She threw herself against the wall behind her and watched them advancing at full tilt on a substantial crowd as it wheeled around a corner. There was the crackle of gunfire and people started to run.

'Dear God,' Raisa gasped out loud. 'The Cossacks are going to run those poor wretches through.'

A passer-by shook his head.

'You misunderstand. Things are changing. Just you watch.'

What Raisa saw would throw the points on her life's track. A police inspector was urging his men to fire on the crowd, but the foremost Cossack cut him down. The city rang with delighted cheers.

'Brothers, Cossacks, join our struggle. Peace is what we want, not conflict.'

'Don't you want an end to this war?'

'Join us,' bawled one man, stepping out of the throng and raising his arms. 'Disarm the Pharaohs'

The women emulated his example and surpassed his courage, enveloping the Cossacks, pleading with them, placing their hands over the barrels of the soldiers' guns or grasping at scabbards to ensure their lethal blades were never drawn.

'Join the side of the workers, Comrades.'

Raisa was torn. Part of her wanted to get away, to return to the boarding house, lie on the comfortable bed and read one of of Mrs Kuznetsova's books, a Pushkin or a Tolstoy. There was also a driving, all-consuming compulsion to be at the very heart of the surging crowd, beseeching the soldiers like the other women. They had something she envied – a cause, a message of human solidarity. There was precious little unity in a bordello. The older women detested their younger, prettier sisters. Both sides detested the brothel-keeper. But look at this, look at these women in their rags, risking injury, even death to demand bread and an end to war. Without another moment's hesitation, she joined the shabby cordon that had formed around the beleaguered horsemen.

'Well, will you look at this,' somebody announced. 'Even the prim young ladies of the Nevsky are joining us.'

It was a moment or two before Raisa realised the comment referred to her. She smiled at the old woman. If only she knew. The Cossacks wheeled around and cantered away to the cheers of the crowd.

'You are all so brave,' Raisa said, amazed to see the notorious Cossacks in retreat.

The man behind her took her wrist. She flinched.

'Don't worry, love,' he said, 'I'm not going to hurt you. I just wanted to show you this. Go on, hit me on the head. Hard as you like.'

Raisa made a fist and rapped on his cap. Everybody burst out laughing as she stared at the tin man.

'That's right, I made a special metal plate to ward off blows.'

The old woman was still relaying news.

'Everybody is coming out on strike. It isn't just the likes of the Putilov. They're always ready for a scrap, that lot. Why, the bread shops are shut. We've waitresses, shop workers, cab drivers, cooks, maids, tram drivers joining us. What do you do, my dear?'

Raisa's mind raced. 'I'm a typist.'

'Hear that, we've even got a typist here. We might need those nimble fingers of yours once the stone-throwing starts again. Your boss won't like that.'

Raisa's mind filled with an image of Andrey's pale, stiff corpse. 'He doesn't know.'

'That's the ticket!'

'Don't leave out the students,' somebody shouted. 'They're with us.'

'And the postal workers.'

'Printers too! Don't forget them.'

'Comrades, it could be a long list.'

That's when Raisa felt a tug on her sleeve and she almost jumped out of her skin. She spun round, expecting to see a policeman. Part of her actually anticipated the ghostly face of Andrey.

'It's only me,' the newcomer said.

Raisa breathed a sigh of relief as she recognised Svetlana, the woman who had first called her into the street.

For the next hour, Raisa mingled with the crowd, listening to their tales. She enjoyed their company, related to their stories. Until this moment, she had almost forgotten the meaning of solidarity. The light was dimming over the Winter Palace and the Kazan Cathedral. Svetlana shifted her feet. 'Hello, they're back.'

Sure enough, the Pharaohs were moving forward. This time, the Cossacks seemed to be with them. There was a sudden charge and people were running, colliding, falling. In the confusion, horses trampled fleeing protestors. There was the rumour of a machine gun being mounted up the road. The authorities' patience had snapped. The only sound was of screaming and running feet.

'Stop! Join us, brother Cossacks. We have the same enemy.'

The latest appeal seemed less successful. There were fewer smiles on the faces of the Cossacks as they move slowly forward, driving the crowd before them.

'Bastards!' somebody yelled, picking himself up off the floor.

'No,' Svetlana said. 'Don't antagonise them.'

He seemed unimpressed by her call for tolerance.

'If the swine gets down off that horse, I'll give him what for.'

The retreating protestors gathered once more around the statue of Alexander III. There, speakers harangued the crowd, gesturing sometimes in the direction of the Pharaohs and Cossacks, sometimes in the direction of the great Imperial buildings.

'Nobody leave the square,' one of the speakers said. 'Shots have been fired, comrades. If the autocracy is to survive, it will have to send the troops against us. It is time to ask the question to our brothers in uniform, will you fire on the people or will you join us?'

There was a loud chant of: 'Join us, join us!'

Svetlana touched Raisa's arm.

'This could get nasty,' she muttered. 'Nobody will blame you if you want to slip away.'

'I am going nowhere,' Raisa told her. 'My mother worked in a mill. My father died on the Front. This is my fight too.'

Svetlana looked surprised. 'You're one of us then?'

Raisa felt slightly uncomfortable in her stolen clothes, her air of petit bourgeois respectability. Before she could answer, there was an interruption.

'Who's your friend, aunty?'

Svetlana's lined face broke into a broad smile. 'Look who it is, my pretty Elena.'

Raisa turned to look at Elena. It was true. She was very pretty. Her beauty shone out, in spite of her drab working clothes.

'You be careful around our Elena,' Svetlana warned. 'She'll have you converted to Bolshevism before you can sneeze.'

'You're a Bolshevik?' Raisa said.

'I am a proletarian woman,' Elena said proudly. 'What other cause would you have me serve?'

'What about you' Raisa asked Svetlana.

'Me too. When are you going to join us?'

Raisa had no answer to that question. For months, she had served only the cause of the mattress and a series of sweating, grunting men. It was a lousy way to live, but it was better than starving on the street. The three women started to walk, night wrapping itself around them like a shawl. But Petrograd was not done with them yet. There was another squadron of horse thundering through the gaslight.

'Pharoahs!'

Svetlana pushed the younger women roughly. 'Run, will you? I know how to take care of myself. I've had enough practice.'

'I won't go without you, aunty,' Elena said.

'You will do as you're bloody well told,' Svetlana snarled. 'If I know men, they're not after an old bird like me. It's fresh meat they're after.'

Raisa couldn't imagine anyone less like an old bird than the beautiful Svetlana, but she and Elena swapped glances then they hitched up their skirts and fled down the street. The Pharaohs were closing, roaring triumphant hurrahs. They would have some good sport this evening. The horsemen were fanning across the thoroughfare to outflank the running pair.

'It's no use,' Elena panted. 'They've got us.'

Raisa darted a flaming look at her. 'You think?'

She skidded to a halt, turned and produced the pistol.

'Think you're going to get your end away, do you?' she yelled. 'How's about I shoot your lousy cock off?'

Without a moment's hesitation, she fired. It was so inaccurate it ricocheted off a wall, but it was enough to send the Gendarmes off in headlong retreat. Elena's eyes were as wide as serving dishes.

'You've got a gun!'

'Perceptive, aren't you?'

Elena's chest was heaving, but it didn't stop her giving a hearty laugh. 'I can see why aunty Svetlana took you under her wing.' She stared at the firearm. 'Where did you get it?'

Raisa tapped her nose. 'It's a secret. Look, we should go. What if they come back?'

Elena looked around. 'I should retrace my steps and find aunty Svetlana.'

'Are you crazy?' Raisa said. 'They could be waiting for you. I just shot at the police. If you can't imagine the consequences, I can.' She hammered home the lesson. 'I know enough about men.'

'But the bridge is that way. How do I get home?'

Raisa hatched an idea. 'You don't.'

'Well, I'm not sleeping on the street!'

'You won't have to.'

Elena fixed Raisa with a stare, as if seeing her properly for the first time.

'You're a funny one, and no mistake,' he said. 'Do you always talk in riddles?'

'I have lodgings,' Raisa explained. 'You can stay with me and make your way home tomorrow. After all, you don't have work. All Petrograd seems to be on strike.'

Elena looked across the frozen river and nodded. 'Lead the way.'

They reached the boarding house without further confrontations. Elena hesitated on the doorstep.

'What's wrong?' Raisa asked.

'You live *here*?'

Raisa tried to look at the house through Elena's eyes and she understood. Elena's plain factory clothes were going to look quite incongruous in the neat, petit bourgeois surroundings of Mrs Kuznetsova's lodgings.

'Don't worry,' Raisa said. 'Let me do the talking.'

Mrs Kuznetsova greeted them in the hall. Her face fell, demonstrating the fact that Elena was not her idea of a respectable young woman.

'Elena is my cousin,' Raisa explained. 'She works on the Vyborg side.'

'I hope you weren't involved in the disturbances,' Mrs Kuznetsova grumbled. 'I steer clear of politics. It's the best way. Keep yourself to yourself, that's my motto. I tell you, I have heard frightful things, quite frightful things.'

'You have no need to worry,' Raisa assured her, maybe a little too quickly. 'Elena had to join the strike. All the other women were walking out so she could hardly stay at her carding machine on her own, could she? I arranged to meet her and take her to her aunty's.'

Mrs Kuznetsova frowned. 'I thought you didn't have any relatives in Petrograd.'

'I have no relatives with suitable accommodation,' Raisa answered, her nimble mind negotiating the minefield of her landlady's suspicions.

'So the two of you ended up here?'

'The crowds were filling the street,' Raisa explained. 'We sheltered in a doorway for hours, trying to stay out of trouble.'

She caught Elena's eye and saw the twinkle of amusement. Not many people stay out of trouble by pulling a gun on the police. That's when Mrs Kuznetsova said something unexpected.

'If your cousin stays for any length of time, I will have to charge her for her board. If you share a room, the rent will be at the full amount for you, Raisa, and half price for her. It is a room for two, after all.'

Elena had just poked Raisa playfully in the backside. Raisa managed to behave as if nothing had happened. She thanked Mrs Kuznetsova and led the way upstairs to her room.

'What do you think you're doing?' Raisa hissed the moment the door was closed. 'Is that your idea of a joke, poking me when I am still negotiating your right to stay.'

Elena pulled a face. 'Sorry.'

She looked like a scolded puppy, waiting for the moment to pass so she could resume whatever game she had been playing.

'You're not sorry,' Raisa said, folding her arms. Then she snorted with laughter. 'Old Mrs Kuznetsova isn't bothered about respectability at all. The only thing she is interested in is hard cash.'

Elena examined her new surroundings and seemed to like what she saw. She tested the mattress on her bed with splayed fingertips.

'I could live like this,' she said approvingly, 'What do you do for a living?'

Raisa frowns away the question. 'Let's say I have a private income.'

'Do you rob banks?' Elena asked light-heartedly.

Raisa pursed her lips and gave her guest a long, hard look.

'OK, I was only joking.'

Raisa approached the window. 'Do you think it will be the same tomorrow? The trouble, I mean.'

Elena moved closer, standing just behind Raisa's left shoulder. Raisa could feel her breath on her neck, her presence as intimate as one of Bagrov's clients. The moment brought it all back, the way a man would stroke her arms, slide his greasy hands to her breasts. The closeness was troubling, but comforting at the same time, maybe because Elena was another woman, not one of Bagrov's mangy dogs. Elena seemed oblivious to Raisa's confusion.

'This is not trouble, Comrade. It is revolution.'

Raisa's hand stole to the nape of her neck, as if soothing away a sudden rush of heat. 'It is frightening, but exciting at the same time.'

'Like life,' Elena murmured. She took one of Raisa's hands in hers. 'You're very beautiful, you know, not like me. I'm a Plain Jane.' With that, Elena released Raisa's hand and danced across the room. 'People like me though. It's my raw, animal energy.'

Raisa wanted Elena's hand back around hers. It reminded her of when she was a child and used to skip down to the corner with a friend. She turned to watch Elena's antics. 'I don't think you're plain at all. You're lovely.'

Elena sat on the edge of her bed. 'That's good. I always wanted to be pretty. My body's too flat, like a bloody washboard. I always wanted a curvy figure… like yours.'

Raisa was self-conscious. She remembered the way Bagrov bought black market food to keep her attractive to the punters. Elena was still talking.

'It doesn't help going hungry all the time. It plays havoc with your breasts. I tell you, if I could get a decent meal inside me, these little poached eggs would be the size of church bells.'

Raisa dropped her eyes.

'Am I embarrassing you?' Elena asked.

Raisa shook her head. 'It's not that.'

'What then?'

'Nothing. Really nothing.'

Elena shrugged 'Well, I'm dog tired.' She pulled back the sheets and crawled into bed in her under garments. 'I'm dog-tired.'

Raisa watched as Elena turned to the wall then she undressed and slipped into her own bed. She remembered Elena's long, shapely legs as she vanished under the covers. It was a long time before she fell asleep, a very long time.

Pavel

Pavel Sergeyevich Kirilenko had heard the reports coming in from the other barracks. Murder! Mutiny! Soldiers firing on civilians, soldiers refusing to fire on civilians. Nobody could make sense of the swirling chaos. The one thing they did know, something was happening. Now, his fellow grunt Mikhail kicked his boot, wanting to talk.

'Did you hear about what happened at my brother's regiment?" he said. "They marched down to the Nevsky, but that isn't the half of it. They bumped into the mounted police and do you know what happened next?'

'Did they feed the horses?' Pavel drawled, feigning boredom.

He was sprawled on the pavement, bored stiff by the complete lack of action. Under a grey sky, heavy with rain, the whole regiment had been waiting for orders since dawn. Some were smoking. One relieved himself against a wall to the disgust of the officers. Pavel had seen this campaign of minor insubordination growing: unbuttoned uniforms, slovenly behaviour, curses under men's breath, the endless drip, drip, drip of low-level resistance to the officers' authority. Until recently, this would have been a disciplinary issue. Now the officer class were reluctant to rock the boat.

'Well, did they feed the horses?'

'No, you idiot,' Mikhail snorted. 'They opened fire, shot one of the Pharaohs dead and killed his mount.'

Pavel flicked the end of his nose with his thumb. 'Pity the nag had to get it. Horses are worth more than any bloody policeman.'

'There were injuries too.' Frustrated by Pavel's casual reception of his thrilling tale, Mikhail nudged him. 'Do you see? Things are happening, but you can't get the full picture. The newspapers are all shut down by the strikes and there's bugger all leadership from the Party committees. No, the initiative is coming from the *Vyborgtsi*.'

'I've heard talk of thirty dead,' Pavel said 'maybe more. We've got soldiers shooting people down like rabbits.'

'I've heard the same,' Mikhail said. 'What the hell is going on? I thought we were going to refuse to fire.'

Pavel shrugged and pulled his hat over his face. 'When you've got more information, let me know.'

Mikhail's voice rose with indignation 'For Christ's sake, Pavel. Don't you care about anything? You're twenty-one and you sound like an old man.'

Pavel sighed, under his hat. What the hell did Mikhail know? Pavel had things going on in his head his friend just couldn't imagine. He closed his eyes and let the sluggish breeze play over his hawkish face.

'You know, I don't believe in much," he said. "I grew out of the Tooth Fairy when I was six. I stopped believing in God the first time I saw a man trip over his own guts on the battlefield and I stopped believing in the bloody Tsar when he couldn't get me any fucking boots. Happy now?'

'Hell's teeth, Pavel, you're in a lousy mood.'

Pavel snatched his hat off again and glared. 'I am when some soft bastard keeps prattling about revolution and does fuck all about it. If there was as much courage in some men's hearts as there is in their mouths, we'd be in Berlin by now.'

'Do you want to get to Berlin? What have you got against your German brothers? Liebknecht is just as much a comrade as…'

'Buggered if I even know where Berlin is,' Pavel interrupted. He shifted his weight.' Get your finger out of your arse and do something about your fine ideals or leave me be.'

But there was no peace for Pavel Sergeyevich that Monday morning in the February cold. An order to form up travelled down the road.

'There you go,' Mikhail said. 'You've got your action.'

Pavel spat noisily on the ground, earning the disapproving stare of one of the officers, a jerk by the name of Galdin. Pavel bristled. He was one of the most combustible men in the regiment, a constant thorn in the officer's side. 'Who are you looking at?' he growled.

A few weeks ago, that would have led to a reprimand at the very least. Now, it just earned him a nervous stare. The officers knew all about the noisy debates that had been raging in the barracks behind their backs.

'Line up, soldier,' Galdin said.

'Fuck off, dickhead,' Pavel snarled back.

Mikhail jabbed him in the ribs with his elbow. 'Have you taken leave of your senses?'

'Have you lost your balls?' Pavel snapped. 'You were quick enough to mouth off last night. There's workers' blood on the street and we are still taking orders from their executioners.'

Rumours were flying around them. When they heard the Semonovsky had joined the revolution, even Pavel sat up. 'Weren't they the bastards responsible for Bloody Sunday?'

'Was that them?' Mikhail wondered out loud. 'I thought it was the Preobrazhensky.'

Galdin approached. 'Stop talking there!'

Galdin's attempt to assert his authority was full of danger. Once you climbed up on your dignity, it was a long way down. Pavel decided he was up for a fight. He shouldered his rifle and planted his fists on his hips.

'You want me to shut up, do you?' he said. 'Why don't you make me, you pathetic streak of piss?'

Galdin's face drained of blood. He was a pasty specimen at best. Now he looked like one of the corpses sprawled in the neighbouring streets.

'This is insubordination,' he yelled, his voice rising.

'No,' Pavel said, correcting him calmly. 'This is go fuck yourself.'

The street was milling with workers, some armed with hammers, nuts and bolts, the ordnance of the factory floor. The confrontation was attracting their attention. In the distance, there was the chatter of a machine gun. Shouts and screams eddied around the square.

'What's happening?' somebody demanded.

'I don't know. It's chaos.'

As if to demonstrate the point, people started to race down the road, shots ringing out behind them.

'They're cutting us down in the street. People are getting trampled to death.'

'Which is it, machine gun fire or panic?'

'What do you think, you moron? It's both.'

The furore allowed Galdin to recover his composure and try to instil some discipline.

'Get in line,' he bawled. 'We have orders to clear the streets.'

Nobody gave a damn about Galdin's orders. The firing continued, sending the crowd crazy with panic. People were smashing their way through shop windows to take cover. A burly, balding man was carrying something in his arms. Pavel realised it was a small child, flopping like a doll.

'Is that your daughter, Citizen?' he cried.

'They are killing us,' the man yelled. 'I need help for my child.'

Pavel didn't want to say, but the little girl was already dead. Instead, he turned on Galdin.

'Is this your Army?' he cried. 'You're shooting children now.'

Galdin reached for his pistol.

'Back off,' he commanded.

Pavel saw where his long-pent up anger was leading. He flicked a glance at his comrades. Everything hinged on this moment. If he obeyed, they would move forward and join in the massacre. If he didn't…

'You will obey my order,' Galdin bawled. 'You will…'

Pavel didn't wait another second. Before the gaping, expectant crowd, he shoved the stock of his rifle against his shoulder and fired a single shot. It spun Galdin round. The officer was dead before his face hit the pavement. Pavel climbed onto the plinth of the nearest statue and raised his rifle above his head.

'We've crossed the unicorn,' he yelled.

'That's Rubicon, you idiot,' Mikhail said, correcting him.

There was a shrill, almost hysterical tremor of laughter in his voice.

'Who gives a fuck. We've crossed something,' Pavel shouted back, hoarse with excitement. 'Here's the thing, somebody put this uniform on my back to serve the Tsar or Holy Mother Russia or some fucking thing.

They put a uniform on my back and a rifle in my hand and pointed me at an artillery battery that wanted to blow my peasant head off. Nobody said anything about shooting working people and nobody mentioned killing a little kid. I say we go down there and take the guns off whatever stupid shit is still doing the officers' bidding. Who's with me?'

A roar welled up. Suddenly, soldiers and workers were mingling. There was no discipline, no distinction between civilian and military, just a river of people flowing towards the sound of gunfire, and Pavel was at its head. Mikhail came panting up to him.

'What's come over you?' he yelled. 'I thought you didn't give a damn about anything.'

'Well, maybe I just started to,' Pavel said. 'These Bolsheviks of yours, are they serious?'

'How do you mean serious?'

'I just shot an officer dead. If this thing goes belly up, I could be put up against a wall and shot. I want to know where I stand. Let me ask you again. I shot that officer in cold blood. Would a Bolshevik do that?'

Mikhail grinned. 'That's exactly what a Bolshevik would do.'

'Then I'm a Bolshevik.'

They reached a street corner and peered at the machine gun post. There were dead and dying men, women and children, their life blood staining the snow. Pavel had never seen such a pathetic sight. He spotted a bare foot, a shoe lying a couple of paces to the right. He put up three fingers and pointed. The soldiers he had indicated run, crouching, towards cover. He issued his orders with a crisp authority that brooked no refusal. He wondered at the instant response. He wasn't even a sergeant and the men were obeying him. Then he broke cover. The muzzle of the machine gun swung round and pointed at his chest.

'Stop right there.'

Pavel shouldered his rifle and raised his arms. There was the ghost of a smile on his face. He was afraid. Every man, woman and child with breath in their body feels fear, but Pavel wasn't going to show it. He had the face of an eagle and a predator's cold single-mindedness.

'All I want is to talk,' he said.

'Say your piece then clear off.'

'See, it's like this,' Pavel began in his lazy drawl. 'We're hearing that you think it's fine to shoot kids.'

He had struck a nerve.

'We didn't shoot any kids.'

'No, so how do you explain these bodies? What are you doing, brother? I thought you put on a uniform to fight soldiers. That's a man's war. This… this is crap.'

'We've got orders.'

'How old are you?' Pavel asked. 'Twenty, twenty-one? My age, I'm guessing. Maybe younger.'

'It's none of our business.'

'Sorry,' Pavel said, 'but when you shot a little girl, you made it my business. I've got a sister her age.'

'Say another word and I'll shoot you where you stand.'

Pavel's gaze travelled to his left where the crowd was waiting. He had men taking cover, awaiting his order.

'You say you're only doing what you're told?'

'That's right.'

'What's your name, soldier?'

This caused some consternation.

'Why do you want to know?'

'Well, if somebody's going to shoot me, I'd like to know his name, you know, take the knowledge to my maker.' He realised he was performing for the watching marchers. 'Then I can wait for the bastard and kick the living shite out of him when he gets to the afterlife.' He asked his question again. 'So what's your name, Citizen?'

There was a long silence then an answer.

'It's Ivan. Now fuck off.'

Pavel folded his arms. 'I'm not going anywhere. You can shoot me or you can stop firing that gun. Now, before you make your mind up, let me ask you something.'

'Christ, do you ever shut up?'

That brought laughter from many in the watching crowd.

'No,' Mikhail shouted, 'this is Pavel. He's got a bear's temper and a parrot's squawk.'

'Shut up!' the machine-gunner yelled. 'You're getting on my nerves, the pair of you. What's your question?'

'It's this, Ivan, my brother,' Pavel replied. 'What's the Tsar ever done for you?'

'What do you mean?'

'Simple question. What's the Tsar done for you? I mean, the war, how's that going?'

'Is this some kind of joke? We're ill-equipped, badly fed and treated like shit. Add in the fact that they're mowing my brother soldiers down like barley and you could say I'm utterly pissed off.'

Pavel started to walk up and down in front of the gun post. 'Yes, that's my experience too. What about the Duma? Those deputies, are they giving you any help?'

'Are you trying to wind me up? No rich man ever gave a damn about a lousy *muzhik* like me.'

'So let's get this straight, the Tsar and his Chief of Staff betray you on the battlefield, the Duma is as much use as tits on a bull and you want to shoot a brother soldier? You're not the brightest spark, are you?'

This time, the silence went on forever.

'Are you still there, Ivan?'

Still nothing.

'Ivan?'

Then two soldiers rose to their feet and walked away from the gun. The taller of the two glanced at his tormentor.

'You must be Ivan.'

'Yes, and you must have the biggest mouth in Petrograd, you crazy fucker.'

Pavel nodded. 'That's about the size of it.'

The crowd surged forward and the first ones to arrive went to lift Pavel and the machine-gunners on their shoulders.

'Put me down! Will you stop this nonsense and put me down?'

Eventually, Pavel struggled free of the wildly-cheering throng. He clambered back onto the base of the nearby statue and called out for quiet. He was about to speak when a group of students sporting green caps stumbled by, bearing a wounded man on a board.

'Comrade soldiers,' one of them panted, 'the killing continues. You've got to help us.'

'Hear that?' Pavel said. 'It sounds like this thing is in the balance. Either we bring the fighting men over to our side or the bloody autocracy will have our heads on a spike. Now, call me selfish, but I'd quite like to keep mine on my shoulders. What about you lot?'

There were roars and a few hurrahs.

'So what do we do?'

'Show us how to fight, Comrade.'

Pavel nodded. 'The men in uniform will provide the hardware. You provide the numbers. We will make the first approach. The soldiers are the sons of the workers and peasants. We reach out our hands to them.

The Cossacks are the same. Some of their troops have refused to charge the people....'

'What about the Pharaohs?' somebody yelled. 'What do we do with them?'

Pavel glanced at Mikhail. 'I'll let you use your imagination.'

That produced a mighty roar. As it subsided, there was another shout from the body of the crowd.

'What about us?' the machine-gunner Ivan asked. 'What do you want us to do?'

Pavel reached out a hand and hauled him up beside him.

'This is Ivan,' he told the crowd. 'His officers told him to mow you down. He has come over to the side of the people.'

There was wild celebration.

'The machine-gunners will join us in addressing our fellow soldiers.'

There were more loud cheers. Flags and banners rippled in the wind. Pavel was feeling dizzy with the rising tide of revolt.

'Does anybody know any good songs?' he asked.

Somebody struck up the *Internationale*.

Pavel winked at Mikhail. 'So what do you think?'

Mikhail slapped him on the shoulder. 'You're a born leader, Comrade. Tonight, I will introduce you to the Party committee.'

Pavel saw a smartly-dressed young woman weaving her way through the crowd in the company of a factory girl. Mikhail followed the direction of his stare.

'I'd rather you introduced me to her,' Pavel said.

'Behave yourself,' Mikhail told him, slapping his shoulder. 'Get your mind back on what I said. Do you want to meet the Party committee?'

Pavel considered his friend's words.

'If we survive the next couple of hours.'

Raisa

'Do you know that soldier?' Raisa asked as they turned into Znamensky Square.

Elena paused to look and wrinkled her nose at the thought. 'No, and I wouldn't be interested if I did. He looks like a brute. Besides, he isn't looking at me. It's you he is interested in.'

Raisa scowled. 'Well, I'm not interested in him. Men are dogs, the lot of them. They only want to hump the first piece of living meat they come across.'

'Oh dear,' Elena said, 'somebody has been unlucky in love.'

'Don't talk about love to me,' Raisa said, her voice dropping. 'I had the love of my mother, but cancer ate her away. Have you seen anyone die of cancer?'

Elena shook her head. 'Do you have a father?' she asked.

'He died at the Front,' Raisa answered. 'He wasn't much of a man, anyway. All he lived for was another bottle of vodka. He beat my Mama, kicked her like a dog.' Her eyes flashed. 'One time I caught him booting her as she lay on the floor. Well, I waited my time. Three days later, when he passed out in his own vomit after a drinking binge. I kicked the shite out of him while he was senseless.' She started to laugh. 'All the next day, he was moaning and whining, saying he was a sick man. He never dreamed it was his little princess did that to him.'

Elena laid her hand on Raisa's arm. Instantly, Raisa felt a charge, like electricity. Her stomach turned over. Her eyes met Elena's and for a moment it was as if the swelling roar of the crowd was melting away, then someone yelled "Pharaohs!" There was a new surge, a press of bodies and the moment was broken.

'Go home. You must leave the square!' For once the mounted police were trying to use persuasion to disperse the crowd. They didn't gallop or charge. They weren't brandishing their *nagaikas*.

'You go home,' came the reply. 'The square belongs to the people.'

A chorus of shouts rose like a flock of birds.

'The soldiers are with us.'

'They will not fire.'

'Workers and soldiers together.'

Raisa watched the soldiers standing not fifty metres away.

'Elena,' she said, 'something is wrong. Look at them. They are still listening to their officers.'

One officer in particular seemed to still have the ear of his men. He marched up and down, pouring out a stream of instructions. Nobody contradicted him.

'You must vacate the square,' he commanded.

Nobody moved. There was some catcalling. Mostly, there was good-natured laughter. The crowd was convinced that the soldiers were with the people.

'Elena,' Raisa said, 'we should go. Look at their eyes. They are going to fire.'

Elena shook her head. 'The soldiers are coming over to the side of the people. Trust me, Raisa. There will be no violence here today.'

The officer before them stood ramrod-straight, face taut with determination. Such are the men who turn the tide of events in the heat of battle, utterly determined, demanding the loyalty of their men.

He drew his pistol. 'On my command, aim and fire.'

The soldiers hesitated, fingers wavering over triggers. Hearts beat fast. Sweat stung eyes. People who moments earlier had thought the revolution was won were in fear of their lives. There was disappointment, anger, fear.

'Fire!'

Screams burst from a hundred throats, but the fusillade was aimed above the heads of the multitude. Nobody fell.

'Damn you, you cowardly dogs,' the officer screamed. He marched along the line. 'That is your shot. Take it. What are you, a little girl? Fire.'

When nobody listened, he aimed and fired himself. Three times there was the crack of the gun, then the rasping, metallic roar of a machine gun followed. Hot steel reaped a human harvest and bodies fell like sheaves. Then there was more gunfire, this time directed at the machine-gunners. Elena clawed Raisa to the ground and they crouched among the crawling survivors. Raisa could feel Elena's thin, cold hand on her face. She is shielding me with her own body, Raisa thought. But why? Where did it come from, this preparedness to sacrifice her own life to save another's? This, thought Raisa, was how a mother gives herself for her child.

'Stay still!' Elena hissed.

'What's happening?'

'I don't know. I think the Cossacks are shooting back. They seem to be the ones who have taken the side of the people.'

There was a motor ambulance here, a horse-drawn one there. They were taking away the wounded and the dead. There were spent cartridges in the snow, blood, shoes, rage.

Before long, Elena squeezed Raisa's shoulder. 'There's your beau again.'

Raisa peered over the mound of the dead and the living before her and saw the soldier with the hawk nose. He was leading a line of soldiers towards the gunners on the edge of the square.

'What's he doing?'

'He is persuading them not to fire.'

'Will they listen?'

'A soldier is more likely to listen to one of his comrades than to the likes of us. We should go.'

Raisa resisted. 'I want to see how this plays out.'

'I see,' Elena said with a twinkle in her eye. 'Looks like you have a soft spot for Soldier Boy, after all.'

Raise pulled a face. 'Will you stop it? I want nothing to do with any man.'

Elena patted her cheek. 'We should go, my flower.'

Raisa scrambled after her. The hawk-soldier was still arguing with his fellow fighters. She wished him well and hurried after her new friend. They were still making their escape when there was a loud crack. Elena stopped at the street corner, staring at the scene behind them with wide, wondering eyes.

Raisa was eager for news. 'What happened?'

Elena told her. 'That officer. He's dead.'

'Was it Soldier Boy again?'

'Not this time. It was his own men.'

A vast roar was echoing back and forth across the square. There were people embracing, hats being tossed in the air, spun on bayonets. The dam had broken. News flooded across the city like a maelstrom. The Preobrazhensky had left the Winter Palace. The Volynksy were killing their officers. By now, the vast and swelling crowds had swept Raisa and Elena along to the Field of Mars. Mutinous soldiers were firing into the air. Raisa clamped her hands to her ears, but Elena took hold of them and guided them down to her sides. She leaned close and her breath was warm.

'Don't be scared, my sister. This is it. This is the revolution.'

As if to give physical form to the momentous events, an armoured car came racing down the road, twin red flags fluttering. It was welcomed with roars and cheering. More rumours, or were they news? Nobody was quite sure. The arsenal had been wrecked. Guns were being handed out as if they were sweets. The prison gates had been torn down. Some even said the police stations were burning.

'This is crazy,' Raisa yelled, twirling and twirling, arms thrown wide. 'It's just crazy. I feel as light as air.'

Elena was dancing too, dancing and cackling with laughter. She slipped her right arm round Raisa's waist and clasped Raisa's hand with her left. They danced first one way, then the other. Some of the old women started to clap and they danced, kicking their heels. Raisa broke away and danced alone, arms raised. Finally, breathless and dizzy, she rested her hands on her knees. Applause fluttered round her. Elena was the last to stop. Raisa straightened up, still breathless, and gasped, 'I didn't know there were so many vehicles in all Petrograd.'

Armoured and private cars raced up and down, draped in scarlet and heaving with soldiers and workers. Suddenly, the smile drained from her face. A shiny, black Russo-Balt had just appeared. Andrey's car, or one like it.

'Something wrong?' Elena asked.

'No, absolutely nothing.'

Keen to divert attention from her shock, Raisa pointed at Soldier Boy, now waving from the running board of a commandeered vehicle.

'I'm going to marry you, Comrade,' he shouted.

Raisa shook her head. 'In your dreams.'

He took off his hat. 'Wear this,' he shouted, throwing it to her. 'One day, you will wear my ring.'

'You're an idiot,' Raisa shouted back as she caught it.

'Handsome idiot,' Elena said bitterly, as he disappeared into the distance.

'Why so serious?' Raisa asked, startled by Elena's tone.

Elena inspected Soldier Boy's hat. 'Oh nothing. What are you going to do with that? You already have a fur hat.'

Raisa swept off the hat she had taken from Andrey's death house and handed it to Elena. 'This is my present to you, Citizen Elena, for services to our great revolution.' She tapped her friend on both soldiers. 'I hereby declare you Countess Elena, Order of the Dumb Hat.'

Elena set it at a jaunty angle. 'I accept this great honour.'

Raisa then planted her hands on Elena's shoulders and kissed her on both cheeks. As she placed the second kiss on Elena's face, she sensed her sister-comrade's lips moving towards her own, sweet breath caressing her like balm. Pretending not to notice Elena's eager response, she skipped away.

'Hey, here's Svetlana.'

Svetlana hurried towards them, eyes wild.

'What is it, aunty?' Elena demanded. 'Are you hurt?'

Raisa finally noticed the bloodied hands. 'Oh God! Are you shot?'

Svetlana seemed to notice the blood for the first time and wiped her palms on her skirt.

'Don't you worry yourself about me, Elena. This is not my blood, but that of a police commander.'

'You killed a Pharaoh?'

'Not all by myself, darling. It was the democratic will of the people to send the bastard to the afterlife. May he rot in hell for the blood he has shed.'

Elena was staring at her aunt as if she was seeing her for the first time. 'I never saw you as a killer, aunty.'

Svetlana crossed her arms across her bosom. 'Well, I never thought I would see the *Vyborgtsi* sweep away years of oppression, sweetie. I never thought I would live to see us avenge Bloody Sunday and the crushing of the revolution. I was there that day. I've waited twelve years for this moment. Look around you, do you know what this is? It's the cleaning of the stables.'

Elena nodded slowly. 'Aren't we supposed to be the fairer sex?' She glanced meaningfully at Raisa, bringing back memories of the pistol shot. 'It seems some of us are deadlier than the male.'

'Will you be home tonight?' Svetlana asked. 'Your mother is asking.'

'Tell her I will be home tomorrow. Raisa is letting me stay.'

Svetlana kissed her niece on the cheek.

'Pay attention to everything Raisa says and does. She has made something of herself. She sleeps between clean, white sheets and lives in a good part of town. All this from humble roots. She is an example you should follow.'

'Aunty, you are talking like a bourgeois,' Elena protested. 'This is a revolution. We are all equal now.'

Svetlana so-so'd with her head. 'We'll see. The autocracy is crumbling. That doesn't mean we're all going to be sleeping on a fluffy cloud, being fed grapes by a young Adonis with fine, hard buttocks and a chest like a wrestler.'

'Aunty!' Elena said, pretending to be shocked.

Svetlana patted Elena's cheek. 'I may be knocking on a bit, lovely girl, but I am still a woman. Here's my advice to the both of you, get yourselves a couple of fine, young bucks and have some fun. Life's short.'

With that, she sauntered away into the crowd, hips swinging. Raisa saw the surprise and embarrassment she felt in Elena's face, too.

'Well, I wasn't expecting that!' Elena managed.

They walked side by side down one of the quieter streets. They stopped to look at the bloodied body of a policeman.

'Looks like the guards of the autocracy are the ones getting shot now,' she observed coolly.

The dead man's wrists were tied behind his back, his ankles trussed. A green-capped student sporting a red neckerchief passed them.

'Long live the revolution!' he shouted.

'Long live the revolution!' Elena responded.

'What about you?' the student demanded, pointing at Raisa 'Do you not support our just struggle?'

He approached her threateningly.

'Leave her alone,' Elena warned. 'She has done more for this revolution than you can imagine.'

'I doubt it,' the student growled. 'She looks like a bourgeois.'

He made a grab for her sleeve. Elena slapped his hand away, reached into Raisa's coat pocket and produced the pistol. The student's face turned white as she aimed it.

'Look at him, sister. Remember this moment. This is what happens to a bully when he's challenged. What, are you going to piss your pants, *boy*!'

The student had his hands in the air. 'I meant no harm, Comrade.'

'Of course you didn't,' Elena said, cold as ice. 'You listen to me. I am a worker-Bolshevik. This is my comrade and my friend. She routed a troop of Pharaohs with this weapon. What have you done, piss-breath?' She waved the barrel of the gun. 'Kneel.'

'Don't shoot me, Comrade,' the student bleated. 'We are on the same side.'

'You should have thought about that before you started throwing your weight about.'

Raisa had been quiet to this point. Now she clasped Elena's hand and peeled her fingers from the gun.

'Run off home, little rabbit,' she told the student. 'Run while you can.'

He scampered away, chastened. When he was out of sight, Raisa put the pistol away and turned to look Elena hard in the eye. 'Are you out of your mind? Don't you ever do anything like that again.'

Elena was shocked at the reprimand.

'You are my friend,' Raisa said, 'my dear sister in revolution, but you had no right to do that.'

'I am sorry,' Elena murmured. 'Please forgive me.'

Raisa embraced her, her body aroused by the crush of Elena's sweet form.

'Always,' she said, then they separated and resumed their walk in complete silence.

Kolya

It was as if he was seeing the great building for the first time. The green cupola and grand, Palladian façade symbolised wealth and power, yet it reminded him of some wondrous cake, easily crushed into crumbs. A huge crowd was gathering outside the Tauride Palace. The white colonnades were now a meeting point for workers, students, soldiers. There was a buzz of excitement you could cut with a knife. Here and there, people were dishing out food to those drawn to the sumptuous building. In a hungry city, people were not sure where it had appeared from. There were dried herrings. There was bread and plenty of hot, sweet tea. There were people squatting, heads sagging, exhausted by the days of protest, still unsure whether they had won and, if so, what exactly they had won. Many were talking excitedly, asking what was going to happen next. While at one end of the building, members of the Duma wondered how to salvage some stability from the tumbling rapids of revolution, in another wing soldiers and workers called for nothing less than a socialist republic and an end to the bleeding of Russia on the battlefield. They cared nothing for the stability of the rich and powerful. They wanted the order of the streets, the barracks, the factories. In the forthcoming weeks, a name was born for this state of affairs.

Dual power.

Everybody wanted to join the debate. 'We have a temporary government,' said one man, a pompous, balding individual who was almost completely spherical.

'It's going to be temporary all right,' said a soldier, flicking his half-smoked cigarette onto the ground. 'If the new ministers come from the same class as the bloody Tsar, nobody's going to listen to them.'

'Kerensky's supposed to be all right. He's only thirty-five. Maybe he's got some fresh ideas.'

'I don't care how old he is. Is he going to stop the war?'

The only news came from a broadsheet called *Izvestiya*. There were some arguments, but mostly the crowd was expectant. Even now, the odd crack of a rifle or chatter of a machine gun could be heard, but the people had become accustomed to gunfire. It didn't spook them the way it once had. In a land of blood and broken bones, the discourse was one that was no longer appalled by violence. Kolya watched the soldiers milling around, red armbands on their sleeves, flouting military discipline by wearing their caps at an uneven angle, unbuttoning their collars, rolling up their sleeves or swaggering along the street – anything to say they were no longer parts of an obedient, submissive mass. Rather, they were individual men making their own decisions about the future of Russia. Kolya marvelled at the change, but he was looking beyond the disorder of revolt to the possibility of a new form of governance, a new life, a new world. He was impatient to throw the door open and march into the future.

All along the quayside there were bundles of documents being burned. Kolya's eyes were stinging, but less from the acrid smoke than the promise of what might be. He approached half a dozen soldiers. They looked up at his approach, suspicion written on their faces.

'What do you want, kid?' one asked. 'Your mum's let you out on your own, has she?'

'I want to talk to you about the revolution,' Kolya told them.

'You talk. We've just made it happen.'

'But what's next?' Kolya asked. 'That's the question you should be asking.'

This earned him a look of disdain.

'What do you mean, next? Didn't you hear me? We made a revolution.'

'The insurrection is victorious,' Kolya explained. 'What power will rise from it?'

'You tell us,' came the answer. 'We've done our bit, shooting the officers, scattering the Pharaohs, protecting the workers. What more do you want?'

'As we speak,' insisted Kolya, "the Soviet of Workers' Deputies is being formed in the Tauride, a real workers' government, elected from the people's democratic councils. It is they who should be running things, not the representatives of the old order that gave us the war in the first place.'

'We had a Soviet before,' said the sergeant. 'It was crushed. What's different this time?'

'The proletariat is victorious,' Kolya said, waving his arms. 'You soldiers are with the workers. We are the power now, Comrades, you, me, the *Vyborgtsi*, the women who called us out of our barracks and factories.'

'I don't see you spending much time in a barrack or a factory,' somebody scoffed. 'I bet you don't even shave yet.'

Kolya's cheeks burned at their laughter, but he was determined to make himself heard. 'The power is not with the Duma. The deputies are yesterday's men. The Soviet has the wireless, the telegraph, the railway stations. It has the people.'

'You'd better tell that to the Duma,' the sergeant grunted 'They seem to think they're the government.'

'Wait until the worker-Bolsheviks become the majority in the Soviet,' Kolya said.

'And when will that be?'

The soldiers were still wary, but they were listening.

'When men like you support us.' Kolya felt the soldiers' gaze following his every move. 'Do you know what I want to hear?' the sergeant said. 'I want to hear somebody tell us how things are going to get better. I want somebody who says, here you go, this is what Russia needs, follow me. Take that to your Bolsheviks, son.'

Kolya heard hope in the soldiers' words. 'I will.'

He was elbowing his way through the press of bodies when he saw a familiar face. Anishin was standing on the running board of an armoured car. He was sporting one of the ubiquitous red armbands.

'Well, if it isn't young Kolya,' he said.

Kolya ignored the patronising sneer of a man just ten years older than he was. 'Do you have any news?'

Anishin patted the armoured car the way a cavalry officer strokes his mount. 'We are establishing workers' militias. We are expropriating weapons. Come with us.'

Soon, Kolya had a rifle slung over his shoulder. He clung desperately to the side of the car, feet planted on the running board. He was terrified of being thrown off and suffering serious injury, but his terror was eclipsed by the thrill of a city in the throes of revolt. They roared up and down, with little sense of purpose other than to terrify any bourgeois that dared emerge from their expensive homes. Finally, they pulled up by a police station. It was being ransacked by scores of soldiers and workers. A bleach-faced commander was being hurried away.

'When do we take power?' Kolya asked breathlessly.

'We don't,' Anishin told him.

'I beg your pardon?'

'The Duma deputies are going to form a government.'

'But we are the revolution! What of the Soviet?'

Anishin shook his head. 'This is a bourgeois revolution, Kolya. You need to read your theory. This historic stage must be completed before we move onto socialism.'

'A bourgeois revolution made by workers and soldiers! Surely we haven't taken power to hand it meekly over to the liberals?'

'Will you listen to this young pup?' Anishin said. 'He thinks he can tell the likes of Shlyapnikov and Molotov what to do. They have forgotten more about revolution than you will ever know.'

'Who are the leaders of this new government?' Kolya demanded, neck ablaze with indignation.

'Rodzianko is President,' Anishin answered.

'The monarchist! Workers' and soldiers' blood was shed to put a monarchist in power? Who is Prime Minister?'

'Prince Lvov.'

'A prince and a monarchist? Is this what we have fought for?'

Anishin was livid. He punched his finger into Kolya's chest. 'Comrade Shlyapnikov became a revolutionary at the age of sixteen. He has been to prison for his beliefs. You will show some fucking respect.'

Kolya was shaken. He half jumped, half stumbled down from the car.

'It's getting dark, *boy*,' Anishin snarled. 'Now you take yourself off home and report to me tomorrow after you have slept off this fit of pique. Do you understand me?'

Kolya nodded.

'When you have made sacrifices for the revolution, maybe then you can mouth off. Now get lost.'

Kolya hurried away, humiliated. As he departed through the darkening streets, his eyes blurred with tears.

'You're a fool, Kolya,' he sobbed, 'a pathetic fool.'

He stuck his boot into a door and yelled at the top of his voice. Then he sensed a presence behind him.

'I can think of better uses for all that energy.'

Kolya's eyes slowly accustomed themselves to the dark.

'Who are you, Mother?'

She planted her hands on her hips. 'Mother you say! How old do you think I am?'

Kolya realised that, swaddled in that drab, almost colourless dress was a body that was still firm. She had a kind face framed by dark hair. Her eyes blazed with life. The longer he looked, the more he saw a warm, attractive woman.

'I didn't mean any offence,' he said.

'I'm forty-five. That may be twice your age, but I'll give you a run for your money any day, my lad.'

Kolya looked her up and down, using his imagination to make the shapeless clothing fall away. 'I don't have any money.'

Suddenly, her face clouded. She walked straight up to him and delivered a slap that made his teeth rattle.

'I am a woman worker,' she told him as he sagged backward, rubbing his cheek. 'I do not sell myself. My husband is dead, crushed by a fucking machine to make the bosses' profits. Now, my old man was a red-blooded guy, if you understand me and I have needs like any woman. I just want somebody to give me a bloody good shagging. So are you up for it or not?'

Kolya was still stroking his cheek. 'That hurt. A man couldn't hit any harder.'

She laughed. 'Don't worry, I'll be gentle with you. I haven't killed a man yet.' She softened and laid a soft palm on his cheek. 'Have you got a room to yourself?'

He nodded. 'I have, yes.'

'Then lead the way.'

He leaned forward and planted a chaste kiss on her cheek. A heavy breast brushed his chest, inflaming his desire.

'Are you a virgin?' she asked.

When he stared back, shock written on his features, she roared with laughter. 'I bagged myself a virgin!' She took his hand and pressed it to her full breast. 'Do you like that?'

He nodded, his throat dry. 'Yes.'

'I'll make a man out of you tonight, Citizen. I'm Svetlana, by the way.'

When they reached his lodgings, he told her to wait outside while he checked the hall for any sign of his landlady, then waved her inside. He fumbled with his room key, struggling to insert it in the lock.

'I hope you do better with your cock than you do with a key,' Svetlana said.

She ran her fingers over the back of his hand, squeezed then took the key off him and opened the door. Once inside, she gave the place a once-over.

'So this is how a student lives, is it?' she said. 'It looks pretty sparse to me.'

Kolya was relieved that she found his lodgings sparse. He wouldn't want a woman of the Vyborg thinking he was well off.

'Your husband,' Kolya said, 'was he killed outright?'

'Was he fuck!' Svetlana retorted. 'They brought my man home in a wheelbarrow. He took three days to die. Can you imagine what it's like watching somebody you love scream in agony for three whole days?'

'I am so sorry, Svetlana.'

'So am I, lad. So am I. Hey, you know my name. What's yours?'

'Nikolai. Kolya.'

Svetlana wrapped a hand round the nape of his neck and kisses him hard. Then her body started to shake.

'Are you crying?' Kolya asked as she slumped against him.

She rubbed at her eyes with the back of her hand. 'Yes, I'm crying. I thought I would live with that man for the rest of my wretched life. I'm lonely, Kolya, lonely and pathetic. I don't want to grab some young buck off the street and beg for sex.' She swallowed hard. 'It's humiliating. Look, I'll go.'

She was almost at the door when Kolya took her hand.

'No,' he said. 'Don't.'

He guided her hand to his groin. 'I mean, I've got something or you. What do you want me to do with this?'

She laughed through her tears and he loosened her garments and stripped her to the waist. The sight of her made his voice thick with hunger.

'You're magnificent.'

'I had a fine pair of tits when I was younger,' Svetlana said, covering herself. 'Gravity starts to do its work after forty.'

Kolya gently removed her hands and enjoyed the blush of freckles on her breasts, the tawniness of the half-light, the shadows.

'I think you're beautiful.'

'Yes, I bet you do when you're about to get your end away for the first time.'

'No,' he said. 'I mean it.'

It was Svetlana's turn to strip Kolya.

'Skinny,' she said approvingly, 'but lean and muscular. When you fill out a little, you'll be a real lady-killer.'

Kolya cupped her heavy breasts and his thumbs felt her stretch marks. 'You have children, don't you?'

'Yes, two. I have to live with the battle scars.'

Kolya smiled. 'I love your stretch marks. They show that you have lived...and loved.' He lowered his voice. 'What's it like, making love, I mean?'

'Bloody good,' Svetlana says, her voice husky. 'Are you ready to find out?'

Kolya nodded so she unbuckled his belt and shoved her hand in his trousers. She leaned her forehead against his chest.

'I see you're already standing to attention, soldier.'

'I'm not a soldier,' he said.

'You're got a rifle.'

He laughed and saluted.

'I am in the workers' militia.'

'Menshevik, Bolshevik… Anarchist?'

'Bolshevik.'

'Me too. I do like shagging somebody with the right politics.' She winked. 'Let's go to bed.'

Pavel

'Well, fuck me!'

Mikhail gave Pavel a long, hard stare. 'What's got into you?'

Pavel waved a scrap of paper, a flyer from the Bolsheviks. 'It's the Kronstadters.'

He had Mikhail's attention: 'They've mutinied?'

'This isn't just a mutiny. They've marched out of the fortress. They've shot some of their officers and joined the revolution. Do you know what's funny? The poor bastards think they moved first. Imagine their faces when they find out we'd already won the revolution before they even crawled out of bed.'

Mikhail raised his eyes to the high ceiling. Even the corridors of the Tauride Palace were breathtakingly grand. It was as if the whole place had been built to dwarf and overwhelm the insurgent people.

'It's hard to take in, Pavel Sergeyevich. We've got the Tsar rattling round Russia in a train like a lost, bloody suitcase, the soldiers and workers in control of the streets, the sailors walking off their ships. It seems his abdication is being negotiated even as we speak. The word is, nobody wants to take his place.'

'Then there's the Soviet,' Pavel said. 'I'll tell you what I don't understand, my brother. We shed blood to find ourselves where we are now. We drive the Pharaohs from the street. What do we get in return?

The power passes from the Tsar to a bloody prince. Is that supposed to be an improvement? What the hell is going on?'

Mikhail was having the same doubts.

'Fucked if I know,' he said with a shrug. 'Have you seen our government? We're still being ruled by some tosser in a frock coat. Kerensky can tear off his collar to look more proletarian, but he's no man of the people. I'm pissed off with all this.'

There were nods and words of agreement from the other soldiers guarding the Tauride. Amid the grumbling, a stranger approached, a well-dressed man in his Fifties. 'Comrade soldiers,' he began, I am Anton Vladimirovich Stankevich.

Some of the soldiers, those of peasant stock, scrambled to their feet in respect for the starched dress-shirt and a frock coat. Others sauntered over, still displaying the insolence of the revolutionary street.

'You are in the saddle in Petrograd now,' Stankevich told them. 'The workers and the soldiers are the sole power.'

'State the fucking obvious, why don't you!'

For a moment, the previously assured Stankevich looked flustered.

'What about these ministers? How does the new government square with the Soviet? You can't have two centres of power.'

'I am here to commend Citizen Alexander Kerensky to you. This man is my friend. Alexander Fyodorovich is a man to be trusted.'

'Another toff,' came a sceptical voice from the back of the mass of soldiers.

'You misunderstand Citizen Kerensky,' Stankevich said firmly. 'He has been jailed in the past on account of his opposition to the regime. He acted as a defence lawyer on behalf of revolutionaries in the aftermath of the 1905 revolution. He is a member of the Socialist Revolutionary party. Does this sound like a toff?'

'Cut to the chase,' Pavel growled. 'What do you want from us?'

'Security,' Stankevich said. 'Citizen Kerensky is vice-chairman of the Soviet and Minister of Justice in the Provisional Government. The situation on the streets is volatile. There is all manner of wildness. I want to know if you are loyal to the new government.'

Pavel and Mikhail looked at each other, none too eager to commit themselves.

'If this Kerensky is as good as you say,' one soldier said, 'then I'm with you.'

'Give us a minute,' Mikhail said, pulling Pavel to one side.

'You're the bloody Bolshevik,' Pavel said. 'What's the word from these comrades of yours?'

'The Vyborg committee called for a revolutionary government,' Mikhail told him.

'So we give our guy the bum's rush, is that what you're saying?'

'Not so fast,' Mikhail said. 'The Central Committee has overruled the *Vyborgtsi*.'

Pavel's face was a picture of disbelief.

'Look,' he said, 'I'm a simple man, just a dumb *muzhik* in uniform. What kind of bloody revolutionaries are you? It sounds to me as if these Bolsheviks can't find their own hands to wipe their arses.'

'It's a difficult situation,' Mikhail said. 'You have got to give the party leadership a chance to settle on the way forward.'

'Difficult?' Pavel leaned in close. 'You listen to me, Comrade. The way I see it, a revolutionary carries out a revolution and if he can't do that he's about as much use as tits on a bull.' He turned and pointed at Stankevich. 'This is a simple question. I want a yes or no answer. Do we trust this man's word or not?'

Mikhail took a deep breath. 'The present position of the Central Committee is that we do not oppose the Provisional Government.'

Pavel shook his head. 'This is all too complicated for me. Give me somebody to fight, something to live or die for and I am a happy man. Just don't feed me horse shit.'

Stankevich approached them. 'Maybe I can help you with your discussions. I have followed the debates in detail. The soldiers are to have the right to elect officers, the right not to be abused by them, their own soldiers' committees.'

Pavel and Mikhail listened to his reassurances.

'These are the demands the soldiers made themselves,' Pavel told him. 'It's like going to a party and you have to bring your own present.'

'The demands rose from the ranks of the soldiers, as you say,' Stankevich agreed. 'That is what gives them their value. They are being drawn up into a charter.'

Eventually, Mikhail nodded.

'You can tell your Justice Minister we won't cause any trouble.'

Stankevich smiled a thank you and left. The hours ticked by. As lights flickered in the darkness, one of the soldier deputies emerged from the discussions in the Soviet and read the outcome. It was called Military Order Number One.

'We have won concessions,' Mikhail concluded.

'We could have won a lot more,' Pavel retorted. 'I'm not happy with this. You know that party membership card, Mikhail? You can shove it up your arse. I'm going for a smoke.'

He walked through the detritus of the workers' and soldiers' occupation: cigarette butts, empty bottles, rotting food, unwashed cups and plates, shredded paper, looted goods, items of discarded clothing. Pavel stared at the sea of filth. A new order, that's what he wanted, a revolutionary order and an end to the slaughter of the war. He looked at the works of the revolution and already he despaired. It was a disappointment. He wandered out into the bitter cold. For a moment, the heavy cloud lifted and it was as if he saw all the stars in the universe.

'This is what I want,' he murmured, 'to see beyond all the crap and know where we're going.'

Then the window of eternity closed and he made his way back to the others.

'Are you all right?' Mikhail asked.

'I'm fine,' Pavel said. 'I just need some sleep.'

But he needed so much more.

The following afternoon, the soldiers got to see Citizen Kerensky with their own eyes. He came striding into a session of the Petrograd Soviet. Pavel watched with a jaundiced eye. He still had the rundown of the new Justice Minister's political career running through his head, but he saw somebody who reminded him of his officers.

'Cocky bastard, isn't he?' he observed.

'He looks very assured,' Mikail replied.

'Assured? That's one way of putting it. He loves himself to bits, that bugger.'

Kerensky was on stage, addressing the audience. His gestures were theatrical and exaggerated.

'Comrades,' he cried, 'do you trust me?'

The crowd greeted him with acclamation. There were shouts of, 'Yes!'

Pavel swapped glances with Mikhail, but didn't say a word. Kerensky was in full flow, flailing his arms.

'I speak, Comrades, with all my soul,' he cried. 'And if it is needed to prove this, if you do not trust me, then I am ready to die.'

Pavel stared coldly at the delegates giving Kerensky their rapt attention.

'Everybody is ready to die,' he said. 'I prefer people who are ready to live. This popinjay should be in the theatre.'

'My first act as Minister of Justice,' the Minister continued, 'is to release all political prisoners.'

Silent amidst loud cheering, Pavel remained sceptical. 'Didn't we already do that?' he asked. 'Didn't the masses release the political prisoners?'

'They didn't just release the political prisoners,' Mikhail reminded him. 'They opened all the prisons. The worst offenders have had to be re-arrested already.'

'Well, I'm suspicious,' Pavel said.

'You sound like a man after my own heart,' a voice crackled behind him.

Pavel turned to see a slim, young man with intense, dark eyes.

'Who are you?'

'I am Comrade Kolya.'

'Didn't I see you talking to some of the lads yesterday?'

Kolya nodded. 'Probably. I am a militant of the Bolsheviks.'

'Like you, Mikhail,' Pavel said, his wary gaze drifting between them.

'So you're suspicious of Citizen Kerensky, are you?'

Kolya remembered the way Anishin admonished him. This time he answered cautiously. 'Kerensky is the fig leaf. The rest of this government belongs to the bosses and the landowning class.'

'But you gave them the power,' Pavel said. 'Why?'

Kolya answered as neutrally as he can. 'It is early days, Comrade.' Instinctively, he glanced over his shoulder. 'I am not the only one who is irritated by all the compromises. We should be agitating for a revolutionary government, bringing an end to the war.'

Pavel winked. 'That's more like it, Mikhail, I'm warming to this guy.'

Kolya found it hard to suppress a smile. At last, somebody was taking him seriously.

'It's like this, Comrades. The Central Committee isn't just the members in Russia. We await Kamenev, Zinoviev, Stalin,' he let their names hang before saying another, 'Lenin. They are abroad or in exile. Sometime soon, our leaders will return and then you will discover what the socialists can do.'

'So, jam tomorrow, that's what you're saying?'

'What I'm saying,' Kolya said, 'is that the likes of you and I, people who made the revolution, we are being treated like children. We have to hope that when our leaders – real revolutionaries with years of experience – return from exile, they will see what is possible.'

'If there are people who know what they want,' Pavel said, 'and have the balls to fight for it, anything is possible.'

Raisa

'So the day has come,' Raisa said, the wind catching her words and carrying them away like snowflakes.

'It's strange,' Elena reflected. 'It seemed to take so long for the Romanovs to fall, but when they did, it was all so quick.' She took Raisa's hand. 'The Tsar of all the Russias, the Little Father, he is now just a common citizen. Fancy that.'

'I thought the landlords and the generals would have fought until their dying breath,' Raisa said. 'When it came to it, nobody lifted a hand to save the autocracy.'

Elena swung her arm and guided Raisa along the street. It must have looked as if they were schoolgirls, wandering their neighbourhood, so young and carefree, and yet they were uneasy. In this world of revolution, a world balanced between the powers of yesterday and those of tomorrow, their lives were little more than grain between great millstones. They didn't understand it, but they sensed it.

Raisa hadn't seen Elena for a couple of days and she was glad of the company. 'What happens now?' she said.

Elena shrugged. 'Even the party committees don't seem to know. One calls for a revolutionary government and an end to the war. Another slaps it down. It is as if people know what they want, but they are too scared to go out and take it.'

Some lounging soldiers whistled at the two young women and shouted obscenities.

'Ignore them,' Elena said, sensitive to her friend's mysterious wariness around men. 'They're all talk.'

'I wouldn't be so sure,' Raisa said. 'Given the chance, men revert to type, grabbing what they can get.'

Raisa knew what Elena must have been thinking, wondering what triggered Raisa's attitude to men. And where did her money come from? She lived comfortably in a clean, tidy guesthouse that charged a rent well out of the reach of an ordinary worker. She must come across as a mystery, all right.

They reached the Nevsky and stared at the confusion.

'What are they doing?' Raisa asked.

Elena led the way. 'Let's find out.'

They arrived just as one of the symbols of the imperial regime came crashing down on the pavement to appreciative roars.

'Down with the Dynasty!'

'Long Live the Republic!'

The two-headed eagle, carved from stone, shattered into pieces. Close by, the pair could see Romanov coats of arms smashed to bits. Paintings and photographs piled up, crushed under soldiers' boots. A soldier unscrewed a brass plaque, another defaced the word "Romanov". A young boy, probably still at school, shinned up the façade of one building to tear down the flag that rippled boldly in the wind. The dynasty was being turned into kindling before their eyes, a bonfire waiting to be lit. Elena saw a Red Guard standing with a can of petrol.

'Is that to light the bonfire?' she asked.

'Give me a kiss and you can do the honours,' he said.

'Try to kiss me and I'll rip your balls off,' Elena retorted, earning applause and laughter from the Guard's friends.

Without another word, she sprinkled the fuel over the detritus of the Tsars.

'Who's got a match?' she asked.

The Guard obliged and flames leapt. Elena made a show of warming her hands over the fire. Red flags were fluttering everywhere, matching the bonfire's greedy, scarlet tongue. Raisa approached and crouched beside her comrade-sister, feeling the warmth of the imperial conflagration and Elena's physical presence. Her skin was hot with both. Strangely, Elena seemed oblivious, unlike that moment, one Raisa would never forget, when Elena's lips had moved towards hers.

'Will you look at what we have done?' Elena sighed. 'Who would have imagined this just a month ago?'

'Who would have imagined it ever?' Raisa said.

She rested a hand on Elena's shoulder and gazed into the glow of destruction. The warmth and physicality of her comrade-sister crept along her arm like flame along a fuse. In one way, the garish light was frightening, the reduction to ash of everything that had seemed to be permanent. In another, it was the mischievous glint of a new world about to be born from the ash of the old. Presently, they walked on along the

Nevsky. People were reading. Newspapers were available again. Posters were appearing on the walls. Everybody seemed to want to explain what had happened, and lecture passers-by on what must happen next. They passed under a huge red banner that proclaimed: 'Long live the republic.'

'Long live the *revolutionary* republic,' Elena shouted, clenching her fist.

'Hear, hear,' said an old man approvingly. 'Getting rid of the bloody Romanovs isn't the end. It's only the beginning. You mark my words.'

Elena gave him a conspiratorial wink and they moved on, picking their way through the wreckage and the burning. Raisa felt the delicious squeeze of Elena's hand.

'I told aunty Svetlana we would meet her,' Elena said.

Raisa nodded and they made for the Liteiny Bridge, where Svetlana was at the heart of a large group, mostly female.

'Here she is,' Svetlana said cheerfully, 'my niece and her cultured friend.'

Raisa almost laughed out loud. Cultured? Isn't it amazing what a bar of soap, a decent set of clothes and a fistful of roubles can do for a girl?

'Have you got any news, aunty?' Elena asked. 'Mama says you've got something to tell me.'

Svetlana gave a naughty cackle. 'Got myself a toy boy.'

'I beg your pardon!'

'Well, don't look so shocked,' Svetlana said. 'I took a handsome student off to bed. He made me feel five years younger.'

Elena blushed. 'Aunty!'

Svetlana scanned the crowd. 'That's him.'

'But he's…'

'What? Half my age. So what? It can't last, I know that, but what's wrong with a bit of fun now and then. He's good for me.' She stroked Elena's hair from her face. 'You should find somebody.'

Elena smiled. 'All in good time. There's no hurry.'

'Really?' Svetlana said. 'You never know how long a soul's got in this world.'

'You're still young, aunty,' Elena said.

Svetlana leaned forward and whispered in her ear. 'A whole lot younger since I climbed between the sheets with my Kolya.'

'Aunty,' Elena scolded, 'you've got to stop, hasn't she, Raisa?'

'Why?' Raisa asked. 'I think it is beautiful. Nobody wants to be lonely.'

'Are you lonely?' Elena asked.

Before Raisa could answer, Svetlana gave her niece some advice.

'Why don't you go and keep Raisa company? The mill hasn't reopened yet. You don't have work in the morning. Enjoy yourself while the factories remain idle. Mark my word, we've got a revolution, but we will still have to go back to work sometime. I'll tell your mother you're staying over.'

Elena tilted her head.

'Can you put up with me for an evening?' she asked.

'Oh, I might just manage it,' Raisa replied.

She felt light headed, giddy the way she felt as a child when she was entranced by some new friendship. Svetlana embraced each of them in turn. They took their leave, waving as they went.

'What do you think of that?' Elena asked as they walked along the riverside, arms linked. She sounded slightly scandalised. 'I have just seen another side to Svetlana. Can you believe it? That's a twenty-year difference.'

Raisa turned her head, watching the way the spectral moonlight washed Elena's strong, attractive face.

'Don't judge her,' Raisa said. 'People need love.'

'I'm not sure it's love,' Elena replied. 'That's not how I would describe my aunt getting hot and sweaty between the sheets with some spotty student.'

Raisa leaned into her friend, giving her an admonishing shove. 'He isn't spotty at all. You make him sound like a leopard. Leave her be. She's having fun.'

Elena seized on Raisa's words to ask a question. 'So when do you have fun, my sister? Who makes Citizen Raisa moan?'

Her face was close. Her eyes were glittering with desire. Raisa blushed. She turned her face away, her heart fluttering in her chest.

'Have I embarrassed you?' Elena asked. 'It's just… I have never heard you mention anyone, though I know you have been with a man.'

Raisa felt the need to confess, to reveal something of her past. 'Promise you will never reveal this to a living soul,' she murmured, turning to face Elena. 'There are things about me you need to understand. Will you listen without interruption?'

'You know I would never betray your confidence,' Elena answered. 'You are my dearest friend.'

Raisa laughed. 'What? We have only known each other a few days.'

'It feels like a lifetime,' Elena said. 'Please tell me the same. It would break my heart if you did not treasure our friendship in the same way.'

'Of course I feel the same way,' Raisa told her. 'I have not felt as close to anyone since my dear mother passed away. And this, with you, it's... It feels like life itself.'

They embraced and Raisa felt that mysterious energy rising fiercely from the depths of her stomach again. Elena's proximity made her heart pound. She eased herself away and rested her gloved hands on the stone parapet to her right, feeling the whip of the wind from the river. Elena joined her after a few moments.

'I am listening,' she said softly, her voice blending into the icy gusts.

'I was alone,' Raisa began, 'little more than a child, with no family, no shelter, no money. The war took my father. Cancer ate away at Mama. My world died with her. I tried sleeping in doorways, foraging for scraps, but winter came... then the men.'

She glanced at Elena, expecting a reaction. When there was none, she continued.

'The first time, a man offered me money to jerk him off. I had never touched a man's cock. The thought disgusted me, but I did it. It was yank his pork, or wither and die. It wasn't hard to work out what to do. I got it over with as quickly as I could.' A tear spilled down her cheek. 'Men are pathetic. He wanted me to be in awe of his sticky little member. I said the words he wanted to hear. It earned me a few kopeks.'

Elena began to massage Raisa's back, offering her some comfort as she unburdened herself.

'One day, Bagrov found me. The things I did for men didn't earn me enough to put a roof over my head, but I didn't want to go all the way. The weather was still warm, but I knew the cold, dark days were approaching. I was beginning to imagine trying to survive a Russian winter without shelter. He said he would provide me with a bed and a roof over my head. He gave me a bed, all right.'

Elena pressed her face into Raisa's neck.

'Oh, my poor darling, my beautiful friend.'

'He took me, Elena, roughly, as if I was a bitch to be fucked from behind. He said it was to teach me how to please his customers. I hated the bastard. I still do. One day, I will settle the score with him and feed his lousy cock to the crows.'

She felt Elena's warm, soft lips on her ear lobe, her neck. They brushed her skin and searched for her mouth as they did once before. This time, Raisa did not resist. She dissolved into the kiss and felt Elena's fingertips moving down her spine. It was a few moments before she withdrew from the embrace. She continued speaking as if nothing had happened.

'There, that's how I survived. You must hate me.'

'Hate you?' Elena gasped. 'I love you more than ever. If you asked me to, I would go and kill those men with my bare hands.'

Raisa was unable to suppress a giggle. 'Do you know, I think you would, Elena with her weaver's hands.'

'These are workers' hands,' Elena said proudly, 'hands that will protect you as long as I live.'

She pulled Raisa close, kissing her brow, cheeks, lips. Suddenly, she stopped, resting her forehead against Raisa.

'Please don't be angry,' she said, 'but there is something I have to ask you.'

Raisa's eyes searched Elena's face.

'You were poor, starving,' Elena said, 'reduced to selling yourself to any dirty bastard who had the money to do the deal. That's right, isn't it?'

There was shame in Raisa's voice. 'Yes.'

'So where did all this money come from?'

Raisa knew this moment had to come, the same way she had to confess about the brothel.

'You have lodgings,' Elena said. 'You have food. You have nice clothes. You can afford to give me a fur hat. You have all this, but you don't need to work.' She frowned. 'Then there is the gun.'

Raisa checked that they are quite alone.

'I killed a man.'

'What!'

Raisa was a little surprised at the violence of Elena's response.

'You know I am capable of it,' she said. 'You have seen me use a gun.'

'You missed by a country mile.'

'I fired, didn't I?'

It was some time before Elena could put her thoughts into words.

'I will never judge you,' she said, 'but I have to know who you are and what you have done. I swear, I will never reveal what you tell me to anyone, not Mama, not Svetlana. You know that, don't you?'

Raisa nodded. 'I would trust you with my life.'

Elena smiled. 'If you tell me your story, that is exactly what you will have done.'

So Raisa told her story, there in the March cold, with the war in the distance and the revolution slumbering ready to rise at dawn and swirl on through the lives of millions. When she had finished, Elena pulled her close and kissed her on both cheeks then on her lips.

'You did what you had to do. Maybe it was your own personal revolution. This man's blood was the price of your freedom.' An icy breeze snapped at their clothing and she shivered. 'Let's go back.'

The boarding house was quiet when they arrived. Mrs Kuznetsova was in her bed, no doubt dreaming of her husband. Raisa led the way upstairs, keenly aware of Elena behind her, watching the movement of her hips. Raisa could barely breathe, remembering the press of Elena's mouth, her fingers stealing along each vertebra, probing Raisa's body.

'It is cold,' Elena said. 'Can I come in with you tonight?'

Raisa's face was turned away. Her emotions bubbled like boiling water in a kettle.

'Elena...'

'It's all right,' her friend said, rushing out her words. 'It was foolish of me to ask.'

They undressed, looking away from each other. Raisa slipped on her nightdress.

'There is one for you in the drawer,' she said.

She heard the rustle of cotton on Elena's skin and the creak of the second twin bed. Lying down herself, she gazed up at the ceiling and the sliver of moonlight that lanced through a gap between the curtains. She lay this way for several minutes, heart thumping, barely able to breathe. Elena's presence seemed to fill the entire room, swarming around her like mist enveloping still woods. Raisa could breathe her, swallow her.

'Are you still awake?' she asked.

Elena's answer made Raisa's throat tighten. 'How could I sleep after our kisses this evening?'

Raisa lifted the sheets. 'You can get in with me.'

As Elena leaned forward, Raisa saw into the V of her nightdress, her gaze drawn to the shadow between her breasts. The tightness in her throat was almost painful. Strangely, Elena was less bold than she was by the river. They lay a while side by side, like fish on a slab. Finally, Elena spoke.

'I want to touch you. I *need* to touch you.'

Raisa couldn't find the words to invite an embrace. Elena took her silence as assent. The moonlight was on their faces as Elena's lips brushed Raisa's cheek once more, seeking out her mouth, prising it open. Raisa yearned to breathe in Elena's warmth, her lust, but her arms were heavy, like iron bars. She lay still, allowing the kiss to happen, as if to another.

'I love you, Raisa. Tell me you love me too.'

A ghost spoke Raisa's words for her, rising from deep inside her like some spirit of the night.

'You know I do.'

'Please say the words to me.'

'I love you, Elena. I love you with all my heart and soul. I never dreamed I could meet someone like you.'

That was all the reassurance Elena needed. She took the hem of Raisa's nightdress in both hands and tugged. Raisa sat up and allowed Elena to remove the garment and toss it across the room where it landed on the other, unused bed. Elena rested her palm on Raisa's shoulder then peeled off her own nightdress, shuddering instantly at the bite of the cold on her skin. Raisa stared at the lean, firm body, the small, high breasts, the whiteness of Elena's flesh.

'Seen enough?' Elena asked, teasing.

'Not nearly enough,' Raisa answered, surprising herself.

She had never spoken to anyone with this huskiness of need and yearning in her voice. Until this moment, she had thought that the pleasures of the flesh were about predators falling upon their prey. Then Elena was next to her, her hardness and flatness against Raisa's own curves. Suddenly her full breasts and flat stomach, plump arse and shapely legs, the goods all those men wanted to purchase and possess, the features Raisa had come to despise in herself, were no longer objects of exploitation and shame. She held her breath.

'You can relax,' Elena said.

'No,' Raisa croaked, 'I can't.'

'Then I will help you.'

Elena's fingers travelled over Raisa's throat and breasts before working down her stomach. Kisses followed, on her lips, her ribs and hips. Raisa tensed once more and she felt Elena's laughter as a tickle on her haunch.

'You have never been with another woman, have you?'

'Have you?' Raisa asked, eyes wide.

Part of her wanted this to be Elena's first time too.

'I will tell you later.'

Elena's fingers worked their way downwards and Raisa gasped. She was trembling, but she wasn't afraid. She felt like a child, sitting on rocks as she steadied herself to plunge into the cold waters of a river. She felt Elena's fingers slide between her legs, stroking, rubbing, arousing.

'You can move, you know,' Elena said.

Laughter bubbled up inside Raisa's chest.

'I don't know if I can even breathe.'

'You just did.'

The movement of Elena's fingers was becoming faster, more urgent. Now, Raisa was moaning, tiny gasps bursting out of her. She seized Elena's wrist, stopping her and gave a little shake of her head.

'Those men,' she said. 'They hurt me.' Her tears were welling up again. 'They hurt me so badly. The things they ask you to do....'

Elena rubbed the tip of her nose against Elena's. 'I will never hurt you. Never. It would be like tearing out my own heart.'

Raisa let Elena's hand go, and soon the tiny streams of pleasure become a flood. She relaxed and laughter rocked her body as she came. After a few moments, she was serious again.

'Tell me I am not a whore,' she said.

Elena stroked her face over and over.

'Don't you ever use that word again,' she said. 'Not ever.' Her face was serious. 'The whores are the men who treated you like a piece of meat to be bought at a market stall.'

Raisa seized Elena's face in both hands.

'You must love me forever,' she said. 'I command you. If you ever stop, I will haunt you every day and every night to the very end of your days. I will make you wild with regret.'

'I obey you,' Elena told her, rolling onto her back. 'Now there's something you must do for me.'

Raisa began to explore the woman who had become everything to her, reacting with wonder to the way Elena trembled with pleasure at her touch.

'Do you know what day it is, my love?'

Elena was moving her hips, luxuriating in Raisa's touch.

'Of course I do. What do you mean?'

'It's my birthday.'

More laughter. 'What a lovely way to celebrate.'

Raisa nodded. 'Because of you and the revolution, I am reborn.'

Part Two

April's Messenger

Part Two

April's Messenger

Pavel

Still they came.

The procession stretched as far as the eye could see. They were filling the great open space known as the Petrograd Sahara. The coffins were draped in red flags. Behind them tramped hundreds of thousands of working people in their drab, heavy coats. No smoke belched from the factories. No roar erupted from their furnaces. No rumble came from their machinery. Proletarian Petrograd had adopted the quiet dignity of mourning. This Thursday, on the Field of Mars, the masses were going to honour the fallen heroes of the February revolution.

'I hear they had to dynamite the frozen ground to dig the graves,' Kolya murmured.

'They did,' Pavel said. 'I watched the whole thing. The Russian winter is a bastard.'

Black and white flags snapped in the wind. Scarlet banners rippled.

'We should have waited a day or two,' Mikhail grumbled. 'Look at it. The bloody thaw has to set in, doesn't it? Now it's a sea of mud.'

'What's the matter?' Pavel demanded. 'Are you worried that the deputies and dignitaries are going to get their fine shoes dirty?'

As they spoke, six mighty columns of humanity were descending on the Sahara. Some Sahara! There was no desert here, just mud and a bleak, brooding sky punctuated by flickering snowflakes as the day dithered between winter and spring. The banners passed by.

'Hail to the Democratic Republic.'

'Eternal Memory to Our Fallen Brothers.'

'Honour the Heroes Who Fell for Freedom.'

'I have to go,' Kolya said. 'I am a pall-bearer for the final stretch.'

'Who are you carrying?' Mikhail asked.

'A machinist, Ivan.'

'What was he like? ...Don't tell me you're carrying the coffin of a complete stranger!'

'I never met him,' Kolya admitted. 'I am doing this for the Party. It is important that we are seen to be at the heart of this.'

Pavel scratched at his stubble.

'We *are* at the heart of this,' he reminded the student. 'The Bolsheviks are the driving force behind everything.'

That was Pavel, serious, severe, but always utterly committed to the cause of revolution. In spite of his initial doubts, he had been a Bolshevik since the revolution. He listened to the strains of Chopin's Funeral March, played by a trudging, sullen-faced band.

'What's that dirge?' he moaned.

'We're at a funeral, my friend,' Mikhail reminded him. 'What do you expect, some bawdy drinking song?'

'You're right, of course,' Pavel conceded, unusually for him. 'It is the right thing to do, but I can't help thinking the best way we remember the dead is to finish what they started. Why don't they strike up the Internationale?' He glanced at a raised stage. 'And why do the representatives of the landlords and the bourgeoisie take their places at the head of the service?'

Mikhail rested his hand on Pavel's shoulder. 'Be patient, Comrade. This is not over. It has hardly even started.'

The cannons of the Peter and Paul Fortress continued to boom out, like the drumbeat of a titan orchestra delivering a hymn to the revolutionary dead. Night fell and Pavel and Mikhail continued their watch, Still the marchers came. Still the coffins mounted up alongside the enormous open grave.

'How many coffins?' Pavel asked.

'Over a hundred. I heard somebody say one hundred and fifty, one hundred and sixty. One thing is for sure, it is a drop in the ocean compared to the numbers of the fallen.'

Mikhail gave a bleak chuckle. 'They're not counting the police who got their just desserts.'

Pavel was unimpressed. 'Even so, we all know more died than there are coffins here.'

'It's symbolic,' Mikhail answered.

Six military searchlights swept back and forth across the taciturn crowds, bleaching the faces that lurked under hats and caps. It was an eerie scene. For the umpteenth time that day, a column trudged into sight, singing the *Marseillaise*. Among them were a group of men in expensive-looking suits.

'How long do we put up with the likes of them?' Pavel said, with a scowl coloured by the clouds that had been hanging oppressively over the city all day. 'The country they govern is not our Russia.'

Presently, Kolya appeared, one of eight men carrying a red-draped coffin. He didn't give them a second glance, but kept his face forward.

'He takes his duties seriously,' Pavel observed.

'Yes, he is single-minded, that one. We need men like him.'

'Do you think he is trustworthy?' Pavel wondered aloud. 'Judging by his hands, he has never worked on the factory floor or had a uniform on his back.'

'Intellectual workers are just as important to our cause,' Mikhail reminded him. 'A revolution needs a brain as well as a fist, you know.'

'What this revolution needs is a kick up the arse,' Pavel said. 'For fuck's sake, why do we need the likes of Prince Lvov anyway, or Kerensky for that matter? The workers and the soldiers should be running the show.'

'We've got the Soviet,' Mikhail said.

'And the Soviet leaves these bloody deputies in charge!'

'We've been through this before,' said Mikhail wearily. 'Can't we call a truce, just for tonight, until the dead are buried.'

'In honour of the dead,' sighed Pavel, 'I will hold my tongue. It won't be for long, mind.'

'Well, that will have to do for now,' Mikhail said. 'Hey, isn't that your girlfriend?'

Pavel was nonplussed.

'You remember. The little blond. You said you were going to marry her.'

Pavel located Raisa and Elena in the crowd and watched them. He saw something in their closeness and the smiles they exchanged that made him wonder whether Raisa might be forever out of his reach.

'I wasn't serious, you know. I fancied her, that's all.'

'Fancied, past tense?'

Pavel nodded. 'Past tense. It was a momentary infatuation, that's all. You've got to admit, she's a beauty.'

'She is,' Mikhail agreed. 'Why don't you talk to her?'

'You know what?' Pavel said, setting off through the crowd. 'I think I will.'

The thought of taking Raisa to one side and getting a proper, close-up look at her filled him with optimism. He caught up with her just as the last coffins were laid by the vast grave.

'May I talk to you?' he asked.

Raisa frowned and glanced at Elena, who seemed amused.

'I'll make myself scarce for a few moments,' Elena said. 'My factory contingent is paying its respects. You'll find me over there.'

Her departure threw Raisa into something of a panic. Pavel saw the fluttering eyelashes and reddening cheeks.

'I only want to talk,' Pavel began....and ended.

81

What the hell was he meant to say to her? He had made sure he found out her name and now he was stumped.

'I am listening,' Raisa said.

'I...' Pavel suddenly roared with laughter. 'Shit! I don't have the foggiest idea what I want to say to you. I like you. There, that's it. I think you're bloody beautiful.' His neck burned. 'Christ, this is inappropriate. On a day of mourning, all I can think about is a pretty girl.'

Raisa tugged self-consciously at a lock of hair.

'You think I'm pretty?'

Pavel blundered on. 'You're the most beautiful woman I've ever seen. Are you...free?'

Raisa surprised him with her answer.

'Are any of us free while the landlords and the bourgeoisie hold the power?'

'Is that what you think?' he said eagerly. 'You want the revolution to continue?'

'I will tell you what I want,' Raisa told him. 'I want an immediate peace. I want world revolution, the dictatorship of the proletariat.'

'Are you with the Bolsheviks?'

'My friend is,' Raisa said. 'I am making my mind up. The Anarchists have interesting things to say too.'

'Not the Mensheviks then?'

Raisa shook her head. 'No.'

Pavel recalled what he had asked her. 'But are you spoken for?'

His stomach tightened. A searchlight beam swept across her face. Just looking at her made his throat dry. Please let her say that she is free.

'I am sorry,' she said. 'I can say nothing to encourage you.'

Instantly, his heart was a thing of lead, his senses laden with despair.

'Comrade, this sweetheart of yours, he is a lucky man.' He gathered his thoughts. 'I am sorry I bothered you. I meant no offence.'

'None was taken,' Raisa answered.

'Then I will take my leave. Who knows? We may meet again as comrades. Or friends.'

Raisa touched his arm, surprising herself that she had just come into physical contact with a man.

'I would like that. Goodnight.'

'Goodnight.'

Pavel pushed his way back through the seemingly endless mass of mourners and ran his hands through his hair. He felt quite defeated. Mikhail discovered him at the edge of the throng.

'Well, is it too early to announce the engagement?' he asked cheerily.

'Oh, just fuck off,' Pavel snapped.

'That's a no then?'

'Fuck the hell out of my sight. You're the one who put me up to it. She's got a fiancé.'

Mikhail gave him a playful slap across the head. 'She's an angel, Comrade. There was always a good chance she had somebody.'

'Well, just don't say there are plenty more fish in the sea. I'll rip your fucking head off if you do.'

'You've got it bad, haven't you?'

Pavel brooded. 'I was sweet on her before I met her. Now I have spoken to her, I don't think I will ever look at another woman.'

'Of course you will, you sad bastard.'

Pavel raised his face to the sky and there was no window of stars tonight, just endless black.

'Sad is right,' he said. 'I could bloody cry. I have liked women before. This is the first time….'

'You can't love her,' Mikhail countered. 'You've only just met her.'

'And when I did, it felt as if I had known her all my life. I swear, my brother, she does something to me in here.' He pressed a clenched fist to his breast. 'She makes me feel better than Vodka, better than good food and a warm fire….'

'Better than revolution?'

Pavel respondsed with a rueful grin. 'Don't make me choose, you troublemaker.'

'Tell you what,' Mikhail said. 'I've stashed a bottle of booze. Let's get pissed.'

Pavel nodded.

'Now you're talking.'

Kolya stared up at Svetlana as she straddled him. There was a sheen of sweat on her shoulders and breasts. A lock of hair was stuck to her cheek. He couldn't have had a better teacher in the arts of passion. She was earthy, honest and kind, even if she did tease him almost without pause.

'You're getting there,' she said, swinging a sturdy limb across his chest and almost taking his head off with her knee.

He reached out and slapped her backside, enjoying the way her flesh trembled.

'Getting there,' he said. 'You screamed tonight.'

'It was a cough,' she retorted. 'Give me a kiss, lover. I'm in work in the morning.'

He pulled her towards him and felt the weight of her bosom on his chest. His lips clung to hers until she shoved him away.

'You're not getting me back in bed,' she said. 'If I don't go home and get some sleep, I will never be up in time.' She laughed. 'Roll on the eight-hour day.'

She dipped a flannel into the white bowl in the corner of her room and wiped away the sweat.

'So when do we expect Comrade Lenin to return?'

'The word is that he will be back tomorrow.'

'I can't wait,' Svetlana said. 'He's going to shake things up and not a minute too soon. What do you think he's going to say?'

Kolya shrugged. 'That all men need a Svetlana.'

She hurled the flannel and it slapped him in the face. It delivered one hell of a sting.

'What was that for?'

'You make it sound as if I sleep around,' she said. 'Listen to me, you whelp. The women workers led this revolution. We deserve the respect of the men, equality, the right to vote. Forty thousand of us were outside the Tauride, demanding our rights. You were there. You read the banners. If the woman is a slave, there is no freedom.'

'Yes,' Kolya said, 'and there were slogans in favour of prosecuting the war.'

'That was from the bourgeois women,' Svetlana reminded him. 'Don't tar us all with the same brush. I am every bit the revolutionary you are, Comrade. Besides, what were the Bolsheviks thinking? The party gave it fuck all support.'

'We were there, weren't we?'

'The party didn't make it a priority. There were Mensheviks and SRs too. I tell you, it isn't good enough.'

She came over and perched on the side of the bed, still naked above the waist. She put her hand on Kolya's chest and made it into a fist, pressing down in the middle.

'That hurts,' he yelped, struggling to get up.

'This is the power of the woman worker,' she told him. 'We work, we queue for bread, we bear the children and we fuck you guys senseless. That makes us every bit as good as any man and don't you forget it. I have been with two men, my Vitaly and you, so don't you ever talk about me as if I open my legs for anybody.'

'Svetlana…'

She unclenched her fist and placed a finger on his lips.

'Best leave it, Kolya, my sweet. You might say something that gets you another slap in that handsome gob.'

Kolya raised his palms in mock surrender.

'I give in, OK?'

Svetlana stroked his face.

'You're a good-looking lad, Kolya. I wonder how long it will be before you kick old Svetlana's fat arse and stretch marks out of your life.'

Kolya sat up, pressing his face between her breasts.

'I would never do that, my love. You are the first woman who ever made me feel alive. And you're not at all fat. You've got an arse like a ripe peach.'

Svetlana shook her head. 'You haven't got much to compare me with. I'm your first woman.' She pulled his face from her chest and kissed him. 'You'll tire of me soon enough.'

'Never!' he said fiercely. 'Come back to bed.'

She skipped away from his hands. 'Oh no, you don't. My sister is getting fed up of looking out for my family. She'sgot better things to do than trawl the barracks checking on them. I'm going home. Bed's for more than screwing, you young scamp. If I don't get some shut-eye I will be falling into one of those bloody machines.'

She dressed and brushed her hair then turned, hands on hips.

'What do you think?'

'You are the most gorgeous woman in all Petrograd,' Kolya answered.

'Flatterer.'

She swerved from his grasp and opened the door just in time to find herself facing a woman ten years older than her.

'Can I help you?' Svetlana asked.

'You can get out of my house,' the woman answered. 'I run a respectable establishment. Now clear off, you whore and take that stupid prick with you.'

'Mrs Turisheva,' Kolya said. 'I can explain.'

'You can explain yourself down those stairs and out of the door and take your prozzy with you.'

What happened next stunned Kolya. Svetlana swung her right arm, landing her fist on Mrs Turisheva's jutting jaw. The landlady was slammed back against the wall opposite. Svetlana was on her in a second, seizing her face.

'You listen to me, you sour, foul-mouthed, old sow. I am no whore.'

Mrs Turisheva struggled, but Svetlana's grip was unshakeable.

'Pay attention, bitch. It may just save your life. Kolya here is with the Red Guards. You are lucky he even pays you rent. We run this city now – Kolya, me and every son and daughter of the revolution like us. If you push it, it won't be Kolya who is out on his ear, but you. Have you got that?'

There was another futile jerk of resistance. Svetlana gave Mrs Turisheva a hard slap across the face that drew blood from her nose.

'I said, have you got that?'

Mrs Turisheva collapsed into a fit of terrified sobs. 'Yes. Yes. You can both stay as long as you like. Just don't take my home from me.'

Svetlana collected her coat and hat and took her leave. When she reached the front door, she shouted up the stairs.

'I'll see you soon, Kolya.' She searched out Mrs Turisheva on the landing. 'When I do, you can make us both some supper, you old hag, and don't go spitting in it or I'll knock your fucking teeth out.'

Kolya knelt down beside Mrs Turisheva with his flannel and cleaned the blood from her face. She resisted.

'Don't touch me!'

'I am trying to help,' Kolya told her. 'I am sorry Svetlana struck you, but she is right. You are in a weak position.'

'The world has gone mad,' Mrs Turisheva groaned. 'I work my fingers to the bone my whole life and you socialists can take it all away from me just like that.' She tried to snap her fingers, but they were trembling. 'Is there no justice in this world?'

'You talk about justice?' Kolya said, suddenly less sympathetic. 'Listen to me. The autocracy slaughtered who knows how many people on Bloody Sunday, at Lena, in Black Hundred pogroms, most of all on the battlefields of the imperialist butchery they call a patriotic war. Now you whine about your precious house! I am going out to a meeting presently. Do not even think about trying to lock me out or touch my belongings. If you do, it will be the worse for you.'

With that he got his coat and left. Within minutes he was sitting in a room thick with the smoke from cheap cigarettes. Anishin had the floor.

'Comrades, may I remind you what is written in *Pravda*? We will support the Provisional Government in so far as it struggles against reaction and counter-revolution.'

'Horse shit,' came the response from the crowd.

Kolya recognised the soldier Pavel.

The chair of the meeting pounded his fist on the table. 'That is uncomradely behaviour. Moderate your tone or leave the meeting.'

'Moderate yourself, jackass,' Pavel retorted.

Soldiers in the audience seemed split about whether the fighting at the Front should continue. Arguments broke out among them. Meanwhile, the chair struggled to make himself heard. He gestured in the direction of Pavel.

'This is your last warning. Comrade Anishin, you have the floor.'

Under his breath, Pavel could be heard muttering. 'If he wants us to support the bourgeoisie and the landlords, he should eat the fucking floor.'

'Thank you,' Anishin began, acting as if nothing has been said. 'Now, on the issue of the war, Comrade Kamenev and Comrade Stalin are clear. As long as the German soldier serves the Kaiser....'

This time, it was Mikhail who butted in. 'You're not giving your own opinion. You're reading from a bloody script.'

'I am explaining the line from the leading party organ,' Anishin insisted.

'You're a leading party organ, you prick,' Pavel muttered, this time loudly enough to be heard.

Amid laughter and protests that he didn't reflect every soldier, the chair pointed him out.

'Comrade, I ask you to leave the meeting. Will somebody escort Pavel Sergeyevich outside?'

Pavel folded his arms. 'The first fucker who lays a hand on me will be spitting out his teeth for a week.'

'Let the comrade soldier stay,' Anishin said. 'He is entitled to his opinion, just as others have the right to a different one.'

There was a smattering of applause at this.

'To conclude my remarks, so long as the German soldier continues to obey orders, the Russian soldier should remain at his post, answering shot with shot and shell with shell.'

Again, there was a mixture of lukewarm applause and enraged protest. This time Pavel was on his feet, pointing.

'What is this bollocks? We soldiers carried out this revolution in support of the women so we could bring the war to an end. We didn't do it to die for a republican government instead of a Tsarist government. Nobody is going to drag my arse off to the Front and I am not shooting my German brothers.'

'The correct term, Comrade,' Anishin said, 'is Provisional Government.'

'How are you different from the Provisional Government?' Pavel demanded. 'First the Soviet Executive Committee hands the power back to the landlords and the capitalists. Now you want us to continue the war. What the hell was the point of the insurrection?'

There was uproar. There was substantial support for Pavel's arguments. Anishin raised his hands, struggling to be heard.

'The autocracy has been swept away,' he replied. 'In time…'

'In time, poor bastards like me will be sent to the Front to die. You're not a revolutionary. You're a…' Words failed Pavel for a moment. 'You're a spy.'

At that, Anishin lost his temper. 'You will withdraw that, Comrade. I am a worker-Bolshevik. Where were you when we were maintaining party organisation in the factories?'

'I was being dragged out of my village to fight the Romanovs' war. I was being called a pig by those bloody officers, damn their stinking souls.'

Now, one or two of the soldiers who had been heckling Pavel were nodding along with him.

'You are new to the party and ignorant of its history. I will forgive you for your outburst…'

'Oh, get stuffed,' Pavel said. 'I'm leaving.'

Pavel barged his way through the workers and soldiers standing around the door. Some patted him on the back and told him they agreed with everything he said. Others gave him stern glances and said he had no right to talk to a man like Anishin with such lack of respect.

Pavel reached the door and walked outside before pounding down the stairs and stepping into the night air. Mikhail had followed him into the chill night and watched his friend pacing up and down, eyes blazing with indignation.

'Did you hear that bastard?' Pavel raged. 'He's a fucking plant, a bourgeois.'

'He is a factory worker,' Mikhail said, 'an engineer in an oil-spattered overalls. You must moderate your temper.'

'I say things as I see them,' Pavel retorted, 'and nobody is going to tell me it is revolutionary to kill German soldiers on behalf of Mother bloody Russia. Why do you think I shot that officer? Why do you think I disarmed the machine-gunners? To carry on prosecuting a rich man's war? This is bullshit.'

'I agree with you,' Mikhail said, 'but you must trust the Party.'

'Why must I?'

It was at this point, Kolya made his presence known.

'I will tell you why,' Kolya said.

'Not you again,' Pavel snorted. 'I don't need advice from a schoolboy.'

Kolya ignored the insult.

'What if I can explain why you should remain with the Party?'

'Go on, Professor, tell me. I am all ears.'

'Tomorrow,' Kolya told him, 'Comrade Lenin returns.'

'Well, if he is anything like Comrade Kamenev and Comrade Stalin, it will be a waste of time. All they are is a couple of canaries chirping the government's tune.'

'Comrade Lenin is the party's brain and guiding hand,' Kolya continued. 'Give the Bolsheviks one more day of your trust. If you are disappointed, walk away.'

'What is this?' Pavel demanded angrily. 'Are you trying to pull the wool over my eyes?'

'I am trying to remove the wool from your eyes,' Kolya said.

'Oh, you're good with words,' Pavel said. 'What I want is action. What I want is...'

'Revolution,' Kolya said, 'revolution against war, revolution in the cities, revolution in the countryside.'

'Yes,' Pavel said, 'exactly that.'

'Revolution everywhere,' Kolya said, concluding his pitch. 'World revolution.'

'Yes!' Pavel cried. 'World revolution. In Germany, France, England. Revolution wherever there are bourgeois exploiting the workers. That's it.'

He embraced Kolya. 'You're talking my kind of language, Comrade.'

Kolya watched the soldiers as they walked away. He felt pleased with his evening's work. That's when he heard somebody clapping slowly, deliberately. Kolya turned to see Anishin. Having given his report, he had left the meeting early.

'That was a good performance, Kolya.'

'It wasn't a performance,' Kolya retorted.

'So what was it?' Anishin demanded. 'Do you really think Comrade Lenin is going to break Central Committee discipline? You're wet behind the ears, Kolya.'

Kolya was no longer in awe of Anishin, the worker-Bolshevik. Was it the revolution that had steeled him, the example of Comrade Pavel, the embrace of a woman worker like Svetlana? He answered firmly. 'The workers and the soldiers are looking for somebody to express their will.'

'I work in a factory in the Vyborg,' Anishin snapped. 'You've got some balls questioning me.'

'I heard some of the comrade workers and soldiers contradicting you in there,' Kolya said. 'There were many voices raised in agreement.'

'The meeting voted to support the Central Committee's position,' Anishin said.

'That's because the cadres dominate them.'

'It's because,' Anishin said, contradicting him, 'we have an authority built on years of struggle.'

'Nobody has greater authority than Comrade Lenin,' Kolya said.

Anishin shook his head. 'To hear you talk, you would think you knew what Comrade Lenin is thinking. Here is what you know, Comrade Kolya.' He held up his thumb and forefinger, indicating the tiny gap between them. 'This. Virtually nothing. Fuck all, in fact.'

The meeting was breaking up. On the way out, a few of those attending wandered over to Kolya.

'You should be representing the party, not Comrade Anishin. He does not speak for us.'

'Who knows,' Kolya said. 'Maybe when Comrade Lenin arrives, things will change.'

A uniformed soldier gave his opinion. 'I just hope you're right. At the moment, we are going nowhere.'

The group was becoming a crowd. Soon, Kolya was making a speech. When he was done, he walked home to an empty bed, the sound of many arguments ringing in his ears. Comrade Anishin was bound to be be furious at his disloyalty. Kolya smiled. If only Svetlana were waiting for him with her warm body and agile fingers to make his night.

Raisa

Raisa stumbled backward as Elena tugged at her dress. They were both laughing.

'Wait for me to take it off,' Raisa protested. 'You'll tear it.'

'That's a woman who's known poverty.'

'Stop being so rough!' Raisa squealed, only half seriously.

Elena ignored her. 'It's more fun this way.'

Raisa's calves came into contact with the bed and she landed heavily on the mattress, flopping back just as Elena started to plant eager kisses on her exposed throat.

'You're crazy,' Raisa cried.

'And you are the most beautiful creature I have ever seen,' Elena told her, running a line of kisses down Raisa's body.

Soon, Raisa was arching her back, squirming and yelping with pleasure as Elena performed her magic. Elena was upon her, kissing her lips over and over, nibbling at her ear, her throat. Then it was Raisa's turn to give pleasure, which she did with gusto, feeling a great fire of lust and adoration for her lover, giggling as Elena's body jerked two, three times then relaxed. They lay in each other's arms for some minutes then Elena propped herself up on her elbow, toying with Raisa's hair.

'We make too much noise,' she said. 'Mrs Kuznetsova is going to throw you out on your ear one of these days.'

Raisa glanced up at the sky through the gap in the curtains. This was when they made love, whenever Elena could make it away from the Vyborg side for a few hours and before she had to hurry back to be ready for work in the huge mill. There was no mill for her today, of course. Soon, they would be crossing the city to wait for Comrade Lenin to arrive at the Finland Station.

'Mrs Kuznetsova knows exactly what we are doing here,' Raisa said.

'She what?'

'She is not stupid. She knows you're more than a friend.'

'And she doesn't mind?'

'She likes the money I give her,' Raisa explained. 'It is as simple as that. I am a steady source of income in an uncertain world...'

'What's wrong?' Elena asked, seeing her expression.

'It's the money,' Raisa said. 'The cash is almost gone. The way things are, I don't think it is going to be easy to find a job.' She threw back the bedding and padded across the room, crouching in a corner before pulling back a mat and easing up a loose floorboard. After some fumbling, she produced a small rosewood box.

'What's that?' Elena asked as Raisa climbed back into bed and into her arms.

'See for yourself.'

The moment Elena opened the box, her eyes widened. 'You mean...'

'When I killed that dog Andrey, I took more than just the household cash.'

'Look at this stuff,' Elena said, examining the jewellery. 'You don't need to worry about working ever again.'

'There's a problem,' Raisa said. 'Where do I sell it?'

Elena flicked through the pieces and closed the box. 'I think I may be able to help there.'

'How?'

'I worked with somebody who knows every thief and cut-throat in Petrograd,' Elena said. 'She tired of the drudgery of the mill. Not everyone is proud of being a proletarian. She hated the bullying of the foremen. They sacked her for punching one of them. Vera ended up running with a criminal gang.'

Raisa heard something in her lover's voice. 'Is she the one?'

'What?'

'You hinted that you had been with other women before me.'

'Another woman,' Elena said. 'Just the one.'

'Was it Vera? Was she the one who showed you your true nature.'

'You are no fool, are you, Raisa?'

Raisa looked into Elena's eyes and wondered that another human being could have made her this happy. Or this vulnerable.

'Would you love a fool?'

They kissed and snuggled up close.

'Tell me about her,' Raisa said.

Elena was reluctant, eyes dimming just slightly at Raisa's words.

'You don't want to do this.'

Raisa play-pinched Elena on the hip. 'I do, you know.'

A sigh escaped Elena's lips. 'Promise you won't be jealous.'

Raisa gave a full-throated laugh. 'I am already jealous, you monster.'

'We worked together,' Elena explained. 'You know how it is. You get close to people, make friends. We would tease each other, have play fights. One day, she dragged me into a corner of the warehouse and thrust her hand up my skirts. I started to struggle, but I didn't want her to stop.'

'How long did your love affair last?'

'Love affair?' Elena shook her head. 'I wouldn't give it that grand a name. It was screwing.'

Raisa wanted it to be true, but she was unsure whether Elena was telling the truth.

'How long did the screwing last?'

'A few months,' Elena said. 'We stole those moments when we could.'

'Do you still care for her?' Raisa asked anxiously, willing Elena to tell her a tale of friendship gone wrong, betrayal, hatred, anything to reassure her that she didn't have a rival.

'She was fun,' Elena answered. 'That's all. I fucked her. She fucked me. I love you. There's the difference.'

Elena's words filled Raisa with unspeakable joy. Then she remembered how the story began.

'Can you find this Vera again?' she asked.

'I think so,' Elena replied. 'She will know how to fence your jewellery.'

She nibbled at her bottom lip.

'Is something the matter?'

'The people Vera knows,' Elena said. 'They could be dangerous. They're the ones breaking into people's houses. I wouldn't put it past her to double-cross you. They are quite prepared to maim or kill.'

'What choice do I have?' Raisa asked. 'I am not going back to Bagrov.'

'I would never allow that to happen,' Elena told her, horrified that Raisa could even contemplate such a course of action.

'How could you stop it?' Raisa sighed. 'You can barely survive yourself. The war makes beggars of us all.'

Elena was suddenly self-conscious about her thin shoes and shabby, threadbare dress.

'It's true,' she admitted. 'Times are still hard. The revolution hasn't changed that. There are already people saying openly that it has made no difference. They are disappointed in the outcome.'

Raisa heard the chiming of a clock somewhere in the distance. 'We should go. I want to see this Lenin of yours, this flame of revolution everybody thinks is so important.'

She dipped a flannel into the bowl on the wash stand, imagining a towering man swathed all in black with a passionate, strong voice and eyes that blazed into his wrapt audience. She tried to anticipate what he would say...

Elena came up behind her. 'Let me do it for you.'

Raisa leaned back, her head against Elena's shoulders, and felt the delicious movement of the flannel over her body. Elena started to work her way down Raisa's stomach then Raisa clamped her hand tight over Elena's wrist.

'That's enough,' she scolded. 'You're not getting me back into bed.'

'What a damned shame,' Elena said. 'I'll get dressed then.'

The Finland station resembled a great forest of red flags. Thousands of people were cramming into its halls, gazing at the banners – red, always red, some fringed with gold – that hung around the walls.

'What if this is a moment of history?' Elena murmured excitedly. 'The great revolutionary returns from exile.'

The *Vyborgtsi* were present in force. Soldiers were there and the Kronstadt sailors, now the very spine of the revolution, who formed an honour guard. Raisa and Elena stared at the scene: the armoured cars and drifting steam, the regimental band and dignitaries. The locomotives lights appeared and more steam rolled through the air.

'Is it him?' Raisa asked.

Before Elena could speak, a working man turned and confirmed that the famous revolutionary was about to arrive.

'Lenin is here,' he said, his voice full of awe.

Soon the train lumbered to a halt amid the beams of the locomotive and those of the armoured cars outside. The military band struck up and a small, stocky man appeared, wearing a woollen coat and a Homburg hat.

'Is that him?' Raisa asked, disappointed. 'He looks like a bookkeeper.'

'Shh,' hissed the man in front.

Raisa spotted people she recognised in the crowd, the soldier Pavel who crazily seemed infatuated with her, his friend whose name she couldn't recall, the student-Bolshevik Kolya. Somebody was speaking. It was difficult to make out his words. They came in snatches: 'Comrade Lenin, in the name of the Executive Committee of the Petrograd Soviet and the whole revolution, we welcome you to Russia.' Then it was just gobbets of speech: 'revolutionary democracy... no disunity... closing of the democratic ranks.'

Lenin was a plain figure against a backdrop of belching steam, almost mediocre in his unremarkable garb. He was shorter than Elena imagined. He looked weary, impatient with the pomp surrounding his arrival. He received a bouquet of flowers, but seemed uncertain what to do with it. Finally, he spoke. His voice was high and almost comic. She caught Elena's eyes and they both suppressed giggles. Their levity earned another glare from the man in front. Then Lenin was in full flow. There were no niceties, no diplomatic touches. Judging by the faces of some in the welcoming party, they thought him rude.

'He snubbed the welcoming party!'

Somebody nearby sounded scandalised.

'What did he just say?'

'I think he accused the Provisional Government... of betrayal.'

Then Lenin's words echoed out from where he was standing.

'The piratical imperialist war is the beginning of a civil war throughout Europe.'

There was consternation at his words, but nothing compared to the reaction that followed his next declaration, delivered in a shrill, harsh voice.

'Long live the worldwide socialist revolution!'

Then there was utter confusion, bedlam, in some quarters. The crowd was surging, people buffeting Raisa, momentarily separating her from Elena. A path was being cleared through the dense throng. Lenin vanished then reappeared outside the station, near the coachmen's café, borne on shoulders. He still seemed embarrassed by all the attention. Raisa was unable to square the romantic figure of her imagination with the squat, forgettable man on the armoured car. He was standing on the bonnet, gazing out across the sea of expectant faces.

It was as if proletarian Petrograd was willing to give the revolution direction, to pluck it from the dull swamp into which it had sunk. Headlights blazed. The revolutionary seemed wildly excited. What's happening, Raisa wondered. Reunited with Elena, Raisa strained to hear. The language sounded extreme, violent even. He was shouting about betrayal and struggle. Then the entourage was leaving, roaring into the distance.

'What happened there?' Raisa asked, confused. 'He seemed angry about something.'

Elena was continuing to gaze after the vanishing vehicles. 'I think he just declared war on the government.' She was running her hands through her hair over and over again, quite beside herself. Raisa found the whole thing bewildering, but Elena's excitement told her she had just witnessed something extraordinary. 'Do you believe it? All this time in exile and he comes back and starts lecturing everybody like schoolchildren.'

'Is that a bad thing?'

'No,' Elena replied. 'It is the best thing in the world. We don't leave the power in the hands of the Provisional Government, the landlords and bourgeoisie. We take it for ourselves, *for ourselves*.'

This sounded to Raisa like an impossible dream. All her life, she had been as helpless as a kitten, buffeted by the bleak winds of poverty and war.

'Are you sure that is what he said?'

Elena pulled a face. 'I'm not sure I know anything anymore.'

Somebody bumped into her from behind, throwing her against Raisa. They clung on to one another, giggling.

'What does it mean?' Raisa asked, wondering at the strange, chaotic scene in the station,

It was as if Comrade Lenin was a naughty child throwing a firecracker into a party, then running off chuckling. Raisa noticed Pavel looking her way and felt the same prickle of embarrassment as on the Field of Mars.

'Let's go,' she said. 'Soldier Boy is giving me cow eyes again.'

Elena noticed the lovelorn soldier and guided Raisa through the crush.

'What do we do now we have seen *the great Lenin*,' Raisa asked.

'You weren't impressed, were you?' Elena said.

Raisa shrugged. 'Not much. He looked like a bank manager. So how do we spend the rest of the evening?'

Elena slipped an arm round her waist and gave her a squeeze.

'I can think of something.'

Kolya

Kolya found Anishin leaning against the wall in the street outside the station. At Kolya's approach, Anishin stood up, ramrod straight. In spite of the proud posture, he looked shattered by Lenin's words.

'I don't need your gloating,' he growled.

'Gloating is for spoilt children,' Kolya said. 'All comrades must work together now. No support for the Provisional Government. Soviet power and an immediate peace. There can be no other conclusion.'

For all his fine words, he was wearing a smirk of superiority.

'This will be discussed,' Anishin said stubbornly.

Kolya was outraged.

'You heard what Comrade Lenin said. All the time you were so keen to call the *Vyborgtsi* rash and poor in judgement, their instincts were right. You are supposed to be one of them, aren't you?'

'I am one of them,' Anishin snapped defensively. 'There are comrades saying Lenin has taken leave of his senses.'

'Are you one of them?' Kolya asked pointedly.

Anishin answered with some caution. 'His words were unexpectedly bold.'

'He called for worldwide socialist revolution,' Kolya reminded him. 'He rejected coalition with other parties and continuation of the war as betrayal. He was bold, all right. He is demanding that the proletariat and the small peasants take the power into their own hands, not in a few years, but now. *Now,* Comrade Anishin.'

Anishin looked grey. 'It is better to wait for the considered view of the Central Committee. Lenin is only one member.'

'It is time,' Kolya insisted, his voice strong and unyielding, 'for the revolutionaries to go into the streets and workplaces and call for the masses to prepare for power. It is time for them to *be* revolutionaries, not just flaunt the word. Bread, an end to the war, land to the peasants. Lenin's words at the station have vindicated every one of us who argued to press on with the revolution.'

'These were words uttered in the heat of the moment,' Anishin answered. 'He has only just returned to the realities of the capital.' His voice was dull and flat. 'I have to go.'

Pavel arrived, bottle in hand. He was already a little tipsy. Mikhail was hurrying after him. He watched Anishin scuttling away then turned.

'Well,' Kolya beamed. 'Did I not say Comrade Lenin would put the cat among the pigeons?'

Pavel clapped Kolya on the back.

'I owe you an apology, Comrade Kolya,' he said, slurring his speech.

To Kolya's surprise, he knelt, extending his arms like a satrap before Great Alexander.

Kolya stared at Mikhail, eyes widening in disbelief.

'What's he doing?'

'He is making a complete idiot of himself,' Mikahail answered. 'The moment he heard Comrade Lenin's words, he was determined to crawl inside a bottle and celebrate. This is the result.'

'All hail the world proletarian revolution!' Pavel roared. 'Comrade Lenin, I salute you. And you, Kolya, my good friend. And you.'

He wrapped a hand round Kolya's leg and rested his cheek against the student's boot.

'Shit, I drank too much, too fast.'

Kolya put a hand under Pavel's armpit.

'Come on, Comrade Mikhail,' he said. 'Give me a hand here. Let's get this soldier to his bed.'

'Bed!' Pavel bellowed. 'I'd like to take sweet Raisa to my bed.' He swung the Vodka bottle. 'She is an angel.' He shook his head. 'But she doesn't want to know. She is engaged.'

'Engaged?' Kolya said. 'That's one way of putting it. Svetlana says she is besotted with that friend of hers.'

'Bee-spotted? Bee spotted? What the hell are you talking about, Kolya? What the fuck have bees got to do with anything?'

'It means she has got cow-eyes for another woman, you clown. She is in love.'

'With a woman!' Pavel groaned. 'A woman! I'm in love with one of those *koshki*, a bloody dyke.' He slapped his own head. 'How could I not see what was going on before my eyes. Well, put it all down to freedom, Comrades.'

Together, Kolya and Mikhail managed to haul Pavel to his feet and soon all three were stumbling down the street.

'Continual revolution!' Pavel roared at an amused passer-by. 'All power to the workers and peasants. Fuck, I am pissed out of my head.'

'Really?' Mikhail said. 'I would never have guessed.'

Once Pavel was installed safely in his bed, Kolya bade Mikhail goodnight and made his way home through another dreary Petrograd night. The thought of Mrs Turisheva blundering out of her flat, whining and moaning about her hard life filled him with disgust, as did the litter he saw around him. Maybe revolution had to go through a period of chaos, but what Kolya craved was revolutionary order, a new, rational world where people were more moral, more decent and good than any time in human history. He wanted nothing less than the remaking of woman and of man. This day, in the Finland station, he saw that his great dreams were possible. They were made flesh in the form of Comrade Lenin.

'How courageous you were,' he muttered under his breath. 'You were single-minded and true to your principles, a true leader who doesn't give a shit about the mediocrities around him.'

In his battles with Anishin, Kolya saw himself as a younger, lesser disciple of the great Lenin. Suddenly, on impulse, he raced down the street, feet thudding on the paving stones. He ran and ran until he was quite exhausted then he stood, fingers splayed out on his knees, gasping for air. This was what he wanted, for all humanity to strain to fulfil its potential.

When he straightened up, he saw that he was not far from his lodgings. He'd never called it home, it was an anonymous room, a base for his activities and for sleep. He smiled. Unless Svetlana was there. He shoved his key in the lock and let himself in, walking quietly so as not to rouse the self-pitying old fool from her lair. He breathed in the aroma of soup and his stomach grumbled. He realised that he was desperately hungry, but he was not going to knock at Mrs Turisheva's door and beg for some. He would rather go without. He trudged upstairs, hoping that his hunger pangs wouldn't keep him awake. That's when he noticed that the door to his room was ajar. He entered and there was Svetlana, ladling the soup into two bowls.

'How?' he asked. 'I don't even have a stove.'

'I cooked on Mrs Turisheva's,' Svetlana explained. 'I kept it warm until I spied you coming down the street then I brought some upstairs for us both. You need to keep your strength up.'

'Why's that, Comrade Svetlana?'

She winked. 'I don't need to spell it out?'

They ate together.

'You got bread,' Kolya said, biting off a mouthful.

'Mrs Turisheva acquired it for us on the black market,' Svetlana explained. 'Since I gave her that sock on the jaw, she has been very obliging.'

'You're a bad woman, Svetlana, and no mistake.'

When she collected his bowl, he slapped her on the backside and earned a clip round the ear in reply.

'What happened at the Finland station?' she asked. 'I had to see my kids.'

'You call them kids,' Kolya said. 'Anna and Volodya are fully grown and working.'

'I still like to see them,' Svetlana told him. 'You're not the only love in my life, you know. So…what happened? Did you see Comrade Lenin?'

'He was an inspiration,' Kolya said, pulling Svetlana to him so she was squatting on his knees, facing him, 'the very flame of revolution. He called for the world socialist revolution, an end to defencism. The Mensheviks were appalled. Oh, Svetlana, it was glorious.'

They kissed, lips pressed hard together then Kolya pulled away as if burned.

'You bit me!'

Svetlana shook her head. 'It was just a wee nibble. You need to grow some balls, my beautiful boy.'

Kolya nipped at her breasts through her dress and she threw back her head, howling with laughter.

'I'll show you who's got balls,' he mumbled into her body.

'Oh, I expect no less,' Svetlana said. She took his face fondly in her hands. 'First, you will tell me everything about Lenin's arrival.'

Kolya recounted every detail. He enjoyed the way Svetlana's eyes sparkled at Lenin's audacity and abrasive confrontation.

'It could happen, my love,' he said. 'Imagine it, a second revolution, a workers', peasants' and soldiers' revolution.'

Svetlana was intent and serious. 'Do you really think it could happen?

'We could be all, my love, my heart, my *comrade*?'

Svetlana reacted with a bemused look. 'Is comrade more of an endearment than my love?'

Kolya tilted his head. 'Are you making fun of me?'

She rested her forehead against his. 'What am I doing, Kolya? Who am I becoming? Can our love endure these restless times?'

'You dwell too much on things,' he answered. 'What is the point of thinking about the future when the German Army is grinding towards us and revolution boils in the very heart of Russia? Every one of us is living on the edge of a bayonet. We could die in the days to come. We live for a greater cause than ourselves. So we must live for today and forget tomorrow.'

Svetlana moved her lips around his face, cheeks, nose, eyes and finally lips. When she pulled away, she breathed against him.

'All of that may be true, but I don't want to live for a dream. I want to know that we will be together some day in a better world. I want to know that there will be a time when our struggles are over and we are not haunted by want.'

Kolya slipped his hands under her thighs and struggled to his feet.

'Very romantic,' Svetlana said, teasing him. 'You can barely lift me. I'm not that fat.'

Kolya smacked her arse and lowered her onto the bed.

'You're not fat at all, but you try lifting somebody out of a seat like that.'

'Any time,' she said. 'I am stronger than you are, Kolya. When we have made love, let's arm wrestle. You'll see what I can do.'

Kolya held up his hands in surrender.

'I believe you, my worker-lover. I have never laboured as you have, given birth as you have, endured as you have. You are the better part of me.'

When they had made love, Svetlana watched Kolya sleeping. She whispered the message that comes from her heart.

'You will leave me, Kolya. I know that. It will break my heart in two, but I have lived through worse.' She brushed his nose with her fingertip. Though he stirred a little, he did not wake. 'You have two mistresses, don't you, time and the revolution. I am just a bit of fun on the side.'

She rose from the bed, taking care not to rouse her lover and walked to the window. There was Petrograd, the city that had given her two children and taken her man away. She was still dreaming of the past when Kolya stirred.

'What are you doing there?' he asked. 'You're naked. You will catch your death of cold.'

'It's April, darling Kolya. It is but a slight chill.'

'Come back to bed.'

She strolled towards him, enjoying the look of desire in his eyes.

'You like what you see, don't you?'

'Yes, a hundred times yes. Do I deserve a woman like you?'

'Probably not, you scoundrel,' she said, slipping into his arms, 'but you have got me, for good or ill.'

'What were you doing over there?'

'Thinking, remembering.'

'Tell me.'

'There have been two men in my life, you and Vitaly. He was a good man. He drank in moderation and he never gambled. Not once did he beat me.'

'You miss him?'

'Like crazy. Does that make you jealous?'

Kolya nuzzled the side of her breast. 'Of course.'

Svetlana considered him for a moment. 'What does the revolution mean to you?'

Kolya frowned. 'I don't understand. What are you asking?'

'My revolution is my children, my sister and niece, the proletarian masses of the Vyborg. They have faces and personalities and histories. What is it to you, Kolya. The revolution is people, warts and all. You never mention your parents. To you, it has to be something pure and perfect. But where on this Earth is there purity, where is there perfection?'

'Svetlana, you think too much.'

He began to move his hand along her thigh, but she slapped him irritably.

'I was asking you a serious question. I want to understand you.'

'And I want to fuck you.'

'Not now,' she said. 'I've rolled around in your bed enough for one night. It's time I made my way home.'

'It's late. Why don't you stay?'

'And I must work tomorrow, while all you have to do is agitate.'

'You're agitating too,' he reminded her, 'and among the advanced workers too. I wish I was a worker.'

'Only somebody who has never seen the inside of a factory would say that.'

'But that's where the future of Russia will be decided.'

'So let me go,' she said. 'I'm no good to the revolution if I go falling asleep at the factory bench.'

Kolya watched the door close and felt a sense of loss. It was his turn to go to the window. He watched her hurrying to the street corner, shawl pulled over her head. That question she asked, it was closer to exposing his motivations and desires than she could ever imagine. He tried to imagine life without her.

And failed.

Pavel

'This is it,' Pavel said, nodding in approval. 'This is my idea of a revolution.'

It was still early morning and the restaurants, offices and shops were closed. The transport system wasn't running. There was not a tram in sight. Already, crowds were surging over the bridges, red banners bobbing against the background of the marching ranks. It was May Day. It was Lenin's arguments that were on the lips of the new Bolshevik members tramping along at the heart of this river of humanity, his will that had tripled the membership of the party to eighty thousand strong.

'Full power in the hands of the Soviet of Workers' and Soldiers' Deputies,' Pavel continued. 'Full power, Comrade Mikhail! Things are going our way now.'

'It's breathtaking,' Mikhail said, following the contingents from the factories with his azure eyes. 'Do you remember how cautious the party committees were only a month ago, the drivel Kamenev was writing in Pravda?'

'He's still writing it,' Pavel reminded him. 'He sounds like a bloody Menshevik. Every time he puts pen to paper, they must be rubbing their hands with glee.' He let his moment of irritation subside. 'Who would have thought that the arrival of one man would have meant so much?' He grinned mischievously and gave his friend a nudge in the ribs. 'Maybe it will finally make you forget about your little Raisa.'

Pavel treated him to a hooded look and finished his cigarette. 'Maybe it will make you keep your mouth shut for five minutes, my friend.'

Mikhail knew when to let it drop. 'The reactionaries are still putting it about that Lenin is a German agent. What a shower of bastards.'

'Forget it,' Pavel told him. 'Lenin destroyed the likes of Miliukov in *Pravda*. If Britain and France wouldn't help him get through, what was he meant to do?'

'Shit sticks,' Mikhail said, not entirely convinced.

'Shit sticks if you don't clean it off,' Pavel said. 'We'll take a shovel to it. We've got eighty thousand pairs of arms to do it. Who is going to care about all these rumours if we give them their peace, bread and land.'

'We'll need more than eighty thousand members,' Mikhail said, indicating the great crowds. 'How many do you think there are, just here?'

Pavel let his arms flop at his side. 'How do you count something like this? It is the sigh of the risen people. It is heaven.'

There were speakers haranguing the crowd from booths and stalls, fighting for the attention of every man and woman present. Sometimes, it reminded Pavel of a flock of squabbling seagulls. Talk, talk, talk! The Nevsky was crawling with book-hawkers flogging books and pamphlets. He had read his share, but what he wanted is action. What he wanted was the masses against the old order, a straight fight, something honest, brutal and true. The sound of a military orchestra thrummed along, framing the torrent of human speech. More banners rippled as they passed.

'Land, liberty, peace, down with the war.'

'Maybe when Kamenev watches this, he will come over to Lenin's way to thinking,' Mikhail said.

'If he's got any gumption he will,' Pavel agreed. 'Lenin is talking the language of the working people.'

Such were some of the conversations buzzing around this city of revolution, Russia's capital that had shivered all winter on the Neva and was now alive with protest and debate. Many of the working men and women had nothing in their bellies but tea, black bread and hope. The Damocles sword of hunger and war still hung over Petrograd. Red was not the only colour of revolt. There were the black flags of the Anarchists. Here there was one sporting a jaunty skull and crossbones, there one proclaiming: *Welcome Anarchy!*

'How do they differ from us Bolsheviks?' Pavel asked, curious.

'Ask Kolya when you see him,' Mikhail advised. 'He's the one who has read all the books.'

'That's true,' Mikhail answered, 'but he can never answer you in a couple of sentences. Christ, you ask him the way to the toilet and he treats you to the history of the city's sewage system.'

Mikhail laughed. 'You nailed it there, Comrade.'

Row upon row of women from the factories followed, singing at the top of their voices. They had their shawls pulled over their heads and wrapped around their throats. Some raised their hands in the air, others punched the sky. Freed from the drudgery of the factories and mills, they were enjoying their carnival of freedom. As they swung along the street, one gave Pavel the eye.

'Talk to her,' Mikhail said. 'It will take your mind off Raisa. I mean, what's the point of making cow eyes at somebody who prefers pussy to your pathetic cock?'

Pavel liked the look of her bright eyes and impish face. 'I might just do that. Have you got your eye on anyone?'

Mikhail gave him a playful punch on the shoulder. 'Two or three.'

Pavel shook his head and fell in step with the women.

'Hello there, comrade-soldier,' said Bright Eyes. 'I'm Nina. And you are?'

Pavel drew himself up to his full height in a show of mock pomposity. 'I am Pavel Sergeyevich Kirilenko. You may call me Angel.'

'Why Angel?'

'Beats the hell out of me,' said Pavel. 'It was the first thing that came into my head.'

'And are you?' Nina asked. 'Are you an angel?'

'When a woman looks at me with eyes like yours,' Pavel said, 'I am whatever she wants me to be.'

'Watch this one,' a friend of Nina's said. 'Never trust a sweet-talker. They're dangerous. Isn't that true, soldier?'

'There's nothing wrong with a bit of danger,' Pavel said. 'For goodness' sake, we've just made a revolution.'

'Did you kill anybody?' Nina ased.

Pavel caught Mikhail's eye and saw the subtle shake of the head.

'I did,' Pavel declared regardless. He made a gun with two fingers and a thumb and squinted as if aiming. 'Click. Right between the eyes. He went down like a sack of turnips.'

Nina made a crooked mouth to express scepticism. 'Did you really?'

'Tell her, Mikhail.'

Mikhail seemed reluctant, but he had factory girls clinging to each arm. 'He did. The bastard ordered us to fire into unarmed men, women and children. Pavel here popped him with one shot.'

It was Nina's turn to link arms with a soldier. 'You can show me your rifle later, Comrade.'

Pavel swapped glances with Mikhail and they laughed. The women around them saw the comedy of the moment and joined in. Before long, the strains of the *Marseillaise* could be heard from behind them. Somebody had rewritten the words:

We renounce the old world,
We shake its dust off from our feet.
We don't need a Golden Idol,
And we despise the Tsarist Devil.

'That again,' Pavel said. 'Why don't they play the *Internationale?*'

'Go on,' Mikhail said. 'Lead it off.'

Pavel was reluctant, but there was somebody who wasn't. Anishin was part of the contingent in front.

'What language do you want it in?' he asked.

'You don't know any foreign languages,' Pavel scoffed.

'I do, you know,' Anishin replied.

'Go on then,' Nina said. 'Sing it in French.'

Anishin raised his fist and threw back his head:

'*C'est la lutte finale*
Groupons-nous et demain
L'Internationale
Sera le genre humain.'

That earned him a ripple of applause.

'Fair enough,' Pavel said. 'You'll have to teach it to me sometime.'

'I'll teach you the *Internationale* on one condition,' Anishin said. 'You teach me to shoot. It's a skill we're going to need for the socialist revolution.'

'Well said, Comrade,' Mikhail proclaimed to the marchers around him. 'Down with the war. Towards the socialist revolution.'

Some of those around him took up the shout. The mood was very different from the atmosphere to commemorate the victims of the February revolution. There was hope and optimism, but everybody knew that the unity of the march, supporters of the Provisional Government, SRs, Mensheviks, Bolsheviks, Anarchists would be sorely tested in the month to come. The march continued most of the day, vast processions filing by. Finally, Pavel slipped away with his new sweetheart and they walked along the French Embankment, past the country's Embassy.

'What about Comrade Anishin, eh?' Nina said. 'Fancy him being able to sing the Internationale in French.' She gave Pavel a saucy wink. 'Oo la la.'

Pavel slipped his arm round her waist and pulled her against him, feeling plump breasts against his chest. She noticed his arousal.

'I see Soldier Boy is standing to attention,' she said.

'You shouldn't be so pretty, should you?' Pavel responded.

'Did you really shoot that officer?' Nina asked.

'I did.'

'What's it like to kill a man?'

'When you've got a gun in your hand,' Pavel answered, 'it is nothing but a squeeze of the trigger. See, with a bayonet or a sword, you would be close-up. You'd have to feel the knife sinking into his flesh, his death throes. The gun puts distance between the man who shoots it and his victim. That's what made all this imperialist butchery so easy.'

'Do you have nightmares?'

Pavel paused, gazed across the river to where the Battleship Aurora was at anchor. He frowned. 'I've never given it any thought. Strange, isn't it? I sleep like a baby every night.'

'I don't think I could,' Nina said, that ubiquitous smile draining away. 'I couldn't kill a fly.'

'What if the fly is an enemy soldier about to bayonet your family?'

She shuddered. 'Some of the girls in our factory helped kill a soldier who was firing on the *Vyborgtsi*. Maybe they didn't have any choice, but I don't think I could do that. The Bolsheviks are saying Peace, Land and Bread. There will be peace, won't there?'

'That depends,' Pavel answered.

'On what?'

'I don't see the bourgeoisie letting us take over the factories without a fight. I don't see the landlords handing over the land without bloodshed.'

'Then the war will never end, will it?'

Pavel put a finger under her chin and raised her face to the dimming light.

'The best way to save lives is to win the war quickly.'

It was Nina's turn to frown. 'I thought you wanted peace.'

'I do,' Pavel replied, a little confused, 'but sometimes the best way to have peace is to win the fight.'

'So why are the Bolsheviks calling for peace if you know there is going to be war?'

Pavel thought about saying it was the imperialist war that they are going to end, not the class war. Instead, he tilted her head and brought his lips down to hers.

'That's enough talk of war,' he said. 'Give me a kiss.'

'What's that in French?'

Pavel smiled. 'I got Anishin to teach me that one before we left the march. This is just for you. Embrasse moi.'

Nina tried to repeat it and then dissolved into giggles at her clumsy pronunciation.

'I can't get it right.'

Pavel kissed away her words and considered her elfin face. 'Your French is pretty bad. Your kisses are great.'

'That's good,' Nina said. 'Let's do it again.'

In the fading light, under leaden skies, they kissed away the dusk and vanished into night.

An hour later, Pavel was strolling home with a smile on his face. He would be seeing Nina again. She was sweet and tender and gentle. Her face lit up at the things he said. He couldn't remember the last time he felt such warmth from another human being. Mikhail was his best friend, but cute he wasn't. Pavel chuckled at the thought before guiding his thoughts back to Nina. Instinctively, he raised his fingertips to his lips, remembering the taste of her mouth, her warm, urgent breathing on his cheek.

'You fell on your feet when you met her,' he said to the booming darkness.

He marched briskly past the shops on the Nevsky then paused at the sight of a dishevelled-looking figure standing in front of a hotel with his arms in the air. The manicured fingers flew to his head in the universal gesture of dismay.

'Something wrong, Citizen?' Pavel asked.

'Don't citizen me, you ruffian,' came the answer. 'One of you bastards has ransacked my room. What's it coming to when you can't go to the theatre without some cut-throat stealing your best suit?'

'So you're one of those bourgeois then?' Pavel asked, not best pleased at the reception he had received.

'If you mean, do I have some self-respect, the answer is yes.' Pavel waited for the man's rage to run its course. 'Why, the waiters refuse tips because they say it is below their dignity. Even the whores have gone on strike! You can't even get laid in this town.'

Pavel still wanted an answer to his question. 'You're a bourgeois then, a bour-geois?'

Realisation was beginning to dawn. Eyes dilated, informed with a new sense of caution. 'Who is asking?'

'My name is Pavel Sergeyevich Kirilenko,' Pavel said, putting a swagger in his voice. 'Soldier, farmer....Bolshevik.'

He accented every syllable of that last word. They thumped into the mind of the bourgeois like a boxer's fists.

'You may have heard of us.' Pavel enjoyed the twitch of anxiety that followed. 'Do you have a top hat, Citizen?'

'What?'

A small crowd was beginning to gather.

'I asked if you had a top hat. Aren't you bourgeois supposed to wear them?'

Hands rose in a plea of supplication.

'I don't want any trouble.'

'Of course you don't,' Pavel said. 'I mean, you wouldn't go calling people like me a ruffian or a cut-throat, would you?'

'I was upset. My room had just been ransacked.'

Pavel was beginning to enjoy himself. 'Ransacked? Such an ugly word, don't you think? I prefer the word liberated. The proletarian masses were liberating their expropriated wealth and distributing to those in need.'

He knew the bourgeois was fuming inside, but terrified of what Pavel might do. Pavel threw his arms wide for the benefit of the passers-by.

'Do I look like a ruffian, Comrades?' Laughter ensued. 'Do I look like a cut throat?'

'Not you, Citizen,' said one onlooker. 'I think you look quite refined.'

'There you go,' Pavel said, leaning close into the bourgeois. 'I'm refined. So why, when all I was doing was holding out the hand of friendship, did you have to go and start calling me names.'

'I'm sorry,' the bourgeois mumbled. 'Don't hurt me.'

The words faded into his chest. Pavel cupped his ear.

'What's that you say? I can't quite hear you.'

'He says he's sorry.'

'There you go,' Pavel said. 'He's sorry. That didn't hurt now, did it?'

Satisfied that he had thoroughly humiliated the bourgeois, he sauntered away to a smattering of applause, his thoughts returned to Nina. That's when the object of his ridicule made a mistake, possibly the worst of his entire life, muttering a rejoinder he thought nobody would hear.

'Piss off, you mutinous dog.'

Pavel turned, his good humour vanishing. His eyes were on the man now, hard and cold as steel. The bourgeois was in a fit of panic, fat hands flailing.

'I didn't mean it, I swear, I didn't…'

Pavel wasn't listening. He marched up to the bourgeois and raised his fists. The first blow snapped the man's nose. The second clubbed him to the ground. The third laid him out unconscious on the pavement. Pavel nursed his knuckles.

'He should have left it at sorry, shouldn't he?'

Without another word, he stepped over the fallen bourgeois and unbuttoned his trousers, pissing on the stricken man. Satisfied with his work, Pavel continued on his way. He summoned Nina's face to give himself something to think about on the way back, but it was Raisa's eyes that swam in his imagination, Raisa's lips that parted teasingly.

'Well, that's a bastard,' he declared to nobody in particularly. 'Even now, I can't get her out of my mind.'

Nina was lovely.

But she wasn't Raisa.

Raisa

A week later, Raisa was killing time, waiting for Elena near the Liteiny Bridge. Her heart was throbbing in her chest. Walking into a gangster's lair was the last thing she wanted to do. The thought of it brought back the horror of Bagrov's brothel, where living felt like pulling back the skin from a putrid carcass and seeing the maggots squirm underneath. She could never, would never return to that. Life at Mrs Kuznetsova's boarding house was good. She had her own room, clean sheets, a door she could shut to keep the predators at bay. While the whole of Piter was going to shit before her eyes, for the first time in years she had something to lose, something to protect. Those precious few weeks of revolution had been the first time she had felt safe since the death of her beloved mother. She would not surrender her security without a fight.

Her mood was flat as she waited. She had walked past long queues in the last hour, all those women standing in the open for the chance to get hold of kerosene, candles and wood, milk and butter, fish, milk and eggs and bread of course, always bread. Raisa had seen the worn, exhausted faces of so many women and heard their complaints. Some of the waiting people were grumbling, weighed down by the everyday struggle just to survive, despairing of anyone ever bringing order to Russia, disillusioned about the effectiveness of protests, strikes and marches.

Elena spoke excitedly of a second revolution, but here, on the street, there was a kind of depression descending upon the people. When would things get better? When would something change? It made no sense to Raisa that the Bolsheviks had not launched their bid for power the moment Lenin arrived. Elena tried to explain it all, but it seemed so complicated, all this stuff about strategy and tactics. Whenever Raisa heard somebody sympathetic to the Bolsheviks retort that people should stop moaning and fight for the transformation of Russia, her heart leapt, but she did not forget the chorus of complaints. What if the great uprising of the women turned sour? What if all the old crap came seeping back?

Finally, Elena came hurrying across the bridge. She embraced Raisa, but kissed her on both cheeks rather than the lips. Why go out of your way to attract disapproving glances?

'Are you ready for this?' she asked.

Raisa let out a shuddering breath. 'I think so.'

'Is that a yes?'

'Yes.'

They took a tram. It was packed with soldiers. The shaking rhythm of the car made Raisa sleepy. Suddenly, she felt a hand stealing along the back of her thigh, probing inwards and upwards. She felt a flush of revulsion and started to resist. What was love and the sweetest affection with Elena was squalid and invasive coming from a complete stranger. Raisa was wedged in between several burly soldiers. She wriggled and protested, but she was pinned between many bulky bodies, swathed as they were in greatcoats.

'Come on, lass,' the culprit said, self-satisfied face just inches from hers. 'Be nice to a soldier who could be sent to the Front any time. All I want is a good feel, something to remember when I am far from home.'

'Leave me alone!' Raisa protested.

The other passengers looked away. Not Elena. She pushed her way to Elena's side and smashed her fist into the perpetrator's face. She hit him just above the left eye and he screamed, hand clamped to his face. Fresh, scarlet blood leaked between his fingers. She had split the skin on the rim of his eye socket.

'You fucking bitch!' he snarled. 'What did you hit me with?'

Before the soldier's comrades could react, Elena seized Raisa's hand and dragged her off at the next stop. The soldiers were bawling abuse as the tram rumbled away. Elena threw back an obscene gesture.

'Scum!' she shouted. 'You demean the revolution.' She turned to Raisa and lowered her voice. 'Are you all right, my love?'

Raisa's cheeks were gleaming with tears. 'I was back in the whorehouse with those men. Oh Elena, will I ever be free of that filthy bed, those groping hands?'

'We will make our revolution anew. I swear it on my life.'

'This is not about revolution,' Raisa sobbed. 'It is about a woman's right to live in peace without these bastards touching us up. It is about me crawling out of the cesspit. I have tried to get my life back and some lousy scumbag wants to violate me. When does it end?'

Elena drew her close. 'The revolution isn't just about the men, my love. We began it. We will take control of it.'

'Promise,' Raisa said. 'Promise me that one day soon we will not live like this.'

'My sweet, my darling, one day there will be the liberation of the women. This is a struggle for all humanity, for all.'

Raisa managed a smile through her tears. 'I am such a fool, so weak while you are strong.'

'You are not weak,' Elena insisted. 'That bastard Bagrov took away all your dignity. What strength you showed coming back to life.' Her voice was thick with emotion. 'Coming back to life and finding me. I will thank the stars for the rest of my lousy days that you came into my life. You are the most precious creature in this whole stinking world.'

She brushed Raisa's tears away and kissed her on the cheek before linking her arm.

'Let's go.'

At that moment, Raisa remembered the soldier's words.

'What did you hit him with?' she asked.

Elena took an object from her pocket, a huge steel nut, still smeared with the soldier's blood.

'I pilfered it from the factory to lob at the Pharaohs during the revolution. It was still in my pocket.'

Raisa's eyes were wide. 'You're full of surprises.'

Elena gave her lover's hip a squeeze. 'Isn't that the truth?'

They arrived at a door with peeling brown paint some twenty minutes later. Elena rapped on the crumbling surface. Presently, boots thudded on wooden stairs and a face appeared. Elena made her pitch.

'I talked to Vera about a...' She thought for a moment. 'It is about a transaction.'

The thug before them reminded Raisa of some of the men who found their way to Bagrov's door. She gave an involuntary shudder, but she did not give herself away. There would be no show of fear.

'Top of the stairs,' they were told, 'first door on the left.'

They took a moment to compose themselves then they entered.

'Good to see you again, Elena.'

The words came from the woman standing next to a male with a pockmarked, almost fleshless face. He was sitting behind a huge desk. Raisa stole a wary glance at the woman. She knew instantly that this was Elena's former mistress, Vera. She was surprised to see a small, slightly plump woman with mousey hair and a snub nose, not attractive at all. That didn't stop her feeling intimidated. This was a rival, somebody who had tasted every inch of her lover's body. Her skin crawled with jealousy.

'We spoke only this week,' Elena said neutrally, keenly aware of Raisa's discomfort. 'You would think we were long-lost friends.'

Vera flicked a glance Raisa's way then introduced the man at the desk. 'This is brother Yozhin.'

Yozhin was fiddling with a huge ring on his right index finger. He didn't even look up.

'You have something for me?'

Raisa rummaged in her bag and handed him a bracelet. When he failed to take it from her, she looked flustered. He didn't even glance at it.

'Put it on the desk,' he said. 'Vera, examine it.'

Vera picked it up and scrutinised it carefully. Raisa felt her stomach tense as she waited for the verdict. Before long, Vera nodded sagely.

'It is a good piece.'

'How good?'

Vera leaned over and whispered in his ear. For the first time Yozhin seemed interested. Raisa thought of him as a kind of reptile, almost completely hairless and somehow predatory. His movements were sharp and quick. After carrying out his own inspection, he named his price. Raisa was delighted, but before she could speak, Elena took the bracelet.

'Put it in your bag, Raisa. They are not taking us seriously.'

Raisa was horrified. It was as if somebody had just burned the promised money before her eyes. Wondering what Elena was playing at, she followed her to the door.

'Stop,' Yozhin said. 'That was just an opening gambit, my little joke. I will double my offer.'

The way he rushed to call them back excited Raisa. So the jewellery in her possession really was valuable.

'Triple it and you're on.'

Raisa was stunned by Elena's audacity.

Yozhin finally made eye contact. 'Two and a half times my original offer. That is my final punt. Take it or leave it.'

Raisa was staring at Elena with wondering, adoring eyes, but Elena did not return the look.

'We'll take it,' she said.

'You have made a wise choice,' Yozhin said. 'Is there more where this came from?'

'Lots,' Raisa said eagerly, sounding like an eager schoolgirl.

She caught Elena's eye and realised that she had made a mistake being so open about her enthusiasm.

'I will take anything you have,' Yozhin said. 'What did you do, rob a bank?'

'I killed a man,' Raisa answered.

Elena was probably going to scream at her later, demanding to know what she was thinking, blurting out the truth like that, but some deep urge made Raisa say it.

'You?' Yozhin guffawed. He gestured at Elena. 'Her maybe. You? No chance.'

'It's true,' Elena insisted. 'She has hidden depths.'

Yozhin watched with his expressionless eyes. 'Pay them, Vera.'

He opened a drawer and handed her a wad of cash. She counted off the correct amount and held it out. Raisa watched as Elena took it. She noticed the way Vera stroked Elena's palm with an outstretched finger. Elena snatched her hand away, taking the money with her. Yozhin saw the brief episode and grinned lasciviously.

'I would like to see the other pieces,' he said. 'You know how to get in touch.' He snapped his fingers. 'Show them out.'

Vera walked with them to the front door.

'Pretty little bitch you've got there, Elena.'

Elena turned, eyes flashing with anger. 'Call her a bitch again and I will knock your teeth out.'

Vera laughed. 'Still got that temper, I see. I was only joking.'

'Well don't. I know what you're doing, Vera. I am not interested in your stupid games.'

'Games? I don't play games, though I seem to remember you enjoyed a bit of cat and mouse from time to time, my little kitten.'

Elena took Raisa's hand and swept her down the street.

'Just ignore her,' she said. 'That woman is poison.'

She didn't see the nod Vera gave to a teenage boy hanging round on the corner. She didn't see him following on the other side of the street, registering their every move.

'Don't let Vera get to you, my love,' Elena said. 'Life with Yozhin's gang has hardened her.'

'It's not that,' Raisa said. 'I am worried that she will get to you.'

Elena stopped. 'You think I still have feelings for her, don't you?'

Raisa was terrified of revealing what lay in her heart.

'Do you?'

Elena shook her head in disbelief. 'How can you even think something like that? I despise Vera and the life she leads. I was young and stupid when I got myself entangled with that scorpion. I was only just discovering myself. Raisa, it is you I love and no other.'

'I believe you,' Raisa said. 'Ignore me. I am being stupid.'

There was something new between them then, beyond attraction or desire, beyond friendship; a kind of instinctive trust, unity in a common cause.

'I have never thought of you as stupid,' Elena told her, 'just a little sad and damaged by your troubles.' She decided it was time to change the subject. 'There is something you may be interested in. The word is going round that an English suffragist is coming to Petrograd.'

'Suffragist?'

'She fights for women to have the vote just like men. She is from Manchester, birthplace of the industrial revolution. Citizen Pankhurst is a leader of the mass movement in Britain to win the rights of women. They smash windows and destroy property.'

'Are they revolutionaries then?'

Elena frowned. 'They are not Bolsheviks. Many of them have supported the war effort.'

'So why should I be interested?' Raisa protested. 'The war is at the root of our misery.'

'It seems they can combine the rights of women with national chauvinism,' Elena answered. 'They have been jailed and force-fed by the English ruling class. For that alone, they merit a hearing.'

Raisa found herself trying to make sense of militant feminists who supported war, but she had little to go on.

'I would like to hear her. Does she speak Russian?'

'I would be surprised if she did. She will have a translator.'

They walked on, still oblivious to the boy on the other side of the road, the ice blue eyes that never left them. Raisa glanced at Elena with undisguised admiration.

'How did you learn to bargain like that? I would have accepted his first offer.'

'My mother worked in a village market before she came to Petrograd to work in the factory. She was good at haggling.

'Well, you are good at it too,' Raisa said. 'I shall learn from you.'

'And I from you.'

Raisa frowned. 'What do I have to teach?'

'Are you joking?' Elena said. 'Just think what you have done. You survived on the streets when you were no more than a child. You survived that filthy whorehouse with all the beauty in your soul unsullied. You fought for your life and emerged stronger. You had the foresight to secure your future. You have a strength inside you that I will never possess.'

Raisa permitted herself a shy smile.

'Look,' she said suddenly, 'there's a tram about to depart from the stop.'

They ran and clambered aboard, jostling into the crush. Their tail raced after them, but he was too late and watched impotently as it pulled away.

Left stranded by the departure of the two women, he paced back and forth, mind swirling with panic. What was Vera going to do to him? She plucked him off the street where he was starving, but he had never been more than a convenient slave. He took his own good time to walk back to Yozhin's place. He climbed the stairs on legs made of lead. Something told him he would pay for losing them. He could run away, but how else would he put a roof over his head?

'Well,' Vera asked, 'where did they go? Do you have an address for them?'

He stood tongue-tied, eyes downcast.

'Well, spit it out? Where do they live?'

'I lost them,' the boy admitted. 'It wasn't my fault, I swear. They ran for a tram. I couldn't catch up in time.'

The lad was trembling. Tears spilled down his cheeks.

'Please don't hurt me.'

'Are you afraid of me?' Vera asked, walking around him.

'Yes.'

'Silly boy. You've no need to be scared of aunty Vera. I have your best interests at heart. Don't you trust me?'

'I do,' he said, the tone of his voice betraying him.

'It's not a disaster,' Vera said. 'They will be coming back with more pieces. You have a second chance to do your job properly.'

The boy relaxed. 'I won't mess up again.'

'I know you won't,' Vera said, stroking his cheek.

The boy relaxed, maybe a little too soon. Vera wasn't finished.

'If you do, I will cut your pecker off and feed it to the dogs. Now piss off and do better next time.'

The boy looked at her with startled eyes.

'I'm going to give you nightmares, aren't I?'

'Maybe.'

'Clever boy. Fear may just keep you alive.'

Svetlana

Svetlana loved the onset of summer. She liked to glimpse her reflection in a window and see an attractive woman in a cotton dress and coloured kerchief. The sunlight seemed to bring her skin alive and add a lustre to her hair. The years fell away and she was almost as she had been when she was newly married with two small children. On this June day, she was full of optimism. Kolya seemed as infatuated with her as ever and the Bolsheviks were gaining ground. Though still a minority in the Soviet, they were no despised sect. They had the ear of the workers, and they were guided by the driving force of Lenin. The outdoor meeting was in front of the Anarchist headquarters. Svetlana swung round the street corner and saw the crowd assembled in front of a huge black flag that hung down the front of the building. She spotted Elena and her friend Raisa.

'Friend?' Svetlana said to herself, a smile on her full lips. 'It's love. That's what it is.' She just hoped they were discreet. It was an unforgiving world. She wondered what it was like, being with another woman. Lying with her husband had been a glorious wrestling match, clawing, kissing, pressing, thrusting. They had exhausted the hell out of each other, those nights between the sheets. So how was it with women? She'd had the usual adolescent crushes, a touch, a stolen kiss, but her desire had always been for men. She liked the hardness of them, in more ways than one, but also the tenderness, sometimes unexpected, that came along with the physical frenzy. Now Kolya, he was not like her poor, dead husband. While Vitaly had been simple and direct, Kolya was complex and unpredictable. There was something both masculine and feminine in him. Svetlana loved his gentleness as much as his power, his tender touches as much as his eager lovemaking.

'It's aunty!' Elena exclaimed.

Svetlana embraced her niece then Raisa, a little embarrassed that she still had an image in her head of the two of them together.

'Has Mrs Pankhurst arrived?' she asked.

'It isn't her,' Elena replied. 'Somebody said she was quite frail because of the force-feeding she went through in prison. Another woman is taking her place, Jessie Kenney. Have you heard of her?'

Svetlana shook her head. 'I just hope she doesn't support the war. The last thing we need is a foreigner giving ammunition to the defencists.'

Svetlana waved to some of the women she recognised in the crowd, such as Albina, her friend from the mill. Presently, Kenney appeared. When she spoke it was in an unintelligible English accent. Svetlana had heard them on the Nevsky, but she had never heard one speak like this. Kenney's words were translated. There was applause when it was revealed she was a working class woman from the North of England, among the hills and moors that were the cradle of the industrial working class. She spoke briefly of her time as a weaver's assistant.

'A weaver!' Raisa said excitedly. 'Just like you, Elena, and you Svetlana.'

'We've got something in common then,' Svetlana said, still sceptical about somebody who might be implicated in the bloodbath of the war.

With the light on her face, Raisa was very beautiful. I may not yearn for other women, Svetlana decided, but I understand her attraction. There was a brightness and energy about Raisa that was desperately appealing. Her heart ached to think that there were people who didn't understand this love, who thought it forbidden and wrong. Svetlana had heard rumours that some of these suffragists, suffragettes, whatever they were called, also preferred the company of other women. It was a world she did not fully understand, but one for which she had no hostility.

The crowd warmed to Kenney in spite of the halting delivery of the translator, who failed to replicate the warmth and fluency of the woman's speech. Kenney spoke about being the only working class woman in the leadership of the suffrage movement, how she had campaigned for women's freedom and had been jailed and tortured many times, force-fed with a tube down her throat. The details made Raisa look away, tears in her eyes.

'You need to toughen up, young lady,' Svetlana said, hugging Raisa. 'The next revolution will be no cakewalk and we've got bastards in this country that make the English ruling class look like angels.'

Suddenly, a gale of laughter interrupts Svetlana's softly spoken advice.

'What was that?' she asked. 'I missed it.'

'Do you know what she did?' Elena said excitedly. 'She went with two other women and roughed up Asquith, the Prime Minister. They smashed his windows too.'

Svetlana grinned. 'I am warming to this woman.'

There was one moment when many in the crowd start shaking their heads. It was when Kenney described the suspension of the campaign of militancy in order to support the war effort.

'That's a big mistake,' Elena said. 'How can women who are so militant support the imperialist butcher? I don't understand.'

Svetlana shook her head. 'Nor do I, but this is Britain. Its Empire stretches across the world.'

Raisa listened. 'She may be wrong about the war, but I like her.'

'So do I,' Elena said, 'but if she was living here in Petrograd, she would be a Menshevik or a SR, wouldn't she?'

Raisa sighed. 'Why must everything be so complicated?'

Kenney finished speaking to loud applause, and vanished from the stage. Svetlana remembered the way Lenin had arrived at the Finland Station and lit a new fire under the revolution. When would the words of women have a similar impact? She approached Albina, her fellow Bolshevik from the mill.

'What do you make of that?' she asked.

'This Kenney is being misled,' came the answer. 'She is a worker. She should be as militant against the war as she was fighting for the suffrage. Do you know where they are taking her next? To meet Bochkareva.'

Svetlana shook her head. 'That's what happens when you don't have a correct view of the war.'

'Like Comrade Kamenev, you mean?'

Svetlana's eyes narrowed at the mention of the Central Committee's main conciliator. 'Good job we have Comrade Lenin.'

'Bochkareva?' Raisa asked. 'I've heard of her, but I don't know much about her.'

'Commander of the Women's Death Battalion,' Svetlana said with obvious distaste. 'She wants women to go and fight for Mother bloody Russia. We should be fighting against the war, not for it. It's your attitude to the war that sorts the wheat from the chaff. Remember that.'

Raisa nodded. 'I will.'

Svetlana laughed and stroked her cheek fondly. 'You're quite the innocent, aren't you?'

For just a brief instant, she saw something pass between Raisa and her niece and wondered what it meant. What was there about this young woman of Elena's that she didn't know?

'Well, I have to be going,' Svetlana said, giving a cheeky wink. 'I have somebody waiting for me.'

'Be good, aunty,' Elena said.

'That's the last thing I intend to be, my love,' Svetlana retorted with a full-throated laugh.

Soon, she was striding along the pavement, kicking aside the rubbish. She attracted admiring glances from men sitting idly under the sullen sky. She enjoyed the attention, as long as it was restricted to stares. Only Kolya got to touch. She was glad of the fresh breeze. It helped to sweep away the stink of the sewers and canals, and reduced the irritation of the flies. There was disease in the city. Come the second revolution, they would clean up this filth, she promised herself. What's the point of power if people are too sick to enjoy it?

At last, she was climbing the stairs to Kolya's room. The door was open and she breezed in, planting her hands on the arms of his chair and letting him gaze into the neckline of her dress. He leaned forward and planted a kiss between her breasts before showering her face with more kisses.

'Where have you been?' he asked. 'I was expecting you an hour ago.'

'I was listening to one of the Englishwomen.'

'Pankhurst?' Kolya said distastefully. 'She is a social chauvinist.'

'Kenney,' Svetlana told him. 'She supports the war, but she is a working woman. She hit the British Prime Minister.'

'She supports the war. You closed the chapter with that statement.'

Svetlana took hold of his ears and shook his head. 'Even defencists can have things to say worth hearing, you zealot.'

Kolya's hands were on her breasts. 'I'm a zealot for you, Comrade Svetlana.'

'And I for you.'

Soon, they were between the sheets, he thrusting away, she digging her nails in his arse. When Kolya's passion was spent, she rolled him onto his back.

'My niece Elena is in love with a woman,' she said.

'Raisa? I know. I have a friend who is sweet on her, poor fool.'

'A woman?'

'No, a man. Raisa attracts a lot of attention, it seems.'

'I worry about them.'

'Don't,' Kolya said, 'once we sweep away all the old shit, love will be as free as a bird on the wing. Forget the defencist feminists. You should be listening to Comrade Kollontai or Comrade Reissner.'

'I do,' Svetlana reminded him. 'You're not alone in having a brain, you know?'

'Of course,' Kolya said, tracing a line down her spine to her tailbone, something that always made her squirm with pleasure. 'You have brains and beauty.'

'And you have a flatterer's tongue. I am a middle-aged woman with stretch marks.'

He found them with his fingertips. 'I love your stretch marks.'

'Yes,' Svetlana said, 'and someday soon, when my boobs are sagging and my face is nothing but a sack of wrinkles, you will be looking for somebody with smooth skin and a tight young butt.'

Kolya frowned. 'Do you think me fickle?'

She took his face in her hands. 'I think you are a man like any other.' She sighed and changed the subject. 'When will the insurrection be? Prices get worse every day. We keep striking for the minimum wage, but nothing seems to change. They've cut the bread ration again.'

'I heard Comrade Trotsky talk recently about just this issue,' Kolya said eagerly. 'The conditions of the workers are intolerable. All the offensives run out of steam. Kerensky can wave his arms and scream all he likes. It is all to no avail. Russia is prostrate before the German imperialists. It will all come to a head before long, my love.'

'Such terrible things keep happening,' Svetlana said. 'Just the other day, a mob broke into a house and beat the entire family within an inch of their lives, just to seize food and a few valuables. There is so much ugliness about.'

'There is ugliness in the death throes of the old order,' Kolya told her, 'but it will not be long before a new world is born.'

Svetlana looked away to hide her face. Why did Kolya have to talk in slogans and generalities? She just wanted him to engage with the things she asked him. She wrapped her arms and legs around him. 'I am impatient for this new world.'

'So am I, but we must win the advanced workers to our side. If we move too soon, we will be destroyed.' He stroked back her unruly hair. 'Make no mistake, before long the power will be passed to the Soviets and the workers will be in the saddle.'

Svetlana threw him down roughly. 'Meanwhile, I am in the saddle when it comes to you, my earnest, bookish stallion.'

Kolya roared with laughter as she bounced on him.

'Forget it,' he said. 'You've worn me out.' He embraced her and nuzzled her ear. 'You always wear me out.'

She grew serious. 'But could we lose? There are times this world scares me. I have no worries about great Petrograd, but it is an island in a sea of peasants. And what of red Russia itself? Say we hold the country, we will be a citadel of socialism in a hostile capitalist world. What of the Germans? What of the *Stavka*? Kerensky thinks he has the generals in his pocket, but they could turn on us all and drown red Piter in blood.' There was a haunted look in her eyes. 'I have children, family, *you*.'

'I tell you what will save us,' Kolya said. 'It is ruthlessness, determination, the kind of iron will you see in Comrade Lenin.'

Svetlana spoke her inner thoughts.

'Some say Trotsky is the greater leader.'

Kolya shook his head. 'Trotsky has immense talents. What an orator! What an organiser! But he is not a party man. It is Lenin who is the brain of the party, the engine of the revolution.'

'And he is ruthless enough to win the power?'

'Yes, yes, a hundred times yes, Svetlana.'

Kolya's eyes burned with excitement and Svetlana searched his face, her expression shading into gloom.

'What's wrong?' Kolya asked.

'I don't know,' she said. 'These words you use: iron will, ruthlessness. They scare me.'

'You're not averse to a bit of ruthlessness. What about poor Mrs Turisheva?'

Svetlana actually blushed.

'There you go,' Kolya laughed. 'And you dare to judge me.'

'I am not judging you, Kolya.'

He sat up and took her hands.

'A few minutes ago, you were talking about crushing our enemies. You can't have it both ways. We concentrate with absolute conviction on victory or we lose. They are the only possible outcomes.'

Svetlana gave a nod, somewhere between agreement and resignation.

'But what if we win the power and lose our souls?' 'Dearest Svetlana,' Kolya sighed, 'where does this come from? Do you know what will make our revolution secure? It's the workers and soldiers, millions strong. We are unstoppable.'

'You're right,' she said, her smile returning. 'Of course you are. How could I doubt you?'

But when he slipped into a deep sleep beside her, she did doubt him, just as she doubted herself. It was as if they were passengers on a runaway train, hurtling on and on at breakneck speed. Did anybody, anyone at all, know where the journey was going to end?

Raisa

This was the moment she had been dreading. The money from the bracelet had all been spent. It was time to return to Yozhin with another piece. She waited impatiently for Elena. This time they had agreed to meet closer to Yozhin's den, at the corner of a working class street on the Vyborg side. She was painfully aware that her clothes made her stand out as if she were some middle-class lady who had strayed into the wrong district. It was a few days since she had seen her beloved Elena. Elena had been caught up in a torrent of strikes, protests and meetings, leaving Raisa in something of a limbo, sympathetic to the Bolshevik cause, but still not quite of it, even though she had formally joined. She was envious of Elena and Svetlana for they were at the very epicentre of the revolution, the eye of the proletarian storm.

Then there was Elena, face lit by sunlight, eyes gleaming with love. Raisa wanted to run into her arms, but she knew better than to expose herself to the crowd. Elena embraced her and kissed her on both cheeks, her hands lingering slightly longer than a friend's would. Her lips hovered close to Raisa's ear.

'I am coming home with you tonight.'

The words sent a thrill through Raisa.

'I feared your feelings for me were cooling,' she whispered.

'Not until the stars fall from the sky,' Elena answered, furtive words dancing in her lover's mind. Then her face was serious. 'We have to go.'

'Did you see her...Vera?'

'I sent her a message. We have mutual friends.'

Terror came stealing through Raisa's body, just as it had on her first visit to Yozhin's place.

'I wish you had no contact with her at all.'

Elena gave her a sober look. 'If we had no contact, you wouldn't be able to sell your treasures.'

'She scares me,' Raisa said. 'She is vengeful, my love.'

Elena shrugged. 'I can take care of myself.'

They turned the corner and there it was, the anonymous, rotting door that led up to Yozhin's makeshift office. The boy was lounging against the wall. Raisa recognised him.

'You looking for Yozhin?' he asked.

'We have business with him,' Elena answered.

'He's out. You'll have to deal with Vera.'

Raisa felt Elena's hand squeeze hers as they climbed the stairs. Vera was waiting.

'Short of money, are we?' There was a mocking look on her face. 'They always come running back. It's like an addiction.'

'Show her the ring,' Elena said impatiently.

Raisa saw Elena avert her eyes from Vera's withering stare. She took the ring from her coat pocket and slammed it on the table. Vera seemed to find that amusing.

'Touchy, aren't we? You shouldn't be jealous, you know? What, are you wondering what Elena and I had together, how I knew every inch of her body? It eats away, something like that. You'll be a bitter old shrew before you know it.'

'Maybe it takes one to know one,' Raisa retorted. Her cheeks were burning with jealousy and humiliation, but she was determined to stand up to this woman.

'Well, well,' Vera said, leaning back in her chair. 'So the little mouse has a voice after all.'

'How much?' Raisa snapped.

Vera named her price.

'Double it,' Elena said.

'Done.'

Raisa was surprised, and a little frightened, at the brevity of it. 'See you next time,' Vera said.

'There will be no next time,' Elena retorted. 'I'm done with you.'

'That's what they all say,' Vera snorted. 'You'll be back.'

Back outside, Raisa walked fast, eyes stinging with tears. Elena raced after her, tearing at her arms.

'Stop,' she pleaded. 'For mercy's sake, stop! What is wrong with you?'

Raisa spun round. 'She will destroy us. I know it!'

'Don't be stupid,' Elena cried. 'She has no power over me, or over you. She is a viper without a bite.'

'I don't believe you,' Raisa cried. 'It's that smug expression she always has. She is like a puppeteer pulling our strings. Why did we ever go to that dreadful place? We will never be free of her.'

Elena finally succeeded in calming Raisa and enveloped her in her arms. 'You have to stop this. She can only have power over us if you allow her into your head. Look at her, for goodness' sake. What do you see, just a dumpy little petty crook with fading looks and a well of bitterness inside her? You should not fear her, Raisa. Don't you understand? She fears *you*.'

Raisa stared, bewildered.

'That's right. She fears you. She fears your life, your beauty, the way you mesmerise me. We will not let her get her way, never!'

'Swear to me that this is more than words,' Raisa pleaded.

'I swear with all my heart. She is nothing.'

Finally, they became aware of the busy street around them, the odd, curious glance from the passers-by. They hurried to the tram stop. This time the tram was only half full. They paid no attention to the boy, who had followed them. So wrapped up were they in each other, they had eyes for no-one else as they left the tram, as they walked along the river, as they opened the door to the boarding house. They did not know, as they tore at each other's clothing and exchanged frenzied kisses that he was still watching from the street, wondering what was going on behind the drawn curtains. As their passion subsided, they had no idea that he was on his way back to Yozhn's den, content in the knowledge that Vera would not be cutting off his pecker.

Because he had done well.

Pavel

There was a time Pavel dismissed the Baltic sailors. Latecomers to the revolution, he thought, trying to steal the soldiers' thunder. Now he was sitting in a room with representatives of the Kronstadters. He listened with growing enthusiasm as one of the sailors, dressed in his striped shirt and jaunty cap, read out the list of regiments supporting the call for a demonstration, armed if necessary.

'We can field ten thousand sailors,' he told the meeting, 'ten thousand armed men committed to a Soviet government. We'll bring our military band along with us and it won't be playing the fucking *Marseillaise*. It will be the *Internationale*.'

When he was finished, there was applause. There had been other meetings like this, other demonstrations against the war, other fiery speeches, but it felt different this time. A mass armed demonstration! Pavel's heart thudded with excitement.

'Did you hear that?' he said to Mikhail. 'It has the support of the First Machine Gun Regiment. The showdown is imminent.'

Mikhail looked troubled. 'Do we have the party's support for this? Lenin said patiently explain. I'm not sure there is anything patient about this call.'

'Patience? What's got into you? Did you hear what the Kronstadter said? Nothing can stop us.'

'I'm not so sure,' Mikhail said in his faltering voice.

'Grow some balls,' Pavel exclaimed. 'Do you want to be shipped back to the Front? There are rumours they are going to transfer the Machine Gunners. Everywhere, our comrades are throwing away their rifles and walking away from the slaughter. The lines are drawn, Mikahil. Which side are you on?'

'You can't doubt my commitment to the cause of revolution,' Mikhail protested. 'This is not about the goal, but the immediate tactics. I don't see the hand of the Central Committee behind this move.'

'I've heard all that bollocks before,' Pavel reminded him. 'Isn't this the kind of talk we heard before the return of Comrade Lenin?' He rested his hands on Mikhail's shoulders. 'If we don't lead the demonstration the bloody Anarchists will, and you know what blowhards they are.'

'We can't let the Anarchists make our decisions for us,' Mikhail insisted.

'And we can't lag behind the buggers,' Pavel answered. 'They're already occupying the premises of the right-wing press.' He beamed. 'Did you hear what Comrade Latsis said? We should be ready to seize the railroads, banks, telegraph and arsenals. Podvoisky says the revolution is only just beginning. For fuck's sake, this is my kind of language.'

Mikhail was still wary. 'What if it's too early? I think we should delay, at least until we hear from Comrade Lenin..'

'How do you work that out? How do we find out how far the masses are prepared to go if we don't dip our toes in the water? The Anarchists are always gagging for action. What if, this one time, they are right?'

Mikhail did not look convinced. The Kronstadt sailors were leaving. A few of them waved, and Pavel returned the greeting, while Mikhail could manage only the most peremptory flap of the hand. 'We should wait for the party committees,' he insisted.

Pavel threw up his arms. 'Wait, wait, wait. That's all I ever hear. There are mouldy skeletons in the graveyard that spent their whole lives waiting.'

Pavel was about to go when Mikhail tugged at his shirt. 'Talking about waiting,' Mikhail said, brightening, 'look who's here.'

Nina was waving from across the street. 'What are you doing setting up a meeting with your girl outside the meeting?'

'She's discreet,' Pavel said, wondering what all the fuss was about.

'She'd better be,' Mikhail said.

Pavel strode to meet her. She reached up to kiss him. He lifted her up and felt her mouth against his.

'You need to grow,' he said, teasing.

'You need to shut up about my height,' she answered. 'I can't help being short.'

'You're getting skinnier,' Pavel observed, "I can feel your ribs.

'Is it any wonder,' Nina said. 'There is hardly any food in the city. They are saying even the hotels and restaurants of the rich are serving only sandwiches. The rats are queuing to get tickets out.'

Pavel put a protective arm round her. She had been slim and tiny to begin with. It was as if she was becoming quite invisible.

'Did you hear about the meat speculator at the Putilov?" she said. "The workers smeared him with his own rotten meat and hauled him through the streets.'

Pavel smiled as he imagined the scene.

'Are you still locked out?' he asked.

Nina nodded miserably. 'We have no food and no wages to buy it even if there was anything in the shops. When are you going to do something about it, you and your brave Bolsheviks?'

'I've just come from a meeting, as well you know.'

'Meetings,' Nina scoffed, 'always meetings.' She made a talking gesture with finger and thumb. 'Talk, talk, talk. What's happened to the great promise of All Power to the Soviets, tell me that.'

'It is coming to a head.'

Nina grimaced. 'I've heard that before.'

That's when she slid a hand down his stomach. 'My friends are going to be out so we can have the room to ourselves. Maybe I can get something else to come to a head.'

Pavel gave a low grunt of pleasure as she brushed his crotch with her fingers. 'You're a mischief and no mistake.'

Nina winked. 'You don't know mischief until you see what I've got in store for you, Mr Revolutionary.'

He patted her on the backside.

'Let's go.'

He was woken the next morning by ferocious banging on the door.

'Who the hell is that?' said somebody on the far side of the partitioning curtain. Nina's room-mates must have returned while she and Pavel were sleeping.

Nina went to the window.

'Pavel. Pavel! Get dressed. It's your friend Mikhail.'

Pavel stumbled to the window, wearing only his trousers. One of the room-mates giggled.

'What the hell do you want?' Pavel shouted.

'We've got to go,' Mikhail yelled. 'The bastards are trying to send us to the Front.'

'More rumours?'

'Not this time, I don't think. One of the lads says the commander has just had a telegram.'

'Well, he can shove it up his arse and so can bloody Kerensky. We're not going anywhere.'

He rushed to kiss Nina and wriggled into his clothes.

'When will I see you again?' she asked.

The roar of an armoured truck rattled the window as a detachment of soldiers thundered by.

'The other side of the revolution, by the look of it,' Pavel answered.

He clattered down the stairs, to see a half-dressed Nina leaning out of the window, waving.

'All Power to the Soviets!' she cried. 'Down with the ten capitalist ministers!'

Pavel gave her a clenched fist salute and hurried off in the company of Mikhail. By the time they reached the barracks, agitators were addressing the men. One of them was Kolya, declaiming from the bonnet of a truck. More trucks were arriving, loaded with more soldiers in uniform. All was confusion. Even as Kolya was speaking, gunfire stammered in the distance.

'Is this it?' Pavel demanded as Kolya climbed down.

'This is it. Comrade Bogdatiev has spoken on behalf of the Putilov factory committee. All workers and soldiers to the streets!'

Mikhail was perturbed. 'What does Comrade Lenin say?'

'There's no word,' Kolya answered. 'But this is in line with his April speeches. The time for caution is past.'

'What if this is just an Anarchist provocation?'

Kolya shook his head. 'Pavel, what the hell is wrong with your friend?'

A car arrived flying a pair of red flags.

'The action is at Suvorov Square,' the driver shouted, 'climb aboard. I reckon we can take four, five at a pinch.'

In the event, half a dozen men clung to the boot and running board as the car careered towards its destination. There were the usual scarlet and gold banners.

'Down with the landlords and bourgeoisie.'

'All Power to the Soviets!'

Mingling with the slash of red were the black banners of the Anarchists. Their car pulled up, blocked by a furious struggle. A well-dressed couple were trying to fight off a group of soldiers in the process of commandeering their car.

'Help us!' the woman cried, seeing them.

'Absolutely!' Pavel said, lifting the struggling woman on his shoulders and dumping her unceremoniously on the pavement. Her husband was sent sprawling next to her.

'You scoundrels!' he bawled as his car sped away, packed with insurgent soldiers.

'Coming from the likes of you,' Pavel shouted as they departed, 'that's a compliment. Down with the bourgeoisie.' He glanced at Mikhail, then added a parting comment. 'And ugly fuckers like you!'

Even Mikhail forgot his concerns then, and burst out laughing.

'OK, Comrade Kolya,' Pavel said, 'what are our objectives here?'

To his surprise, Kolya was stumped.

'Well, is it revolution?'

'We are responding to the move of the *Stavka*.'

'Well, stop bloody responding and show some leadership.'

As they roared along the Nevsky, there was chaos. Thousands of workers were swarming around the shops. Some windows had been broken. There were seizures of alcohol. Suddenly, firing broke out and bullets ricocheted along the street. There was the zing and whine of more shooting, this time from the opposite direction. Pavel saw a muzzle flash and returned fire.

'Who were they?' Mikhail demanded as the attacker became a blur.

'Fucked if I know.'

'So why did you fire?'

'Because he shot at me, you moron!'

They screamed to a halt on the square, but already the crowds were thinning there. Mikhail bawled a warning as a panicking, riderless horse clattered past.

'This is crazy,' he yelled. 'Where's the organisation? Where's the leadership?'

Pavel grinned. 'At least the Anarchists will be happy.'

In the dusk, they saw a city on the move. Bayonets glinted in the dying rays of the sun. Silhouetted figures climbed on walls and shouted slogans. It was as if the Bolsheviks had simply melted into the formless throng.

'Well?' Pavel glared at Kolya, 'have you made your mind up yet? What the hell are we telling the comrades on the street.'

Kolya was leaning over the vehicle, talking to somebody.

'I don't believe you.'

'What's that?'

'The word is, the Central Committee has voted against participating in the demonstrations.'

'And you believe it?'

'I don't know what to believe.'

There were more rumours, this time conveyed by a woman fresh from taking part in a street meeting near the Troitsky Bridge. The Petrograd side was awash with protest and gunfire as the people of the Vyborg side swept across the bridges and over the ice – scarlet banners, tramping feet, revolutionary slogans and class war.

'This comrade says that Trotsky and Lunacharsky have made a statement for the Interdistrict Committee. They are calling for All Power to the Soviets.'

'Didn't we already know that?' Mikhail asked.

'Well?' Pavel demanded, not in the best temper. 'What the hell are we saying?'

'All Power to the Soviets,' Kolya answered. 'We stay on the streets until the government falls.'

Kolya

The river of revolution was once more in full spate. Vehicles roared up and down, red flags fluttered. Men clustered aboard each private and armoured car yelled political slogans. Tyres rumbled over the detritus of revolt: broken glass, hats, umbrellas, crumpled banners, even shoes. Kolya didn't see wreckage, only rising hope.

'It's happening,' Kolya hissed. 'It's actually happening.'

'You mean this is it?' Pavel removed his rifle from his shoulder. 'We take the power?'

Kolya nodded, quiet excitement written in every line of his face. 'We take the power.'

'Where are the calls to action from the Central Committee?' cautioned Mikhail. 'Has Lenin spoken?'

'Sometimes leadership lies with the masses,' said Kolya.

Mikhail scowled. 'What textbook did you get that little gem from?'

Rifle fire crackled a few hundred yards up the road followed by the dull, pounding pulse of a machine gun. The gunfire was accompanied by an enormous crash. They ran towards the sound, to discover a large crowd had overturned a tram. Glass glittered everywhere, like sunlight on the ocean. Impressed with their handiwork, people started rocking a second tram, trying to dislodge the wheels from the runnels. Then there was a shout, loud and panicky.

'Cossacks!'

Hooves thundered and Cossacks scattered the crowd. Sabres glinted like bright crescent moons, and flailed left and right. A slash of steel carved open the scalp of a man as he fled. His scream was gut-wrenching.

'Lousy fuckers,' Pavel growled. 'Are they with us or against us?'

Kolya saw the horsemen closing on them and he knew that revoluion was fluid, a molten floe to be tempered, shaped, channelled by the beat of the hammer, the pump of the bellows. This was the moment for a man of destiny. Pressing his rifle inexpertly to his shoulder, he fired a warning shot. The recoil almost knocked him off his feet, but he held his ground, desperate for the respect and acceptance of the masses.

He had aimed two metres above the closest rider's head, but the shot grazed the officer's ear. The charge began to waver, one or two riders restraining their mounts. Horses whinnied and reared. Pavel and Mikhail started to lay down fire. Amid the cordite smoke, a deeper, more throaty chorus of gunfire opened up. Rounds from an unseen machine gun tossed up dust and concrete debris. The skirmish was over. The Cossacks wheeled away, tails between their legs, but without casualties.

Pavel rested an approving hand on Kolya's shoulders.

'I thought you were another bloody intellectual wanker, all talk, but you did well. What a shot and from a novice too.'

Kolya didn't disabuse his comrade about the accuracy of the shot. He knew he had to take command. His mind was already racing ahead.

'Let's go.'

'Where?'

'To round-up these machine-gunners and clear the streets of counter-revolutionaries.'

Pavel nodded. 'Sounds good to me.'

They approached the sailors in their blue uniforms and striped shirts. The Kronstadters nodded to them.

'When did you fuckers arrive?' Pavel asked.

One of the sailors thumbed back his cap and gestured to the river, where barges and steamers were still arriving, and crowds of workers cheered the disembarking sailors.

'We're tied up all along the Nikolaevsky and University Quays,' he said, 'Comrade Raskolnikov is at the head of the insurrection.' He pointed at a fluttering scarlet banner. 'That's the watchword, comrade.'

The slogan read *All Power to the Soviets*.

'I'm not too sure the Soviets want power,' Mikhail grumbled. 'They're asking for protection from the people.'

'They'll take it even if we have to shove it up their arses,' the sailor answered. 'They are meant to be the voice of the workers and soldiers.'

'What's your name?' Kolya asked.

'Are you joking? This is an insurrection, Comrade. No names. If we don't succeed there will be counter-revolutionaries wanting to put me in front of a firing squad. Call me Pissed off with Fucking Around.'

'Well if you're pissed off, come with us. We're going to clear the Liteiny of counter-revolutionaries.'

Pissed Off nodded to his comrades. Now they had a red company advancing towards the fashionable quarter, the centre of power. People were lying face down on the ground. Others were pinned against the wall.

'What's happening here?' Kolya asked.

A voice mumbled against the cobbles. 'Some bastard is shooting at the crowd. There are two dead.'

One of the dead was sprawled on the paving stones, the black flag of the Anarchists flapping around him. Somewhere, the Kronstadt sailors' marching band was still playing, as if leading a village wedding parade. Pavel scanned the rooftop with a practised eye. There was a loud crack. People screamed and ran. Those on the ground covered their heads and squeezed their eyes shut.

'Can you get to the shooter?' Kolya asked.

'Oh, we'll get to him,' Pavel said, squinting as the sun stabbed between parting clouds. He ran zigzagging across the road and kicked the front door. Three times he kicked at the lock, then the door burst open. Kolya watched fascinated as Pavel entered, followed by Mikhail, Pissed Off and a couple more Kronstadters. There was the loud *dum dum* of shots. By the time Kolya reached the hallway of the house, there were two dead men sprawled on the floor in a pool of blood.

'Counter-revolutionaries?' Kolya asked.

'How the fuck should I know?' Pavel snapped 'I didn't have time to ask.'

One of the men was old, the other was wearing a concierge's uniform. Neither seemed to be armed. Pavel saw the look on Kolya's face.

'If you're going to throw up,' he said, 'get it over with. You think I shot the wrong men? Listen to me. If I hesitate, I'm the dead guy. War is shit, Comrade. Innocents get caught in the middle. Get used to it.'

Kolya's face was white.

'Are you all right?' Mikhail asked.

'I'm fine,' Kolya answered. 'Just clear the building.'

Pavel nodded and mounted the stairs. Five minutes later there was a shot, a pause, then a second shot. Gun barrels were trained on the staircase when he re-appeared.

'Don't shoot me, you fuckers,' he laughed.

'The sniper?' Kolya asked

'Dead.'

'I heard two shots.'

Pavel gave him a graveyard smile. 'I wanted to be sure.'

Soon, they were making their way past the State Bank. The streets were seething with people, in spite of the fighting, but there with no sense of purpose or organisation, just endless talk of gunfire and insurrection. There was more shouting, slowly coalescing into a single chorus.

'To the Tauride!'

Every banner proclaimed *All Power to the Soviets*. – All power to the very body that refused to take it. Under a foul, inky sky the swirling maelstrom of people headed for the seat of government. There, Anishin was addressing an impromptu meeting. Pavel interrupted his flow to yell a question.

'Any word from the Central Committee?'

'I heard comrade Lenin speak not half an hour ago,' Anishin said, not without an element of self-aggrandisment.

Pavel tensed with anticipation. 'And?'

'He urges the people to adopt vigilance and self-restraint.'

'He what?'

'He hopes to see the slogan *All Power to the Soviets* become reality.'

'He *hopes*?' Pavel snapped. 'What kind of bollocks is that? I hope for a thousand hectares of land, a cellar full of gold bullion and a sturdy wench yanking my cock every night.'

There was some laughter, cut short by the arrival of dozens of Kronstadters, their faces bleached with tension.

'Cossacks,' one yelled. 'All fighters to the Field of Mars.'

It had begun to rain, now a drenching downpour swept the packed streets. When they reached the Field of Mars, it was already a battlefield. There were Cossacks standing in their stirrups, their lances tilted at the Kronstadters.

'Look at the lousy bastards,' Pavel said. 'We'll deal with them.'

Kolya hurried to issue his own orders. 'On my command,' he yelled.

He heard the beautiful sound of rifles being aimed.

'Fire!'

The volley tore through the Cossack line, spraying blood through the rain. Men and horses screamed. One of the animals, hit by machine gun fire, was instantly kicking in its own entrails. Pavel strode over to put it out of its misery with a single shot. With tears in his eyes, he finished off a second stricken animal.

'You kill a man without compunction,' Kolya said, 'but you weep for a dumb beast?'

'Men have free will,' Pavel answered, stroking the neck of one dead horse. 'This poor creature couldn't help the twat on its back.'

'A truer word has never been spoken,' Mikhail said.

The Cossacks attempted one more ragged charge, but this attack suffered the same fate as the last. When Kolya led his makeshift platoon from the scene there was blood swirling in many puddles, around the corpses of fallen men and horses, and all the debris of battle. People were stripping the carcasses of their bridles and saddles.

'Let's see what's happening at the Tauride,' Kolya said grimly.

The palace was besieged.

'What's happening?' Mikhail asked his neighbour.

'They've sent out Chernov to speak.'

'Who's he?' Pavel asked.

'The Socialist Revolutionary,' came the answer. 'He's a brave man to expose himself to this crowd.'

The moment Chernov appeared there was heckling and not a few shouts.

'Are you the bastard that sent out the Cossacks?'

'He shoots the people,' somebody bellowed.

Sailors rushed forward to pull him down from his makeshift stage. He was a pinched, pale face amid the blue uniforms. Were the Kronstadters going to lynch him on the spot? A burly worker emerged from the crowd. Shaking his fist in Chernov's face, he snarled a challenge.

'Take power, you son of a bitch, when it's given to you!'

The mood was getting uglier, but there was a sudden movement. Somebody with authority was barging his way to the front.

'Who's this?' Pavel asked, as the second figure took the stage.

'Comrade Raskolnidov,' one of the sailors said admiringly.

Pavel knew the name. This was the senior Bolshevik at the Kronstadt base.

'So that's Raskolnikov, is it?'

But there was a still more important figure to be introduced to the crowd. Though Kolya had only ever seen the former leader of the 1905 Soviet from a distance, there was no mistaking Comrade Trotsky. Kolya registered the mop of dark hair, the moustache, the steel-rimmed glasses, the hawkish stare. He remembered Anishin saying that the trouble with Comrade Trotsky was that he loved himself too much. Trotsky began to speak, standing beside the whey-faced Chernov.

'Comrade Kronstadters!' he shouted, his voice strong enough to hush the crowd. 'Pride and glory of the revolution!'

'Cut the flattery,' Pavel grunted, 'tell us what's happening.'

Trotsky's voice was hard and metallic, the kind that could cut through any hubbub, no matter how unruly. Even so, he struggled to get a hearing from the milling sailors.

'You've come to declare your will and show the Soviet that the working class no longer wants the bourgeoisie in power.'

A roar of approval.

'But why hurt your cause by petty acts of violence against casual individuals?'

Then he was involved in an exchange with somebody at the front of the crowd.

'Can you hear what they're saying?' Kolya asked.

Pavel shook his head.

Before long, Trotsky straightened up and shouted at the top of his voice. 'Those here in favour of violence, raise your hands.'

Suddenly, everyone was turning. Not one hand was raised.

Pavel was enjoying the moment. 'Cunning bastard, isn't he?'

Kolya was learning lessons from a master. 'That was brilliant. See how he put the sailors on the back foot.'

Trotsky seized on the ensuing pause in hostilities and ushered Chernov to safety.

'He's good,' Mikhail said. 'I don't think there are many men who could have saved Chernov's sorry arse.'

Fighting continued throughout the heart of Petrograd. Riderless, wild-eyed horses clattered along roads. The acrid stench of cordite and smoke hung in the air. Blood swirled in puddles, stained walls, mired the earth. Persistent rain drove the masses from the streets. Kolya allowed it to play on his face. So this was insurrection. A pure flame, cleansing the world? No, it had been slain innocents, screaming animals, confusion. Revolution was meant to be order, a people remade in the furnace of struggle. Instead, all he could see was chaos.

'What's the matter with him?' Pavel asked.

Mikhail shrugged. 'I think he's ill.'

Kolya opened his eyes. 'I am not ill. I am… disappointed.'

'So am I,' missing the point. 'Looks like we'll have to finish the job tomorrow.'

'Where do we sleep?' Mikhail asked.

Pavel indicated the smart shops and government buildings. 'Take your pick. All we have to do is kick the door in.'

Kolya nodded his assent and they found premises where they could get dry and snatch a few hours' sleep. The vessels of the Kronstadt flotilla bobbed on their moorings, the workers returned to their mean barracks and wooden shacks, the soldiers and sailors found somewhere to eat and rest in the barracks. In the darkened city there were skirmishes and outbreaks of sporadic gunfire. In the Tauride Palace, the debates rumbled on well into the night. The revolution would resume in the morning.

But the day broke over a transformed Petrograd. Sometime in the night, there had been the tramp of regimental boots. As battle-hardened troops arrived from the Front, the Central Committee had called a final halt to the demonstrations. The July revolt was hamstrung and hobbling into oblivion. It was still raining steadily as Kolya's band emerged from an uneasy night's sleep. The square in front of the Winter Palace was an armed camp. There were field kitchens, armoured cars, ambulances, artillery. Sentries were posted on every street corner. Like a horse refusing a fence, the revolution had fallen back. 'How the fuck did this happen?' Pavel raged. 'Why didn't our military organisations intercept them? We've blown this. We've thrown away our best chance.'

They watched in despair as seasoned troops withdrawn from the Front dragged machine guns into place. Seeing the concentration of troops challenging every passer-by, they retreated along the rain-slicked street only to walk into another checkpoint. They were at every junction.

'Where do you think you're going?' one of the guards demanded.

'We're returning to barracks,' Mikhail answered, thinking on his feet. 'What are you doing here?'

'I'll tell you what we're doing,' one of the officers told him. 'We're cutting the head off this fucking Jew-Bolshevik conspiracy.'

'What are you talking about?' exclaimed Kolya. This was the filth of the Black Hundreds, belching from the man's foul mouth.

'This bastard Lenin,' the officer told him. 'He's got no patriotism, like all these yids.'

He produced a newspaper cartoon. It featured Lenin dangling from a noose. Kolya knew he should button his lip, but the word *yid* made his flesh crawl. Were the pogromists about to spread their terror through the streets of the capital?

'Lenin isn't Jewish,' Kolya said grimly.

A glint of interest sparked in the guard's suspicious brown eyes. 'You seem to know a lot about him. Are you a fucking Jew-Bolshevik yourself?'

Kolya knew he was on thin ice. 'Lenin isn't Jewish, that's all I'm saying.' He glimpsed Pavel's warning stare.

'Most of them are,' the officer said, his gaze never leaving Kolya. 'There's Kamenev, Zinoviev, that piece of shit Trotsky. Did you know they took German gold to get the exiles back into Petrograd. They serve the German cause.' He turned his attention to the Kronstadters. 'You sailor boys are being disarmed. You'll be sent back to base.'

'If you try to take my weapon,' growled Pissed Off, 'I'll blow your shit-for-brains head off. Get me?'

That was signal enough for Kolya. He drew his pistol and shot the officer between the eyes. He turned and shot a second soldier. The others followed his example, firing rapid rounds.

'Now we get the fuck out of here,' Kolya yelled. 'We're outnumbered.'

Pavel and Mikhail gave the retreat cover then loped after the rest of the company. In the surrounding streets, workers in their blue tunics were smashing windows. Howls of panic filled the air.

'Should we speak to them?' Pavel wondered.

'And say what?' Kolya asked. 'They need to take it out on somebody.'

Pavel was furious. 'The insurrection is trickling away like rainwater!'

'The CC has hung us out to dry. We had power in the palms of our hands. Now the government has brought in battle-hardened troops, they'll gun down the lot of us. I tell you, I can handle losing a fight, but here's what I can't handle: jacking it in without giving it my best shot. I mean, what the fuck? Where were the bloody CC when we put our arses on the line? Where were the party committtees?' He turned to face Kolya. 'You told us everything would be different when Lenin returned. Well, it looks like the same bag of horse crap to me.'

'This is not over,' Kolya said. 'The revolution wasn't ripe.'

'Not ripe!' Pavel collapsed into mocking laughter. 'This isn't a bloody apple. It's a revolution.'

Kolya sighed. 'There isn't time for this now. Soldiers, sailors, my socialist brothers, you need to get back to your bases.'

'They'll have our balls for this,' Pavel said. 'The Kronstadters will be confined to base. As for Mikhail and me, they're going to ship our sorry arses to the Front.'

'We will rise from this setback,' Kolya told the rest of the men.

'Yes, and Rasputin will rise from the depths of the Neva and bang the Empress,' Pavel snorted. 'I tell you what, Comrade Kolya. Everybody fucks the soldier. The officers fuck him. The revolution fucks him. I believed in you and your bloody Lenin. It's a game for you. We could get shot for this.'

'You must stay strong,' Kolya told him.

He reached for Pavel's arm, but the furious soldier shrugged him away.

'That's easier said than done,' Pavel said. 'Oh, don't worry,' he added bitterly, 'if all this passes, I'll be ready to rise again. You don't see Pavel ducking a fight.' He shook his head in a mixture of defeat and resignation. 'Don't mind me, Kolya, I'm just tired. This is going to be bad. See you on the other side.'

Kolya watched the soldiers and sailors dispersing, returning to their units. He felt hollow. He passed a mangy dog tearing at what was left of a horse. The viscera were hanging out.

'What a balls-up,' he groaned.

When he got home, Svetlana was waiting for him. Her eyes were red and swollen. Kolya took her in his arms and felt the grief and bitterness wracking her body.

'The revolution is dying,' she cried. 'They're already hunting our leaders like vermin. They are saying Lenin is a German spy. It can't be true, can it?'

'Of course it isn't true, dear Svetlana,' he said, covering her face with kisses. 'We will recover from this. I swear on my life.'

There was no move to the bed. In the ashes of defeat, there was no time for lovemaking.

Raisa

She saw the flash of anger in Elena's eyes and squeezed her hand to restrain her. Elena gave a brief nod. She would hold her tongue, whatever the provocations from the gloating bystanders around them.

'...The power of the Bolsheviks is broken,' one paunchy man said, continuing his steady barrage of commentary He was talking loudly to his wife as they joined the onlookers along the English Embankment. 'Our loyal troops have smashed up the Pravda offices. We've got them on the run. I just hope the government finally has the balls to execute the ringleaders, the whole bloody lot of them, and save Mother Russia from this anarchy.'

His wife was shushing him, but it just made him bolder, louder. He was quivering with bombast. 'It is time to root out this Leninite contagion for once and for all. I hear they got Trotsky today. They need to put him against a wall along with the other Jew-Bolsheviks, that's what I say. Let the Black Hundreds loose!'

His wife hissed something about moderating his language. Maybe she wondered whether victory over the enemy was quite as complete as her husband believed.

'...He plunged our capital into chaos once before. These monsters have tried our patience once too often.'

Raisa and Elena watched the procession passing, the rites of ancient Russia. Raisa felt as if she was lying on the ground with a boot pressed to her chest. All that she hated was now in the ascendant. The loud man removed his hat as a mark of respect as the coffins appeared on carts.

'That's the mark of these Bolshevik scum,' he said. 'They used machine guns against cavalry armed only with sabres. What wretched cowards they are!'

'What about the cowards on horseback who used their sabres to slaughter unarmed innocents?' Raisa hissed under her breath.

There was a guard of honour for the coffins of the fallen Cossacks. Each one was covered with silver cloth. Black pennants fluttered over them. The red flags of revolt had given way to the time-honoured colour of mourning. The livery of revolution was being taken down. Before long, the dead men's mounts followed their masters, riderless and patient. Cheering echoed along the street as a limousine joined the cortege.

'Who's that?' Raisa asked.

The loud man gave her a severe look. 'Do you not recognise our new Prime Minister Alexander Kerenksy?'

Raisa dropped her eyes, determined not to give herself away.

'Bravo!' the loud man shouted, beating his palms together like orchestra symbols. 'Bravo! I hope you shoot these Bolshevik criminals. Shoot every one – exterminate them like rats. Only blood will cleanse the sins of the past.' He leaned over to his silent, sullen wife. 'With Kerensky leading the government and the great General Kornilov in charge of the south-western front, our homeland will rise again. Only blood will cleanse us of the Bolshevik plague. Bravo! Bravo!'

Elena gave Raisa a nudge. 'Let's get out of here before I tear that shitbag's head right off.'

Raisa gave the spectacle of the Cossack funerals one last glance then accompanied her friend along the crowded pavement. This time it was not proletarian Petrograd turning out, but the old order, the defencists, all the would-be executioners of the revolution.

'Aunty Svetlana is distraught,' Elena confided to her lover. 'Did you know that the Vyborg Executive Committee has called on our leaders to give themselves in? Yes, the very heart of red Petrograd is advising surrender. What treachery!' Her eyes were welling with tears. 'Now all our dreams are in tatters.'

Raisa squeezed her arm. 'It will pass. You'll see.'

'How can you be so calm?' Elena cried. 'Did you hear that old bastard dancing on our graves?'

The bells of St Isaac's tolled. The strains of an anthem swept the streets: *How Glorious is Our God in Zion.*

Elena shook her head. 'Do you hear it? All the old shit is back. We're done, my love. We are quite ruined. Death would be better than this.'

'You must not talk this way,' Raisa said, her heart breaking. 'You must live for me.'

Elena permitted herself a wounded smile. 'But for you, I would throw myself at the enemy bayonets and go down fighting.'

They passed a street corner agitator. His eyes bulged as he shrieked more conspiracy theories about the Jews.

Elena watched him with cold, resentful eyes. 'Do you see what I mean? The filth is bubbling up again. They're looking for scapegoats now. It is only a matter of time before they begin their pogroms. What are we doing, letting him rant without opposition?'

Raisa feared Elena was about to storm the pogromist's platform and lay about him with her fists.

'You must be calm,' she insisted. 'What if some counter-revolutionary hears you? We will be in great danger. Please don't risk your precious life. Let's go home. You do have time to spend a few hours with me, don't you?'

Elena brightened a little. 'I always have time for you, my sweet girl.'

They walked arm in arm and tried to put thoughts of reaction and pogrom out of their minds. When they reached the boarding house, Raisa fished in her bag for the key. The moment she tried to put it in the lock, the door creaked open and her eyes widened.

'What is it?' Elena asked.

'It was already open,' said Raisa. 'Mrs Kuznetsova always keeps it locked.'

'Let me go first,' Elena told her. 'I have heard about these raids. Criminal gangs break in, even in broad daylight. They are willing to kill the householders to come away with their valuables.' She peered down the hallway. 'Give me your gun.'

Raisa looked around to make sure nobody was watching and handed over the weapon, slipping it discreetly into Elena's hand. Elena hadn't gone far when she gave a moan of dismay.

'What is it?'

'Your Mrs Kuznetsova,' Elena answered. 'She's stone dead. Her neck is broken. It looks like she fell down the stairs.'

Raisa didn't believe in accidents. Somehow, Vera and Yozhin had discovered where she lived.

'Or somebody pushed her.'

Suddenly, Elena's face drained of blood. 'The jewellery!'

She was gone before Raisa could restrain her. Within moments, Elena reappeared at the top of the stairs, quite distraught.

'The bastards have ransacked your room. It's gone. It's all gone!'

'Elena, you must calm yourself.'

Elena wasn't listening. 'Don't you understand, Raisa? This is everything you possess, all you have to live on.'

Raisa stepped over Mrs Kuznetsova's body and climbed the stairs, slipping her arm round Elena's waist.

'It is you who do not understand.'

Elena's panic was beginning to ebb as she witnessed Raisa's curious composure.

'Why are you talking in riddles?'

Raisa managed a smile in spite of the grisly sight in the hall. 'I came home one day and found Mrs Kuznetsova in my room. She said she was changing the linen, but I didn't believe her. It had only just been done the day before…'

Elena tilted her head. 'So…?'

'I waited for her to go out and hid the jewellery.' Pulling back an old chest, she tugged at a section of skirting board and felt behind it. 'It's still there.'

Elena breathed a sigh of relief then she knelt beside Raisa and whispered in her ear. 'You do know what this means, don't you? This isn't the work of ordinary criminals.'

Raisa nodded. 'Vera ordered it.'

'The avaricious bitch has been planning this since she saw the bracelet,' Elena said, 'and you can be sure she will be back with that monster Yozhin. They would torture you to get the information. We can't do this alone. Yozhin has a small army of cut-throats. We need help.'

Raisa looked down at Mrs Kuznetsova.

'Who will help us?' she asked. 'I have no mother or father, no friend but you.'

'You have one,' Elena said, correcting her.

'What are you talking about?'

Elena met her eye. 'Your soldier boy, Pavel.'

So it was that Raisa came to be standing outside the barracks like a soldier's sweetheart. She approached a number of soldiers, but they walked on by without paying her much attention. Each man looked subdued. Raisa had heard that the revolutionary units had been disarmed. Political meetings had been banned. *Soldatskaia Pravda* had been shut down. One man muttered he could show her a good time. Then she struck lucky.

'Do you know a soldier by the name of Pavel Sergeyevich Kirilenko?' she asked.

'Yes, I know Kirilenko.' The man gave her the once-over. 'You're not Nina. Don't tell me the dirty dog has two young ladies on the go.'

'I am not his sweetheart,' Raisa said. 'I'm his sister.'

'Yes,' the soldier said. 'His sister. Of course you are. Darling, you couldn't look more different.' He spoke over her protests: 'If you're related to Pavel, I'm the Queen of Sheba. Don't tell me, he's got you in the family way.'

Raisa stuck stubbornly to her story, pressing on without a stumble. 'Will you take him a message?'

The soldier folded his arms over his chest. 'What do I get out of it?'

'My gratitude.'

The soldier laughed. 'I can't eat gratitude. Now something tells me Pavel would rip my head right off if I asked you for a knee-trembler, so what about money?'

Raisa looked at him, disappointed. After a few moment's consideration, she peeled off a few notes from the money in her bag. The soldier reached for it, but she withdrew her hand.

'Half now,' she said. 'The rest when you bring Pavel to me.'

The soldier grinned. 'You look like butter wouldn't melt in your mouth, but there's a calculating brain in that pretty, little head. Give me the money. I'll be back presently.'

Presently turned out to be almost half an hour later, but finally the soldier returned, accompanied by an uncertain-looking Pavel. Raisa handed over the rest of the money.

'This is something of a surprise,' Pavel said. 'I didn't think I would see you again.'

'It's not what you think,' Raisa said.

'Do you know what I think?' Pavel asked.

Raisa saw the look on his face and wanted to hurry away, but she would have to swallow her pride.

'I need your help.'

To her surprise, Pavel softened. Maybe he didn't just want to possess her, like every other man she had encountered in her short life. Were there men who didn't have their brains in their cock?

'I'm listening,' he said.

Raisa explained, omitting nothing. When she had finished, she waited, expecting Pavel to say something. He met her tale with silence.

'Have I offended you?' she asked after some time. 'Please express what is in your heart, Pavel Sergeyevich.'

'I am not offended, 'he answered. 'There is a good reason for my silence. I don't know what to say to you. Why me?'

Raisa blushed. 'I will be honest with you. There was nobody else.'

Pavel nodded. 'Well, that is pretty brutal.'

'I am sorry.'

This appeared to amuse him. 'No need to apologise,' he told her. 'If you had lied, you wouldn't have seen me for dust.'

'So you will help me?'

Pavel's face was unreadable. In the extending silence, a part of Raisa's mind began wondering if this man was capable of the kind of self-effacing love Elena always showed her.

Finally, he spoke. 'It is hard. We are confined to barracks.'

'You are here with me now,' she reminded him. 'I don't see any officers ordering you back inside.'

Pavel smiled wryly. 'In spite of everything, the officers don't have much control over us. We thought it was over when the loyalist regiments returned, but they still seem wary of us. Maybe this new Prime Minister isn't all he is cracked up to be. The war effort has already gone to shit.' He fell silent again, then; 'Fuck it, I'll help. What can they do to me?'

'Shoot you?'

'Cheerful, aren't you?' He turned to go. 'Give me the address of the boarding house. I'll be there when I can.'

As it turned out, Pavel arrived two hours later, with Mikhail his reluctant companion. Raisa unbolted the door and stepped back to reveal Mrs Kuznetsova's body, covered by a white sheet. One bare foot was peeking out.

Pavel knelt to examine her.

'Broken neck.' He raised her right hand. 'Seen this, Mikhail? She scratched her attacker's face. She's still got his skin under her nails.'

'It might not be a man,' Elena said, making an appearance.

She explained about Vera.

'Can you help us?' Raisa asked.

Pavel said nothing. He rose to his feet, pushed open doors, looking around. 'Who else lives here?'

'Only me,' Raisa said.

He nodded, glanced at Elena. 'What about her?'

'I have my own room,' Elena said, 'in the Vyborg where I work.'

Pavel seemed curious about Elena, attentive to her every word, her every change of expression. The tension between them made Raisa uncomfortable.

'Here's the deal,' Pavel said at length. 'The way things are going, we're going to be shipped back to the Front any day. It's suicide. Nothing is going to stop the German offensive. Desertion is looking like an attractive option.'

Mikhail was horrified. 'Pavel Sergeyevich...'

'What's the matter with you? I thought you were sick of the war.'

'I am, but we have suffered a crushing defeat. The officers are in the driving seat. They will shoot us for desertion.'

'Only if they find us,' Pavel said. 'I'm for fucking off and where better to fuck off to than rooms like this. I can't remember the last time I slept in a decent bed. We could lie low for a bit.'

'Pavel...'

'It is your choice, but my mind is made up.'

Raisa interrupted the exchange. 'You can have Mrs Kuznetsova's room if you can just get rid of the body.'

Pavel glanced at the window. 'It's almost sunset. We will wait for the cover of darkness.'

'Did you just say *we*?' Mikhail asked.

'I did,' Pavel replied. 'It's like this. We're going to wrap this old girl up, take her to the Neva, tie rocks to her body and chuck her in. You can say a few words if you like. As far as I'm concerned, death is death. There is no Mrs Kuznetsova now, just a body.'

'You can be a cold-blooded bastard sometimes.'

Pavel nodded. 'It wasn't always the case. The war made me this way.'

Mikhail looked less than happy, but he didn't protest. Instead, practical as ever, he went looking for something to wrap the body in. He returned with a blanket and some thin cord.

'Help me truss her up.'

It took less than an hour to wrap the body, lug it to the river and return to the boarding house. Raisa was shocked by Pavel's businesslike, dispassionate efficiency. But he was a soldier. He dealt in death. It made her wonder what all the bloodletting had done to the *muzhiks* in uniform. Do any of them emerge unscathed from the experience?

'I get the bed,' Pavel told Mikhail. 'You can have the sofa. If we stay long, we will swap places each night. Deal?'

'So we're officially AWOL then?' Mikhail replied.

'That's about the size of it. Is that a problem?'

Mikhail considered the question then shook his head.

'No, fuck it, half the soldiery in Russia is disobeying orders. I can live with it. Or die from it. It's the same shit however you look at it. We are most likely corpses if they send us to the Front anyway.'

Pavel looked at the two women. 'We take turns to keep watch. Can either of you handle a firearm?'

Raisa drew her pistol. 'Like this, you mean?'

Mikhail rolled his eyes. 'Full of surprises, isn't she?'

'I'll take first watch,' Pavel said. 'Then it's my friend Mikhail here.'

'When the time comes, Raisa and I will keep watch together,' Elena said.

Pavel started to unbutton his tunic. 'I may as well make myself comfortable.'

'Thank you for doing this,' Raisa said. 'I feel guilty asking you, but there was nobody else to turn to. It could be dangerous.'

'Compared to fighting the Germans or the Cossacks,' Pavel told her, 'it's a piece of piss. Life's cheap. Live it while you can.'

Pavel

He was sitting on the stairs, rifle resting on his knees. The weight of the weapon was comforting. The officers had done a rudimentary sweep of the barracks but, truth be told, they had lacked the confidence to challenge the men's access to their guns.

'Too fucking scared to hang around,' was Pavel's verdict.

The rifle barrel had a cold insolence that said the revolution was not over, merely in abeyance.

'Stupid fuckers,' he thought. You were going to crush us and all you managed is a slap on the wrist.' He peered down the rifle to sight it. 'They'd made a revolution halfway. He'd thought they were done for. Now, look at the morons. They made their counter-revolution halfway. All it needed was an iron heel, and they didn't have the guts.'

The door to Raisa's room was ajar and he could hear the sound of the two women sleeping. He imagined them lying together, their rhythmic breathing, their intimacy. Christ, what the hell is wrong with you, Pavel my lad, he thought. Raisa belongs to another. You've got a sweetheart. He tried to conjure Nina's face, but it was Raisa's eyes he saw, Raisa's lips he imagined. He got to his feet, taking care not to make a sound. He checked the barricading of the door. Satisfied that it was secure, just as it had been the last time he ran a check, he padded to the rear entrance in his stockinged feet. Anyone who tried to come through either way was going to face significant obstacles, giving him time to rouse Mikhail.

The minutes ticked by and turned into an hour. The wind soughed in the eaves of the house, wheezed around the windows, whistled under the door, intrusive and inquisitive as a cat pawing to be allowed in. A few raindrops pattered against the windowpane. Pavel passed the time recalling his early years in Kazan province, the broad Kazanka river and quiet creeks where he'd played. He remembered the scent of pines in the rain. He'd thought he would spend his whole life there, until the boom of the guns ended his childhood and forced him to be a man. He found himself thinking of his parents, and brushed away a tear.

'Shit, what's got into me?'

That's when he heard it, in the silence after his words, the resting of a boot on litter, barely a sound at all, but enough to alert Pavel. He shook Mikhail awake. He saw the whites of his comrade's eyes in the gloom, and the nod. They were ready for battle. Mikhail positioned himself at the bottom of the stairs and eased back the trigger of his weapon. Pavel crept upstairs. His voice sidled into the room where Raisa and Elena were still sleeping.

'They're here.'

Once the four of them were assembled in the hall, Pavel touched Mikhail on the arm and gestured for him to cover the back door. He pulled an officer's pistol from his pocket and handed it to Elena. Raisa was already armed. Bracing himself, Pavel removed the barricade, a table, a chair, a cupboard. He wanted to control how the intruders made their way inside. There was a click on the other side of the front door. Slowly, it began to creak open. There they were: two men, faces masked. Pavel pistol whipped the first and dragged him roughly inside. Without a moment's hesitation, he pressed the barrel of his gun to the eye socket of the second intruder, screwing it into the vitreous softness.

'Anyone else?' he hissed.

The intruder's gaze was hard with terror. 'No, just us.'

'Lie to me and I give you a slow, painful death. Got that?'

A nod of submission.

'Get the fuck inside.'

The man he'd clubbed to the ground was nursing his damaged face, blood dripping between his fingers.

'Who sent you?' Mikhail asked. 'You speak directly to me and you do it quietly.' He pointed to the wounded man. 'He keeps his mouth shut.'

'Yozhin gave the order.'

Elena leaned in close. 'What about Vera?'

'Yes, her too. She said it would be a piece of piss, like taking candy from a baby.'

'Yes, it's a bastard when the baby is armed to the teeth, isn't it?'

The captive's eyes were flicking back and forth, assessing the amount of shit he was in.

'Where are they now?' Pavel demanded.

The would-be assassin was making a rapid calculation of his options.

'Are they in Yozhin's den?'

Silence.

'Fine, you want to do it the hard way. There's a hammer in the back room. I want you to imagine it coming down on your joints, one at a time. Left elbow, right elbow, left knee, right knee. Then I get hold of a knife and I start on your balls. I take my time over things. I'm a country boy, see. I whittle on wood so I can whittle on a man just as easy.' Pavel snapped his fingers for Mikhail to get the hammer. 'So what do you have to say to me?'

'There's no need for this. I'll spill my guts.'

He told Pavel everything he needed to know. Yozhin and Vera were in a looted shop a quarter of a mile away. If the two gunmen failed to return in half an hour, they were going to go in mob-handed to find the stash of jewellery.

Mikhail nodded. 'That gives us fifteen, twenty minutes. How many men do they have with them?'

The prisoner gave them the answer without hesitation. 'Two.'

'Gag them,' Pavel said. 'Tie their wrists to their ankles and pull the rope tight.'

Satisfied the men were silenced and trussed up, he rested his hand on Raisa's forearm.

'You're staying here. If either of them so much as twitches, you put a bullet through both their brains. Got that?'

Raisa nodded. 'Can't Elena stay with me?'

'Sorry, 'but we need her. It's a tall ask, storming somewhere with equal numbers. The three of us have got a chance. Any less, it'd be impossible. This has to finish tonight.'

'You're going to kill them?'

'What do you think? Dead men don't take revenge.'

Elena embraced Raisa. 'I won't be long.'

'Don't get yourself shot,' Raisa told her. 'I forbid you.'

Pavel interrupted their goodbyes. 'We've got to go.'

This is my fate, he thought, to walk into the gates of Hell for a woman I love, but will never love me.

They had reached the building without encountering any government patrols. There was no light in the shop, nothing to betray the four people inside. Pavel reached in his pack. Mikhail recognised the stick concussion grenade.

'The moment this fucker detonates,' he murmured, 'we go in fast, do the job and retire. Got that?'

'Got it.'

Mikhail smashed a window. Pavel removed the safety catch and threw, releasing the pin. There was a moment's delay then the loud thud as the grenade went off. Pavel led the way inside, shooting the first man he saw, once, twice. Mikhail pushed a room door, leaned inside and saw moonlight flash on a gun barrel. He ducked back. The man's weapon roared then Mikhail was inside, peering through the haze of cordite.

'Did you get him?' Pavel hissed.

Mikhail nodded.

They turned their attention to the other rooms.

'Downstairs clear,' Mikhail announced.

'Shit,' Pavel said. 'They'll be on the landing, aiming down at us.'

There was no time to waste. The burst of gunfire was bound to have alerted a patrol. The counter-revolutionaries would be looking for troublemakers to kill. Elena read her comrades' faces and rushed the stairs. It brought Yozhin out on the landing.

'Out of the way!'

At Pavel's command, Elena flattened herself against the wall. His first shot tore out Yozhin's throat, leaving him gasping through a spurt of blood. The second hit him in the chest. Elena ripped herself away from the wall, defying all instinct. A vehicle was approaching outside.

'Find Vera,' Pavel yelled. 'We've got company.'

Elena kicked open a door. The room was empty. She turned to the second room. The creak of a floorboard stopped her. She spun round. She had missed something.

'So you thought you could take out old Vera, did you, bitch?' Vera emerged from behind the curtains, firearm raised. 'You never were much good at the rough stuff, Elena.'

Even as the last word left Vera's lips, Elena felt a strong hand drag her back. She fell against Pavel's chest as Mikhail put a bullet between Vera's eyes. She was dead by the time she hit the floor.

'Now let's get the fuck out of here,' Pavel said, his voice as calm as if he had just finished milking the cows. They had only reached the hall when gunfire roared. Silhouettes loomed in the doorway.

'Back!' he bawled.

They pounded to the rear door. Mikahil twisted the handle. Locked. Elena spun round and fired, slowing down their pursuers. While the soldiers scrambled for cover, Pavel and Mikhail kicked and shouldered the door. At the fourth attempt, it gave way and they were in the alley. More shadows darted to their left so they turned right, running fit to burst. Pavel swept the street with frightened eyes.

'He spotted a door opening. 'This way.'

A scrawny man in his mid-fifties emerged. Pavel was on him in a second, pressing the barrel of his gun against the terrified householder's head.

'I'm not going to hurt you. We just need to hide out for a few minutes. Keep your mouth shut, do as I say and you will be all right.'

Once inside, Pavel inspected his surroundings.

'Anyone else here?'

'My wife. My daughters.'

'Fine, here's the deal. You stay shtum and leave them in the land of nod and we are all happy. Any attempt to wake them or get the attention of the soldiers out there on the street and you are one dead father. Do you understand me?'

The man responded with astonishing calm. 'I understand you perfectly.'

'Good man.'

That's where they stayed, listening to the scrape of boots, the hoarse voices outside. Finally, the sounds of pursuit died away.

'We're going now,' Pavel said. 'Any attempt to follow us and you die. Any attempt to alert the soldiers and you die. One false move and....'

'I die. Yes, I understand. Please, just leave my home.'

Pavel led the way down the street, hugging the shadows. They reached a junction and Pavel turned towards the boarding house. He felt a tug on his sleeve.

'I have to go,' Elena said.

'You what?'

She handed him her gun.

'I have work. Tell Raisa I am safe.'

Pavel inspected her face for a moment then he nodded. 'Take care. The soldiers may stop you, ask what you are doing on the street.'

'I can take care of myself.' She laughed. 'I'll flutter my girlish lashes and flatter their manhood. Works every time.'

Pavel rewarded her with a smile for the first time. 'I'm sure it does.'

He watched while she negotiated her way through the wakening streets. Before long, she was no more than a dark blur in the hazy, ochre dawn. They dumped their arms in a doorway and reached the boarding house by a circuitous route that kept them away from the prying eyes of the loyalist troops occupying the city.

Raisa was making breakfast when Pavel entered the small kitchen.

'Mikhail and I have talked things over,' he said. 'We will go back to the barracks once we have had a few winks of sleep.'

'Will they not punish you?'

'Possibly,' Pavel said, 'but our regiment is an unruly bunch. Something tells me the officers won't want to do anything drastic in case it lights the touch paper to more trouble. Don't worry about us. We'll take our chances.'

'But you said…'

'What, become outlaws? Live on our wits? That was a pipedream. No, we stand a better chance at the barracks. Besides, if the revolution is going to rise again, we need agitators pressing the Bolshevik cause.'

'I thought you despised the Bolshevik leaders for their failures.'

Pavel gave a weary shake of the head. 'Comrade Lenin is the best we've got. If there is hope, it lies with him. Nobody else wants to call a halt to the war. Nobody else is offering land and bread. Ignore me when I'm mouthing off. It's my way.'

He watched Raisa's reactions. She seemed self-conscious, as if even talking to him was a betrayal of Elena.

'What happens now?' she asked.

'What happens? Why, nothing. We return to soldiering. We do what we can to persuade our comrades that all is not lost. You live, freed from the threat of Yozhin and Vera.'

Raisa stretched out an arm and pointed.

'What about those two in the hall?'

'Their paymasters are dead. They'll find another way to make ends meet.'

'Are you sure they will not be back?'

'I would stake my life on it.'

Raisa handed him the plates of food. 'These are such terrible times. There are too many horrors, too much suffering. I fear my heart will burst.'

'You'll survive,' Pavel said. 'I can see it in you, a kind of light.'

With that, he took the meal to Mrs Kuznetsova's room. Raisa was gone by the time he returned the empty plates.

The sun was climbing in the sky. The rain had cleared. Pavel tried to imagine life with Raisa in another, different world, one where dreams came true. He met the dawn with three simple words.

'Life goes on.'

Kolya

At the sound of the door opening, Kolya sprang to his feet. He had been in hiding since the July days, since Mrs Turisheva had alerted the counter-revolutionaries to his activities. That one act had elevated him from student activist to dangerous Bolshevik, moving from room to shabby room, mistrusting every creaking floorboard. This time, it was only the woman assigned by Anishin to hide him. He knew her only as Comrade Olga

'Any news?' he asked.

'You are to stay put.' She handed him his food and made for the door. 'Oh, there is one thing. It's quite funny really. Kerensky has had an anonymous message from a well-wisher. Do you know what it says?'... It is meant for the entire Executive Committee of the Soviet: *Please drive out that fucking son of a bitch, General Kornilov, or else he's going to take his machine guns and drive you out.*

Kolya barely responded. Olga had a most peculiar sense of humour.

'The papers say eight hundred Bolsheviks are in prison,' she told him.

To compound his misery, it was days since he had last seen Svetlana. He missed the warmth and comfort of her body, the press of her lips, her hands arousing him. Imprisonment would surely kill him. He counted the blows the revolution had suffered: the suppression of the Bolshevik press, the driving of many of them into hiding, the restoration of the death penalty for soldiers at the front. Worst of all, there was the slander against Comrade Lenin, that he was a paid agent of the German imperialists. Were people believing that? Kolya paced the floor.

He quizzed Olga the way he did every time she entered the airless room to hand him a meal and take out his slops.

'Don't you have any good news. Is there resistance? Are there strikes, demonstrations, anything? Are the reactionaries having it all their own way?'

Olga's news was mostly bad.

'The bread queues are lengthening. The rations have been cut back again. Sanitation is worse than ever.'

On it went, the litany of problems. There was TB, scurvy, typhus in the city. Kolya had his own problems. He was being eaten alive by bed bugs. His skin was covered in itchy, livid red welts. He slumped heavily in his chair and stared at the yellowing propaganda sheets they laughably called newspapers. Lenin's real name was Zederbluhm said one, Mytenblad claimed another.

'Anti-semitic filth,' Kolya moaned. 'How can people believe this shit?'

Lenin had been arrested in Finland. He had returned to exile in Switzerland. He was even in Copenhagen.

'Maybe he is perching on a stone on the Langelinie Promenade'

'What are you talking about?' Comrade Olga asked.

'Have you never heard of the statue of the Little Mermaid?'

'Can't say I have. Have you finished?'

Once Olga had gone, Kolya leapt to his feet and tore the newspapers into tiny pieces before slumping to his knees with his face in his hands. How had the revolution retreated so meekly? Was it so lacking in substance, so shallowly rooted in the population? Kolya walked to the window and peeked outside. There were children playing in the summer heat, people going about their business. The factory chimneys belched in the distance.

'Is there nothing left?' he murmured.

Despair filled him, dark and bleak and poisonous. He was about to force himself to read what was left of the shredded newspaper, when there was a tread on the landing.

'Olga?'

There was no answer. Was this it? Would the soldiers of the counter-revolution burst? Would they carry him off to a bare cell to be beaten? His blood raced. He snatched up a vase. What a pathetic weapon! Comic as he must look, he knew he must fight, if only for his own pride. He breathed in the fetid air and braced himself. The hinges whined as the door opened and he prepared to swing the vase… and then lowered it, heart still racing. The newcomer was familiar.

'Grigory!'

Grigory pressed a finger to his lips, checked the room, the landing, the street then he embraced Kolya.

'How are you surviving, you rogue?'

Kolya grinned. 'I'm doing all right. The food is crap and I am crawling the walls with boredom. Otherwise, I'm surviving. Do you have any news?'

'It isn't all bad,' Grigory told him. 'There is a section of the leadership arguing that the counter-revolution has us crushed. It's complete bollocks. I was talking to the delegate from the Vasilevsky Island district only yesterday. Do you know how many members they've lost during the repression, a hundred. A hundred! That is out of four thousand, Kolya. Our members are tough buggers. It's a bit premature to write us off.'

'That's good,' Kolya said, 'yes, very good.' He waited a beat then asked the question that had been on his mind for days. 'Have you heard from Svetlana?'

Grigory's face filled with pleasure. 'I've got a surprise for you.'

Kolya's eyes drifted to the door.

'That's right,' Grigory told him. 'I'm only here as a bodyguard. Svetlana is with me. I'm going to keep look out while you two talk.'

Without another word, he left, passing Kolya's lover on the landing.

'Svetlana! Oh, Svetlana, my love!'

Kolya took her in his arms and showered her face with kisses, seeking out her lips. His mouth fastened on hers, as greedily as a man denied water taking his first sweet swallow to slake his thirst. Finally, he broke away and searched her face for an explanation.

'Has something happened?'

'Not yet,' she told him, 'but it will.'

'Oh, don't tie me up in riddles. What is it?'

Svetlana shoved him into his chair and straddled him, plucking at her skirts.

'The hold of the reaction is not as strong as the generals would have us think,' she told him. 'A few days ago, I was in attendance when our party held its Sixth Congress.'

This was news to Kolya.

'It went ahead! Olga didn't say anything.'

'She didn't know anything.'

He was overjoyed. The life had returned to his face.

'It did not just go ahead, my love,' Svetlana told him. 'There were 150 delegates from across Russia.'

'Did I hear you right? One hundred and fifty?'

Svetlana laughed gaily, her voice musical and fresh, belying her forty-five years. It was as if the guttering flame of Bolshevik organisation had burned away the passage of the years and made her young again. 'Larin and Martov were there. Mensheviks!'

'Then the party's isolation is not complete?'

Svetlana ran her fingers down his arms. 'The party is resilient, Kolya. The Congress reported two hundred thousand members across Russia, almost three times the figure in April. There are forty-one thousand of us here in Petrograd alone. The sinews of the party are strong.'

'It is so good to see you,' he said. His face is suddenly serious. 'Is it safe for you to be here with me?'

'I have come to move you,' Svetlana told him. 'The danger has not passed, but we are not crushed either. The district Soviets all over the city are passing our resolutions. Our influence stretches far beyond the Vyborg. The revolution lives, Kolya. It lives!'

'How can that be?' Kolya asked. 'Just weeks ago we were crushed.'

'We were never crushed,' Svetlana objected. 'We carried out an orderly retreat. We lay low. Every time there was the lash of repression, the working people closed ranks. It won't be long before we are back.'

Kolya pulled her close and kissed her again. Suddenly, he paused, running his fingers over her brow.

'What's this?' he asked tracing the line of a deep, barely healed cut.

'It's nothing,' Svetlana told him.

'If somebody has hurt you, why I'll....'

'Don't fly into a rage,' she tells him. 'It happened when I was addressing a factory meeting.'

'Our own people did this!'

'Some of the women at the next mill to mine were tearing up their party cards. They believed the stories about our exiled comrades being German spies. I went to explain.' She laughed. 'They pelted me with nuts and bolts. One caught me above the eye. It wasn't just me. Comrade Tarasova got the same treatment. She found out the Mensheviks had been stirring up trouble.'

'Bastards!'

'Forget it,' Svetlana said. 'We had our bad days, but we rode it out.'

'That's my Svetlana,' Kolya said warmly. 'Tough as nails.'

He started to tug at her dress but she wagged a disapproving finger in front of his face.

'Now don't you be a naughty boy,' she told him. 'We can't leave Grigory waiting for us. He might attract the attention of the reactionaries. There is time for hanky panky later. We have to get you to your new lodgings. You are quite the blue-eyed boy all of a sudden.'

'I am? Why?'

'Why do you think? Pavel Sergeyevich put a word in for you. So did Anishin.'

Kolya couldn't believe his rival had praised him.

'Anishin spoke up for me?'

'You have earned his respect, Kolya,' she told him. 'Your role in the July events did not go unnoticed, the way you led the assault on the sniper's nest, the leadership you showed against the Cossacks. They are saying that you conducted a retreat in good order, preserving the party's reputation and standing with the masses.'

It sounded as if she was reading straight from one of Anishin's stale reports.

Kolya's neck burned. 'Are you sure there isn't time for some fun?'

'None at all,' she said firmly. 'Do you want to mess up my fine dress?'

He realised for the first time that she was looking very smart. She was wearing a crisp white blouse, buttoned to the neck, a dark green skirt and black boots. She had deposited a wide-brimmed hat on the table when she came in.

'Aren't I quite the bourgeois lady?' she said.

'Svetlana, you could pass yourself off as aristocracy.'

She pouted. 'I draw a line at that. Now, get yourself dressed.'

She tossed him a bag. It contained a dark suit, white shirt and sober tie.

'We are going to pass ourselves off as a well-heeled couple. There is a party sympathiser, a professor. He has a summer home in the Crimea. He has given permission for you to have the run of his home until the party can return to open activity.'

Kolya removed his shirt and enjoyed the cool touch of Svetlana's fingers.

'You can't keep your hands off me, can you?'

She blushed and withdrew her hand. 'Finish getting dressed. We have to go.'

'Why the urgency?'

'Olga is not to be trusted. Her son is sick. We fear that she is preparing to hand you over for a few roubles to pay for his care.'

As they emerged from the building, Grigory gave the street a final glance and nodded. They hurried past him to the tram stop.

'Isn't he coming with us?' Kolya asked.

'He's done his bit,' Svetlana said.

They boarded the tram and watched the streets rushing by. The sun rippled over them and Kolya felt alive in a way he had thought impossible for weeks. Svetlana tapped his arm and they alighted. The lights were stuttering to life along the Nevsky. Kolya peered into the doorway of one of the hotels as they passed and scowled at the sight of women in silk dresses, men in suits and cravats. He heard the gay laughter spilling onto the street. This was the ruling order at play.

'Let them have their fun,' Svetlana whispered, arm linking his. 'They think they are back in charge. The fools think this moment of excess will last forever. Well, we have a surprise in store for them. The revolution isn't dead, merely sleeping, recovering its strength.'

'Oh, let it be true,' Kolya said yearningly.

They passed the Smolny Institute and Kolya stared at the banners.

'This is where the Soviet does its deliberations now,' Svetlana explains, 'not the Tauride.' Machine guns protruded from the neoclassical façade.

'So it's all change?'

'The Soviet majority think they are in charge,' Svetlana replied, 'but the SRs and the Mensheviks are losing ground. Kornilov is manoeuvring to dispense with Kerensky altogether. Things are on a knife edge.'

'And all this has happened while I have been in hiding?'

'It has. The world does not stand still, not even for Comrade Kolya.'

Presently, they were walking up the stairs to Kolya's new home, a bachelor apartment overlooking the Neva.

'Will you look at that view!' he said. 'And this belongs to a Bolshevik?'

'A sympathiser.'

From outside the window came music. Kolya put his arm round Svetlana's waist and took her hand.

'May I have this dance, your ladyship?'

'Why, my lord,' Svetlana responded, 'we have not been properly introduced.'

'I am His Highness, Nikolai Filthy Rich.'

'And I,' Svetlana breezed haughtily, 'am Lady Caviar Gobbler. How gallant you are.'

They danced around the room, he relishing the feel of a woman's body after so long, she graceful and young again with her pinned up hair and swirling skirts. Suddenly, Kolya trod on the hem of her dress and they stumbled backwards. Svetlana guided him to the bedroom, laughing as she propelled him to their inevitable destination. Kolya sprawled on his back, arms outstretched. Svetlana was straddling him just as she had in the dingy flat in the Vyborg. She could feel his cock stirring between her legs and pulled at his shirt, popping the buttons. She ran her hands over his bare chest.

'Now you,' Kolya said eagerly.

He exposed her breasts and rolled her onto her back.

'You can't imagine how I have missed you,' he said.

'If that bulge in your pants is anything to go by,' she answered saucily. 'I think I can.'

Svetlana wriggled out of her skirt and underwear and gloried in the feel of his hands on her arse, his fingers sliding between her buttocks, teasing her. She stripped him naked and coaxed his erection back to life.

'Don't disappoint me, Kolya,' she said. 'I've been looking forward to this.'

'No more than me,' he replied.

Outside, the bourgeoisie smoked and drank and danced and deep in the heart of working class Petrograd, like Kolya and Svetlana's desire, Bolshevism was recovering itself, ready to rise again.

Part Three

October Mists

Pavel

He was addressing his fellow soldiers, armed with the results of the Petrograd City Duma elections. He was having fun, bantering with the men.

'In first place are the SRs,' he said, teasing his brothers in arms. 'Here's the figure, comrades, 205,659 votes. As for the Kadets...' There was some booing, so Pavel allowed it to continue before raising his hands. 'That's right, the great liberal party limps home in third place, 114,483 votes.'

He allowed expectation to grow in the ranks of the soldiers.
'Would you like to know who came second? Was it the Mensheviks?'
'No!'
'Was it the Anarchists!'
'They don't even stand for elections, do they?'
Somebody protested, but he was treated with derision.
'So who came second, comrades?'
There was a great roar. 'The Bolsheviks.'
'Got it in one,' Pavel said. 'Lenin's Bolsheviks.' He put a finger to his lips. '183,624 votes.' He stood nodding as the cheering continued. 'Don't let on to the officers what I just said. They might pee their beds and you know what a bugger it is to dry out a mattress.'

There was more laughter and some catcalling.

'The party of the workers and the poor peasants is reeling in the SRs,' Pavel told the crowd before him. 'We stand on the verge of power. We are revolutionary defenders of the idea of rule by the Soviets, the elected bodies of the working people.' He allowed time for his words to sink in then he read from *Proletarii*.

You must vote for our party because it alone is struggling bravely alongside the peasantry against large landowners, alongside workers against factory owners, alongside the oppressed everywhere against the oppressors. There you have it, lads.'

He let the applause run its course.

'They said we were routed. They said we were in retreat, traitors, foreign agents. They said we had our pockets filled with German gold.' He pulled out his pockets. 'Have you ever seen me with any bloody money? Have you noticed me handing out any bullion lately?'

There was more dark humour, then Pavel said: 'The election results are not all I have to tell you. It isn't all good news. The German Army is getting closer. This time I am not telling any jokes, lads. Riga has fallen.'

There was a groan of dismay and incomprehension.

'That's right, Riga. Do you know how far that is? Three hundred miles away, that's all. Oh, Kerensky breathes fire about war, perpetual war for Mother Russia, but he can't even deliver military success and he certainly can't deliver peace. Prices climb ever higher, saboteurs cause explosions, the transport system is in chaos.'

'Yes, and children are starving to death!'

'You're absolutely correct, Comrade,' Pavel agreed. 'Do you know what the choice is now? It is the Cossack general Lavr Kornilov or it is us, the Bolsheviks.'

He leaned forward conspiratorially and he was delighted to see so many of the soldiers pressing forward to hear what he has to say.

'Do you think we are going to stand idly by while the landlords and the bourgeoisie impose their strongman, their counter-revolutionary? They hunt the Bolsheviks today. It will be the Soviets tomorrow, no matter where they stand or who they support. Then it will be war against the very idea of revolution itself. Are they going to get away with trampling over every freedom we have squeezed out of the bastards?'

He didn't wait for a theatrical reply this time.

'This Kornilov, this hard man, he wants to restore the Army. Well, you know what that means, don't you? It means restoring the officers' right to bully you, insult you, beat you, humiliate you, shoot you if they feel like it. It means you're worthless, cattle to be herded into the meat grinder of war.' He stuck his thumbs in his belt. 'Well, I won't stand for it and I don't think you lot will either.'

His words were met with cheering. As he made his way through the ranks, the men patted him on the back and shouted encouragement. Some stopped him to give their opinion. Finally, he disengaged himself and walked away with Mikhail.

'Is there anything else on the grapevine?'

'There is always news,' Mikhail told him. 'We've got panic over Riga, people besieging the railway stations so they can get a train out of the city and stay with relatives in the country. Everybody thinks Kerensky is fucked. He plays his little counter-revolutionary games, but if Kornilov enters the city, he won't just shoot us Bolsheviks. He'll have Kerensky up against the wall too. Do you know what the Kornilovites are saying?

They're going to hang all the Lenin spies and that means the Soviet leaders too.'

'Stuff Lenin and the Soviet,' one man in uniform commented. 'They'll stretch our fool necks too.'

When the meeting finally came to an end, Pavel joined Mikhail. That Sunday morning, they walked under a cloudless, azure sky and felt the sun on their faces.

'At least if they do put us in front of a firing squad, we'll get shot in warm weather,' Pavel said. 'I wouldn't want to go shivering with the cold and make them think I'm scared. I wouldn't give them the pleasure.'

Mikhail's face was a mask of non-commitment. 'You know what, citizen,' he said. 'You've got a bloody funny sense of humour.'

They stood at the entrance to the barracks, smoking. For ten minutes or so, they lounged against the gate, watching the pedestrians go by, identifying a particularly pretty girl here, an expensively-dressed man there, one they could subject to mockery or send scurrying away with a flea in his ear.

'Yes, scurry away, you bourgeois scum,' Pavel bawled at one man. 'We know what you're up to, calling for the restoration of your bloody Tsar. Well, the Romanovs come back over my dead body.' He threw in one final comment. 'Do you know what they say about your beloved Kornilov, 'the heart of a lion and the brains of a sheep', and that's his own side talking!'

The mood had changed in the last few weeks. Nobody was cowed any more. Nonetheless, there was anxiety. The soldiers, sailors and Red Guards were drilling, preparing for the defence of red Petrograd. The workers' militias had rearmed. It was as if the whole city was holding its breath and oiling its weapons. Finally, they saw the man they had been waiting for.

'Greetings, Comrade Kolya,' Pavel announced breezily. 'It has been a while. You look well.'

'I feel well,' Kolya told him.

Mikhail stretched. 'It looks as if Svetlana has been putting you through your paces. You've added some muscle, I see.'

Kolya laughed. 'She's a fierce taskmaster, Comrade Svetlana. What dedication to the cause. She has me at it night and day.'

When the banter subsided, Pavel asked what was needed.

'I could do with a company of men,' Kolya said. 'We're digging trenches to set up defensive positions.'

Pavel nodded. 'Mikhail will organise that for you.'

Mikhail set off to muster the men.

'They're saying Kornilov has four thousand Caucasian cavalry at his disposal,' Kolya said.

Pavel whistled. 'Four thousand. We'll need machine guns and artillery.'

Kolya nodded. 'You'll have them if I've got anything to say in the matter. Petrograd will not fall to reaction.'

Pavel noticed a change in Kolya. He'd been little more than a boy when they first met. Now he was confident, issuing orders without hesitation. He looked older and had filled out physically.

'It looks like you're moving up the party hierarchy,' he said.

Kolya shrugged, but not without a glow of pride showing in his fleshless features. 'We all do what we can.'

'Is there anything else?' Pavel asked.

'Oh, we've got something special for you,' Kolya said.

'And what's that?'

'There's a crowd of officers, Kornilovites.'

'Where are they?'

'The Astoria. If we leave the bastards in the city to stir up trouble, we'll come to regret it.'

'Say no more,' Pavel told him. 'I don't fancy a bullet in the back myself.'

'When you've placed them under arrest, wait for me at the hotel,' Kolya said. 'We need to talk.'

Within the hour, he was approaching the front door of the hotel at the head of a column of armed men. They marched straight past the startled hotel staff and entered the dining room where the officers were singing and carousing, to the distaste of some of the other guests. The celebrations came to an abrupt end the moment they saw the infantrymen filing in. Forks clattered on plates. A glass rolled here. A chair scraped there.

One officer rose to his feet, summoning every ounce of dignity he could muster. 'What's the meaning of this? You have no right to interrupt a private regimental function.'

'Is that right?' Pavel said. He noticed a chicken drumstick and picked it up. 'Will you look at this? I can't remember the last time I ate chicken. Fuck me, you boys do well for yourselves.'

'How dare you use profanities in the presence of a senior officer!'

Pavel drew his pistol and put the barrel to the head of the man facing him. There were screams from some of the diners.

'I'll tell you how I dare,' Pavel said. 'See, I have had enough grief from shithouses like you to last me a lifetime. My friend Kolya, he's a Bolshevik you understand, same as me. Kolya asks me to go down to a nest of reactionaries.' He paused. 'Reactionaries. That's you lot. Kolya says, place them under arrest so the fuckers can't get up to any mischief. Fuckers, by the way, that's you lot too.' He let them digest the calculated insult. 'So I would advise you to sit down and shut up, because if you don't I might just blow your brains out all over your beetroot soup.' He watched the suppressed fury in so many faces and luxuriated in their impotent rage. 'Do I make myself clear?'

There was no answer.

'Do I make myself clear,' he bawled, 'you rotten sacks of shit?'

His voice crackled across the room. For a few moments the only sound was the mellow tick of the clock on the mantlepiece by the window.

'You have made yourself perfectly clear,' the officer replied, trying his best not to sound flustered.

'Good,' Pavel said, 'now I am going to finish my chicken and you are going to watch me eat because I have a gun and you don't. When I am good and finished, we will take you to Peter and Paul Fortress.'

'You are detaining us! On what charge?'

'Let's see,' Pavel drawled. 'Oh yes, that would be plotting against the revolution.'

His armed men stood behind the officers, weapons presented.

'Are you not eating?' Pavel asked casually. 'What's your name, by the way?'

'I am Officer Balayev of the...'

Pavel cut him off with a wave of his hand.

'Do you think I give a shit what regiment you are from? I asked your name. That is all I asked.'

Balayev looked outraged.

'So, what do you think of this clown Kornilov?'

There was consternation around the room, but only one voice of protest.

'General Kornilov is a brave and talented son of the Russian Motherland. You owe him more respect.'

'Oh, respect. I remember respect, citizen Balayev. It's what you bastards have never showed to us soldiers.'

He slapped Balayev across the temple, hard enough to make his ears ring.

Balayev shot to his feet. 'How dare you strike an officer?'

'Sit the fuck down,' Pavel warned him, 'before I knock you down, you daft bastard.'

Balayev sat, and stewed in his own resentment.

'You look a bit aggrieved,' Pavel said. 'Now I think that's a bit odd, myself. You see, it's this Kornilov of yours who is going round, throwing his weight about, promising to hang all us grunts from the lamp posts.' He glanced at his men and addressed them one by one. 'Do you fancy dangling from a lamppost? What about you? No, it is looking unanimous here. Not one of my lads wants his neck stretching. Isn't that funny?'

Finally, Pavel tired of his fun and snapped his fingers. 'Get this counter-revolutionary scum out of my sight.'

He trusted the men to march the officers off to their cells without any help from him so he rocked back in his chair, hands behind his neck in the time-honoured gesture of idleness. The staff crept around him, wondering what he wanted now. He requested a coffee, but that was all he had to say to them. Kolya had asked him to wait. So he waited. And waited. Then he waited some more. Finally, Kolya hurried in.

'I am sorry I kept you waiting all this time,' he said.

'Don't worry about it,' Pavel told him. 'It's been nice just sitting here, killing time.' He laughed. 'I finished off the counter-revolutionaries' lunch for them. So what did you want to talk to me about?'

'The situation is dire,' Kolya said. 'There is genuine panic. General after general declares for Kornilov.'

'That's to be expected, he's a career soldier.'

'The military schools are with him. He is advancing on the city.'

'At least the Cossacks are opting to stay neutral,' Pavel observed. 'That could be important.' He set all four legs of his chair down and leaned forward. 'Is there any more good news, because right now it all sounds pretty shit.'

'Well, this might not sound like it, but the party organisations have been a hornet's nest. Furious arguments have been breaking out.'

'That's good?'

'Let me finish. One side says the leadership is fucking useless. The other side wants to lie on the bed sobbing because we're all going to die.'

Pavel cocked his head. 'I still don't hear much optimism, you know.'

'It is an opportunity,' Kolya said. 'There is a mood abroad in the city, a sense of impatience even with the Bolshevik leaders. The workers, the soldiers, they are not fleeing the city, like the better off. They are up for a fight.'

'It's true of our lads too,' Pavel agreed. 'We've been here before, haven't we, with the rank and file running ahead of the leadership?'

'This is our chance to drive cowardice and defencism out of our ranks. Shift the party to the left, throw Kornilov back into the swamp where he deserves to be, and pave the way for the revolution, the *real* revolution, Pavel Sergeyevich.'

'Why are you telling me all this?'

'I will tell you why, comrade. I want men like you to put yourself and anyone who is with you at the head of this movement, to join the spearhead of the advanced workers and soldiers. You need to be visible. What do you say?'

Pavel looked up at the ceiling, following a crack as it meandered across the plaster.

'Well, that means I'll be one of the first in front of the firing squad, I suppose.'

'Front of the queue,' Kolya confirmed.

'They might even torture me first.'

'Squash your nuts between two bricks,' Kolya said. 'No doubt about it.'

'So it is all pain and no gain. I put my head on the block and hope a rag tag band of working folk and rank and file soldiers can beat the best the professional soldiery can offer?'

'Yes,' Kolya said, nodding. 'That's about the size of it. So you'll do it?'

Pavel shook Kolya's hand. 'Too fucking right!'

Kolya poured two glasses of water.

'A toast.'

'With water?'

'It's all we've got. To revolution.'

'To revolution!'

By the end of the day, the city was on a war footing. Factory sirens wailed and whistles blew. Pavel was one of the soldiers helping to drill the workers' fighting detachments. The resistance to the Kornilov coup had a name: the Committee for Struggle against Counter-revolution. Soldiers sympathetic to the revolution were drilling the Red Guards. From time to time, a red soldier would collapse into helpless laughter at the inability of the would-be workers' militia to march in time. Kolya arrived to review one detachment.

'How are they doing?' he asked Pavel.

'We're getting there,' Pavel answered, 'but look at these skilled guys. Why the hell do they turn up in their suits? Look at this fucker. He's wearing a bowler hat like some English gentleman.' He reached out a hand, guiding Kolya to a car. 'Let's take a spin.'

They toured the streets. Pavel explained the defences. There were armed workers erecting barricades, others stringing our rolls of barbed wire. Everywhere they looked there were teams digging trenches.

'You can't have organised all this yourself,' Kolya said.

'Of course not,' Pavel answered. 'Proletarian Petrograd has risen, The people know the choice is successful defence of the city or military dictatorship. Kolya. I can't keep up with the buggers. Every worker wants a grenade or a rifle. Some of the Red Guards had weapons they had made themselves in the armaments factories. They're making cannon for us. I tell you, some of them would fight Kornilov with their bare hands if they had to.'

'So you think we can pull this off?'

'Too fucking right. Kornilov is dead meat.'

Raisa

She was alone that morning, alone and gripped with anxiety. If only Elena were lying here beside her, so strong, so courageous, but Elena was with Svetlana at the barricades. Raisa had promised to join them. She swung her legs out of bed and looked down at her feet. They were tiny and white against the wooden floor. Never had she felt her frailty more keenly. The thought of thousands of General Kornilov's troops bearing down on the city terrified her. What if all the brutishness, all the bestial appetites she experienced in Bagrov's wretched brothel were to be unleashed on great Piter? Kornilov was a monarchist and a warlord. He would stain the streets in workers' blood if he could.

She went to the washstand and splashed her face. The image of bloody streets stayed in her head. The watery sunlight failed to warm her. As she brushed her hair, she examined her reflection in the mirror. Was this the face of a fighter? A revolutionary? She dressed, resting her palms on her flat stomach. You're getting thinner, Raisa girl, she told herself.

Finally, she sat down to lace her boots and peered along the landing. It did not seem to matter that Vera and Yozhin were both dead. Since the gunmen invaded her home, she had been afraid at night, eyes snapping open at each brush of wind against the window pane, each creak and groan of the house. In spite of her unease, she gave a wry smile at the word home. Yes, this was her home now.

'I have somewhere I can call my own.'

So why did she feel guilty?

Guilty!

There was only one way to assuage her guilt, and that was action. She checked that her pistol was loaded and slipped it back into her coat pocket. She sipped a little water and headed for the door, glancing just for a second in the direction of Mrs Kuznetsova's living room, as if, at any moment, the old lady was going to rise from the grave and hobble out to greet her. She needed to be bold, audacious, the way she had been when she defended herself from Andrey, when she scattered the Pharaohs.

She paused at the door. Pavel had fixed the lock and added extra bolts at the top and bottom. Instinctively, he understood how vulnerable she felt. It was strange having a man care for her after all the men who had used her, treated her as if she was not human at all, just a thing, a piece of meat, a toy to be set through its motions for their pleasure.

She stepped into the warmth of another August day and the first thing she noticed was the normality around her. She'd expected armed men on the streets, an inexorable menace beneath a brooding, leaden sky, but here was sunlight, birdsong, a light breeze. She walked two streets before she came across the first sign of anything unusual. There were half a dozen men loafing by a newly dug trench. One whistled at her. Another treated him to a disapproving shove and gave her a cheery wave, calling her comrade. She paid some attention to their faces and saw little evidence of tension. They seemed almost carefree. Could it be true? Just hours after there had been blood-curdling talk of civil war and counter-revolution, there was this casual cheeriness. By the time she reached the French Embankment, there seemed to be something approaching a carnival atmosphere. There was a woman in arms.

'May I ask you something, Comrade?' Raisa asked.

The woman swung her rifle strap over her shoulder. 'How can I help you?'

'Nobody seems afraid,' Raisa said. 'Do they not fear Kornilov?'

'Nobody can find the bugger,' came the reply. 'They're saying he's stuck with his troops in the sidings somewhere.' She puffed out her cheeks and adopted a deep, gruff voice. 'I am the great Kornilov, crusher of skulls, hammer of democracy.' A pause. A smaller, mouse-like voice: 'Oh dear, does anyone know the right way to Petrograd?'

There was appreciative laughter from some of the other fighters. Raisa cocked her head, still unsure what to make of the new optimism.

'You should have been up earlier,' said the woman. 'The rumours are fairly flying. It's the railway workers, you see. They've been having some fun, jamming points, tearing up lines. These bloody counter-revolutionaries can't even get out of the sidings, never mind launch their offensive.'

Her neighbour nodded. 'They can't even contact each other. The telegraph workers won't send their messages. It's true, love. They're stuffed.'

Now, Raisa felt as light as air. She fairly skipped across the ground, stopping occasionally to ask for more news. She got snippets of information, rumours, pure gossip, but a picture was forming. Thousands of armed soldiers had surrounded the Cossacks at Luga, making sure they kept their promise not to take sides. Muslim revolutionaries had been sent to persuade the Savage Division to withdraw from the fight. Raisa began to run, not because she had anything to run from or run to – she had plenty of time – but because she wanted to feel her blood pumping through her veins. She was still running when she saw a familiar figure among the crowds of Red Guards.

'Svetlana! Is it true? Has the coup collapsed?'

'It has run away into the sand,' Svetlana confirmed. 'Who knows, we might be conducting one of the world's least bloody revolutions. The bastards can't kill us if they can't get to us.'

They embraced, then Raisa searched her surroundings for some sign of Elena.

'She's over there,' Svetlana told her. 'She's been haranguing some of the factory girls. They're not taking their defensive duties seriously. You should hear Elena scold them.'

Raisa beamed. 'That sounds like my Elena.'

Thinking she may have said too much, she grimaced.

'There's no need to try to hide things from me,' Svetlana told her. She leant forward, lips by Raisa's ear. 'Love should have no boundaries, my sweet. Our revolution will sweep away all the old muck and allow people to live as they wish. Go where your heart takes you.'

Raisa was shocked that her secret was out. 'How long have you known? You're not going to say anything, are you?'

The answer humbled her. 'You can rely on aunty Svetlana to be discreet. What business is it of mine?' She squeezed Raisa's arm. 'Don't I have my own guilty secret in Kolya? Go and find Elena.'

Raisa discovered her lover returning from her impromptu, open-air meeting. They embraced and found a quiet spot, which was not easy because the streets were once again swarming with workers, soldiers and sailors from the Kronstadt fortress. Everybody wanted to be seen taking part in the defence of red Petrograd.

'They fell apart,' Elena exclaimed. 'All that talk of drowning the city of revolution in blood and they couldn't even get here! There is a warrant out for Kornilov's arrest.'

'So we've won?'

'Bolshevik soldiers are fraternising with the Kornilovites. We haven't just repulsed the counter-revolutionaries, my love. We have strengthened the revolution. Do you see?' She pointed out the cheering, swelling crowds and uplifted faces. There was the same glow of euphoria in hers as in theirs. 'Do you see what the working people can do when they are united?'

Raisa was bewildered. Mere hours ago, she had left home with the expectation of pending tragedy. Now all she saw was hope and celebration. It was as if somebody had tampered with the points on the track of time. The old rules no longer applied. Everything was spinning, swirling, refusing to fit into expected patterns.

'It isn't just Kornilov who is finished,' Elena said. 'It's Kerensky too. He appointed the general. He tinkered with the possibility of counter-revolution himself. He can't avoid responsibility for this.'

'Quite right, Comrade sister,' a passing sailor said. 'It is time to transfer power into the hands of the proletariat. If you get a chance, you should go and listen to Comrade Raskolnikov. He will put it much better than I can.'

'Thank you,' Raisa said, as if expressing gratitude for the delivery of a cup of tea.

'I swear,' Elena said, 'you are the politest of revolutionaries.'

Raise frowned. 'Are you teasing me?'

Elena pulled Raisa into another embrace. 'Oh, definitely.'

That's when they were disturbed by a klaxon. A vehicle was pulling up next to them.

'Do you want to do something to serve the revolution?' Svetlana called.

She was in the passenger seat of a car. Kolya was beside her, eyes blazing with optimism.

Raisa scrambled into the back seat after Elena, Half a dozen more soldiers and workers clambered onto the vehicle, almost crushing them in their eagerness to spread the message of Soviet power. Then they were bouncing along the road on the barely existent suspension. On arrival, Elena rubbed at her backside.

'I'm going to be black and blue!'

'Oh, stop moaning.' Svetlana told her. 'Not so long ago you thought that pretty little arse would be sitting on the point of a Caucasian bayonet. Be grateful for small mercies.'

Elena treated her to a rueful look. 'I think that is quite a big mercy. I'm fond of my arse, thank you very much.'

Raisa gazed up at the factory. The chimneys were dormant, the sound of machinery stilled. She followed everyone into a vast, open space inside the factory. There, hundreds of workers were listening to a speech from a man who stood framed by an enormous skeletal structure made up of scaffolding festooned with the ubiquitous scarlet banners with their revolutionary slogans. She recognised the speaker, but his name had slipped her mind.

'Who's that?'

'Don't you know Comrade Anishin?' Elena hissed. 'He is a friend of Shlyapnikov.'

Raisa simply frowned, making Elena laugh. Somebody in front put a finger to his lips. Raisa's gaze strayed to a stack of pallets, draped as were so many parts of the hall with a red banner. A workman saw her looking and lifted a corner to reveal a stack of rifles. He winked and laughed. She returned her attention to Anishin's speech.

'There is this from the Second Machine Gun Regiment,' he shouted, his voice hoarse and sometimes barely audible at all. He read the statement. *'the only way out of the present situation lies in transferring power into the hands of the working people.'*

There was thunderous applause. Anishin raised his right hand for silence.

'From all over the Vyborg, from all over the city, it is the same message. The masses want the unity of socialist forces, not a coalition with the bourgeoisie. Neutral units are declaring for the transfer of power. Military units that initially refused to take sides between Kornilov and the Soviet are coming over to our side.'

There was more cheering and clapping. This time, it was harder to restore order.

'Kornilov promised the mailed fist of the bourgeoisie and the landlords. As it turned out, thanks to our comrade railway workers, he had nothing to punch but air. When he dreamed of fields of slaughter, all he could see through his carriage window was a siding. There is now a firm determination to crush the counter-revolutionaries and establish a government of the workers, peasants and soldiers that will finally bring this bloody, imperialist war to an end.'

Wave upon wave of applause swept the room. Anishin clasped his hands behind his back and basked in the approval of the gathering.

Kolya winked. 'He isn't finished, you know.'

'There were those who prevaricated,' Anishin continued. 'There were those who said we could only hand the power to the landlords and the bourgeoise.'

Raisa overheard Kolya whisper in Svetlana's ear. 'Cheeky bugger. He was one of them.'

It produced first a snort of laughter then a mock disapproving stare.

'Under the lash of counter-revolution,' Anishin yelled, 'the revolution has found its voice and this is what it is saying, 'All power to the Soviets.''

The applause went on and on. Anishin struggled down from the raised platform, spotted Kolya and fought his way through to join him.

'You spoke well, Comrade,' Svetlana said.

There was a glint of mischief in her eyes that Anishin failed to notice. Raisa watched the metalworker's face. He was stealing furtive looks at Svetlana. Did Kolya have a rival?

'Thank you, Svetlana,' Anishin purred, luxuriating in the praise. 'Is there any more news, Kolya?'

'It's the same story everywhere,' Kolya replied. 'In every barracks, every mill and factory, on every street corner, people are crying out for an end to the war. The people have had enough of this government of civil war.'

Anishin nodded dismissively. Kolya was not telling him anything new.

'Let's go,' he said.

'Where?'

'There is a meeting at the Carriage Works in twenty minutes.'

That was the pattern of the rest of Raisa's day, a dizzy round of meetings. Anishin had work for her, along with the rest of the group delivered by car to the industrial district. They were going to leaflet the workers and distribute copies of Pravda. With each new task, Raisa felt the dark tide of fear ebbing. Not so long ago, she had been a plaything tossed to the men who came to Bagrov's door. Then, the night she slew Andrey, baptised in the monster's blood, she became human. Elena had reminded her of the meaning of love and she had never been alone since that moment. Then there were Svetlana, Pavel, Mikhail. She is determined never to be alone again.

Never.

At the end of an exhausting but thrilling day, Raisa stood waiting for Elena outside the last factory they visited. She was a rock amid the stream of workers leaving the meeting, and she finally felt like a true Bolshevik. She searched the throng for Elena, then there she was. Her heart leapt and Elena made her way over, waving with both hands.

'Isn't it wonderful!' she cried. 'Tomorrow, we will do it all over again, solidifying our support among the masses. I'll have to be up early to tour the factories. Darling, that bastard Kornilov has done us a favour.'

Raisa's face fell at the mention of an early start. 'I thought you might come home with me.'

Elena squeezed her arm. 'I will be with you soon, my love, but the task is urgent. We are Bolsheviks. This is our time.'

Raisa nodded, while inside she felt empty. 'Of course.'

'I would ask you to stay, but I share a room with two other girls.' She whispered in Raisa's ear. 'You could share my bed, but I might not be able to keep my hands off you. I don't think they would understand.'

At that, Raisa felt her skin tingle. She wanted to be with her beloved Elena every moment of every day, every second until the last day of her life.

'I understand.'

'You must,' Elena told her. 'You really must. We have to make sacrifices. What are our lives compared to the future of all Russia? Russia! What am I saying? Soon, the workers in France and Germany will rise, Finland, Italy and Britain. The world revolution is imminent and we are in the vanguard. Our happiness depends upon it. If woman is to be free, we must liberate all mankind. You do believe me, don't you?'

All Raisa heard was slogans, but she knew that Elena believed every word. But why, why couldn't they have both? Why couldn't they have revolution and personal happiness? She wanted a few minutes of Elena's time in the storm of activity. Was it too much too ask?

'I will always believe in you,' Raisa answered. 'I had better go.'

'You can't walk all that way!' Elena protested. 'Do you know what is happening on the streets? There are criminals waiting to waylay unwary citizens. Raisa, there are cars we can use. Somebody will take you home.'

She spotted a familiar figure.

'Pavel Sergeyevich,' she called. 'Will you drive Raisa home. She was actually thinking of walking. She can't be allowed to do that, can she?'

Pavel sauntered across to them and shoved back his cap. 'Always at your service, comrades.'

He strode to the car and opened the door. Raisa followed him hesitantly. She remembered the last time she was alone in a car with a man.

'What about you, Elena?' Pavel was saying.

He was clearly intrigued that Elena would permit Raisa to go home with a man who loved her.

'I am staying in the Vyborg tonight. It is just Raisa who needs a lift.'

Pavel drew a breath, flicked his cigarette butt into the gutter and slid into the driver's seat. As he pulled away from the kerb, Raisa turned and waved. She continued waving until Elena was lost in the shadows.

'Are you uncomfortable with me?' Pavel asked, when she turned round.

Raisa glanced at him, aware of the rigid way she was holding her body. 'No, not at all. Why?'

'I am uncomfortable Raisa, well, a little.'

'Why?' she asked. 'Why would you be uneasy in my presence? Truly, I do not understand.'

She marvelled that this tough, resourceful soldier, this leader of men, could find her intimidating. Sometimes, she thought she would never understand people.

'I made a fool of myself,' Pavel reminded her, 'when I declared my love for you.'

Raisa marvelled that he had built one moment of embarrassment into something of importance. She had barely given it a moment's thought since. She started to giggle.

'Love?' she said. 'I don't remember it like that at all. Are you sure that is what you said?'

His face remained serious. There was a thump in her throat as she realised he meant it.

'Oh,' she said.

'Oh indeed,' Pavel said. 'I thought you knew. It is not something that has gone away, Raisa.'

'But you have a sweetheart.'

She saw the shadow of guilt pass across his face and she knew that everything he had told her was true.

'Nina is sweet,' Pavel told her. 'She adores me and I betray her every time your face comes into my mind. I loathe what I have become.'

'But you are good, Pavel Sergeyevich. You are a good man.'

His face was hidden from her.

'I am a man who strings along a wonderful, generous, loving woman when I know I would betray her instantly should another ever show me the slightest encouragement.'

Raisa was grateful that they had almost arrived. 'Pavel, you should not speak like this. You must understand...'

'That you love somebody else? That you will always love her? I do. I wish it was otherwise, but honestly I do. It doesn't mean I can change my feelings.'

He stopped the car in front of the boarding house. Raisa watched him staring straight ahead and wondered what feelings were tearing at him.

'I have to go,' she said.

'I know. Ignore me. I am just a fool.'

She was standing on the pavement now, with her hand resting on the door. 'You're not a fool, Pavel. Men like you are the heart of this revolution.'

'Isn't the revolution meant to make us happy?'

She heard him put the car into gear. Simultaneously, his words spoke to her, echoing her own thoughts.

'We will be happy, Comrade Pavel, when the world is made anew. It will be like Heaven on Earth. It will be just as Comrade Anishin said, Kolya too.'

Pavel still didn't look at her. 'Anishin is a bag of wind. He has no independent thought. He does what others tell him, depending on who he spoke to last. As for Kolya, oh, he's a dreamer. Heaven on Earth? Raisa, I'll believe that when I see it.'

Kolya

There was something artificial about Petrograd under cover of darkness. It was like an ice sculpture, hard and solid at first glance, but horribly impermanent and false when exposed to light. The Kornilov coup had disintegrated, the seeming military might of the generals reduced to plumes of retreating mist. The revolution was nourishing itself on the renewed unity of the workers, soldiers and peasants. Kolya could almost taste victory.

Comrade Slutsky had it right. Kolya had heard his speech at the Petrograd Committee. It still made his skin tingle: 'For us to consider compromises now is ludicrous. No compromises!'

How unequivocal. How insistent and firm.

'Ours is a proletarian revolution. Our task is to clarify our position and to prepare unconditionally for a military clash.'

Those words in his head, Kolya stood in the imposing heart of the Petrograd, and the city reminded him of some cheap, tawdry, travelling fair. Everything was a painted façade. There were shop windows full of mannequins, draped with expensive dresses, corsets and wigs, hats and accessories, as though the entire population had nothing more to think about than what to wear at their next, grand ball.

Yet the people still hovered on the brink of starvation. Not so very far from here, women stood for hours in line to feed their families. All winter long, they shuddered in poor quality coats or just thin, worn dresses. The respite of summer was coming to an end. Another winter was approaching. Some could barely afford a decent pair of shoes. He thought of Svetlana. Only once, when she came to him in disguise, had he seen her dressed in the style this beautiful, vibrant woman deserved. What did the working people know of flutes of sparkling champagne, cabarets, fashion catalogues and the latest American movies at the Pikadilly Cinema on the Nevsky? What did they know of jewels and furs and gambling clubs?

Kolya remembered the officers' dinner he instructed Pavel to break up. Even now, as red Petrograd emerged from the July days of retreat and repression, gathering itself for an assault on power, the self-satisfied dregs of the old order caroused and laughed off the possibility of their imminent destruction. You complacent, fools, Kolya thought. Do you not sense it? Do you not feel the winds of change?

He walked alone, pistol stowed in his jacket pocket, running a jaundiced eye over the gaudy lie that was high society. Once, when he had been a precocious schoolboy, he aspired to this mirage, this world of wealth, status and fame. What he wanted now was the pure flame of revolt, the withering fire of history consuming all this filth and corruption. He heard footsteps behind him and turned. A prostitute was approaching, exaggerating the sway of her hips to get his attention. She was finely dressed and attractive. Her clientele, he guessed, was well-heeled.

'Would you like me to show you a good time, Sir?' she asked.

Well, well, so they did actually talk like that, these women of the night. Kolya shook his head. This poor creature was, for him, an example of all that corruption that had to be consumed in the furnace of insurrection. She had to be cleansed of exploitation. The words she had just used to approach him were so self-caricatural he'd almost laughed out loud. Not that high class then. He ran his eyes over her. She was slim, even elegant, with blond hair and hazel eyes. He had always imagined that the women who plied this trade would be heavily made up, but if he had seen her in different circumstances he would have taken her for a secretary or nanny, even a lady. Christ, listen to me, he thought, still swimming in the filthy pool of capitalist prejudices. What is a lady but a woman raised up by an accident of birth? What is a prostitute but one cast down by the same vagaries of fate?

'We could go to your room.'

'No, thank you,' he said.

In spite of himself, in spite of Svetlana, he was tempted. He was attracted to the slope of her back, the curve of her buttocks, the haughty glint in her eye. This was a woman who defied the judgement of the world. In spite of himself, he imagined loosening her corset, pressing his lips to her bare shoulders. After the whirlwind of meetings, leaflet drops and speeches that had occupied him all day, he felt as if possessed.

Inside him, there was a beast that must be fed. He wanted to drown himself in Svetlana's hair, her soft, brown eyes, the gasp that came from her parted lips when they made love, but she was not here. Why did she have be such a dedicated comrade? She had insisted on remaining in the Vyborg, where she could help drive the shift to the left. Oh yes, you are the very pulse of the struggle, dear Svetlana, Kolya thought, and he was going to have to jerk himself off alone in his room. The prostitute clearly sensed his interest. She seemed to find him equally intriguing.

'*No, thank you*?' She examined his face carefully, lips pursed in bemusement 'I don't meet many chaps as polite as you. Most of them know exactly what they want and it isn't an intellectual discussion.'

'You should not demean yourself, Comrade,' he told her. 'No woman should have to sell herself to make ends meet. The revolution will free you from this misery.'

She looked at him as if he had just grown a second head.

'I'm not miserable,' she told him. 'I like what I do.'

Kolya was appalled. 'How is that possible?' he asked her. 'This is the most terrible oppression.'

'I'm a high-class girl, see. I only go with the best. You don't catch me lying on my back in some cheap brothel. That's why I took a shine to you. I know class when I see it.' She played with a lock of her hair. 'In your case, I'd do you for free.'

Kolya wondered how she could see a gentlemen in his pale blue smock, white trousers and leather boots. He was enticed by her offer, but laughed it off. 'The revolution will give you dignity,' he told her.

'Revolution!' she snorted. 'Disruption of trade, that's all I see. Nothing will change. You mark my words. The gentlemen who use my services, you know what they're after? They want to forget the worries of the world. I take them out of themselves. That's where we are different, Sir. The likes of you, you want to rub people's noses in the worries of the world. I give them the opposite. I allow them to escape. Believe me, I can open the gates of Heaven to a man.'

Kolya looked away, maybe a little too quickly.

'You can keep your revolution,' she said. 'It won't change anything.'

Kolya shook his head. 'What do you know of what we are planning?'

'You'd be surprised who uses my services,' she chuckled.

Kolya ignored that. 'We will change everything.'

'You think?' She turned to go. 'You'll have to change yourself first.'

He watched her as she wandered away, putting herself in the shop window. Already, she was attracting the interest of a middle-aged man in a suit. The thought of them together produced a twist in Kolya's gut. After a few moments, he called after her, voice echoing in the damp streets.

'What's your name?'

'It's Klara. Why, are you having second thoughts?'

Kolya's neck burned. He wished to be seen as the very torch of revolution, but her gaze was stripping him naked. She knew men and she saw his weakness. Somehow, she knew how to place her finger into the blue heart of the fire and come away unburned.

'You're no different to other men,' she said, in a knowing, sing song voice. 'You may get your revolution, but the world will remain the same.'

She reached the street corner and gave him a coquettish flutter of the eyelashes. He was incensed that she had got the better of him.

'Everything will change,' he shouted. 'You wait and see.'

She waved dismissively. 'Good luck with that.'

He did not need luck! The Bolsheviks were in the ascendant because they had a programme, a firm plan of action and, driving them on, the iron will of the great Lenin, the talents of the likes of Trotsky, Krupskaya, Lunacharsky, Kollontai, Raskolnikov. The revolution would be the fulfilment of history, it would! The completion of the rise of man, the achievement of absolute reason. The shackles restraining human progress would be broken. Kolya felt the warm, dank air on his face. Though it mingled with the stench of poorly maintained sewers and rotting debris, he looked beyond the corruption of the city streets to the possibilities of its people. A better, mightier society was about to emerge from these savage struggles. He returned to the car, ran his fingers along the paintwork and instantly imagined the touch of Klara's flesh, the contours and mysteries of that unknown, unseen body. Fancy that – the penniless student drove around Piter in a car requisitioned from some bourgeois and caught the eye of a pretty girl, a lady of the night who was willing to ply her trade for free. He smiled. Yes, the ironies of history.

He slid into the car seat. He missed Svetlana. It was easier to sleep when she was beside him. She helped soothe the fever that overtook him when he was left with his thoughts. Abandoned to his own devices, he swung from elation to depression, lying awake hour after hour, haunted by doubts and uncertainties. He craved Svetlana's sensuality, her earthiness. Their passion seared away all doubt.

'My love,' he murmured, 'How I need you now.'

He started the car and listened to the drumming of the engine. He sat there, reliving Anishin's speeches, the wild applause of the factory audiences, the endless discussions of slogans, strategy, tactics. How he feared the night, when he was alone with his ghosts and his fears. After several moments, he killed the engine and walked down the street once more. At first, all he could see was the litter dancing in the breeze and settling in doorways. Then he spotted Klara, watching him from the corner.

'Changed your mind, lover?'

'I'm not going to pay.'

He knew exactly how ridiculous he sounded He thought for a moment that Klara was going to change her mind. Then she kissed him on the cheek.

'I told you,' she said. 'You don't need to. I like you. What's your name?'

He was tempted to give her a false one, but instead he told her. 'I am Kolya.'

'Klara and Kolya,' she said. 'What fun.'

Then she took his hand. 'Let's go…Comrade.'

Next morning, Kolya sat on the edge of the bed, buttoning his shirt.

'Must you leave so early?' Klara asked, tracing a line down his spine.

He was tempted to lie back and let her use those delicate, agile fingers to please him the way she had the night before.

'I have to be in the Vyborg in twenty minutes,' Kolya told her, rejecting the idea. 'The bosses have locked out workers at several factories. I am giving a speech at the protest meeting.'

'Why don't you give me a speech?' Klara said, teasing him. 'You could tell me about all the women you have had.'

Kolya stood, tucking his shirt into his trousers. All the women! Imagine how she would react if she knew that it was Svetlana who took his virginity.

'I think we did our talking last night,' he told her, checking his appearance in the full-length mirror.

'What's all this about?' Klara asked. 'What is somebody like you doing rubbing shoulders with factory workers?'

Her words brought Svetlana to mind and he felt the sting of guilt.

'We're expecting a government militia to be used against the *Vyborgtsi*,' Kolya answered. 'I will be joining a unit of Red Guards to protect them.'

'Red Guards?'

'Armed workers.'

'Do they need protecting?' Klara wondered out loud. 'I hear your wonderful workers have been breaking into houses to steal food.'

'Starving people do desperate things,' Kolya reminded her. 'If we want to put a stop to such outrages, we must give the people hope for a better world.'

Klara climbed out of bed and stood before him without any self-consciousness about her nakedness. 'Shall I see you again?'

Kolya planted a kiss on her lips. 'Is that what you want?'

Klara ran her fingernail along his bottom lip. 'I can think of worse ways to pass the time.'

He lingered, enjoying her touch for a moment, then he walked to the door.

'Let yourself out,' he told her, 'and please don't steal anything. The apartment doesn't belong to me.'

As he left, a pillow slapped against the door.

'Temper temper,' he shouted gaily.

He was walking to the car when Klara appeared at the window. 'You're a cheeky bastard, Kolya.'

He blew a kiss up to her. 'Maybe that's what you like about me.'

By the time he reached the protest, Svetlana was already addressing the locked out engineering workers.

'...How many of you have enough to eat? There, I don't see many hands going up. Do any of you have sons at the Front? Fine, here's the next question. Who trusts Kerensky to give you bread? Who trusts him to end the war? We can't go on living in the old way, working long hours, standing in endless queues, seeing the war drag on month after bloody month.'

She spotted Kolya watching at the back of the assembly.

'And who bears most of the burden?' she said, her voice rising. 'Why, it's the working women. Well, we are going to throw off the burden. There is no emancipation of women without socialism and no socialism without the emancipation of women.'

Her words were greeted with warm acclamation. Kolya loved listening to his Svetlana addressing the women workers. Her heart beat in tune with the rhythm of their hopes and dreams. He didn't deserve her. She must never know of his night with Klara.

'I am going to invite Comrade Kolya to address you. He is speaking on behalf of the party committee.'

There was a prolonged round of applause. Kolya climbed onto the platform and launched into a prepared tirade, one he had given a number of times before.

'The actions of the Kornilovites were those of enemies of the people,' Kolya told the workers before him. 'But does anyone think Kornilov was acting alone? He and Kerensky were two faces of the same conspiracy against your interests.'

He watched the reaction of those before him, saw the nodding heads, heard the approving murmurs. Emboldened, he delivered a damning verdict on Kerensky and the government:

'Either the power lies in the hands of this clique of landlords and bourgeois,' he yelled, 'meaning the continuation of the war, of hunger, of repression of the working masses, either that...' He paused. 'Either that, or the power passes to you, the workers, to the peasants and the soldiers. All power to the Soviets. Peace, bread and land!'

Then he stalked from the stage to renewed applause. Svetlana was waiting for him. She embraced him and kissed him on both cheeks, before checking whether they were being watched and throwing him against the wall to kiss him on the lips. Kolya felt the press of her body and he returned every touch, every embrace with his traitor's kiss. She searched his face.

'Is something wrong?'

'Of course not. I am not sure this is appropriate when people can see us.'

Svetlana accepted his explanation and released him. As she did so, she winked.

'We'll talk about appropriate later, at the apartment.'

He wondered what state Klara had left it in.

'So you can get away?' he asked. 'We can spend time together?

'I'll make time,' Svetlana told him, 'then we can be as inappropriate as we like.'

He watched her as she went over to a large group of women workers. They embraced her one by one, exchanged smiles, talked eagerly about their concerns. People like her were the heart and soul of the revolution. She was organic to them in a way he would never be. Kolya ached to be accepted the way Svetlana was, but he would always be one of the intellectuals, with the working people but not of them, respected but not loved.

After a few moments, Svetlana stole a look at him with such a smile of love and warmth that he despised himself. What was he doing?

He had a decision to make and he had to make it soon.

Pavel

'Why did it take so long to get a message to me?' he demanded, putting his hand to Nina's forehead. 'What is wrong with her?'

The elderly woman who had come to alert him looked at him with pity.

'You mean you don't know?' she asked. 'What kind of village idiot are you?'

Pavel was struggling to understand why she was being so hostile. Hadn't he rushed to Nina's side without a moment's hesitation?

'She fainted in the food line,' he answered. 'That is all I know. It is getting colder. Is that the problem?' He remembered the sharp gusts that had snapped at his clothes as he had hurried to Nina's lodgings. 'Is it exhaustion, exposure?'

'It is new life,' the woman told him, with a stony glare. 'Honestly, you men. You dip your wick and never think. She is pregnant, you young fool.' She registered the look of shock that washed across his face. 'That's right, she is pregnant and she is barely eating enough to keep herself alive, never mind a baby.'

Pavel stared at Nina's wan face in disbelief. 'You mean she is having my child? How?'

This earned him another wintry stare.

'I think you know exactly how.'

'She is having my baby,' Pavel bleated, still struggling to absorb the information

'Well, she isn't going to give birth to a bloody kitten, you great oaf!' She gave him one last sideways glance, dripping with hostility. 'I will leave you two to talk. You had better take care of this precious girl. She deserves better than lying half-dead in this cramped, cold room, waiting to drop your sprog.' She swept past. 'She deserves better than *you*.'

Pavel took her reprimand on the chin and turned to Nina as the door closed. 'Why didn't you tell me?'

Nina stretched out a desperately thin arm and stroked his face. 'I feared that you would toss me aside. Men abandon women all the time, as soon as they lose their figures.' She sobbed. 'Please don't give up on me, Pavel. I beg of you. Don't desert me.'

His eyes stung. Would she see the emotion and believe it was on account of her, rather than his lost hopes?

'I will never leave you, Nina.' He rested his hand on her stomach. 'I would never have guessed. There is hardly even a bump.'

She wept again. 'Don't say that, Pavel. Please don't say that.'

He was startled by the force of her reaction.

'What's wrong?'

Her features were taut with misery.

'Nadezhda's right, I don't eat enough to sustain the child,' she told him. 'What if he is harmed somehow?'

Pavel assumed that Nadezhda was the woman who had been insulting him for the last five minutes.

'The baby could be a girl,' he reminded her.

'Oh Pavel,' Nina said, her voice shaking, 'so many babies are stillborn.'

'I will make sure you are well fed, even if I have to steal to do it, even if I have to kill to keep you alive.'

Nina threw her arms around his neck and clung on. 'Don't say that, my love. Please don't talk this way. You are good, Pavel. You are gentle. So many men become monsters in bad times. This war is driving people crazy. Promise me that will never happen to you.'

'Of course it won't,' Pavel told her. 'It's just talk. You know me. It's a way of getting things off my chest.' He glanced at the door. 'That bitter old crone – Nadezhda, how do you know her?'

'Don't talk about her like that,' Nina begged. 'She has been so good to me. Do you remember the girls who share with me? They're twins. Nadezhda is their mother.'

Pavel digested the information. 'Can she take care of you, get you better I mean?'

'I don't think so,' Nina told him. 'She works long hours in the mill. She can barely keep herself. Pavel, I'm scared. What if I lose our baby? I think I would kill myself.'

Seeing the way her body shook with bitter sobs, he wrapped his arms around her. He could feel her ribs. How could he not have realised how thin and frail she was, how fragile her health? He let her weep until she was exhausted and fell back on the mattress. To his surprise, she slipped into a fitful slumber, and he watched her as she slept. Even now, when he gazed down at the mother of his unborn child, it was Raisa's face he imagined, Raisa's body he craved. He would have torn out his own heart if he could.

'What's wrong with me?'

His voice echoed in the mean, dingy room. He hung his head and tried to banish Raisa from his thoughts. Presently, Nadezhda returned and seemed to approve of the effect he had had on Nina.

'She needs to sleep,' she told him. 'Even more, she needs some decent food inside her.'

'I will get it,' he told her. 'Just give me a list of what she needs and I'll find a way.'

That drew a look of scepticism and distrust.

'Is something wrong?' he asked.

'Oh, there's quite a lot that's wrong,' came the answer. 'There's this bloody war. Then there are you Bolsheviks, waiting like vultures to exploit it.'

'We're trying to stop the war,' Pavel answered.

'You're trying to stop one war,' Nadezhda told him, 'but you're stirring up a different one. I've heard what your rabble-rousers say. They want class war, insurrection, world bloody revolution. How's that going to give us peace? Tell me that.'

'Without an international revolution, backward Russia is lost. You have to fight to take the weapons out of the hands of the capitalist reactionaries…'

'Oh, keep your slogans for your meetings,' Nadezhda interrupted. 'You're no better than bloody Kerensky. You're warmongers, the whole bloody lot of you. You want different wars, different victims, but you're all the same. It's the women who have to pick up the pieces.'

Pavel felt as if he had been transported into a different world from the certainties he shared with his comrades. 'All the same! How can you say that?'

Nadezhda's voice was hard as steel. 'Because it's bloody true! I know you Bolsheviks. I work with enough of you people. The poor mug at the factory bench thinks she is going to get what you promise: land, peace and bread. Well, fuck you, you lying bastard. You're going to unleash anarchy and it is the working people who will suffer.'

'That's complete nonsense!' Pavel objected. 'I told you. When we take power, we will end all these imperialist wars.'

'By calling for world revolution? How does that work? Do you think the generals will stand idly by while you try to create your socialist paradise, these capitalists you hate so much? Bollocks! There's going to be a civil war, brother against brother. The whole of Russia is going to run with blood. So you can stick your revolution.'

Pavel was shocked. 'What's your solution? Which party do you support?'

Silence fell between them. When Nadezhda replied, her voice was softer, defeated.

'I don't have solutions. I am just an ordinary woman, trying to survive. The Tsar was a dog. Kornilov is a dog, Kerensky too. Yes, and your beloved Lenin. He's a dog too.'

'So you don't trust anyone?'

'No, not one. I trust in God.'

Pavel opened his mouth to argue, but he saw the sadness in Nadezhda's eyes. He would let her have her faith. Nadezhda seemed to understand his decision. She rested a hand on his arm.

'You get some food inside that poor girl and maybe I will have a different opinion about you.'

'I will do it. I told you. You have to believe me, I didn't know!'

'Well, you bloody well should have done. If you cared for her one iota, you would have picked up the signs.'

She saw his face twitch.

'That's right, you neglected her, didn't you? You know it's true. You're a user, Pavel Sergeyevich. I know your type.'

'You sound bitter,' he retorted. 'Maybe you are just transferring your own bad experiences onto Nina. Not all men walk away.'

'We'll see,' Nadezhda said, eyes blazing. 'You said you would get her some decent nourishment. Do it.'

Then she was gone, slamming the door behind her.

Two hours later, Nina was sitting up in bed, eating borscht and a large chunk of black bread. Pavel's speedy actions had even mollified Nadezhda.

'Where did it come from?' Nina asked.

'I know people,' Pavel told her.

'People who can get you scarce food at the drop of a hat,' Nadezhda grunted. 'They've got to be political.'

For the first time, Pavel felt ready to confront Nadezhda's constant sniping.

'Thank you for all you have done to help my fiancée,' Pavel said. 'Now I would like you to go.'

'Fiancé!' Nina cried. 'Do you really mean it?'

'This child is my responsibility,' Pavel told her. For as long as I live, I promise to be as good a father as it is in my power to be. I will never let you down, either of you.'

'So you love me that much?' Nina cried, pressing her knuckles to her mouth. 'Oh, my dear love.'

As she sobbed against him, all her hope and grief and hunger pouring out, Pavel folded her in an embrace, stifling grateful words that shamed him to his core.

'When will we be married?' Nina asked, slipping away from him.

'We will do this as soon as we possibly can,' Pavel told her. 'My good friend and comrade Kolya says the times are changing. Man and woman will be truly emancipated.' He saw the flicker of doubt in Nina's eyes, but ploughed on. 'Our marriage will be a union of equals. I will not be a bully to rule over you.'

'There are so many new ideas,' Nina told him. 'All this talk of revolution and freedom, it makes me dizzy.'

Pavel clasped her hands in his.

'My feelings are the same as yours,' he said. 'I am learning so much from Kolya.'

The way Pavel talked about his friend brought a jealous glint to Nina's eye. She blinked it away. 'My dearest Pavel, my love, you have made me so happy.'

'I have arranged for you to receive all the support you need during the pregnancy,' he told her. 'I can't be with you every moment as I would wish, but you will never be alone and you will never be neglected. The future is ours. In our new Russia, life will be good.'

'Don't fill me with false hope,' Nina said, her eyes pleading. 'I know you have great things to do, Pavel. I support you in everything you seek to achieve. You are my comrade, my love…now my husband to be. Bring down the exploiters and oppressors, Pavel Sergeyevich. Do what you must to usher in this new world for our child.'

'I will,' Pavel told her, his voice raw with emotion. 'Our baby will grow and thrive in a better, brighter world. I promise, he will never go without.'

He kissed her gently and walked to the door, ushering Nadezhda back into the room.

'You take care of her,' he told her, expecting another broadside.

Nadezhda met his gaze unflinchingly. 'You too, Comrade soldier. I will be holding you to account, believe me.'

Once out in the open air, Pavel lit a cigarette and watched the moving storm clouds through a haze of acrid smoke. What he saw was a city nailed to the crucifix of hunger, war and neglect. The air was colder now, damp and miserable. Grass grew between the cobblestones. The sky was heavy with rain. It was a place of potholes, dirt and clinging mud. Factory after factory, barracks after barracks, soviet after soviet declared for revolution, but the insurrection never came. Like a menacing dog on the other side of the door, it growled and barked, scratched and threw itself at the obstacle, but never quite broke through, never bit. Lenin fretted and wrote and argued, at odds with many in his own party leadership, who were demanding that they take the power. Pavel felt like sobbing with impotence.

'So why does it never happen?'

Those foot-draggers Zinoviev and Kamenev were making mischief again. He had their statement in his pocket. To launch an insurrection would 'put at stake not only the fate of our party, but also the fate of the Russian and international revolution.'

'The lousy fuckers!' Pavel barked, earning a curious look from a passing adolescent.

Frustrations boiled inside him. Where was this new world when even Central Committee members could speak out openly against the revolution? They broke party discipline and still they were not expelled.

Where was happiness when there was this child growing inside Nina's belly, tying him into a loveless marriage for the rest of his life? Oh, the party was promising to make divorce legal and easy, but how could he walk away from Nina after everything she had said to him and everything he had promised to her?

'My child, my unborn child.'

He brushed away a tear of despair. Unsteady legs carried him to the tram stop. He didn't even remember climbing aboard or fumbling for the fare. The tram rocked. Bodies pressed in on him. He was a sleepwalker, hemmed in by the suffering, impatient citizens of red Petrograd. He tried to clear his head. He examined the faces around him. They were tired. But when he reached the barracks, his mind was still a confusing maelstrom of conflicting emotions. He elbowed his way through the crush, earning a few protests, one in particular from a bearded man with pockmarked skin.

'Fuck you!' Pavel snarled, the look in his eyes warning the protestor not to say another word.

He found Mikhail perched on the edge of his bed, reading *Novaya Zhizn*.

'What's the matter with you?' Mikhail asked, the moment he saw Pavel's glowering expression.

It was as if a dam burst. Pavel pressed his fists against his temples.

'It's Nina. She's pregnant.'

'And the child is yours?'

Pavel glared, eyes black with fury. 'Of course it's mine. What? You think she's some common slut. She loves me. The poor girl loves me and I am the lowest creature on Earth. I am fathering a child and I love another woman.'

Mikhail tossed the newspaper at him. 'This isn't going to improve your mood.'

Pavel caught it, straightened the pages and cursed loudly. 'They write in a Menshevik rag! Jesus Christ, it was bad enough when they argued this shite in party organs, but this, this is treachery.'

He poured all the rage he felt into this denunciation of the comrade-traitors.

'Why can't we just get this bloody insurrection over and done with? Is this how we make a revolution, with votes and divisions? I didn't join a debating society! It is an armed action by the people!'

'You're shouting, Pavel.'

'Of course I am fucking shouting. We've got cretins like Kamenev wanting to maintain Kerensky and the bourgeoisie in power. He should be thrown out of the party. He should be shot. Zinoviev too.'

'They say Stalin backs them on the quiet.'

'They should deal with that stupid Georgian shit too!'

'So you want to shoot half the Central Committee?'

'If that is what it takes to summon the masses to action, why not?'

Mikhail sighed wearily. 'Pavel, you must calm yourself.'

His attempt at settling Pavel was received like petrol on a flame.

'Calm myself! How am I meant to be calm when we've got some of our own leaders siding with the enemy and boasting about it in another party's press?'

'Lenin is fighting a struggle against the vacillators. My brother, this is party democracy. We argue things out.'

'Well, I wish we would stop arguing and start acting,' Pavel yelled. 'This whole thing makes my senses spin.'

He drove his fist into the frame of the bed then cursed, hopping away to nurse his throbbing knuckles.

'Better now?' Mikhail asked

'I nearly broke my fucking hand!'

Pavel finally burst into self-mocking laughter, his fist still throbbing. 'I look stupid, don't I?'

'You look quite ridiculous. *Have* you done any damage to your hand?'

Pavel flexed his fingers. The momentary smile drained away.

'I'm a clown, Mikhail, a pathetic, fucking clown.'

'You're hurt, my friend. You are in despair about Nina and the child. Do you know what you should do? Get yourself a bottle of Vodka and drink yourself stupid.'

Pavel fell back on his bunk and stared up at the ceiling.

'Drink doesn't do me any good. I just turn mawkish.' He put his hands behind his head. 'Forget it. I'll find another way to handle my shit life.'

Mikhail walked from the room, shaking his head. 'Think carefully about what you just said, Pavel Sergeyevich. What kind of man discovers that a woman who loves him is giving him a child and then bemoans his lot with such bitterness? You're my friend, Pavel, but you really are talking bollocks. You should count your blessings rather than cursing the world.'

The door slammed and Pavel stared at the peeling woodwork for the longest time. His head told him that Mikhail was right.

But his heart was torn in two.

Raisa

This was the time.

Raisa was at home, elbows on the windowsill, chin cupped in her hands. This was the time all right. She watched the autumn leaves as they drifted to the ground the way wild geese did when they settled on the surface of a lake. Her life had become a whirlwind of meetings. She had even drilled with the Red Guards, one of the few women present, usually as a medic, but sometimes under arms. She had shouldered a facsimile rifle made of tubes from the steelworks, in expectation of being handed the real thing. As was to be expected in a Russia that was still in many ways a masculine world, it was the men who were the first to lay their hands on working firearms.

Part of her was tingling with the thrill of the meetings and the drilling. Her senses were fairly spinning with all the new words and ideas that had come buzzing at her like a swarm of hornets. She knew the arguments for restraint coming from Kamenev and Zinoviev. She knew the counter arguments, demanding action, from Lenin, from Trotsky, from Latsis and the Vyborg, from the factory committees, the Red Guards and the Kronstadt base. This was the time for revolution. If the Bolsheviks didn't strike soon, so Svetlana said, the city would descend into violent anarchy. There had been so many terrible stories: a woman having her throat slit in a robbery, a father and his three young children murdered in their home. Either the revolution went forward, or the Neva would be full of grey carcasses and the lampposts would be acting as gibbets.

How could she, a Bolshevik, be anything other than full of joy? The party stood on the very brink of power. A new world was taking shape before her very eyes. Belonging to a great cause had given her back her dignity and self-belief. She was not the despised little whore on a filthy, soiled mattress any more. She was not a piece of meat to be used and cast aside. She was a comrade in her own right, equal to any other comrade, a fighter, a human being. Because of all this, surely she should be content.

And yet.

And yet….

There was a hole in her life and it was Elena. Not so very long ago, it was as if they were inseparable. Raisa had even thought about inviting Elena to move into the boarding house. With Mrs Kuznetsova gone, there would be nobody to disapprove of their togetherness, nobody to spy on them or expose them. It had only been a few days, but it felt as if Elena had moved on, leaving Raisa behind. She had her own meetings, her own circle of party comrades, her own commitments. Suddenly, there was no time for love. Raisa watched the leaves, auburn, brown and gold swirling across her view of the river and she sighed. For a moment, she was about to tell herself that she would give up the revolution itself to have Elena here with her. She was about to brush her hair and undress ready for bed when she heard a dull scrape downstairs in the hall.

Raisa's body burned with fright. She raced to the drawer where she kept the gun, her bare feet flying over the carpet. How did they get in? She didn't hear the tell-tale sounds she had feared so long, the splintering of the door frame or the smashing of a window, but they were inside, intruders, cut-throats, maybe even the two gangsters Pavel released. Raisa groaned inwardly. Why hadn't they finished those two off on the spot? Mercy could cost her life. Pavel had even thought about executing them. Why didn't he? She had the butt of the pistol firmly gripped in her hand as she edged to the door. She rested her face against the surface, listening intently. There it was again, movement downstairs. You little fool, she thought, you forgot to bolt the door. She knew she must act. Taking a deep breath, she raced to the top of the stairs, pointing the barrel of the gun at the intruder.

Then her whole body relaxed. 'Elena!'

'Who did you think it was?' Elena fairly bounced up the stairs, seizing Raisa in a bear hug. 'I have missed you so much.'

Then she pulled back and looked at Raisa with a twinkle in her eye. 'Who did you think was coming in?'

'Criminals,' Raisa answered honestly. 'Maybe even Yozhin's thugs.'

'Were you afraid?'

'Oh, desperately so. My heart was almost out of my chest.'

Elena rested a hand on Raisa's breast and nodded. 'Oh yes, your heart is pounding.'

'It is now,' Raisa said, her voice softer.

'Are you sure you weren't expecting somebody?' Elena teased. 'Maybe I have a rival in love.'

Raisa reacted earnestly.

'I would never be unfaithful to you!' she cried.

Finally, Elena kissed her passionately on the lips. 'Of course you wouldn't, you little goose. I'm taking a rise out of you.'

Raisa was wary for a moment then she returned the kiss. 'I have missed you.'

'Oh, I've missed you too,' Elena said. 'Since I met you, I hate sleeping alone. I can't wait to slip between clean sheets. For the last few days I have been sleeping sitting up in chairs, even on the floor. I spend half my time at the Smolny.' She pulled Raisa into her room and sat her on the edge of the bed. 'Guess who I saw speak today?'

Raisa waited patiently. She didn't like guessing games.

'Only Trotsky!' Elena cried. 'He addressed the crowd with such passion. His voice had wings. Before him, the people raised their arms like this.'

She demonstrated, her face lit with something like ecstasy.

'Why?' Raisa asked.

'They were hailing Trotsky. They were summoning the revolution. Oh, it was glorious.'

'Did you stay to hear him?' Raisa asked, curious about the great Trotsky, second only to Lenin in importance.

'Of course I stayed,' Elena answered, seemingly astonished that Raisa could have asked such an idiotic question. 'Let this vote be your oath,' he said.'

'Oath?'

'Oh, I forgot that bit. They were promising to fight for the workers and peasants to the last drop of their blood, to sacrifice themselves for the Soviet and fight for peace, bread and land. It was so exciting.' She pulled the ribbon from her hair and let it fall loose. 'What about you? Have you got any news?'

Raisa failed to mention Pavel's declaration of love. Instead, she stumbled through a description of open-air meetings and her struggle to march in time with the men.

'It's their long stride, you see,' Raisa said. 'I have such little legs.'

Elena slid her hands under Raisa's skirt. 'You have beautiful legs.

Feeling her lover's cold hands chill her calves, knees, thighs, Raisa shuddered, a little with cold, mainly with desire. She felt a sharp lurch in the bottom of her stomach, an unstoppable throb of pleasure.

'Do you know what I'm going to do to you?' Elena asked, face lit with the first beams of moonlight.

Raisa shook her head, eyes full of wonder at Elena's beauty.

'Shall I show you?'

Raisa nodded and Elena rolled up her skirt until she was entirely exposed below the waist. She stared up at the ceiling while Elena planted kisses on the insides of her thighs. At last, Raisa gave a cry of pleasure and her body shuddered. Without any self-consciousness, Elena peeled off her clothes and left them in a pile on the floor. She slid into bed and rolled onto her back.

'Now it's my turn.'

'Why did you stay away so long,' Raisa asked in the grey light of morning. 'I feared there was someone else.'

'It was only a few days,' Elena said, lying on her side and propping herself up on one elbow. 'We have both been so busy. Did you miss me that much?'

'More than you can ever imagine!' Raisa cried. 'You are my life.'

Elena saw the tears glistening on Raisa's cheeks. 'Hey, hey. What is all this? Did you really think I had found someone new?'

'Don't ever say that!' Raisa cried. 'I could not bear it.' A cloud came across her face. 'Am I wrong to want only you?'

Elena's face was a question. Raisa answered it: 'There is all this talk about free love, sleeping with somebody being as simple as drinking from a glass of water.'

Elena snorted. 'There are plenty of men who like the idea of free love. They think they will be like children in a sweet shop. It means they can have more women.' Her gaze rested on Raisa's. 'You must read Comrade Kollontai. Woman must be freed from economic necessity to make her own choices.' She smiled. 'And I am free to love you to bits.'

'So we can always be together?'

Elena slapped her playfully on the haunch. 'Well, you've no need to worry on that score. I would never look at another woman.' She grinned. 'Well, I might look. Do you want to hear some gossip? Pavel has only gone and got Nina pregnant.'

She reached for the glass of water on the bedside table and sat up, sipping it.

'I wonder if this is the glass of water everyone's talking about, the vessel of free love?'

Raisa squatted beside her.

'Forget the glass and tell me about Pavel and Nina. I didn't think he was that serious about her.'

'I don't think he is,' Elena said. 'The poor little cow thinks he is in love with her. I tell you, he will clear off and leave her in the lurch the first chance he gets.'

Raisa shook her head. 'No, I don't think so. He is an honourable man.'

Elena examined her lover's features. 'What's this? I thought you hated men. Got a soft spot for Pavel, have you? Now, I'm jealous.'

She yawned, proof that she wasn't the least bit envious.

'You have no need to be,' Raisa told her. 'I don't have those kinds of feelings for him. I don't for any men.'

Elena squeezed Raisa's shoulder. 'I should hope not. So what kind of feelings do you have?'

'He is like a big brother,' Raisa said. 'He is protective towards me. I feel safe with him.'

'That's good,' Elena said. 'We need friends we can trust.' She became serious. 'The revolution is only days away.'

'I thought you would be happy,' Raisa said.

'I am. It's just...'

'Yes?'

'What if we lose?'

'How can we?' Raisa asked. 'You said yourself, Kerensky's power ebbs away by the day.'

'There are still the generals,' Elena reminded her. 'Do you know what happened to the losing side in the Paris Commune?'

Raisa had heard the stories, but she let Elena tell the tale.

'When the barricades fell, the victors started shooting the workers. They just put them up against a wall and gunned them down. The slaughter was indiscriminate. Bodies soon filled the parks.'

Raisa wrapped her hand round Elena's.

'They bayoneted the women in the street. Thirty thousand revolutionaries died in the bloodbath. I could not bear to see you die.'

'Nor I you,' Raisa cried. 'Surely you don't think it could happen here.'

'Of course not,' Elena answered, 'but victory is never guaranteed in advance. I can't sleep for thinking about it. I swear, this whole thing is like a runaway locomotive. Sometimes I think I can't stand it anymore.'

Raisa could barely believe that it was her reassuring the bold, courageous Elena.

'I didn't know you had doubts like this.'

Elena leaned her head against Raisa's shoulder. 'Anyone who doesn't have doubts is a fool. We are so close to heaven and so close to hell. How do you explain that?'

'I can't,' Raisa said. 'I just try to live for each new day.' She hesitated before putting her question. 'You don't really think the revolution could fail, do you?'

'Ignore me. I was just being stupid. There is nobody left to defend Kerensky. The railwaymen dealt with Kornilov and the rest. As for Kerensky, Svetlana says it will be like knocking over a snowman.'

Elena's words were brave, but her voice shook as she delivered them.

'Will you come with me this evening?' Elena asked. 'There is an important meeting in the Vyborg.'

Raisa realised that she was being allowed at last into Elena's circle. Until that moment, she had been sent on errands, like a child. At last, she would truly be trusted.

They walked through slushy snow to the meeting. Large flakes swirled against ebony night.

'Is this it?' Raisa asked.

Elena didn't answer. Instead, she rapped on the door to be admitted. The debates were already underway, echoing similar ones in the Central Committee. Raisa recognised Anishin's gruff delivery before she made him out in the fog of tobacco smoke.

'The risk is too great,' he argued. 'I am with Comrade Kamenev and Comrade Zinoviev. A premature insurrection would risk the very revolution itself.'

There were jeers and catcalls.

'If we rush into action, we may regret it. We must patiently explain that…'

Another familiar voice cut him off. It was Kolya.

'Rush!' His voice dripped with contempt. 'Rush! Do I hear you right? We have dithered so long, a sense of depression is spreading among the masses. Kamenev threatens resignation. Stalin asks him to retract. Do none of them have the balls to act?'

This produced uproar.

'We must transfer power immediately to the Soviets and establish a government of the workers and poor peasants. Surely you have heard Comrade Lenin's arguments by now. Not only is the time right for revolution, it is overripe. Anyone who stands in the way…' He looked straight at Anishin. '…is a traitor.'

Anishin was almost beside himself with fury.

'Withdraw that slur,' he yelled.

'I demand that the vote be put,' Kolya bawled.

Raisa stared at the confrontation. There had been a time when Kolya had always in Anishin's shadow. Now the apprentice was taking on the master.

'Does anyone else have anything to say?' the chair asked. 'No? Then I...' His voice trailed off and he stared at Raisa. It was a moment before she realised that he was staring at a raised hand.

Hers.

'Do you wish to speak, Comrade...?'

He searched his memory for a name.

'I am Comrade Raisa.'

The chair looked around. There was some laughter then: 'Oh, let the Comrade sister speak.'

Raisa stepped forward, feeling Elena's astonished gaze on her back.

'I am a new comrade,' she began haltingly. 'I don't work in the Putilov. I have not served at the Front. I...'

She glanced back at Elena and received a smile of reassurance.

'I can't quote Marx and Engels. I don't know what Comrade Lenin said in his letters. But I do know this: I have been treated with contempt in my life. I have been told I am nothing, just a piece of dirt.' She remembered the look on Andrey's face that night in his rooms. 'I have seen the look of hatred in the eyes of the bourgeoisie. I am sick of lying in the mud while our rulers wipe their feet on us.'

There was a murmur of agreement.

'Comrades, the revolution is in danger. Every day we delay we encourage the counter-revolutionaries. If we don't go forward, we will go backwards and they will smash us to smithereens.' Her eyes flashed. 'It is there for the taking. The enemy is weak. You know it. I know it. But if we continue to hesitate, they will destroy us. I refuse to return to slavery. I will not go back to the shit life I led before February.'

This earned throaty cheers. Emboldened, Raisa yelled the rest of her impromptu speech.

'Most of you will think I am just a bit of a girl, a child, but I have seen things most of you can never imagine. I have suffered. I am a mere woman in the eyes of many of you, but I will fight to the death and that means I've got more balls than any of you cowardly bastards arguing that we should wait.'

There was laughter and cheering.

'So for fuck's sake, let's do it. Let's get on with this revolution.'

As she stumbled back to stand besides Elena, Raisa caught Kolya's eye. The look she saw there told her she had sealed the deal, at least in this part of the Vyborg.' The meeting would support the call for an immediate seizure of power. Once the congratulations and backslapping that followed Raisa's speech had subsided, Elena approached to whisper in her ear.

'I am coming back with you tonight,' she said. 'My love, we are going to make history.'

Kolya

'You're no gentleman,' Klara complained when Kolya climbed out of bed.

'I have a revolution to make,' Kolya answered, a wry smile playing on his lips. 'Everything else pales into insignificance compared to this.'

'Including me?'

Kolya lifted her chin with his fingers. 'Even you.'

Klara pouted. 'Revolution. Pah, you know what I think of you boys with your silly games?'

Kolya was already dressing. There was no time to wash. He wondered if the scent of Klara would be on his skin as he joined his comrades. He teased the curtains open and looked at the lightening dawn sky.

'Are you listening to me, Kolya?'

'Yes,' he told her. 'I'm listening. How could I do anything else when you're prattling away at me.'

She rolled onto her stomach, crossing her ankles. 'You're a mean Bolshevik. Why can't you stay with me?'

'I've told you.' He slapped her on the backside. 'The insurrection is imminent. I have things to do.'

'Am I *things to do*?' Klara asked. 'You arrive in the early hours of the morning, you take me, you leave. You are not a man. You are a beast that satisfies its appetite then creeps away without a single thought.'

'I have just explained,' Kolya told her. 'I am needed.'

'But I need you.'

'Klara, you are being tiresome.'

In truth, he was getting bored of her already. Except for their time together between the sheets, there was little about Klara that entertained him. At least Svetlana was a comrade. They could discuss politics. They shared a common purpose. All Klara did was complain and demand ever more of his time. She was a spoiled child. She also endangered what he had with Svetlana. Though he saw no future with a woman twenty years older than him, Kolya found it hard to imagine life without Svetlana. She kept his feet on the ground.

'Anyway,' he said, 'I have to go.'

Klara immediately flew at him, leaping from the bed and tugging at his sleeve. 'I won't let you go. I refuse to let any man treat me like this.'

'My dear,' Kolya said brutally, 'you really don't have a choice. You're a whore. Any man who pays you enough can treat you as he likes.'

Klara stared at him in horror. 'They pay me. It is different with you.'

'Is it?' Kolya demanded. 'What is marriage but legalised prostitution? How would we be any different?'

'Do you not believe in love?' Klara asked.

'Oh, this is rich. A whore who believes in love! You are a product, my dear, just like any other commodity in a capitalist market. Socialism will sweep away all that. It will do away with the likes of you.'

'How can you be so cruel?'

Kolya shrugged. He was telling the unvarnished truth. 'To be brutally honest, Klara, I am tiring of you and your little tantrums. This isn't love.' He saw the shock in her face. 'Don't be here when I get back.'

She tried to claw at his face, but he hurled her backwards. Her calves thumped against the side of the bed and she tumbled onto the mattress where she lay sobbing.

'I thought we had something.'

'We screwed,' Kolya retorted. 'That is all we did.'

He didn't even look back, striding to the door, rushing downstairs and out of the door to his car. He drove towards the Vyborg and stopped at a street corner where a group of Red Guards was waiting.

'You're late, Comrade,' one of them complained.

Kolya shrugged. 'Are you sure you weren't early?'

'They say Kerensky is threatening an offensive,' the complainant informed Kolya.

'Let him come,' Kolya said. 'We will disperse his forces just as we dispersed the Kornilovites. Kornilov was the real thing. Kerensky is nothing but a screaming actor.'

They drove through streets filling with people. Armed soldiers and sailors were drilling or standing around bonfires. Working class Petrograd was waiting for something to happen. The skirmishes of the last few hours had left the smell of cordite everywhere, giving the streets an air of tension.

'Who's been shooting?' Kolya asked.

'Nobody knows.'

They passed roadblocks where men saluted from armoured cars. They picked up reports, discussed, argued. A picture began to form of the accelerating seizure of power. The Marinsky Palace was surrounded. The Central Telegraph Office was occupied, the Post Office too. Reports of other key facilities under revolutionary control came in as they stood smoking, waiting for news. The word was that Trotsky had issued an order. This was not insurrection. It was self-defence.

'Sure,' Kolya said, winking at the men under his command. 'Defence, that's what it is.'

The Red Guards were still laughing when more news came in.

'They are raising the bridges. They're trying to cut the city in half.'

Kolya rushed to the riverside and saw the bridges yawning open, stopping workers from the Vyborg side crossing to the heart of red Piter.

'I don't like this,' Kolya grumbled. 'It happened during the July days too.'

'These are not the July days,' somebody said. 'This time, we are not going back.'

Kolya turned. Pavel and Mikhail were approaching.

'Do you have any news?' Kolya demanded.

'All the shops are closing. The trams have stopped. It looks like the counter-revolutionaries are trying to take the initiative.'

'Bollocks to that,' Kolya said. 'The bridges are ours. Whoever controls the routes across the river controls the city. Come with me.'

By the time they reached the Liteiny Bridge, they could see that the working people were ahead of them, rushing to confront the cadets. The crowd was loud and angry. Kolya strode to the head of the Red Guards

'I call on you to surrender,' he told the artillery cadets. 'If there is any bloodshed, you will be held responsible.'

That ended any resistance. Like so much of the old order, the cadets didn't have any stomach for a fight.

'Lower the bridges,' Kolya commanded.

Before long, the pulleys started to groan into motion. Pavel watched with satisfaction and turned to Kolya.

'Would you have shot them?'

Kolya ran his fingers through his hair, still thinking of Klara and her idiotic tantrums. 'Too fucking right. This is revolution, not a chess game.'

He looked at the gathering dusk. 'Put men all along the bridge. We hold it, no matter what. What's happening elsewhere?'

'The Troitsky Bridge is open, so two out of four.'

Kolya nodded and leaned on the railings, overlooking the dark waters. 'Fuck knows how we lost control of two bridges, but two will do.'

Everybody was tense. There were all kinds of rumours. The Kerensky advance was proceeding. The restaurants and cinemas on the Nevsky Prospect were open as if nothing was happening. The insurrection was under the command of the Military Revolutionary Committee. Kolya clapped Pavel on the shoulder.

'It's begun.'

'No sleep tonight then,' Pavel said.

Kolya nodded grimly, determined not to betray any anxiety, any emotion at all. 'None.'

It was in the early hours of the morning that Mikhail roused Kolya and Pavel from a fitful nap. 'You need to see this,' he said urgently.

They followed him past wary machine-gunners, squatting soldiers and sailors, small groups of workers in black tunics and round hats.

'What is it?' said Kolya.

A steel leviathan was making its way down the river. Kolya took in the masts, the three great funnels, the raised guns, the searchlight beams swinging through the darkness. 'Whose side are they on?' he murmured.

'For all our sakes,' Mikhail said, 'let's hope it's ours.'

'The sailors won't let us down,' said Pavel, as they watched the cruiser's steady progress. 'It's going to anchor by the Nikolaevsky Bridge,' he said. 'Let's get down there in case the reactionaries try to retake it.'

Kolya found himself falling in behind Pavel. Much as they were meant to be comrades and friends, he couldn't help resenting the soldier's presence. So many times, Kolya had assumed leadership and so many times, Pavel had acted when his efforts fell short. Fine, Pavel seemed to have no ambition to subvert his authority, Kolya mused, but he did it without thinking. By the time they reached the Nikolaevsky Bridge, hundreds of sailors and Red Guards were already there. Kerensky's shock troops hovered in the distance, their numbers drifting away. The insurrection continued to advance. The bridge's defenders kept watch, gazing down the road in case there was an attempt to take it, then out at the battleship.

'It's not doing much,' Pavel observed. 'Do you think it's just for show, you know, a display of strength?'

As if to answer his question, the guns opened up. Soon, the cannons of the Peter and Paul Fortress were joining the barrage on the Winter Palace. The ground under their feet shook.

'I'll tell you what that is,' Kolya said. 'It's the death knell of the old order.'

They listened to the scream of the shells and watched the flash as they arced through the gloom.

Beside him, Mikhail was smiling with satisfaction. 'And bugger-all resistance.'

Pavel nursed his weapon. 'Yes, nobody wants to save the government. It's all a bit disappointing really.'

'Would you rather have bloodshed?' Kolya asked.

Pavel grinned. 'No, this suits me down to the ground.'

A Red Guard arrived on a bicycle and handed Kolya a leaflet.

'You won't be disappointed anymore, when you've read this,' he said.

'Well,' said Pavel, 'share it, will you?'

Kolya smiled. 'Citizens!''

'Comrades would be better,' Pavel interrupted.

'Shut up and let him read,' Mikhail grumbled.

Kolya's words were punctuated by more firing from the Aurora.

''The Provisional Government is deposed. State power has passed into the hands of the organ of the Petrograd Soviet of Workers' and Soldiers' Deputies.''

'Well, fuck me, if we haven't made a revolution,' Pavel said, face beaming, 'and we didn't even notice it happen.'

Kolya slipped his rifle from his shoulder and embraced each of his comrades in turn. 'This is it,' he said, tears in his eyes. 'The end of prehistory and the beginning of the time of man.'

Judging by the look on the other men's faces, this little speech didn't mean much to them. Presently, he was overshadowed by an old rival. 'Comrade Anishin,' Kolya said, adopting a serious tone. 'I see the revolution went ahead after all.'

Anishin scowled at the reminder of his support for caution. 'When did I ever oppose the revolution? I questioned its timing and preparation, that's all. I have been a revolutionary since the age of fifteen. I thought you would have been at the Congress of Soviets.'

'I held my position here,' Kolya answered.

Anishin scratched his stomach. 'I tell you, I could sleep for a week, but it will have to wait. I am on my way back there now.'

Kolya watched him go, his excitement at the victorious revolution fading.

'It looks like we might have been in the wrong place,' Pavel said. 'Comrade Anishin seems to have been nearer the action than we were.'

'We did our job,' Kolya said. 'We held the bridge.'

'Aren't you just a bit jealous?' Pavel said. 'I mean, that's history being made,'

'We have all made history today,' Kolya reminded him.

Here was the blue and gold cupola of the Smolny Institute. Kolya was dog-tired after his vigil at the Neva quayside, but he had to be at the Second Congress of the Soviets even if it was only to say he had been there, a witness to the birth of a new world. He entered the grey, three-storey building, flanked by Pavel and Mikhail. They could hear the roars of acclamation from the far end of the corridor. The sound echoed and reverberated. It reminded him of a train entering a tunnel. Over a sign that read Teacher's Room, somebody had taped *S-D-Bolsheviki*. Rain was drumming on the windows and there were muddy footprints everywhere. The Assembly Hall was heaving with people in their shabby clothes. He looked around, trying to spot people he knew. Svetlana ought to be there.

Pavel nudged him and said, 'Trotsky's speaking!'

Sure enough, the eagle-faced man was roaring his address with his customary theatrics and conviction: 'A rising of the masses of the people requires no justification. What has happened is an insurrection and not a conspiracy.'

His voice echoed around the hall. *A victorious insurrection... The backing of the people... What use did the revolution have with compromisers?...* Kolya's eyes gleamed with adulation. Yes, this is what he wanted. Absolute conviction. The purity of revolution. Trotsky did not disappoint. He was a true man of action.

'A compromise is supposed to be made, as between two equal sides, by the millions of workers and peasants represented in this congress.' his next words were lost in the roar of approval. '...To those who have left and to those who have told us to do this we must say: you are miserable bankrupts, your role is played out. Go where you ought to go, into the dustbin of history.'

Pavel met Kolya's eye and rocked with laughter. 'Fuck me, that's telling them.'

The Menshevik Martov rose and retorted indignantly. 'Then we'll leave.'

It was hard to see, but there was some jostling as Martov departed, followed by some of his comrades. Then there was more applause.

'What's that?' Kolya demanded.

Mikhail conveyed the information from somebody to his left. 'The Left SRs have stayed in the hall. We have allies.'

The proceedings continued. The speakers came and went. Lunacharsky had taken the stage, spoken and returned to his seat. Arguments have been breaking out on the floor. Now Kamenev was on his feet.

'The leaders of the counter-revolution, ensconced in the Winter Palace, have been seized by the revolutionary garrison.'

Pavel and Mikhail wrapped their arms round one another and did a ridiculous dance. Kolya stood stiffly, buffeted by the joyous tumult. A government of the working people was about to take shape. A document would be presented to the Congress. The decisive moment was still to come. A rumour travelled around the hall.

'What is it?'

'Lenin.'

The crowd witnessed a different kind of speech to Trotsky's. There was no waving of arms. There was little drama in his gestures, his facial expression or the tenor of his voice. His hands rested on the rostrum before him. Finally, in the wake of announcements about land, peace and workers' control of production he leaned forward. 'We will proceed to construct the Socialist order.'

The applause that followed was elemental, like a force of nature. When it began to subside, Kolya remained still, absorbing this moment. It vindicated his entire existence. True human history began here.

'We did it,' Pavel said, with tears in his eyes. 'After all the pissing about. We did it.'

When they eventually filed out into the hesitant, bleary dawn, Pavel shook both men's hands and set off down the street under a canopy of grey cloud.

'Where are you going?'

Pavel kept walking. 'To see Nina. She needs to know what I have witnessed here today.'

Mikhail was about to say farewell when a smile lit his face.

'It's a good feeling, isn't it?' Kolya said, misreading his expression.

'That's not why I'm smiling, comrade Kolya,' Mikhail told him 'You've got a visitor.'

Kolya was mystified until he felt the press of a familiar body against his back. Svetlana's arms wrapped round his shoulders.

'Were you in the hall?' she asked.

'Of course.'

'Wasn't it wonderful?'

'It was beautiful,' Kolya answered, turning to face her.

Mikhail shoved his hands in his pockets and sauntered away. 'I'll leave you two lovebirds to it.'

'We've made a revolution,' Svetlana said. 'Now let's make love...if you've still got the energy.'

Kolya grinned. 'Just the thing to help me sleep.'

Raisa

While Kolya was occupied securing the bridge, Raisa had found herself at the eye of the storm. There had been times recently when she felt like a fallen leaf, swirling in a great maelstrom. Things happened to her. History roared around her. The storm was elemental, beyond her control. Now, still fearful, still unsure, she fully understood its raging power. She was truly, finally part of it.

'You won't leave me on my own, will you?' she pleaded, clutching Elena's sleeve in the crush.

She felt like a child again, afraid of being lost in some great crowd. Her heart thudded at each crackle of gunfire. Her terror was not of losing Elena in this moment, but of losing her for all time. For all that, she would not hang back. She was no longer a mere witness to revolution. She possessed it and it possessed her. For good or ill, it was hers, she would see it through.

The sky was black, the throng dense and grey as it surged along the street. Raisa wondered if they all remembered another day, twelve years earlier, when another crowd was advancing on the Winter Palace, and was gunned down in cold blood. She couldn't be the only one who was afraid, but somehow fear had stopped numbing her. It no longer deterred action. The multitude had its own momentum. Were there leaders? If so, it was hard to make them out or know what they wanted. Elena said the Bolshevik Antonov was in charge, but they hadn't seen him. Somebody did mount a makeshift podium and yell an instruction, but nobody in this part of the multitude could make it out. Instead, they allowed themselves to be channelled towards the palace.

'Be brave,' Elena told her. 'All my doubts are gone now. This is our time.'

They were moving past the posts of the soldiers and Red Guards. Bonfires lit faces and made them garish and alien. Raisa found herself looking for Pavel, but he wasn't among the men. Why would he be? Petrograd was a great city and men like him must be needed at many strategic points. Near the Kazan Cathedral, shouts went up. The occupants of the Winter Palace were taunting them. No, somebody countered, they wanted the crowd to give them an excuse to surrender. Maybe it was a trap.

'Shouldn't there be more of us?' she whispered to Elena.

She looked at the crowd. How many were there, ten thousand, fifteen thousand? There had been much bigger demonstrations. Was this all it took to make a revolution?

'All proletarian Petrograd supports this moment,' Elena answered. 'We are acting on their behalf.'

Raisa splashed after her through muddy puddles into a dark court, and saw muzzle flashes. Nobody else stopped so she ploughed on, swept forward by the will of the working masses around her. Her fear didn't leave her. The gunners would cut them down like sheaves of wheat, as they had done twelve years earlier. Strangely, the firing deterred nobody, wounded nobody, killed nobody. Was it directed at anyone at all or was it celebratory gunfire, into the air? Are we winning, Raisa wondered. There were so many rumours, so many counter-claims. It was impossible to work out the truth.

'Elena, look...' She pointed out an artillery piece.

'It's one of ours,' Elena said, giving Raisa a playful pinch. 'At least, I think it is.'

'Don't tease me,' Raisa protested.

Her heart was pounding so hard she could barely breathe. There was another push, this time so powerful the torrent of people fell into a forward dash, rapid, unstoppable. Raisa was penned in so tightly she was lifted off her feet. She clawed the air, trying to cling to Elena, but it was a fruitless task. Something thumped against her shins and she started to scramble over the unseen obstacle. They were scaling a wooden barricade. Finally, she located Elena once more.

'Are the defenders firing at us?'

'Do you hear gunfire?'

She shook her head. 'It's stopped.'

'Didn't I tell you? They've got no will for the fight.'

Gunfire resumed briefly and there was talk of casualties, but nothing deterred the forward push of the crowd. What barricades they encountered were mere tokens. They came face to face with the palace's defenders, but there were no clear lines. As the Red Guards washed around the defenders, nobody could use their rifles, their grenades. Everyone was so close. Elena tore a rifle from a defender's hands. Following her example, Raisa raised her pistol and instructed another to take his hand away from the grenades hanging from his belt. Everywhere, the will of those entering the building was stronger than the will of those meant to protect it. The foremost ranks stumbled through an imposing pair of doors and spilled into a vast hall.

'This is it,' Elena said breathlessly, 'the heart of the Romanovs, the seat of the enemy's power.'

Raisa looked around. There was a time she had found even Mrs Kuznetsova's lodgings wondrous after the grim claustrophobia of Bagrov's brothel. But this! Corridors branched in every direction like the tentacles of an octopus. There were gilded portraits on the walls, chandeliers, glittering gold leaf and fine ornaments everywhere. Doors swung open to reveal yet more passageways. Staircases climbed to the upper floors, labyrinthine and confusing.

'We need a map to find our way round this place,' Elena remarked.

'You don't need a map,' one man said. 'You need deep pockets. I feel like a kid in a fucking toyshop.'

He thumbed his coat pocket open and something glinted.

'No, Comrade,' Elena told him sternly. 'You must put that back. We are revolutionaries, not thieves. This palace and everything in it is the property of the people.'

'Oh, fuck you,' he snapped. 'You might be a revolutionary. I'm here for the ride. I'm taking as much stuff as I can get my hands on.'

Raisa drew her pistol and pointed it at his knee.

'Put it back,' she said, 'or you will be walking with a limp for the rest of your life.'

The thief spat on the tiled floor and emptied his pockets. 'Women used to know their place.'

Elena laughed in his face. 'That was before we made a revolution, Citizen.'

'I'm not your citizen,' he snapped, moving away. 'I'll remember your faces, you bitches.'

'What's he doing here?' Raisa asked.

'Scum will attach itself to any movement,' growled Elena.

There was a crash, and they rushed into the next room to see that it was not just one man, but many who were looting, breaking into packing cases and chests, emptying them of their contents. There were more shouts from Bolsheviks among the people storming the palace.

'Comrades. This is wrong. You must return everything you have taken.'

But while some hesitated or returned their loot, others carried on regardless. The old authority had collapsed and the new one had yet to assert its authority. Before long, Red Guards were moving among them, trying to clear the building.

'Why are we leaving?' Elena protested. 'Where are the defensive positions? Are we falling back?'

'Falling back?' one worker scoffed. 'Most of the bastards just walked away. Nobody wants to defend the government anymore. We've won. They've surrendered, the lot of them, the Junkers, the Women's Battalion. The cycle regiment just buggered off first chance they got.'

Raisa was dumbfounded at the news. 'But we didn't do anything! Do you mean we just walked to power.'

The Red Guard laughed, 'That's about the size of it, Comrade.'

They heard the deep, baritone boom of the *Aurora*'s guns and the walls trembled.

'Come on, Citizen' the worker said. 'Be a good girl and move.'

Raisa's eyes flashed. 'She is not your *girl*. She is Comrade Elena, a worker-Bolshevik and she deserves your respect.'

That provoked an instant retreat. He raised his hands and begged their forgiveness.

'I meant no offence, Comrade,' he told Elena. 'Please accept my apologies.'

'No offence taken,' Elena said, winking at Raisa..

As they allowed themselves to be guided down a long corridor, Elena thumped her hip against Raisa's.

'They should make you an officer in the Red Guard. You'd show them how it's done.'

A huge pile of swords, trinkets jewellery, porcelain and statuettes had been confiscated and now sat in the middle of the floor. Pathetically, some of the invading citizens had stolen cakes of soap as if they were treasure.

Then, at last, the defeated counter-revolutionaries appeared, flanked by soldiers, sailors and Red Guards.

'Oh, here they are,' somebody growled. 'Bloody Junkers.'

Shouts of derision echoed around the vaulted ceiling. 'Kornilovites, enemies of the people.'

A punch was thrown here, a gob of spit landed there, but it was half-hearted. The Red Guards had little difficulty subduing the angrier onlookers.

'No violence, Comrades,' Elena shouted. 'These men have surrendered. You must observe the honour of the revolution.'

Then the strangest thing happened. The Red Guard officer addressed the prisoners.

'Do you promise not to take up arms against the people?'

There were mumbled promises and the officer waved with an open palm.

'Then you may go.'

Elena was furious. 'Have you taken leave of your senses? What if they do take up arms against us?'

'They promised not to,' the officer told her.

'And you take them at their word! Do you want them shooting you in the back?'

His eyes smouldered with resentment. 'I give the orders here and I say we should be merciful.'

'I am not asking you to shoot them,' she cried. 'Just arrest them. It is basic common sense.'

Her words earned several glares from the departing Junkers.

'Since when do you give the orders?' he asked her.

'I don't,' Elena replied, 'but maybe I should when there are idiots like you letting our enemies walk free without interrogating them.'

'They said they wouldn't fight us,' he reminded her.

Elena and Raisa swapped disbelieving glances.

'And you believe them? Just like that?'

One of the officer's comrades pulled at his coat. 'Let's go. Why waste time on them?'

More men appeared at bayonet point.

'Who are they?' Raisa asks. 'They don't look like fighting men.'

'Members of the Provisional Government, by the look of it,' Elena answered.

'They look so…ordinary.'

'That's because they are,' Elena told her. 'They may wear frock coats and preen like peacocks, but strip them of their finery and they are no better than you or me.'

Raisa watched the group tramp past, eyes downcast. The old power looked so pathetic and powerless. Some of the onlookers wanted to rough up the men before them, people they blamed for the continuing war, the hunger that stalked the streets, the coup attempt, but the Red Guards restrained them and the moment passed. Raisa was unsure what to make of all this. Defenceless people should be protected, but was it wise to let soldiers walk free without a proper interrogation? Could the new order afford to be so magnanimous?

The commonest objects being stolen were clothes. It seemed pathetic. There was all kind of loot glinting on every wall, on every surface, stored in every cupboard, yet it was something as simple as clothing that they took. It said something about the wretched state of the working people that this was their priority. They came across couches that had been torn apart. That seems like pure vandalism.

'Why did they destroy the furniture?' Raisa wondered out loud.

Elena stopped and took her hands. 'Do you know why they want the leather?'

Raisa shook her head, unable to think of a reason.

'It's to make shoes. Just let that sink in for a moment. Our people can't even afford footwear. Can you think of a better argument for the revolution?'

Raisa's first instinct was to run back to the boarding house and set off around the streets, handing out whatever money she could gather, but she knew it would soon run out. What good would the money she got from Andrey's house do when there were so many poor people in Petrograd?

'How can we ever solve the problems of all Russia?' Raisa wondered out loud. 'There is so much poverty...' Her eyes misted. 'There is so much despair.'

'The working people of Russia will rise to the task,' Elena assured her. 'Think what we have just done. Did you ever dream that working people could take the Winter Palace just by walking through the doors? Together, we will storm the gates of Heaven itself.'

Raisa tilted her head. 'I thought you didn't believe in God.'

'I don't,' Elena told her. 'It's a figure of speech. Heaven on Earth, that's what we are after, peace, food in every belly, land to the peasants.' She paused. 'Yes, and shoes on every pair of feet.'

Raisa grinned. 'Is that the new slogan: Peace, Bread, Land and Shoes?'

'It could be once winter sets in.'

As they wandered the rooms of the palace, several things struck Raisa. The first was the amount of wealth the Romanovs had accumulated.

'They must have bled Russia dry to be sitting on this mountain of gold,' she murmured.'

Then there was something else, she felt the enormity of the task facing the revolution like a great stone weighing on her shoulders. The old order stood humiliated in that moment, but beyond those walls, in the vast spaces of Russia, it would surely gather its strength. There was hunger and ignorance in the land.

'Can we hold the power?' Raisa said, looking around. 'The German Army is almost at the gates of the city.'

'We have each other,' Elena said. 'We have Svetlana, Pavel, Kolya, Mikhail. Surely, if there are thousands, millions like them nothing is impossible.'

The crowds who had entered the palace were beginning to disperse, emerging blinking into the night, their minds still trying to cope with what they witnessed in the palace, the wealth, the grandeur, the sheer scale of ancient power. Some set off along the Nevsky Quay. Others headed in the direction of the Smolny or the Kazan Cathedral. It is as if they were unable to make sense of what they had done. Was that it? Was that what a revolution is like? Raisa had imagined it as a great struggle, hundreds of bodies lying in the street, a bitter war to the death. Yet they had wandered into the palace rather than storming it. All these great buildings, all this show of pomp and ceremony. It was a mirage. Faced with a risen people and a determined leadership, it had disintegrated once the final blow was delivered.

'Let's go,' Elena suggested. 'Maybe we will catch some of the speeches. Maybe we can find out what is happening in Moscow, Rostov and Ekaterinburg.'

Raisa followed, but stopped as she passed a side street. 'I have to pee.'

Elena laughed. 'Even the revolution has to wait for a girl to do her business. I will wait for you.'

Raisa found a quiet corner and relieved herself. A smile spread across her lips. They had just flipped the world from its moorings and the old routines carried on regardless. You needed shelter. You had to eat. You had to pee. Life went on. Smoothing her skirts, she was making her way back when she heard a sound. It was a kind of whimpering, like the pleading of a frightened child.

'Elena, is that you?'

That's when the pleading became an intense, terrified scream. It tore at the night like a razor. It was definitely Elena's voice. Now she was running. Raisa knew that sound. She had pleaded. She had begged. She had known the bleak hopelessness when it was to no avail.

Raisa saw something, a moving shadow and edged forward, drawing her pistol.

Finally, in the gloom of a service bay she discovered the source of the cries. She recognised the looter Elena had confronted in the palace. He was pushing her roughly against the wall and tugging at her clothing. There was another man looking out for him.

'Stop fighting me, you bitch, or it will be worse for you.'

Still Elena resisted him, kicking and squirming. She managed to wrench a hand free and clawed his face, blood spilling over her fingers. In fury, he showed her the back of her hand. Before the blow could fall, Raisa stepped forward, arm outstretched, pistol aimed straight at his face.

'Touch one hair of her head, you bastard,' she said, her voice a splinter of ice, 'and I will blow your fucking brains out.' Something occurred to her and the barrel of the gun glided downward. 'Better still, I will blow your balls off first so you have time to understand pain before I finish your shit life for you.'

'Oh, fuck off, you little bitch before I come over there and spank your backside for you.'

The second man was already moving towards her. Raisa felt the flames of anger licking her insides and pulled the trigger. The gun roared. Instantly, there was a scream of agony.

'You blew my toe off, you bitch!'

Another cry of agony followed, then a stream of groans and expletives as he rocked back and forth in pain. Meanwhile, Raisa flicked the barrel of the gun at the second man.

'Piss off before you get the same.'

Abandoning his friend, the man ran.

'No honour among rapists then,' Raisa said.

Elena plucked her foot from the looter's grasp and made her way unsteadily to the safety of Raisa's welcoming arm.

'Are you all right? He didn't…?'

'I didn't let him.'

Elena was shaken and she was sporting a bruise on her cheek. Otherwise, she seemed unharmed.

'The bastards jumped me from behind,' she explained.

The looter was still raging at her. 'I should have killed you when I had the chance, you bitch!'

'Keep insulting her, Citizen,' Raisa told him. 'Go on, give me an excuse to put another bullet into you.'

By this point, he had crumpled to the ground, pawing at his ruined toe, his face twisted in a rictus of disgust and self-pity.

'Look what you've done to me. Are you crazy? All this for a quick screw?'

Elena spoke at last. 'It's called rape, you ignorant shit.'

'So which is it to be?' Raisa asked, incensed that he didn't even understand what he had done wrong, 'Choose. Ankle, kneecap, arse, balls, which would you like me to shoot first? I'd make it your pecker, but it's too small a target.'

Finally, he raised a hand in a gesture of surrender.

'OK, OK, you've made your point. Get me a doctor, for fuck's sake.'

'Get one yourself.'

Even now, his eyes were full of confusion and self-pity.

'You're not going to help me?'

'Clever boy,' Raisa replied. 'We'd help bloody Kerensky before we'd help you.'

'I'll have you shot, both of you.'

'Is that right, Citizen?' Elena asked. 'Maybe you know a friend of ours. His name is Comrade Nikolai Martov, Kolya to his friends.'

At Kolya's name, the looter's face drained of blood. 'Kolya? The one who advises the Red Guards.'

'That's him. Maybe you would like to explain to him how you pollute the revolution.'

He squatted in the mud, nursing his foot.

'Just clear off, you lousy bitches. I'll take care of myself.'

'I should finish you off right here,' Raisa told him, 'but I am better than you. I will never descend to your level.'

They had gone several streets when Elena crumpled against Raisa and began to sob.

'I am so grateful you found me,' she moaned into her lover's shoulder. 'When I felt the blow from behind, when his hands covered my eyes...I thought I was going to die.'

Raisa comforted her, caressing away her pain and fear. Finally, Elena withdrew and began to speak. 'You have never talked about it,' she said at last, 'what those men did to you…at Bagrov's place.'

She avoided the word brothel.

'There is nothing to say,' Raisa answered. 'You find a way to live with it. You survive.'

'That's what worries me sometimes,' Elena said. 'How much of you survived? If something like that were to happen to me, I don't know how I could carry on.'

Raisa turned and embraced Elena, whispering into her ear. 'You carry on because there is no choice. All of me survived, my love. No matter what they did, how sordid their filthy games were, they never took my soul. They never broke my spirit. I would never let them do that.' She was about to release Elena when a question came to her lips. 'What about that looter?'

'What about him?'

'Are there Bolsheviks who think like him?'

Elena considered the question. 'Not many, I hope.'

They sat down on a bench together while the sounds of insurrection still eddied around the city, shouts, gunshots, factory sirens.

'I was already afraid of the dangers facing us,' Raisa said, 'hunger, war, the counter-revolutionaries, I know they are my enemies. What if there are men like that in our ranks? He has heard of Kolya. How many like him are ready to poison our cause?'

The wind was on her cheeks, chilling the glistening tears.

'I don't know, my love. I honestly don't know.'

'Maybe we should. How can I believe in a better future if we have comrades who are no better than Bagrov's customers?'

'He wasn't a comrade. He admitted it.'

Elena raised her eyes to the night sky and watched the glitter of the stars through the drifting clouds.

'He was the product of all the filth the old world created. Raisa, my darling, do you think one act of insurrection will cure all the ills of the past? It will take time.'

'How long?'

'Years,' Elena. 'Many years, maybe, but not all men are like that dog. What about Pavel, Mikhail, Kolya? Even that bore Anishin is respectful of women.' She laughed. 'Especially Svetlana. Poor sod. She only has eyes for Kolya.' She returned to the question. 'We will make this world anew. Our march to freedom didn't end today. This is the moment it began.'

Aware that prying eyes could be upon them, Raisa planted kisses on Elena's cheeks.

'I pray that you are right, my love. That man frightened me.'

Elena pulled a face. 'He bloody terrified me!'

'Are you sure you're all right?'

'Yes.' She waited a beat. 'Oh, and if we ever meet him again, we kill the fucker.'

Pavel

He swung his legs out of bed and felt the bite of the morning cold. Nina's hand slid down his back and flopped onto the mattress like a stranded fish. When he glanced behind him she was sleeping like a child, the ghost of a smile on her lips, a similar ghost of the stomach swell housing his baby now visible. Behind the grey curtain strung across the room, Nina's roommates were sleeping. Soon, the factory siren would summon them. It was not clear how much work they would have. The bourgeoisie had still not accepted their loss of power. Pavel had heard stories of well-dressed men and woman walking down the Nevsky stopping the Red Guards and screaming at them.

'You think you are still in the saddle,' Pavel murmured, speaking to nobody but the yellow morning.

He dressed quietly, collected his rifle and departed, pulling the door to so gently there was barely a click. In the front hall he rested his back against the wall and gazed at the ceiling, following the cracks with his eyes. How had his life reached this point? A year ago he had been a soldier from a distant village, plucked from the backwardness of rural Russia to fight in the service of his Tsar. Now, he was a member of the shock troops of a republican revolution and soon, he would be a father. All this, and he had barely turned twenty.

He emerged into the slow awakening of the Vyborg district. There was mud, litter and debris, a cart here, an armoured car there, throbbing and shuddering, awaiting orders. He made his way to the Red Guards leaning against the vehicle and chatted to them about the security situation.

'Any word of Kerensky?' Pavel asked.

They shook their heads. 'They say he has scarpered to take refuge with the Cossacks.'

'The generals? The Germans?'

More shrugs and shaken heads. Maybe the relative peace and tranquillity were a mirage. Pavel wondered whether they were all just living in a bubble, about to be popped by the waiting counter-revolution. He asked about his comrades. Kolya? Anishin? The street pickets waved lazily in the direction of the river. Eventually, after some searching and a lot of misdirection, he discovered a purposeful-looking Kolya giving orders.

'What's the news?' Pavel asked.

'The rumour is that Kerensky is trying to reach the Cossacks at Gatchina. There is fighting in Moscow too. We are the advance guard of the revolution.'

Some of the Guards and sailors were hanging ammunition belts over their shoulders or oiling their weapons.

'Are we shipping out to Gatchina then?' Pavel asked.

Kolya shook his head. 'Not yet. We've got a more pressing problem closer to home.'

'Which is?'

'Fucking cadets.'

Pavel was confused. 'I thought they were under arrest, banged up in the Fortress.'

Kolya shook his head. 'You would think so, wouldn't you? Well, some dickheads in a Red Guard unit got them to promise to be good boys and let them go. Now they are attempting a counter-insurrection. Can you fucking believe it? We've got people on our side who think this is a bloody game. You can't have a revolution without firing squads.'

A cyclist arrived and conveyed the latest news. Kolya cursed and hung his rifle over his shoulder by its strap.

'Now they've occupied the Astoria. Every bloody bourgeois who wants to strangle our workers' government will be cheering. What a balls-up.'

Mikhail approached them.

'You got out of bed then?' Pavel said, teasing.

'You're the one who's in his pit until the sun burns his eyes out,' Mikhail countered good-naturedly. 'I've just been to the Telephone Exchange on Morskaya. They used false papers to get past the Guards. A bunch of bloody kids!'

'Kids or not,' Kolya said. 'We clear out this nest of vipers. Enough amateurism. It is time for us to get ruthless.'

'Maybe we should send in negotiators,' Pavel suggested.

'You go and talk if you like,' Kolya snapped, 'yes, and get your fool head blown off. I intend to get this job done, by any means at my disposal.'

Within moments, a convoy of armoured and private cars, many commandeered from the wealthier parts of the city, were roaring towards the heart of Petrograd. Pavel was astonished at the difference in Kolya. He remembered when the student-Bolshevik was wet behind the ears and started at every crack of a rifle. Now, he was assured, cool-headed in an emergency. At the Telephone Exchange, the fighters fanned out, opening up from every direction. Hot lead ricocheted off the soon pock-marked walls. Windows shattered with a loud thud. Motor trucks, laden with Guards, rumbled up the road to supplement the attacking force.

Seeing that the resistance was pathetically weak, Kolya ordered his shock troops into the building. Soon, Pavel was kicking down flimsy barricades, inexpertly constructed from boxes, packing cases, boards, even firewood. He worked in tandem with Mikhail, picking his way inside. Already, the cadets were surrendering. One lad looked more child than man. Pavel seized him by the shoulder and kicked his backside.

'Get the fuck out of here,' he said, 'before some over-eager Guard blows your stupid, young head off.' He saw Mikhail looking. 'How old was he?'

'Sixteen, seventeen,' Mikhail answered.

Pavel thumbed back his cap and wiped his brow with the back of his hand. 'What the fuck are we doing fighting kids?'

Mikhail gave a troubled shrug. 'You fight what's put in front of you.'

'Let's get this over and done with,' Pavel snarled.

He kicked down the next barricade, just a pile of useless debris. Accompanied by three Kronstadters, he entered a room. Instantly, the two lads surrendered. One had been cutting the buttons off his coat. The other had ripped off his gold braid and epaulettes. They were roughly dragged away. One of the sailors cuffed the older cadet over the back of his head.

'Hey, there's no need for that,' Pavel said. 'He's already surrendered.'

'He should have thought of that when he took up arms against the revolution,' the Kronstadter replied. 'Soft hearts mean dead men. Take it from me.'

'What are you going to do with them?'

The sailor wasn't saying. 'Let's clear the building, Comrade. We can talk about this later.'

There was a crash from upstairs then a loud shout rebounding off the walls of the stairwell.

'They're getting out onto the roof. We could have snipers firing down on our men.'

Mikhail shook his head. 'I don't think these kids have got that much nous. They're trying to get away across the rooftops.'

They climbed the stairs and emerged blinking into the light. Immediately, one of the cadets fired and a puff of masonry dust rose. Infuriated, one of the Red Guards rushed him and hurled him from the rooftop.

'Fuck!' Pavel yelled. 'There was no need for that.'

'Little bastard tried to kill me. What do you want me to do, give him a hug and a kiss?'

Pavel gazed impotently down at the body spread-eagled on the ground below and he felt sick. The rest of the cadets were already surrendering, broken by the fate of their friend. Before long, the building was cleared, but there was no end to the fighting. The high-pitched braying of a machine guns mixed with individual gunshots. Kolya was already in the car he seemed to have commandeered for his individual use as a commander of the Red Guard units.

'Get in. There are more at the Vladimirksy.' Seeing the blank look from some of the Guards from the Vyborg, he added; 'It's a military school. I'll direct you.'

They raced through chaotic streets. Skirmishes were continuing elsewhere. The sound of combat echoed back and forth in shapeless waves. By the time they reached the Vladimirksy, there was fury among the attackers.

'They repelled the first assault with machine guns,' a Guard explained. 'Here's our answer.'

It came in the shape of three field guns. Kolya nodded approvingly.

'Flatten the entire building if you have to. We crush the resistance.'

While the artillery pieces did their work, Anishin put in an appearance.

'It looks as if you've got everything in hand,' he said.

A shattering impact tore a hole in the façade of the building.

'Shit!'

Anishin's face had turned ashen. Kolya laughed.

'Maybe you need to get yourself some earplugs, Comrade Anishin.'

The Red Guards launched their attack, supported by the soldiers and sailors, but withering fire from inside the school cut down many. Others sprawled on their bellies, returning fire. Kolya stared in fury at the dead and wounded.

'Lay down covering fire!' he bawled.

Pavel watched his comrade directing one strand of the attack, leading by example.

'Let's go,' Pavel told Mikhail. 'He knows what he's doing.'

'Too fucking right,' Mikhail answered, ducking low as a lethal volley of machine gun fire tore up the ground in front of him. 'Learns fast, doesn't he?'

'He's a natural.'

Pavel only had one doubt. Kolya could lay his hands on power, but would he know how to use it? There was something cold about him. To Kolya, an idea was worth as much as a flesh and blood human being.

Maybe more.

They were moving forward, taking casualties, but within touching distance of the door. Armoured cars were cruising back and forth, spraying fire into the building. The field guns continued to pound the walls.

'On my command,' Kolya yelled. 'Go, go!'

Pavel had to kick at the lock three times before it burst open. He fired twice as he entered. He heard a scream, but couldn't locate its origin. Inside, everything was anarchy, a dark lair peopled by death. There was shouting. Mikhail had a hand on his shoulder.

'Some Commissar from the Smolny is saying we should talk to the defenders.'

'We've got dead men,' Pavel retorted. 'I'm done talking. Who is this fucker?'

'Name of Kirilov.'

'Well, tell Kirilov we're going to finish this.'

He rushed a barricade and came face to face with a startled cadet, jabbing at him with a bayonet. Pavel took aim with his rifle and a bullet smashed through the man's skull. By now, the cadets were starting to surrender, but the scores of Red Guard dead had inflamed the minds of the attackers. Screams reverberated through the building as they bayoneted to death anyone they thought was responsible for their losses. Pavel's blood rage was ebbing.

'Stop!' he cried. 'There's no need for any more.'

'Is that right?' one sailor spat back. 'One of my mates is dead. Another has a shattered knee. Go on, tell me I should be merciful.'

Pavel stepped between the sailor and a group of cowering cadets.

'You can stick mercy up your arse,' Pavel told him. 'This is about what kind of revolution we are making. We are not going to massacre kids when they've already surrendered.'

'So what are you going to do, let them go, the way some wanker did in the Winter Palace? They just marched straight down here and started shooting revolutionaries.'

'So we arrest them,' Pavel said. He slowed the tempo of his voice. 'We don't kill them, Comrade. We arrest them. Yes?'

The sailor waivered at last. 'Fine. I respect your wishes, Comrade.'

Pavel guided the surviving cadets out of the building. To his horror, a group of seven or eight more were crumpled on the ground. He saw Kolya.

'What happened?'

'What do you think?' Kolya replied. 'They killed the sons of the proletariat. The people dealt summary justice.'

'Why didn't you stop them?' Pavel demanded. 'There was no need for this.'

'Why should I deny the people their verdict?'

'You talk as if this was a court of law! They beat these boys to death.'

Kolya was unimpressed.

'These cadets are no innocents. They killed our comrades without hesitation.'

With that, he walked away. He had gone maybe fifty metres when he shouted an order.

'We are moving on to the Telephone Exchange.'

As they drove away, Pavel saw two Red Guards marching one of the cadets down to the river. The lad knelt, arms tied behind his back. A shot rang out and he fell face first in the river.

'He was just a fucking kid!' Pavel protested.

Kolya turned. 'He was a counter-revolutionary.'

'Shit. You are one heartless bastard.'

Kolya seemed to take it as a compliment.

'We've had this discussion before, Pavel Sergeyevich. I seem to remember you being the ruthless one then. Well, I learned my lessons at your side.'

Pavel listened with horror, remembering his part in the hardening of Kolya.

'You saw what happened when we handled the buggers with kid gloves,' Kolya continued. 'They cut down our guys without mercy. Now you ask yourself, Comrade. Do we do it my way and win or do we do it your way and leave hundreds of our brothers dead on the street?'

When Pavel was unable to come up with an answer, Kolya turned to look at the street and gave the driver some directions. The resistance at the Exchange was weak. There was the same tearing off of epaulettes and buttons, the same pleading for overcoats to disguise uniforms, but the cadets were allowed to surrender without further violence.

'What's in there?' Kolya asked.

'The switchboard room.'

The sailors led the way inside then the forward surge came to a halt.

'What is it?' Pavel demanded angrily. 'Why aren't you clearing the place?'

He barged his way through to the front then stopped himself. There were no cadets, just the young women who worked there. As soon as they saw that they wouldn't be touched, the women started to shout insults at the men who had stormed the building.

'Animals!'

'Pigs!'

'Look at them. They don't even clean their boots before they come in.'

Emboldened, one woman walked up to Pavel. 'Look at this common *muzhik*. You think you've taken power, do you? You will ruin the country in a week.'

To begin with, Pavel felt intimidated. Then he reacted.

'Sit the fuck down. Your bloody Romanovs, landlords and bourgeoisie have been ruining this land for centuries.' He saw the shock in her face. 'Pogroms, Bloody Sunday, Lena, the war, Kornilov, do you want me to go on?'

She returned to her seat without a word.

'That's right,' Pavel growled. 'Before you judge me or any of these working men here, just give some thought to what it is you have been supporting all your lives.' There was silence in the room. 'You call us dark people. Well, maybe we are, but we call the shots now.'

He walked from the room without another word, passing Kolya on the way. Kolya applauded.

'Well said, Comrade Pavel.'

Pavel met his eye then glanced back at Mikhail. 'I need some air.'

While they were smoking on the pavement, a well-heeled couple walked past.

'You think you're so clever, don't you? Wait till the Cossacks come, you bastards. You'll shit your pants and run.'

Pavel blew smoke from his nostrils. 'We didn't run last time. What makes you think we'll do it now?'

He leaned against a lamp post and closed his eyes, his mind filling with thoughts of the dead cadets, the insolent switchboard girl, Nina and the baby, most of all Raisa, always Raisa. Time passed and he achieved a kind of peace. Mikhail would not disturb him. He knew Pavel's moods. It was Kolya who did of course, dishing out orders.

'Kerensky is at Tsarskoe Selo. We may yet be required to repel an attack.'

Pavel opened his eyes.

'It was never going to end with the insurrection, was it? Something tells me we are in for a long fight.'

Raisa

Raisa had been standing at the window for some time when Elena climbed out of bed and embraced her from behind. Raisa instinctively stroked her lover's arms and closed her eyes as fond, familiar fingers stole over her midriff.

'I love you so much,' Elena told her. 'Before you, all this, it was a physical need.'

'Vera?'

'Yes, Vera, but there was no love in that. What I feel for you, it is, I don't know, completeness. It is as if we are one being, one life.'

'I know that feeling too. Before I met you, I had only ever loved one human being in my whole life. I feared my father, but I adored my mother. After I lost her, I swear I thought I would never feel love ever again. I would continue to exist, without emotion, without warmth until the moment of my death. There was no joy in life, but I was too much of a coward to hasten death. Now I love you so much my heart could break. If I were to ever lose you…'

'That will not happen,' Elena told her, pressing her lips to the nape of Raisa's neck. 'We shall grow old together.' After a few moments, she patted Raisa's shoulder. 'We should go.'

Once they were dressed, they admired themselves in the mirror.

'We are like twins,' Raisa said.

They were sporting identical red cross armbands and they had both packed kitbags of first aid accessories. It was Svetlana's idea that the women's auxiliaries, providing nursing support to the Red Guard units, should become more professional, though she had discovered later that other units had adopted the same idea. Svetlana didn't mention the firearms that both women are also carrying.

Because Elena had stayed at the boarding house the night before, they had to leave before dawn to reach their unit. Even so, many checkpoints and streets were closed by minor outbreaks of fighting men. They were late on the scene outside the Military School. They saw the bodies of cadets, soldiers, sailors, Red Guards.

'What happened here?'

A young woman, an office worker judging by her crisp, white blouse, was tending to a passer-by, struck by glass or debris during the fighting.

'I'll tell you what happened,' she said in a curt, resentful voice. 'Your Bolsheviks happened. Do you see what they have done?'

Raisa's gaze travelled across the fallen.

'I see working people,' she said, 'Bolsheviks, Red Guards, Kronstadters, soldiers. Do you only see the bodies of the cadets?'

'I see the fruits of your revolution.'

Some of the surviving Guards were beginning to move the bodies of the fallen.

'Look at this mess,' the office worker said. 'You Bolsheviks leave our poor boys where they died and remove their own.'

The argument attracted one Red Guard. 'What's that bitch saying?'

'Comrade, control your language,' Elena advised him.

He was still trying to force his way past her. Elena stood her ground.

'But what's she saying? We've got you bloody bourgeois weeping over these cadets. You think we started it, do you? They took the buildings over in an act of treachery. They fired on us, not the other way round. If they had come out with their hands up, there would never been any of this.'

'You stormed the Winter Palace! You carried out the coup.'

'It was no coup,' Raisa replied. 'It was the will of the masses, expressed through the Soviets.'

'It was the will of hooligans!' The office worker was furious. 'That man talks about treachery. What do you call overthrowing the government when the Germans are at the gates?'

The indignant Red Guard was moving his finger towards the trigger of his rifle.

'What do you know about fighting? My son died at the Front.'

'I advise you to go,' Raisa told the woman. 'I really advise you to leave now.'

'Because of him?' In a show of defiance, the office worker thrust out her chest. 'Go on, you Bolshevik scoundrel, shoot a woman through the heart if you have the guts.'

The Guard was bewildered. It was clear he didn't know how to respond. It was Elena who found a solution.

'Oh, do put your tits away and piss off,' she sighed, as if talking to a troublesome adolescent.

Amid the laughter that followed, the office worker reddened and stalked away with at least some of her dignity intact.

'I wonder if she knows you just saved her life,' Raisa whispered.

'She knows,' Elena answered. 'Come on, let's do our job.'

A doctor, a Bolshevik sympathiser, was dealing with the worst injuries. Raisa and Elena bandaged the lightly wounded. They had little equipment or expertise, but did what they could. Raisa discovered one man sitting alone.

'Are you all right, Citizen?' she asked.

When he looked away, she knelt down and gently turned his face towards her. It was covered in blood.

'Let me clean this for you,' she said.

She snapped her fingers and Elena brought some boiled water.

'The Red Guards have been making tea,' she explained. 'It is tepid now.'

Raisa dabbed at the man's face, slowly cleaning away the dried blood. Still, he tried to turn away from her.

'What is it, Citizen?' she asked. 'Would you prefer somebody else helped you?'

'Maybe he is embarrassed by a woman's presence,' Elena suggested. 'Shall I ask a male comrade?'

Finally, the man spoke. 'It's not that.'

He turned his gaze towards Raisa and she reacted as if her skin had been touched by a branding iron.

'What's wrong?' Elena asked.

Raisa had her hands over her mouth. The wounded man dropped to his knees.

'Forgive me, Comrade. Please forgive me.'

'What's he talking about, Raisa? Why, you're trembling.'

Raisa was indeed in shock. It was some time before she could speak. When she did, it was Elena's turn to exhibit distress.

'This man,' Raisa groaned, 'Yuri, he was a client, a regular. He came to Bagrov's brothel.'

The man, now revealed as Yuri, continued to beg, shuffling forward ridiculously on his knees.

'Please forgive me, Comrade. I am a weak, sad individual. Please don't blame me. Pity me.'

He reached for Raisa's hands, but she drew back from him.

'Stop!' she said. 'Don't touch me.'

Some of the Red Guards were staring, bewildered by the scene. Elena addressed them.

'It's all right, Comrades. He is very upset. We are dealing with it.' She leaned forward, hissing in his ear. 'Get the fuck up, you sick bastard. You're not going to embarrass Raisa in front of these men.'

Yuri nodded obediently and perched on a box. He was hanging his head.

'I lost my wife, my child. I sought solace at Bagrov's place.' He gave Raisa a sideways look. 'You must hate me.'

'Too fucking right,' Elena said, cuffing him across the head.

'No,' Raisa said, 'Don't. There is no need to abuse him.'

Elena was indignant. 'He abused you!'

'Maybe in a better world,' Raisa said, 'I would not have had to sell myself and he wouldn't have had to purchase my services.'

'Are you saying you forgive him?' Elena asked, appalled.

'I don't know what I feel,' Raisa answered.

Yuri began to sob, his shoulders heaving.

'Now he's feeling sorry for himself,' Elena said, shaking her head. 'Well, I don't feel any pity. I think you're a piece of shit, you dirty, horny old bastard.'

Raisa caught up with Elena at the street corner. 'You're taking this worse than I am.'

Elena had tears in her eyes. 'If I could find all the scum that used you, I would cut their balls off and feed them to the crows.'

There was a long silence then Raisa laughed. 'I think you would too. Come on, let's finish our work.'

By the time they finally discovered the Vyborg Red Guards mopping up resistance, they were quite exhausted. They rested among the workers, soldiers and sailors. There was a general buzz of optimism. Red Petrograd had crushed its internal opponents, it was time to look outward – what of Kerensky, the Cossacks, the forces the toppled government could call upon in the wider country? Agitators moved among the weary fighters, summoning them to another battle. One of them was Kolya, flanked once more by Pavel and Mikhail. Raisa saw something in Pavel's face, a new reflection and caution, and wondered what had happened. Kolya started to speak. He seemed older, much older, than when Raisa first saw him.

'You are tired, Comrades. Your limbs ache. You mourn your fallen brothers.' His fiery gaze swept back and forth, seizing on a returned glance here, a reluctant stare there. 'Our fight is not yet done. There is bloody fighting at Pulkovo Heights. Krasnov's Cossacks number at least a thousand sabres.'

'I heard two thousand,' came a voice.

'I heard five.'

'Would it matter if it was ten thousand?' Kolya answered.

'Too fucking right it would!' The comic was rewarded with a gale of laughter.

'No,' Kolya retorted, utterly humourless. 'It would not. The counter-revolution has engaged our forces, the forces of the workers and peasants' government, the shock troops of the coming world socialist revolution. We must go to their aid. We must crush those who would rekindle the war and stamp out our infant revolution. Will you rally to the cause of Lenin and Trotsky, the cause of the working people?' He took a breath. 'Will you fight?'

If Kolya was expecting a roar of acclamation, he was in for disappointment. It was more a rumble of resignation. One man expressed the mood.

'If we have to,' he grunted, 'but you knew that before you asked us, didn't you, Comrade?'

'Who's commanding?'

'There has been a garrison conference,' Kolya answered. 'That honour has fallen to Colonel Muravyov.'

'A colonel? We've been carrying those pigs on our back for three fucking years. Why not an elected man?'

'We need military expertise,' Kolya explained.

'We've had their military expertise for three bloody years. That's why the Germans are just days away from Petrograd.'

Kolya raised his hands for silence, struggling with the mood just as Anishin started rousing the Red Guards on the far side of the square.

'The decision is already made, Comrades. If you have points to raise, you can do so once we have repelled the enemy. That is the time to discuss such things.'

'That's right,' one man grumbled. 'We discuss and you make the decisions.'

'That is not the way it will be under the Council of People's Commissars. You are the rulers now.'

'Put that in writing, Comrade,' came a shout. 'I'll have Lenin's office.'

'I'll have his coat. It's freezing.'

It was Pavel who rescued Kolya from the sullen scepticism of the Guards.

'That's enough, you arseholes,' he shouted. 'Do you want Kerensky back in Petrograd or not? Well, simple answer, do you?'

'Of course not.'

'Fine. So stop giving Comrade Kolya grief and get into line. Let's go and kick some Cossack ass.'

That got a grudging cheer and the Guards started to shuffle into unruly ranks.

'Do we join them?' Raisa asked uncertainly.

Elena inspected her kitbag. 'I am just about out of bandages.'

While she was doing a quick stocktake, Svetlana arrived, bearing supplies and a broad smile.

'This should keep you going,' she announced, 'and if you run out of bandages again, tuck your hair into your cap and use your weapons to support the assault on Kerenksy.'

'Will the men let us fight?' Raisa asked.

'If they try to stop you, threaten to shoot the fuckers,' Svetlana said, with a beam as broad as a searchlight. 'It usually works.'

The trembling curtain of evening was on the hills by the time the reinforcements joined the battle. In the distance, just fourteen miles to the north, was red Petrograd. Here, on a plain before the hills, revolution and counter-revolution faced each other amid smoke and the rush of working people and artillery fire. There was the heart-driven amateurism of the masses and the grudging professionalism of officers attaching themselves to the cause of the Soviets. There seemed to be people rushing towards the action and away from it.

'Where are the Cossacks?' Kolya demanded.

A forest of arms pointed in response. Fingers, hands jabbed through the smoke haze.

'How many?'

'Fuck knows.'

'Loads of them.'

'Shit loads.'

'Stop spreading panic. They've no stomach for a fight.'

'For people who don't want to fight, they've killed enough of our lads.'

Pavel was some way to Raisa's left. His words floated through the crowd. 'You watch Comrade Kolya. He was born for this moment.'

It sounded like praise, but somehow it was tinged with criticism. Pavel's voice was husky and low. He was not a man at ease with himself. Raisa caught his eye for a moment. She wanted to make some sense of his behaviour, but she doubted whether he was in any mood to talk to her. They remained wary of one another, strangers with a curious bond. There was no time anyway. The Red Guards started to hurry forward even before Kolya, Anishin, Svetlana could suggest that they act. They paid little attention to these grassroots leaders, never mind the unseen Colonel Muriavov. Roads and lanes swarmed with soldiers, sailors, Red Guards, purposeful and ragged, the chaotic product of hope – not an army, but a chaotic, enthusiastic mob. As artillery batteries opened up again, tearing into distant counter-revolutionary ranks, Raisa feared for the people milling about her. There were screams, combining with the hysterical whinnying of horses. The dull thump of the guns continued, suppressing the terrified shrieks of man and beast alike.

'That's our artillery,' Elena said, voice brimming with excitement.

'Is that right?' a worker said. 'I thought it was Kerensky's. I didn't know we had any.'

'But still you came to fight?'

'I would have tackled the bastards with a hammer if I had to.'

There were nods around and encouraging shouts. Kolya and Anishin rushed ahead, trying to give form to the forward march. There was a warning cry, followed by confusion.

'Cossacks!'

Kolya was shouting, trying to impose order on the attack, but before he could make an appeal, the Cossacks were among them. Screams ripped the through the cold. In the choked confines of the narrow lane, a brutal struggle began, sabres slashing, bayonets jabbing, rifles spitting lead.

'Raisa!'

'Elena?' Raisa turned to see a Cossack rider closing on her, sabre pointed at her heart. She fumbled for her pistol, but somebody crashed into her from behind and she fell heavily to her knees. Two more sharp blows from the struggling crowd left her dazed. Unable to draw her pistol, she stared at the rearing horse, the glinting blade. But the sabre never fell. A blurry form intervened. There was a spray of blood and a dying man lay at her feet.

'Yuri?'

She saw him struggling to breathe as he drowned in his own blood. His words would not form, but she saw his shocked eyes and knew what he wanted. Seizing his hand, she squeezed tightly.

'Yuri, you're forgiven. I swear, I forgive you.'

The old man died there on the heights overlooking Piter.

'He sacrificed himself to save you,' Elena said, dragging Raisa to her feet.

The attack had foundered against the workers' ranks. Sabres failed to sweep through air or tear through flesh. Raisa sensed that the Cossacks had already lost any heart they had for the fight. Maybe they hadn't really been attacking the revolutionary positions at all, but trying to hack an avenue of retreat through their lines. Could it be they were simply fleeing the artillery ordnance? Hemmed in, they were being dragged from the saddle. Some were beaten, a few shot on the spot. Others were simply disarmed and sent on their way. One fresh-faced rider crumpled to the ground, weeping.

'They told us Petrograd would hail us as liberators. They said we would be heroes.'

'Well, now you know,' Kolya said. 'They are using you, brother Cossack, as a battering ram against the proletariat and the peasants. Take a good look around you. The battering ram is splintering at Pulkovo, at Tsarskoye Selo, in the hinterland before Petrograd. The counter-revolution is being smashed before your eyes.'

Though the sounds of distant fighting continued for some time, it soon became obvious that the enemy had been repulsed.

'So what do you make of it?' Kolya asked Pavel.

'I think we ended up piggybacking somebody else's victory,' Pavel answered. 'The bloodiest fighting was over by the time we got here. It's time to go home.'

There were hundreds of workers, soldiers and sailors tramping in the direction of Petrograd now,

'So we've won?' Raisa asked.

Instinctively, Elena turned to Svetlana.

'We've won,' Svetlana confirmed, 'this battle at least.'

'So there will be more, aunty?' Elena asked.

'There will,' Svetlana said softly. 'Many of these men you see, they think we can persuade the counter-revolution of the justice of our cause. They think a revolution is settled with reason and soft words. They're in for a rude awakening. Out there…'

She gestured at the hills and vast Russia beyond. It is as if she could hear the counter-revolution like a wounded beast, groaning across plains and mountain ranges, swamps and lakes and forests.

'Out there, the reaction is already gathering its forces. The capitalist nations will stuff their mouths with silver so they can strangle our revolution at birth. You can take my word for it, we will have to fight our enemies to the death.'

Raisa shuddered visibly, causing Elena to wrap an arm round her.

'What's wrong?' she asked. 'Did somebody tread on your grave?'

'Don't make jokes about it,' Raisa said. 'I fear for the future.'

'It's the counter-revolution that should be afraid,' Kolya said, overhearing them.

He planted a kiss on Svetlana' cheek.

'No matter how long it takes, we will smash the enemies of the proletariat.'

'We promised the people peace,' Raisa reminded him.

'We meant it,' Svetlana said, 'but our enemies are set on war.'

Kolya was cleaning his spectacles with the hem of his tunic. 'They will regret the day they bore arms against the revolution. For every martyr who falls, we will slay ten of them.'

Raisa caught Pavel's eye. He opened them wide for a moment in a silent, cryptic comment on Kolya's words.

'So how do we get home from here?' Raisa asked.

'As soon as I work out where here is,' Svetlana answered, linking Kolya's arm, 'I'll tell you.'